A DEEPER WELL

Books by Jill Eileen Smith

THE WIVES OF KING DAVID

Michal

Abigail

Bathsheba

WIVES OF THE PATRIARCHS

Sarai

Rebekah

Rachel

DAUGHTERS OF THE PROMISED LAND

The Crimson Cord

The Prophetess

Redeeming Grace

A Passionate Hope

The Heart of a King

Star of Persia

Miriam's Song

The Prince and the Prodigal

Daughter of Eden

The Ark and the Dove

Dawn of Grace

A Deeper Well

When Life Doesn't Match Your Dreams

She Walked Before Us

$\mathscr{A}$ DEEPER WELL

The Story of the Woman at the Well

JILL EILEEN SMITH

Revell

a division of Baker Publishing Group
Grand Rapids, Michigan

© 2026 by Jill Eileen Smith

Published by Revell
a division of Baker Publishing Group
Grand Rapids, Michigan
RevellBooks.com

Printed in the United States of America

Library of Congress Cataloging-in-Publication Data
Names: Smith, Jill Eileen, 1958– author.
Title: A deeper well : the story of the woman at the well / Jill Eileen Smith.
Description: Grand Rapids, Michigan : Revell, 2026.
Identifiers: LCCN 2025023465 | ISBN 9780800744809 (paperback) | ISBN 9780800747961 (casebound) | ISBN 9781493452798 (ebook)
Subjects: LCSH: Samaritan woman (Biblical figure)—Fiction | LCGFT: Bible fiction | Novels
Classification: LCC PS3619.M58838 D44 2026 | DDC 813/.6—dc23/eng/20250620
LC record available at https://lccn.loc.gov/2025023465

Scripture quotations are from the Holy Bible, New International Version®, NIV®. Copyright © 1973, 1978, 1984, 2011 by Biblica, Inc.® Used by permission of Zondervan. All rights reserved worldwide. www.zondervan.com. The "NIV" and "New International Version" are trademarks registered in the United States Patent and Trademark Office by Biblica, Inc.®

This is a work of historical reconstruction; the appearances of certain historical figures are therefore inevitable. All other characters, however, are products of the author's imagination, and any resemblance to actual persons, living or dead, is coincidental.

Cover design by Laura Klynstra

Published in association with Books & Such Literary Management, www.booksandsuch.com.

Baker Publishing Group publications use paper produced from sustainable forestry practices and postconsumer waste whenever possible.

26 27 28 29 30 31 32   7 6 5 4 3 2 1

For the misunderstood and misrepresented
and for those who wish they could
undo all the mistakes of their past,
this story is for you.

Prologue

I'll never forget the first time I saw him. He sat on a grassy knoll near Jacob's well, eyes closed. He wore an undyed mantle over a long, plain tunic with his blue and white tzitzit visibly hanging below his knees. A Jew. What was he doing here in Samaria?

I couldn't tell if he was sleeping or praying, but the closer I came, the wearier he looked.

I did not fear him. I probably should have. He was a man, after all, and I a woman alone. My only defense was the jar resting on my shoulder. I could have thrown it at him and run back to Sychar. But I was not a fast runner. Besides, what could he do to me that my previous husbands had not already done?

I had no idea why he was sitting there, but I didn't really care in that moment. The sun beat down on me, and sweat trickled down my back, reminding me that if things were different, if I had not made the choice I had made that morning, I wouldn't be here at the hottest part of the day.

And I wouldn't have felt the knot in my middle the moment he lifted his head and gazed at me. His presence unnerved me, but I tried to ignore him as I tied the rope to my jar and lowered it until I heard the distant splash and gurgle of water filling the jar. I waited, avoiding the man yet ever aware of him. If he moved toward me, I would run, jar or not. But he simply sat there until I had pulled the rope and dragged the jar over the lip of the well.

He shifted slightly, facing me. "Will you give me a drink?"

Those eyes. I will never forget the way he looked at me. As if he knew me. But why was he speaking to me? His exhaustion was evident, and I did not doubt his thirst. Still, I hesitated.

"You are a Jew," I said at last, "and I am a Samaritan woman. How can you ask me for a drink?" I mean, honestly. Hadn't I heard over and over through the years that Samaritan women were unclean to Jewish men? If he so much as took a cup of water from me, he would be unclean, though why we were so maligned, I'd never understood. We weren't *always* ritually unclean. Still, why was he even here, talking to me? It made no sense, and I wanted no part of him or his reason for being here.

He straightened. Nothing in his appearance stood out as remarkable. He didn't strike me as anything like the men I had married or the one I had always loved.

"If you knew the gift of God and who it is that asks you for a drink, you would have asked him and he would have given you living water," the man said after a brief pause, as if waiting for me to fully listen.

Living water?

I had no idea then what he meant or where our conversation would lead us. I did not know that this Jew would be my undoing, would completely change my life. My pathetic, mostly loveless, bitter life, which had cost me much and always would. If only things had been different. If only my father had made a better match for me from the start, I wouldn't be in this situation. And I would never have been at Jacob's well in the hottest part of the day, talking to a Jew.

But before I continue with what happened with that man, let me tell you my story from the beginning.

1

kicked at the stones along the path as I lugged water from Jacob's well to my parents' home in Sychar. I glanced behind me at Gali, my best friend, who always lagged behind, and caught a glimpse of Mt. Gerizim in the distance. The sun had dipped below its summit, signaling the need to hurry before darkness fell. Before the young men bent on harm emerged to roam the streets or we had an unfortunate run-in with a Roman.

"Come on, Gali," I called over my shoulder. "They're going to close the gates on us."

"I'm coming." Hurried steps hit the dirt path behind me, but Gali's shorter legs could not keep up with my longer strides. "Slow down, Ness."

I dropped back a bit, but my heartbeat quickened at the distance we still had to cover. "We should have come sooner," I said, shifting the weight of the jar to my other shoulder. My back ached from the cycle that had begun that morning, proof that I was now able to beget, to wed. How relieved Ima had been, though I did not see the urgency. True, I was thirteen and could have married sooner, but I was in no hurry to leave my father's home as my older sisters had done.

"I had to finish helping my ima," Gali said, puffing with the effort to pick up her pace. "You could have come without me if you're that worried about the sun setting."

"You don't have to sound so irritated." I frowned as Gali came alongside. "The other women came earlier, but I couldn't let you come alone and you know it." Best friend or not, sometimes Gali could be so annoying.

"You talk like you're a woman like the others. We're still girls." Sweat trickled down Gali's narrow face. She was a year younger and not yet a woman, and I didn't have the heart to tell her the truth. Why trouble our friendship? And yet, if my mother had her way, I would be betrothed before the next new moon.

I drew my headscarf closer to my face and released a sigh as the gates to the city drew near. We did not speak as we passed the lone Roman guard standing at the entrance. Though the Romans had never bothered us, there was talk of what they had done to other women who walked alone. I breathed easier once we were well past him.

"We made it." I smiled at Gali, whose scarf blew behind her in the evening breeze.

We continued down the narrow street through the city to a section of homes on the east side. Dusk settled as we stopped in front of my courtyard.

"Tomorrow I'll try to get away earlier," Gali said as she turned toward her home next door. She entered her courtyard and lowered the jar to the indentation in the ground near the front door.

I moved through our courtyard and set my jar near our door, then scooped some water into a smaller clay jar resting nearby and carried it into the house. Lamps burned at the window, where white linen curtains fluttered, and also lit the table where Ima and I would set the food.

"I was beginning to worry," Ima said, looking at me with fondness. "Did the pain slow you down? There is always pain with these monthly cycles, but you'll get used to it."

"Gali was late getting away. Tomorrow we will do better," I promised.

"Set the dishes of cucumbers and olives on the table. And don't forget the bread," she called over her shoulder. "The men will be in soon." She carried a large clay pot of barley stew and placed it on the table where Abba, my brother Chen, and our cousin Lavi would recline. Lavi worked with Abba, and his presence around the table normally brought laughter as his humor was contagious.

I courted a secret smile at the memories of the fun we'd had when we were younger. Lavi often teased me beyond reason, but I didn't take him seriously. His tone never carried the sting of hurt that came from my sisters when they made fun of my appearance.

"Don't listen to them, Ness," Lavi had said. "They're jealous because you're so beautiful. You know I'll marry you one day and they're jealous of that too."

Was I really as beautiful as Lavi had said? When I stared in the bronze mirror, it was hard to truly see my reflection, but I had begun to notice the way the young men at synagogue looked at me. Gawked was probably a better description. It made me feel strange inside.

The door opened as I placed the last dish on the table, the men laughing and talking all at once. The nagging pain in my back made me long to lie on my pallet, but I could not leave Ima alone to serve. Besides, I didn't want to strain this sudden affection Ima showed me. Was becoming a woman so important that it warranted such a change in attitude? Was this what it took to gain my mother's love?

"Come now," my father said, taking his place among the cushions surrounding the table. "Let us give thanks."

I knelt, as did my mother, and the men bowed their heads. "Blessed are You, Lord our God, King of the Universe, who brings forth bread from the earth," they said in unison.

I stood, filled the cups with wine from the skin, and took my place at the end of the table near my mother.

"We have good news to share with you all," Ima said after dipping her bread into the stew. She looked fondly at me again, making my heart skip a beat. She wasn't going to tell the men, was she?

"Our Nessa is a woman today!" she said in triumph. "Adonai be praised!"

"Ima!" Mortified, I felt my cheeks grow hot under the scrutiny of the men.

"A woman at last," Chen said, laughing. "So, you will soon be off to a home of your own like our sisters."

I studied my food, unable to lift my head to look at any of them.

"Meital, Yaffa, and Adva were thrilled when this day came. Where is your joy, my child?" Ima asked, touching my arm. "Lift your head. You are a woman now!"

"Good," Lavi said, his tone softer and more serious than normal. "Now you can marry me."

I gave him a sharp look, then glanced at Abba reclining at the head of the table. He had always favored me and treated me kindly. Would he treat Lavi the same and give him my hand in marriage?

"I'm sure we still have plenty of time to discuss your betrothal," Abba said, his gaze shifting from me to my mother. "There is no hurry."

My mother opened her mouth as if to protest, then shut it again and looked away. They would discuss this later, no doubt, when I couldn't hear them, and in the end, as she always did, my mother would win. But would Lavi? Did I want him to?

◆ ◆ ◆

Lavi's hopes had soared the moment Aunt Lihi announced that Nessa was a woman now. At last! He'd known nearly as soon as Uncle Raanan had taken him in after the death of his parents that he would marry Nessa. Cousin or not, he could not imagine loving anyone more.

He'd been so sure that they belonged together and never once doubted she would be his. Until he'd seen the look pass between Lihi and Raanan after his declaration. While he had always spoken his mind around the family table, he realized in that moment he should not have spoken.

Now as he walked from his room to the building where he helped Chen and Raanan build tents, his heart pounded. If Raanan would listen and allow him to state his case, surely he could convince him that he was the only one who could truly love Nessa, not for her beauty—though there was no denying she was a rare gem in a city of ordinary women—but for herself. Raanan would see that, wouldn't he?

He smoothed his hands on his tunic and blew out a long-held breath as he approached the building. The cool mist of morning air brushed the skin on his arms as the damp grass tickled his feet. He glanced about, remembering the many hours he and Nessa had chased each other here as children in the early days of his loss.

The prick of grief never really left him, but quietly and patiently loving Nessa, waiting for this moment, had made his life bearable, even hopeful. Now, if he could convince his uncle to seal their betrothal, life would be perfect.

He opened the door to the shop and was grateful to find Raanan alone. His uncle looked up and gave Lavi a slight nod. Raanan was a man of few words, and Lavi often found it difficult to talk at length with him.

He cleared his throat and approached. "Uncle, may I speak with you?"

Raanan set the flint knife on a table beside him and met Lavi's gaze. "Yes?" His puzzled expression did not help ease Lavi's anxious thoughts.

"It's about Nessa." He swallowed hard past the sudden lump in his throat. "It is no secret that I would like her to become my wife. Now that she is . . . able to wed . . . I would like to formally request her hand in marriage."

Raanan studied him as he stroked his beard. Lavi dare not breathe too deeply, lest it cause his uncle to look on him with disfavor.

"You have no means to support her, my son. If you marry her, you would both be living here, and I would be the one to support you both and any children you have. You are not ready to begin a business of your own nor to purchase a house. Did you plan to live under my roof all of your days and have my daughter as well?" Raanan's voice remained steady and low, not angry or heated, yet he quashed Lavi's hopes with every word.

"I would work hard to find a way to support us both. Even if we are betrothed soon, we would have a year. I will prove myself to you," he said, his words rushed. "I love her, Uncle. I would treat her well." The pleading in his voice could not be lost on his uncle, yet he saw no change in the man's expression, though a deep sigh lifted his chest.

"My son, Nessa is a favored daughter, and many men in Sychar have watched her for the past year. Lihi has had mothers approach her, and I've had fathers speak to me after synagogue and at the city gate. Every one of them can give us a hefty bride-price, whereas you have nothing to offer either me or Nessa. How am I to answer that?"

"Isn't my love worth anything?" Lavi hated the plaintive quality in his tone.

"You cannot live on love, my son."

Lavi's hopes fell, and he could think of nothing else to say that might convince his uncle.

Raanan motioned to the area where Lavi normally worked. "I will consider your request, but I cannot promise. Now get to work and show me that you have the ability to one day do as you say and give my daughter the life she deserves."

To thank him for what felt like nothing did not sit well with Lavi, but he muttered the words just the same. He moved to his area of the building and began to stretch the fabric over the frame to be sure it was the right size, his mind whirling. What more could he do to prove his worth when his uncle had never paid him more than food and a place to live? The few coins he occasionally received could never add up to enough for a bride-price for any woman. Why hadn't he considered that problem years ago?

But he hadn't, and now he would be competing with the men of Sychar, who would not see Nessa for the caring, funny, happy young woman he knew. They only saw her outward beauty— her thick dark hair, large and expressive dark eyes, and heart-shaped face. He didn't need to imagine much to know that she had curves in all the right places and lips that caused him to dream of kissing her when he lay on his mat at night. Men watched her, and he knew they did not have pure thoughts as she passed them in the market or sat with the women at synagogue.

Would Raanan truly allow her to marry one of them? The thought made him suddenly nauseous. No. He couldn't. *Please, Adonai, don't let him give her to another.*

Would God hear his prayer? He had never really thought to pray before this moment, but now it felt as though his future depended on more than himself. He needed all the help he could get, and God seemed like the best choice since he had no one else.

❖ ❖ ❖

I lay awake long into the night, listening to my parents argue in the next room, though I could not hear their actual words. At last sleep came in spurts, and I woke early, no longer able to lie abed. Restlessness filled me, and with it the need to speak to my father. Surely he would listen to me and not just marry me off to anyone my mother had chosen.

I bided my time as I worked with my mother to grind the grain and sweep the stone floors. The men had left to go to the shop, where they made tents for those who could not afford brick homes and to sell to passersby. For my part, I spun the goats' hair my mother wove to make the colorful rugs, material for the tents, clothing, and other household goods.

"You must take my place at the loom today," my mother said, basket over her arm. "I'm going to market. Be sure to finish the piece I began yesterday."

"Yes, Ima," I said, taking her place at the wooden loom.

"Good girl." Ima left the house without a backward glance, but I caught the determined set to her jaw and knew that this trip would mean more than a casual outing to buy spices or some other product she needed. She was off to tell the whole town of Sychar that I was now able to marry, and I had not yet even told Gali.

Irritation spiked with the embarrassment I still felt from last evening's meal. I walked to the door and peered into the street, making sure my mother was out of sight, then quickly slipped into my plain leather sandals and ran to the back of the house. I needed to tell Gali, but I needed to speak to my father more.

I found him alone, thankfully, carving a piece of wood that would make one of the beams for the tents. "Abba?" I said, coming alongside him.

"Nessa. What are you doing here?" He set the wood aside and faced me. "Did your mother send you?"

I looked behind him to be sure Chen and Lavi were not close enough to hear. I shook my head. "Ima went to market. I hoped to speak with you."

He cupped my cheek with a gentle hand. "You are worried. Tell me, my child."

16

As his youngest child and fourth daughter, I should not receive special attention from him. After all, his first three children had been a sore disappointment in that they were girls and not beautiful. When Chen came along, I later learned, there was great rejoicing in the household. And when I came a year later, the sting of disappointment was no longer there. For reasons I did not understand, I found greater favor in Abba's eyes than Meital, Yaffa, or Adva ever had. And except for Yaffa, they did not treat me all that well because of it. Couldn't he see that he should not show favoritism? And yet, I needed that favor now.

"Are you going to betroth me to Lavi, Abba? Or has Ima picked someone else I don't know?" I wouldn't mind marrying my cousin, though I wasn't sure my parents felt the same about him. Lavi was humorous and a decent worker, but I'd heard complaints about the friends he ran with when he was not working.

"Do you want to marry Lavi?" He tilted his head to peer into my eyes.

I shrugged. "I don't know. I think so."

"Your ima has had the mothers of other young men approach her for the past year, and she put them off," he said, revealing what I knew but never wanted to ponder.

"Can we put it off a little longer, Abba? I'm not sure I'm ready." I searched his face, and he studied me in return.

"Put it off? For how long?" He frowned and ran a hand over his speckled beard.

"A few months perhaps? Until I adjust . . ." I looked beyond him, avoiding his gaze.

He patted my shoulder. "My dear girl. You are already thirteen." He paused, and indecision flickered in his eyes.

"Please, Abba. Until we are sure about Lavi at least?"

"He already approached me this very morn."

The news surprised me. "I didn't know he was so anxious." I bit my lower lip, suddenly wondering why I was so hesitant about this cousin I had known all my life. A flash of memory clouded my thoughts of Lavi stealing a loaf of bread from a merchant when I was eight and he was ten.

"Put that back," I had hissed in his ear. "You shouldn't steal. They could stone you for it."

Lavi laughed as he grabbed my hand and ran toward home. "No one saw me." He tore off a piece and popped it into his mouth, offering me one as well.

I had vehemently shaken my head. "I will not share in your thievery, Lavi ben Erez. It's wrong!"

"Nessa? What are you doing here?" Lavi's voice at that moment pulled me up short. I whirled about, then looked back at my father and gave him a pleading look.

"I will consider your request, my daughter. Now return to your work." He shooed me away, and before Lavi could speak again, I picked up my skirts and ran back toward the house.

I paused at the narrow path between my house and Gali's. We would see each other that evening, but I couldn't wait for her to hear my news from someone else.

I hurried to the door and knocked, and when Gali opened it, I knew she had already heard. Were there no secrets in Sychar?

"Why didn't you tell me yesterday?" Gali crossed her arms over her narrow chest. "I had to hear it from Ima this morning, along with the disappointment that it wasn't me."

"I didn't want to hurt your feelings." Misery swept through me. Everything was happening so fast simply because I was a woman now.

"Well, you did. You know you can tell me anything. You *should* have told me first." Gali lowered her arms, then suddenly smiled and pulled me into a hug. "We're supposed to do everything together, you know. Can you get your father to wait so we can marry at the same time? At least don't go and marry Harel. He's mine!"

Harel was a handsome young farmer who lived with his

father's large family on the outskirts of Sychar. Gali had fallen for him when we'd seen him at synagogue.

"I have no plans to marry Harel." Though we both knew that Harel had shown no interest in Gali. I couldn't bear to let her think her choice was impossible.

"Ima will probably pick someone else by the time I am ready to wed," Gali said, her voice low. "But come in and let's talk about it. Who do you want to marry? Will it be Lavi?"

"I can't," I said. "I have to get to work weaving while Ima is at the market or she will be angry. We can talk on our walk to the well tonight." I touched Gali's arm, then turned and ran back home, my mind spinning.

Why did growing older have to make everything so complicated? I would turn back time to be a child again, if only I could.

2

ime passed quickly over the next week as I completed my ritual purification and returned with my family to the synagogue for the reading of Torah and singing of our hymns. The day after Shabbat, I worked with my mother to finish the weaving of her famous colorfully designed rugs, then stood beside our donkey laden with the load of them. Abba, Chen, and Lavi accompanied us and shared our excitement of seeing a passing caravan.

"Ima!" my sister Meital called, hurrying through the market toward us.

"Meital!"

The embrace they shared caused a twinge of hurt to quicken my heart. My oldest sister had always been Ima's favorite, and everyone knew it.

"Yaffa. Adva. You're all here," Ima said a moment after she released Meital and the others ran toward us.

I acknowledged them all with a cursory hug, then focused my attention on the camels bedecked with jewels and ornate saddles. They carried wares from as far away as Syrophoenicia, a place to the north of Samaria and all that I knew. What would it be like to travel to distant places?

"Your mother seems happy to see your sisters again."

I jumped at the sound of Lavi's voice so near. "Lavi." My

heart skipped a beat at the way he looked at me. "You scared me."

He laughed outright. "Scared of me, Nessa? Why?" He looked a little annoyed by my comment amid his humor.

"Surprised would be more accurate." I met his gaze, smiling. Had he truly asked my father for my hand so soon? While Lavi had his problems—the stealing when he was young and his quick temper at times—I loved him as much as I did Chen. But could I marry him? "Isn't this exciting?" I said, changing the subject from my wayward thoughts.

Lavi's fingers brushed mine as we walked closer to the camels. "Let's take a look," he said.

I hurried to keep up with him as children darted between the adults in the crowd and men and women bartered with the caravan driver and the merchants accompanying him. The scents of camel dung and sweat mingled with the sweeter smells of pomegranates, spices, and oranges. Leather goods carried a rich, deep scent, drawing my attention. Piles of white wool hung tied on one side of the nearest camel.

"So many things," I said barely above a whisper. "I hope Ima and Abba can sell their wares for a fair price."

"Is there anything you see that you like?" Lavi touched a strand of beads hanging from one of the camel's necks. "These would look beautiful on you." His dark eyes probed mine, causing my heart to flutter. "But then anything you wear only enhances your beauty."

My cheeks grew hot. I smacked his arm. "You shouldn't say things like that. Someone might hear you." I turned away, both embarrassed and secretly pleased.

"I don't care who hears me, Ness." He touched my shoulder, coaxing me to meet his gaze. "You know I want you to be mine."

I could not pull away. "I know," I said softly. Shyness swept over me all of a sudden, and I stepped back. "But we are not yet betrothed. We should not assume."

Lavi scoffed. "Your father knows me, Nessa. Who else would make a better husband to you?" He fingered the earrings that matched an even brighter necklace, one with jewels like a bridal crown. "But I know your mother is also talking to the other mothers in town. I don't have anything to offer your father as a bride-price. I think he hesitates because of that." He drew a hand down the scruff on his chin, not yet a full beard. "You know, it would help if you told your father that you want me. He listens to you."

I found my sandals fascinating at that moment. Anything to avoid the pleading in his eyes. "I asked him to wait a little." I lifted my head, urging him with a look to really hear me. "I'm not ready, Lavi. Give me a little longer."

"But why?" He frowned. "Have I offended you?"

"No, no! I'm just adjusting to the idea of marriage, that's all." Was that really my reason?

"But we've talked about this since we were young. Aren't all girls anxious to wed once they are able?" His confusion matched the feelings in my heart.

"Well, yes. I suppose so. That is . . . I'm not sure everyone feels the same—"

"Nessa! There you are!" Gali rushed up to me. "Why didn't you wait for us?" She looked at Lavi. "Am I interrupting something?" she whispered, leaning close.

I shook my head. "You're fine." I faced Lavi. "I will be back." Grabbing Gali's hand, I pulled her toward the cheese maker's booth. "Come with me."

"Are you running from him?" Gali asked when we were out of earshot. "Aren't you supposed to marry him?"

"He wants to marry me," I corrected. "I don't know what I want. Or what my father wants."

"But he is already part of your family. Your father shouldn't have any reason to hesitate." Gali sized me up with her typical no-nonsense expression. "What's going on, Ness?"

I lifted one shoulder in a half shrug. "I don't know. I asked my father for a little time to adjust. It's not like I can wait for you to . . . you know . . . so we can wed at the same time. But I had hoped to be planning our weddings together, and now everything is changing so fast!"

Gali patted my hand. "I want the same thing, but I'll be one of your maids, and when it's my turn, you'll be mine. You can't slow down what is determined to come, Ness."

"I know." The thought simply brought more misery. "I don't know what's wrong with me. I can't imagine marrying anyone else. I guess I should tell that to my father."

"Definitely," Gali said.

A commotion of loud voices and boisterous laughter pulled us out of the cheese maker's booth. I turned to see my father embracing an older man, apparently someone he hadn't seen in a while. I studied them a moment. The man had a familiar look, but I couldn't place him.

"Let's go back to the camels to see the things the merchants have brought," Gali said, tugging my arm. "They will be gone before we know it."

I nodded, still watching my father talking with the stranger. My sisters were clustered around my mother, and Lavi had found Chen again. They appeared to be haggling over a large bundle of wool.

Gali stopped at the side of a camel, where beads and jewels hung. "I wonder how much these cost," she said, her eyes alight. "Maybe they have a bridal crown you could ask your father to purchase for your wedding."

I scoffed. "My father is not going to spend money on me. He will tell me to wear the bridal crown worn by my mother and sisters. Our family is not going to purchase something new just for me." Not that I minded. There was something good in knowing I would be wearing my family's traditional jewels

23

when that day came. But would a necklace as Lavi had shown me be so wrong to want?

I touched one of the sparkling necklaces and matching earrings as a woman approached from my right. "Ahh, I can see you have good taste in jewels, young woman. But they are quite costly."

I took a step back. "They are beautiful, but I could never spend money on jewels."

The woman tsked. "For you? I give you necklace and earrings for two denarii, eh? It is not so much." She lifted her hands in a dismissive gesture, as if such a large amount should mean nothing to me. Was she serious? "Are you betrothed?" she asked, looking beyond me. I did not dare follow her gaze in case Lavi stood there listening. But she seemed to be directing her words at someone other than me. "Perhaps your young man should come and see me so he has a proper gift to give you on that day." She searched my face. Her smile showed slightly yellowed and crooked teeth, but her eyes were kind.

"I am not betrothed yet," I said. "And I do not know who my betrothed will be, so I could not send him to you." I bowed to the woman. "But I thank you."

"Come now. Why don't you at least try them on? With your beauty, these jewels would shine like the stars." The woman took them from the camel's side and held them out to me.

"I couldn't." My protest sounded weak.

"Come on, Ness. You know you want to." Gali was not helping.

The woman draped the shining beads over my neck and slipped the earrings into the holes in my ears, then pulled me toward a bronze mirror to see myself, however imperfectly.

"Oh, Ness, you look amazing," Gali breathed, a hand to her heart.

I wanted to scoff, but one look in the glass and a glance into Gali's earnest face, and I held my response in check.

24

"Nessa?" Ima's voice from behind made me jump nearly out of my skin.

"Ima!" I yanked the beads and earrings off me and thrust them into the hands of the merchant. "I was just looking."

My mother, with my sisters crowding around, looked at the jewels then at me. "We have plenty of jewels for your wedding," Ima said. "There is no need to wish for more when your sisters were perfectly fine with what we have."

Meital lifted her chin and Adva scoffed, and they both turned and walked away. Yaffa gave me a compassionate look and touched my arm. "Don't worry, Ness. They're just jealous."

I had always sensed it was true but thought Yaffa felt the same way. Was I wrong about this sister?

"Come on, Yaffa!" Meital called over her shoulder. Ima had already followed her and Adva away from the camels to another part of the market.

Yaffa leaned in close to my ear. "You're Abba's favorite, Ness. That affects us all." She turned and left then.

I looked at Gali. "My family hates me."

"They don't hate you, Ness," Gali said, linking arms with me. "You're just prettier than they are, and for some reason they think your abba loves you more. That would make me jealous too, you know."

I shook free of her grasp. "Well, it shouldn't. I have no control over such things." I stalked away, and Gali hurried after me.

"Ness! Stop!" She reached my side and grabbed my hand. "Please. The merchants are only here for today. Forget your sisters and the jewels and even Lavi. Let's just look around."

I drew in a breath. "You're right. Let's go."

Gali led us back to the market, and we spent the day looking at things we could not afford to purchase.

Later that evening I helped Ima in silence, listening as she chattered about my sisters and possible suitors who might come calling any day now. I placed the food on the table as always, and when the door opened with my father and brother and Lavi, the man I had seen at the market was in their company.

"Hurry and set another place," Ima hissed as the older man settled on the cushions next to Abba. I ran to the cooking area, found a dish and cup for wine, and set them before the man.

"And this is my youngest daughter, Nessa," Abba said as I backed away from the man. "Nessa, this is Amichai, an old friend of mine."

I bowed. "Shalom. A pleasure to meet you," I said, then rushed from the room.

"She's a quiet one," my father said. "But she's a good young woman. Always helpful."

Why was he singing my praises when they weren't even true? I didn't feel helpful most of the time. Or good. Not with some of the thoughts that ran through my mind.

The men continued to talk, and Ima and I carried the flatbread and sauces to the table and took our seats at the end of the table. I chewed a piece of flatbread that was tasteless despite the spices Ima had added to these loaves.

Chen spoke with Abba and Amichai, but Lavi remained unusually silent. One glance in his direction showed me why. Fear flitted in his gaze, and he kept looking at Abba's friend as if he was another suitor. But he was simply an old friend of Abba's, not someone who wanted to marry me.

But Lavi's misery worried me. I would speak to Abba on his behalf tomorrow. Put Lavi's fears to rest and begin to plan our betrothal. Yes, that was truly what I wanted. I couldn't bear to see him fear losing me, especially when there was nothing to fear. I loved him. I did.

Tomorrow I would make sure he knew it.

3

I rose from my bed as the sun lit my room, then stepped outside to retrieve water from our cistern. Voices came to me from the inner courtyard where we cooked our food. I stepped into the house and tiptoed closer, listening as my mother and father argued.

"You can't possibly be serious, my husband," Ima said, her tone stern. "Amichai is old enough to be her father! And we've known Lavi all his life."

"Precisely why Lavi is not the right choice for her." Abba blew out a breath. "I haven't told you this, but I caught him stealing from me. I warned him the first time and have not seen him do so again, but one of my tools went missing a week ago and I have yet to find it. I cannot trust him, Lihi."

I covered my mouth to stifle a gasp. I was certain that Lavi wouldn't do such a thing to my father. Why would he? Confusion whirled inside of me as I pressed my back to the wall.

"But Amichai! Let me find someone better suited to her, closer to her age," Ima insisted.

Yes, please, Abba. Listen to Ima. I could barely breathe for the fear pumping through my veins.

"Amichai is a good man, Lihi. He is grieving the loss of his wife, and Nessa would be the perfect distraction for him. To help him get over his grief." Abba's tone changed, and I recognized his stubborn resolve. When he acted like this, my mother usually did not get what she wanted, though normally she could convince him of anything. Why was he pushing so hard to see this man marry me, his favorite daughter?

Desperation warred with anxiety within me. I'd asked Abba to wait, and now all of a sudden he wanted to wed me to this unattractive old man. Why?

"Humph. Let him grieve and marry a woman his own age. A widow would understand him far better than a young virgin. You can't do this, Raanan."

Silence followed Ima's outburst, and for a moment I hoped. Surely Abba would listen to reason.

"I already promised him," Abba said, his voice dropping so low I barely heard him.

"You what? Without asking me? How could you? You know that I've been talking to the women whose sons are interested in her. I've simply been waiting for one to offer the best bride-price."

My stomach dipped at Ima's words, and I pressed a hand to my middle, certain I would be sick.

"Amichai can offer more. He is a wealthy potter, Lihi. And he wants Nessa. He is captivated by her beauty. He will treat her well." The sound of Abba's footsteps made me move quickly away from where he might see me. "The matter is settled, Lihi," he said as he walked in my direction.

I fled down the hall to my room and sank onto my pallet, heart pounding. Why were they doing this to me? Was my father so concerned about money that he would sell me to such a man?

Lavi. Why had he stolen from Abba—if indeed he had? My father would not lie about such a thing. Would he?

How would I face Lavi knowing that my father had rejected him for a man three times my age? And a potter? I was a weaver and knew nothing about the life of a potter, and I had no interest in finding out.

Despair threatened to overwhelm me as I stared at my hands, wondering if I would be expected to turn the potter's wheel instead of work with threads. And how could I become a wife to someone who nearly repulsed me?

I lay my head on my pillow and curled onto my side, wishing I could go back to sleep and not wake up. Or wake up and find out that this was all a dream. A very bad dream.

All attempts at forgetting or sleeping again vanished in a moment, and I resolved I would not let this happen without speaking to my father. I jumped up and ran barefoot from the house before I could even tie on my sandals or my mother could stop me. I rushed to the back of Abba's shop and slowed to catch my breath at the entrance.

Lavi and Chen looked up from their work on one of the tents. I nodded at them both but turned away to face my father.

"Abba, may I please speak with you?" I willed myself to give him my brightest smile. "Please."

He gave me a curious look, but after a moment, he set his tools aside. "What is it?"

I glanced at Lavi and Chen. "Might we speak outside?" The last thing I needed was for one of them to overhear.

My father released a heavy sigh but led me away from the shop to a copse of trees. He faced me, brows drawn in concern. "What is it this time, Nessa?" He glanced at my feet. "Where are your sandals?"

I swallowed my fear of speaking my mind. I searched his face. "I left in a hurry. I heard you talking to Ima."

"You should not have done so." He crossed his arms over his chest.

"I know, but I came upon you and couldn't pull away. You can't possibly send me off to marry that man instead of Lavi." I kept my voice low and glanced back at the shop, fearing that Lavi had followed us. "Why would you do that to me, Abba? You know Lavi has wanted to marry me for years."

"It seems to me that a few days ago you were not so sure about Lavi and wanted to wait to marry. Now you are so certain?" His scowl did nothing to aid my confidence.

"I thought about it and decided that there is no one I want more than Lavi. We've known each other most of our lives and he will be good to me, and I . . . I love him, Abba." I gave him a pleading look, searching for a glimpse of compassion in his eyes.

He dropped his arms to his sides. "Nessa." He motioned for me to sit beside him on a fallen log.

I obeyed and twisted my hands in my lap.

"Nessa," he said again, "you think you know what is best for you. But you are young. Too young to know your own mind."

"But not too young to wed? And you would betroth me to a man three times my age? I am old enough for that?" My voice rose with the emotion clogging my throat.

He shook his head. "You put me in a difficult position. You were not certain but now you are? It shows how little you know your own mind. It is a father's obligation to choose the best man for his daughters. I have made my choice."

"You would assign me to a miserable life simply because this man is wealthy?" I could not keep the hurt from my tone or the tears from slipping down my hot cheeks. I had never talked so openly with my father, or so boldly.

He patted my arm in an awkward gesture. "You will not be miserable, my daughter. Amichai has a large home and even a few servants. You will be mistress of a home larger than mine, and one day you will thank me for it. Wealth has its benefits, and I would give you that. Lavi can provide you nothing. You would both end up living under our roof all of your lives, and when Chen takes over my business, who is to say that he might not send Lavi away, and you with him?"

He was making excuses now. "Chen would never send us

away." Didn't he want me to stay with him? Living under their roof had not been so bad all these years, had it?

Abba lifted his hands in an imploring gesture. "When I'm gone, I have no idea what Chen will do. But, Nessa, if you heard me speaking with your mother, then you know my concerns about Lavi." This time he glanced toward the shop. "I care for the boy like a son, but I'm not sure I trust him. If I cannot trust him with my tools, how can I trust him with my daughter?"

"But we would be living right here. What could he possibly do to me?" I was pleading now, even amid my own doubts. "I don't want to leave you." I lowered my voice. "Abba, won't you reconsider?"

He rose from the log and pulled me to my feet. Placing both hands on my shoulders, he held my gaze. "Amichai is a good man, Nessa. He needs someone right now and you need a husband. It is a good match."

The set to his jaw and that same tone he had used with my mother accompanied his words. He would not back out of his promise to this man now, even if it meant my whole life's happiness.

I could not stop the tears then, and suddenly I could no longer bear to be in his presence. I broke free of his grasp and ran weeping all the way home.

❖ ❖ ❖

By evening everyone in Sychar had heard the news, even though the betrothal had not officially taken place. The date had been set for the following week, and while the household was nearly mourning with Lihi moping and Nessa taking to her bed, Lavi sought Raanan, anger pulsing through him. He clenched his hands, not caring what his uncle thought of him. This decision regarding Nessa was wrong. All wrong.

He came upon Raanan and Chen carving wood into tent

pegs. He stopped in front of them both. "How could you?" he demanded, arms crossed, voice raised.

Chen took a step back and Raanan faced him. "How could I what, my son?"

"Don't call me your son! You could have made me your son by letting me marry Nessa. How could you even think to betroth her to someone else? And a man your age at that?" His breath came in hot spurts and his heart pounded.

Raanan stood, extending a hand toward Lavi as if to placate him. "You need to calm down, Lavi. Whatever decisions I make for my daughter are up to me, not you."

"But I asked you first. You've known I wanted to marry her for years. I see now what you really think of me!" He glared at his uncle.

"You are young, Lavi. You will find another girl when the time is right. My decision stands." Raanan returned Lavi's firm look, though his tone gentled. Of course, what did he have to be angry over? He was getting exactly what he wanted.

"I don't want another girl. Nessa is my cousin and I want her. I will take her and we will run away if you insist on going through with this." His threat surprised even him, and he swallowed hard, wishing back the words. If he did run away with her, he would do so in secret. Would Nessa even agree to go with him?

"You are dangerously close to crossing a line you do not want to cross, young man. I could have you stoned for doing such a thing."

Chen sidled next to his father, and Lavi knew he was defeated. Chen would never agree with him, even if he had been sympathetic until now.

"Nessa doesn't want that man," Lavi said, weaker now. "You know she doesn't. She wants me."

"Nessa will obey my wishes," Raanan said. "She has no say in this and you know it."

"Do you care nothing for your daughter's happiness? You just want the money this man can give you." At Raanan's guilty look, Lavi rushed on. "That's it, isn't it? I'm a poor orphan who works for you and can offer nothing but love for your daughter, but you would rather have the gold of a rich man to fill your pockets and send Nessa off to live unloved in the house of a man with children older than she is!"

"Enough!" Raanan curled his hands into fists. He took one step closer to Lavi. "You will either stop this ranting right now or you can take your things and find somewhere else to live and work. The choice is yours."

Lavi felt as though he'd been punched. Somewhere inside of him he had actually thought he could convince his uncle to change his mind. But he'd come on too strong. Nessa had warned him often about his temper. Why hadn't he considered that?

He shifted from foot to foot, staring at this man who held his fate. Should he take his things and leave? Where would he go? He didn't want to live on the streets or leave Sychar with nothing. He would need funds before he could leave. But his uncle paid him so little.

Perhaps it was time to return to selling some of his uncle's things here and there when no one was aware. Maybe even help himself to some of the gold this Amichai was going to give Raanan to take Nessa away from him. Yet stealing wasn't right. He knew that and Nessa didn't like it, but what else could he do? Run away with the next caravan, which might not come through for months?

The thought held some interest, but he wasn't ready.

"Well, what is it going to be, Lavi?" Raanan tapped a foot.

"I'll stay," Lavi said at last, letting his arms drop to his sides. Defeat settled over him, but he lifted his chin, hiding his thoughts. "Until I can find other employment," he added, his anger still simmering under the surface.

He whirled about and stalked off. Yes. He would seek employment with someone else. Apprentice under someone who did something besides build tents. Somehow he would find a way. And hope he could forget Nessa in the process.

4

ome on, Ness, stop frowning," Yaffa said as she helped me dress for the betrothal a week later. "Your mouth will settle with lines you don't want if you don't smile again." She touched my shoulder and bent to peer into my face. "It will be all right."

I swiped my eyes. I had thought my tears were spent, but obviously not. "It's not even the wedding day, so why do I have to dress up for it? I just have to accept his gifts and watch them sign the ketubah."

"You are the bride, dear one. We only do this once, so enjoy the process. I know he isn't the man you wanted. But it won't matter once you're mistress in your own home. He might not even come to you that often. They say older men don't care so much."

My eyes grew wide as I stared at my sister. The gossips at the well did not have good things to say about the marriage bed, something I feared.

"He won't love me." I was pouting, but I didn't care.

"Love doesn't matter. You'll have money and power—more than all of us—and he will probably treat you like one of his daughters most of the time. You are younger than his children, after all. What matters is that he's kind. If he's not, you can bring a case to Abba and let him deal with him." Yaffa sounded so sure of herself.

"You don't know what you're talking about. You got to marry the man you wanted, as did all of you." My sisters had been given their choice, and yet I, the supposed favorite of my father, had not. Perhaps I had not truly been his favorite but simply the one who could bring the greatest price because of the beauty everyone claimed I had.

"Well, I know that Abba is his friend and Amichai won't want to anger his friend by mistreating you." Yaffa adjusted the flowers in my hair. "There. You look perfect. Now come. He will be here and Abba won't want you to keep him waiting."

I stood, but my legs felt weighted and my whole body had lost its energy. I drew in a deep, steadying breath. In the distance, I heard a knock on the door, and male voices drifted down the hall to me. Ima and my sisters talked quietly where they prepared treats for us, and I knew everyone awaited my appearance.

Trembling, I allowed Yaffa to lead me to the main sitting room to a seat prepared for me. Servants followed Amichai into the house and laid gifts at my feet. A carved chest to house the garments I would weave. A ring for my finger and the very jewels and earrings I had tried on when the caravan had visited Sychar a week ago. Wool of the finest kind to be dyed and woven and a variety of baskets. At last Amichai presented me with a flask of costly perfume and then presented my father with a sack of gold coins.

I nodded and offered a small smile with each gift, and finally forced myself to say, "Thank you," when he finished.

Amichai smiled wide. "It is I who must thank you for being willing to wed an old man." He knelt in front of me. "I will treat you well, Nessa." He stood and quickly put his seal to the ketubah alongside my father's.

So, it was done. I sat in numb silence while Amichai and my father drank and laughed at their good fortune.

My mother and sisters produced food and drink for all, but my stomach recoiled at the thought of either. I longed to run far from this place. Chen drank with the men, but Lavi was nowhere to be seen. It was just as well. Would I ever see him again, or would he leave us now?

It didn't matter, I told myself, but in my heart it did. I watched Amichai from across the room, and with every word spoken, every laugh, and every glance my way, all I could think of was what I didn't have. What I had lost with this night and could never get back.

❖ ❖ ❖

Amichai stopped by after work each night after the betrothal to dine with us—something my father had readily agreed to but that had not pleased my mother.

"The man could wait until the wedding," Ima told me as we prepared the normal barley stew and baked the flatbread in the clay oven. "You're supposed to have a year until the wedding. We need time to prepare, to weave the clothes you will need. I don't like him coming so often."

"Nor I," I said just above a whisper.

I caught Ima's compassionate gaze. I was not used to affection from my mother, but in that moment, she touched my cheek and cradled it in her palm. "I'm sorry, my daughter. I know you wanted Lavi."

"Or anyone younger," I admitted. "Am I the only one who thinks this whole arrangement is wrong?"

Ima turned back to the stew, stirring it over a small fire in the courtyard. "You are not the only one," she said, not looking my way. "But there is nothing to be done about it now."

I knew that, but a shudder worked through me just the same.

An hour later Abba and Chen came into the house, and

Amichai knocked on the door. Lavi joined us only moments before my father pronounced the blessing. Misery lined his face, but he said nothing throughout the meal.

I pushed the food around my plate, barely eating, listening to Amichai's grating voice talking and laughing with my father and brother. Once I moved to his home, I would live with his two sons and daughters-in-law. Would they make life more bearable? Or worse?

I'd heard he also had two daughters, but they lived across Sychar with their husbands. All of them were much older than I was, with children of their own. How could I marry a man who was already a grandfather? *Oh Adonai, why?*

"I would like to take Nessa to meet my children," Amichai said, jolting my thoughts to the conversation. He glanced at my father for permission and received a slight nod. We were legally wed, but for custom and propriety's sake, I should not be alone with him yet. Nor did I want to be.

My father glanced at Ima, whose mouth was pinched in a slight frown. I took small comfort in that.

"If one of her sisters is free to accompany them, I see no problem," Ima said at last.

Lavi snorted, but low enough that only I could hear. His anger had not abated, and when Amichai visited I felt the tension growing between them, affecting us all. If Lavi was not careful, my father would send him away. I could not bear that for him.

"I will be happy to go," I said quickly, lest Lavi say something he would regret. I looked at Amichai but could not return the smile on his thin face. Hard lines accentuated his features, and his hair was too long and graying. "If Yaffa will come with us," I added, meeting Ima's gaze.

"Better yet," Amichai said as he dipped Ima's bread into the stew and held it, "why don't you all come—your daughters included—to a dinner party next week? Since we were not all able to meet at the betrothal, this will be a good time for our families to get better acquainted."

Why hadn't his children attended our betrothal? I had simply accepted that the business was between my father and my new husband. The family would come together at the wedding. I was in no hurry to meet his children but said nothing to this new idea.

"A dinner party sounds lovely." Ima stood to refill the cups of wine.

"Then it's settled," Amichai said around a mouthful of food. His talking and chewing at the same time made me turn away. My father ate the same way, and I'd never gotten used to it. Perhaps it was the way of older men.

I fought the urge to release a troubled sigh and focused instead on the food I continued to push around my plate.

"Next week," Abba said.

"On Shabbat," Amichai added. "Let us celebrate the day together."

"All of us?" I glanced at Lavi. Would he be welcome in my new home?

Amichai seemed to follow the direction of my gaze. "All of you," he said after a moment. But by his look and tone, I wasn't sure he meant it.

❖ ❖ ❖

I walked between Yaffa and Adva as we hurried along Sychar's streets before the sun set on Shabbat the following week. Meital walked with Ima, and Chen and Abba and my brothers-in-law led the way. Lavi had disappeared after work the day before and had not yet returned.

"I wish he would have come," I said, worrying my lower lip. "I'd like to think he would feel welcome when we wed."

Adva laughed and Yaffa gave me a pointed look.

"What's so funny?" I should be used to their teasing and

picking on me, but Meital and Adva could be unkind, and I knew better than to trust either of these sisters with my thoughts.

"You're so naive, Ness. Lavi is never going to be welcome in Amichai's home. Amichai won't allow it." Adva flipped the end of her belt as our feet tapped the stone streets.

"Why not?" I looked at Yaffa.

Adva continued laughing, but Yaffa touched my arm. "Men do not want other men around their women," she said softly. "Amichai knows you wanted Lavi. Lavi will be a threat to him and Lavi knows it. I'm sorry, Ness. You just need to accept what is and let Lavi go. He should probably move on. We would all be happier if he did."

I wouldn't. "I think he wants to, and he will when he can afford to live somewhere else."

"Perhaps Father can put in a word for him with another tentmaker or he can apprentice for some other trade." Adva offered me a conciliatory smile. "Don't fret so much, sister."

I frowned, but when Amichai's house came into view, I drew myself up and forced a smile as Amichai welcomed each one of us.

"Nessa, my love." He led me ahead of the others. "These are my sons Arieh and Ezra and their wives, Hila and Rina."

I nodded to each one.

"Welcome to our home," Hila said, though Rina merely smiled. Both looked older than Meital.

A moment later, three children, probably three or four years old, ran up to their mothers and grabbed their skirts.

"And here are my daughters Devora and Elke and their husbands, Melek and Shalev. You will not see them as often, though we do try to keep Shabbat together each week." Amichai fairly beamed at his offspring, all men and women much older than me. Devora held a toddler on her hip, and Elke bent to speak to another three-year-old.

"Welcome, everyone," Amichai said, turning back to my family. "Please, take your seats."

I glanced at the opulent room with its wall tapestries and soft rugs to cradle our feet. Embroidered cushions were placed about an ornate oak table where the men reclined at the head and the women at the foot. My father could have never afforded such decor, nor would he have thought to spend any extra money on such things. The wealth just in this room took my breath.

Amichai's daughters and daughters-in-law served us basic Shabbat fare, though the pistachio sweets were the best I had ever tasted. Even the pottery, no doubt made by Amichai and his sons, boasted bold, colorful designs. I stole a glance at Yaffa, saw her raised brow, and knew she was feeling as overwhelmed as I.

About an hour later, as the meal came to an end, I longed to return to my father's home to escape this house, this man, and his offspring. To think. To process all I had tasted and seen.

Hila approached me. "You are nervous about joining us, yes?" She took my arm. "Walk with me." She led me further into the house and pointed out each of the rooms. More tapestries draped the walls, and colorful rugs covered the wooden floor, another expense few in Sychar could afford. Furniture filled each room, even those obviously set aside for the children. "I'm sure you know that the sons stay with the father and their wives join the father's family while his daughters live in the houses of their husbands' fathers. You will be the mistress of this house because you are taking Ahuva's place, peace be upon her. But don't expect that role to be easy." She turned back to where we had been but stopped short of the eating area, where the rest of the family remained talking.

"I don't have any expectations." I searched Hila's face, noting kindness in her dark eyes.

"Rina isn't happy that you are so young," Hila said, glancing beyond me and leaning close to my ear. "You are old enough to wed, of course, but no one would have guessed that Amichai would choose someone younger than his own children. We thought he might remarry because he is lonely, but we thought he would choose one of the older widows in town. It would have been a better choice for everyone."

I couldn't have agreed more. "Then why did he want me?" And why was I trusting this woman I did not know? Could she be trusted, or would she end up acting like Adva and Meital often did?

"Have you never seen your reflection in a glass?" Hila laughed softly, a pleasant sound. "You are strikingly beautiful, Nessa. I am honestly surprised that your father didn't take the highest bidder rather than settle for an old friend."

"You make me sound like a slave to be auctioned." Pouting didn't become me, so I told myself to hide my expression behind a smile.

"You might feel like that sometimes, but Amichai is a decent man. He will treat you well. Just be sure to treat all of us the same way. Rina will come around, as will the others. In time."

Time. Something I did not have. If Amichai had his way, I might be living here far too soon.

5

*L*avi rose before dawn and gathered everything he had to his name, along with some of his uncle's tools and the gold coins Amichai had paid him the month before to assist him in finding somewhere new to live. He couldn't truly fault the man for wanting him out of Nessa's life, though he still could not shake his resentment. Was that why he'd waited another month before making the decision to leave?

He fingered the pouch with the gold, his face heating with the memory of that encounter with Amichai. He shouldn't have returned home and taken a few gold pieces from the pouch Amichai had paid for Nessa. Nessa deserved better from him, and Amichai would provide well for her. It wasn't like she needed the gold, and he was not about to let Ranaan keep it all after what he'd done.

A soft curse aimed at his uncle escaped his lips, but a moment later, he shook himself, tied everything together in a bundle, and attached the load to his back. He slipped into his sandals and tiptoed out of the house. He closed the door gently behind him and passed the brick oven on his way to the courtyard gate.

"Lavi?"

He nearly jumped out of his skin at the soft voice. He whirled about. "Nessa? What are you doing up at this hour?" His heart pounded against his ribs.

"I could ask you the same thing. Where are you going?" She looked deeply into his eyes, then noted the pack on his back. "You're leaving us," she whispered.

He nodded. "I can't bear to lose you, Ness, and to stay and watch you marry that man is too much."

She released a breath, glanced back at the house, then faced him again. "Where will you go?"

He shrugged. "I haven't thought that far. Away."

"But you have to have a plan. You can't just live in the wild." Worry lines etched her brow, and he took comfort in knowing that she cared for him.

"I'll make one as I walk. Right now I need to leave before anyone else knows it. Don't say anything, please, Ness. If your father discovers that you saw me leave and didn't tell him . . . I don't want you to get into trouble." He swallowed a sudden lump, emotion welling within him. He tamped it down, focusing on his anger instead.

"I won't tell. But please, somehow, keep in touch with me." She stepped toward him and reached up to kiss his cheek.

The kiss was his undoing. He clung to her and kissed her gently, all of his longing pouring into a kiss that could never be more than that. When she didn't pull away, he deepened the kiss until she melted against him.

"Oh, Lavi, don't leave," she said, resting her head against his chest.

He held her close, breathing in the scent of her, longing to take her away with him. To keep her forever.

"I have to," he said at last. "I'll never forget you, Ness. I love you. I always have."

"I love you too," she said.

The gray light of predawn shook him out of this moment

44

of bliss. "I must go." He grasped her hand and squeezed, then noticed lamplight coming from the house. "Keep our secret," he whispered, then turned and half ran away from the house, away from Nessa. Away from love.

He shouldn't have kissed her like that. He would have taken her completely in a heartbeat after that kiss. Would God strike him for such thoughts?

No. God didn't care about him. If He did, none of this would have happened. His parents would still be living. Nessa's father would have accepted his request to marry her, and they would live together happily forever.

He picked up his pace as the gates of Sychar drew near. Once he was past the guard, he would find a solitary place and think of where to go next. He was free to do what he wanted.

Why did that thought not make him glad? But there would never be anything to make him glad without Nessa.

❖ ❖ ❖

I lifted the water jug to my shoulders and followed Gali through the streets of Sychar toward Jacob's well. The evening breeze lifted my veil and blew it behind me, a welcome relief to the heat of the day. The sun's rays began painting the sky in reds, oranges, pinks, and yellows as it worked its way behind Mt. Gerizim.

Had Lavi gotten away? How far had he traveled? Would I ever see him again? How would he live? Would he be forced to steal to survive or, worse, be caught and stoned for it? A heavy weight settled in my middle as the fear of what could happen played in my thoughts.

"You're moving slowly today," Gali said, walking beside me. "Is your time upon you that you seem so sluggish?"

I shook my head. "No. I'm just . . ." I glanced away. I'd promised Lavi. I couldn't tell anyone.

"Are you worrying about your wedding?" Gali stopped,

forcing me to do the same. "You can tell me anything, Ness. You know that."

I nodded. "I know. I just don't know what to say. I wanted Lavi but I can't have him. Is God punishing me that my father would choose Amichai of all people?"

Gali's eyes widened, and she began walking again.

I hurried after her. "That's why I didn't say anything. The wedding is only five months away now, and I don't know where the time went or what I'm going to do when that day comes."

"You're going to marry the man, that's what," Gali said. We reached the well but held back while a line of other women filled their jars.

"I know. But I don't want to. And Abba said that Lavi is missing and we don't know where he went." I could say that much because I was only quoting my father.

"When did this happen?"

"Just this morning."

"Did he not even say goodbye to you?" Gali searched my face. "He did. That's why you're so upset."

"No. He didn't. That's why I'm upset." The lie tasted sour on my tongue, but I'd promised.

Gali sighed. "I'm sorry, Ness. I would have thought that he would at least tell you, even if he didn't tell anyone else."

I shook my head, trying to look confident under Gali's scrutinizing gaze. "He was gone before anyone was up this morning. Abba checked his shop, but there was no sign of him. He and Chen searched the city, but no one had seen him."

"Amichai will be glad about that," Gali said, frowning. "You don't think he had anything to do with Lavi's disappearance, do you? He wouldn't hurt him? Or maybe he paid him to leave."

If only he had. "No. Abba asked Amichai if he had seen him. He knew nothing. For all his faults, I think he would have told my father if he'd paid Lavi to leave."

"I'm not so sure . . . I mean, he knew you wanted to marry

Lavi and how angry Lavi has been. How well do you know Amichai? Not well enough to know if he would do such a thing."

"Well, I don't think he would have." I weighed her words as we moved closer to the well, the line dwindling. "Of course, it is possible." Would Lavi have kept such knowledge from me? How could I know? Lavi was gone, and I truly did not know Amichai despite his many visits. He talked to my father more than he did to me.

"I guess you'll never know then," Gali said, lowering the jug into the deep well, waiting to hear the splash at the bottom.

"I guess not." I glanced at Mt. Gerizim in the distance. We would have to hurry before the sun descended completely. How was it that we always seemed to barely make it home in time?

But today I didn't care. The memory of Lavi's kiss still lingered, and I would never forget the way he made me melt in his arms. I would have gone with him in a heartbeat if not for the knowledge that my father and Amichai would find us.

If he did take the tools my father said were missing, Lavi would be in danger wherever he went. I could never have gone with him. But I couldn't stop my heart from doing so.

6

*H*old still, Ness," Yaffa said, attempting to place a veil over my head and fit it with a narrow headband. "You're fidgeting like a restless doe."

"You don't want to squirm out of Amichai's embrace tonight, so calm down, sister." Adva's tone held no rebuke, causing me to look up and meet her gaze. "All will go well if you just relax."

"Adva's right." Meital approached and placed on my head a simple golden bridal crown with a few colorful gems of carnelian, jasper, and amethyst. While many brides wore their own crowns, a gift from their betrothed as part of their dowry, my family had preferred the groom give the dowry in gold coins. My mother liked the tradition of passing down her crown for each of us to share. I think it had more to do with my father wanting the gold. "Amichai will be a fine husband, and after tonight you will be wealthier than all of us. Be grateful."

Grateful? How could I possibly be grateful for something I had dreaded for nearly a year?

"Here. See how beautiful you look, my daughter?" Ima held the silver glass up for me to see, though my reflection told me little through the veil.

48

"There," Yaffa said, placing a colorful shawl over my shoulders. "You look perfect. Now come. We should wait in the sitting room for his knock."

The sounds of my sisters' young children laughing and running through the house reached me. How old I now felt in comparison to them.

I let my sisters lead me to the bench each of them had used on their wedding day, silently praying for some kind of peace. Did God answer such prayers? I had prayed often in the synagogue and at Passover when our family had traveled with the whole town to the top of Mt. Gerizim, where the ruins of our temple reminded us of what used to be. But no matter how much I cried out to Him, God never answered.

Gali burst into the house, followed by nine of my cousins and friends who would be my maids. They surrounded me with exuberant giggles, then took up a song to the bride as I sat listening.

"Smile, Ness," Gali said, bending low to my ear. "This is your wedding day."

"How do you know I'm not? The veil hides my face," I said, feeling cross but hoping I didn't sound that way.

"The veil is thin. Besides, I can tell," she said softly. "If you smile, you will lift up your head and at least seem happy to receive your groom."

I complied but said nothing more. I knew the smile did not reach my heart. It seemed to satisfy Gali, though, and I released a breath, thankful to have appeased her. I could do this. No one need ever know that I was unhappy with this marriage or that I still pined for Lavi. No one.

But surely God knew my heart, and I struggled with bewilderment and anger at Him for either not hearing or not caring to answer my desperate prayers to change my circumstances.

God had not given Lavi back to me nor sent Amichai away. He had given me no joy in my upcoming nuptials, nor cared when I cried myself to sleep in the darkness. I had a thirst for something I could not name, something that I was certain Amichai could never satisfy, but I told myself over and over that I was probably simply being childish. I was a woman now. I would learn to accept what I did not want. Maybe my longings were not as important as I thought they were.

I stayed seated on the bench while my sisters and mother left me to prepare the food we would take to Amichai's house. The actual ceremony would take place there with the rabbi's blessing and our coming together in the bridal tent.

A shudder passed through me, and I pulled the shawl closer. But the air was warm and the chill was not coming from outside of me. I was cold deep down in a place I could not define.

Dusk settled over the house too soon, and while many grooms waited until darkness shrouded the town, Amichai's knock jolted me before the sun had completely set.

Abba and Chen had just returned from the shop and freshened themselves when the knock came. Ima hurried to my side, and Gali and my maids surrounded me.

"Don't be nervous, Ness," Gali whispered as my father opened the door. "All will be well."

"I'm not nervous," I said, again offering a smile she could barely see.

"Your hands are shaking," Gali said, taking her place beside me.

I clasped my hands in my lap to still them as Amichai approached. He reached for me, and I extended a hand, allowing him to pull me to my feet. The virgins lifted their lamps as he led me to a wooden litter draped in a colorful canopy and helped me inside. Male servants lifted me up and led us to Amichai's house set in the hills on the city's west side.

Amichai's sons and the men of the town walked with him, while my maids and sisters and mother walked beside my litter. The lanterns held high and the jubilant voices of the townspeople tried to permeate the wall I had built around my heart. I should be joyful and laughing with them on this wedding day. But I could not bring myself to feel anything other than fear and a sense of numbness.

Would Amichai's kiss feel anything like Lavi's? But I could not think thus. I must marry this man and choose to like him, whether I would ever love him or not. I must bear his children and rule his household, as Ima had spent months teaching me to do.

The procession stopped, and Amichai helped me from the litter and led me toward the huppah. He took my hand and we stood before the rabbi. Normally, a groom's parents would bless the union, but given my new husband was widowed with no living parents, he called upon our rabbi to say the traditional words.

I listened attentively to all seven blessings, which ended with "Blessed are You, Lord our God, Ruler of the Universe, who creates happiness and joy, groom and bride. Exultation, delight, amusement, and pleasure, love and brotherhood, peace and friendship. Blessed are You, Lord, who makes the groom rejoice with the bride."

When Amichai lifted my veil, I finally met his gaze. "Welcome to your new home," he said, his tone gentle. He took my hand and rubbed his finger along my palm, wooing me. "I trust you will like it here."

I noted vulnerability in his gaze for the first time, and I wondered if he feared me as much as I feared him. "I hope so," I said, pulling away and clasping my hands beneath my cloak.

His look held kindness as he took my elbow and led me to a large white tent that stood in the middle of the inner courtyard. We would not feast until we had consummated the marriage, the part I dreaded most.

He held my hand and lifted the flap for me to enter. Lamps were hanging from poles that held the tent sides taut, and a soft wool carpet cradled our feet. We removed our sandals, and he took my hand again and led me to a raised bed in the center of the room. A finely woven linen cover threaded with strands of gold covered the bed, and the scent of lavender wafted from a small incense burner sitting on a table. I took in the simple beauty of the room, though the moment he turned me to face him, heat filled my cheeks and my heart nearly galloped from my chest.

He slowly removed my bridal crown and veil, pulling the combs loose to reveal my glorious length of dark hair. He breathed in its scent, his lips lingering near my ear. He stroked my cheek, and I smelled his warm breath. Had he chewed a mint leaf to sweeten his kiss? My breath hitched, and I desperately tried not to worry my lip.

He pulled back and searched my face, saying nothing, then one by one removed each piece of bridal clothing my sisters had so carefully placed on me earlier. I stood before him, heat flooding my face, but he turned to pull the covers from the bed and bid me to wait for him there. The bridal sheet to prove my virginity lay beneath the cover, but thankfully a thin sheet lay above it to cover my embarrassment.

Did all brides feel this way? Would I have felt embarrassed to marry Lavi? I couldn't imagine it.

Amichai turned away from me as I lay there with my troubled thoughts. He removed his own robes and slowly joined me. Again, that feeling that he was as nervous as I surfaced. He gently pried the sheet from my tight fingers, and I blew out a breath, forcing myself to look into his dark eyes. He looked almost youthful in the lamplight, and perhaps in his eagerness?

I drew in another breath, and he pulled me to him. He kissed me and stroked my cheeks. "Do not fear, Nessa," he whispered.

"I won't," I said, whether to appease him or to convince myself, I wasn't sure. I closed my eyes, trying to imagine Lavi's kiss all those months ago. The kiss that had been my undoing.

Amichai's kiss, however loving he might think he could be, did not compare to the stolen kiss I could not forget.

Though Amichai was gentle with me and I'm certain he wanted to please me, I simply could not feel the way he did. The marriage bed was not what I had pictured, but perhaps it was not the act itself that troubled me. I knew in my heart that I was here because Amichai had paid a high price to have me. A price Lavi could never have afforded, and I wasn't sure I could ever accept that fact.

7

A month following my wedding, I jolted awake and sat upright, listening. What was that? I glanced at the place beside me where Amichai still snored. Moonlight shone through the windows, telling me that dawn was not near. I strained to hear and decided it must have been Amichai who had awakened me.

Would I ever grow used to sleeping with a man, and one who snored louder than my father, whom I'd heard faintly through the walls? I lowered my body again to my side of the bed, shifting closer to the edge, away from Amichai's touch. While I had learned to tolerate him, I could not bring myself to want him. If only I could claim uncleanness every day instead of only a few days each month.

I closed my eyes, attempting to sleep again, but my mind raced as I remembered all I had planned to do that day. Amichai had promised that after I prepared food with Hila and Rina, I could visit my mother and Gali, though he'd insisted I take the young servant girl, Dana, with me. Part of me felt as though he didn't trust me, but I know he only wanted Dana to accompany me for my own safety. Two were better than one, he said. I couldn't argue with that point.

At the first hint of dawn, I rose quietly, careful not to disturb Amichai. He was expecting visitors to purchase his pottery later in the day, so he needed his rest. If he awakened too early, which he often did, he would be too tired, and I didn't wish that for him. He needed his wits about him to work the potter's wheel. I didn't want him to accidentally crush a jar or hurt his hand because of me. He was not young, after all.

I moved on tiptoe to the cooking area, carefully pulled out the jar of flour I had ground the night before, and set it on the table. I took the jar of leaven stored in one of Amichai's more artistic pieces of pottery, mixed the two together with oil, and set it to rise.

I examined the various jars Amichai had made over the years, housing all manner of spices, oils, and grains. I had to give him credit for his ability to decorate his pottery in ways I had never seen before. Perhaps one day he would teach me to paint the designs, to give me more to do than cook and clean and draw water from the well.

But I missed weaving the most. Hila had claimed the loom long before I arrived, and while I did help with the spinning and dyeing of wool, I missed the loom. Rina spent most of her time caring for the children, but she also enjoyed dyeing the wool Amichai purchased from nearby shepherds.

Was there nothing I could offer to this household that they didn't already have? The question troubled me when I lingered on it. Clearly, I was here more to please Amichai than to add anything to the value of his house. What happened if he grew tired of me or if I stopped pleasing him?

"You're up early," Rina said, rubbing sleep from her eyes as she stumbled into the cooking area. She poured a cup of water and drank. "I was up half the night with Amira. She's cutting teeth."

"I didn't sleep well either," I admitted. "I heard something, I think, but it might have been a dream." I would not complain about Amichai's snoring or suggest that Rina's daughter had awakened me, but perhaps the child's cries were what I'd heard.

"Well, we're up now." Rina set the cup on a table, took a block of cheese, and cut it into squares. "We might as well make the food for the others."

"Yes." I took a knife and began chopping olives and removing the pits. I'd quickly learned that Amichai did not like spitting out the pits as everyone else did. What else would I discover about him as time passed?

Silence settled between us, which suited me. I was in no mood to talk and struggled to understand Rina. She could be kind, but she often seemed to look at me as a child rather than wife to her father-in-law.

"My, my," Hila said, entering the room. Voices came from the back of the house as the men roused and the children chattered. "And I thought I would be the first one up. I think we were all kept awake by Amira's cries." She glanced at Rina and I braced for Rina's rebuke, but none came. "You must be exhausted, sister. I'll watch the children so you can nap later if you like."

How skilled Hila was at appeasing. I took note, telling myself I must do the same.

After the meal, as Amichai headed to his workshop, I followed him, feeling the need to be sure he still approved of my visit to my mother. "Can I help you with anything today, my husband? I know you said that I could visit my mother, but I would be happy to stay and help you entertain your customers instead." I smiled, hoping he believed me, despite the way my heart felt at giving up my plans.

He stopped and looked into my face, touching my cheek. "You honor me, my love. But no. I am a man of my word. I said you could visit your family, and I meant it. It will do you good to see your mother again." He smiled, showing clean but crooked teeth. He was not a handsome man, but I was grateful for the kindness in his eyes.

"Thank you, my lord," I said, bowing my head. "I will be home early enough to prepare the food. And if you need me

56

sooner, please send a servant to tell me and I will come." How gracious I sounded. How awful I felt.

"We will be fine, Nessa. We managed without you before. A few hours won't make a difference. Go. Enjoy yourself. But remember—take Dana with you." He kissed my cheek, then waved me away and turned to leave.

Amichai had purchased Dana to assist me a few weeks after our wedding. Why he had done so I could not understand, and now I would have no choice but to bring the girl. Irritation rose at the thought that I would not have complete privacy even with my mother, but if I sent the girl away, Amichai would surely know.

I found Dana putting the leftover food in its respective jars. Amichai's food preparation area was bigger than any I had ever seen, with wooden shelves and his decorative jars filling them. One even held butter freshly churned.

"Come with me, Dana," I said, grabbing my shawl from a peg near the entryway. "We're going to visit my mother."

Hila came from the sitting room and Rina joined her, bouncing Amira on her hip. "So soon?" Rina asked. "Only married a month and you're already running home?" She gave me a pointed look.

"Leave her alone, Rina," Hila said. "You remember what it was like to be newly wed. Amichai said she could go." She looked at me. "Have a pleasant visit."

Her smile warmed my hurting heart. Why did Rina have to be as unpleasant as my sisters sometimes? She was tired, to be sure. But so was everyone else awakened by her daughter.

"Thank you, Hila." I glanced at Dana. "Bring your spinning." I nodded toward the door. The girl grabbed a basket with a spindle and distaff and followed, easily keeping pace with my strides.

When we reached the main street at the bottom of the hill where Amichai's house sat, I looked at Dana. The girl was still a child, not old enough to wed, with skin the color of dark almonds. Her large brown eyes seemed too big for her petite face, but when she smiled, she was pleasing to look upon. No doubt she would be beautiful when she was grown.

"How did you end up a slave, Dana? Were you taken from your family?" I smiled at the girl.

"My father had too many mouths to feed and we were poor. He had no choice but to send some of us away." Dana watched her feet as if she were afraid of her next step or, more likely, ashamed of her plight.

"I'm sorry." I touched her arm. "I'm glad you're here. If you're kind, I will make sure you are treated well."

"Yes, mistress. I am yours to serve."

We walked on in silence as I pondered her words. Was my father's shop doing so poorly that he thought selling me to Amichai, who gave the most gold as a bride-price, was his only option? He'd never paid Lavi much at all when he apprenticed under him. An occasional coin, Lavi had said, but his payment was a place to stay and food to eat.

As we approached my father's house, I noted with sudden clarity that they didn't live in the wealthiest section of town. Amichai's home was large and ornate while my father's was adequate, humble.

Perhaps I wasn't so different from Dana as I first thought.

"Nessa!" Gali burst from the house next to my father's and ran toward me, pulling me from my wayward thoughts.

"Gali!" I set my basket down and hugged her. "It is so good to see you."

"And you." She held me at arm's length and looked me over. "You don't look like a married woman." She laughed. "Why are you here?" She looked at Dana. "Who is she?"

"This is my maid, Dana. Dana, this is my best friend, Gali." I pointed to each one in turn. "But come, Ima is waiting for me." I motioned for both of them to follow me and led the way into the house. "Ima?" I poked my head in the door. "I'm home!"

I found Ima seated at the loom. She stopped the shuttle, stood, and hurried to take me in her arms. "Nessa, my girl. I've missed you."

I breathed in the scent of her, loving this moment, memorizing everything I'd missed about this place.

"Come, sit with me."

I obeyed, and Dana sat in a corner while Gali ran home for her spinning and then returned. Our busy hands kept time with our chatter, and I relished hearing about all the gossip from the well and how my sisters were doing.

The time went too quickly, and when I bid them farewell to return to my new home, a lump settled in my middle. I had a good life. Hadn't Meital told me so? I was the wife of a wealthy potter whose wares brought good prices. I had my own personal maid and what most people would consider a pleasant life, despite being married to an old man and living with his adult children.

But my visit home brought a longing for all the things I missed, including Lavi, whose memory lived in every room. What was he doing now? Did he miss me?

All of a sudden, longing filled me. I missed him more than I'd realized in my attempt to make myself care for Amichai. I knew I should be grateful for Amichai and all he had given me, but I wasn't. And I didn't know how to change that.

8

I walked down the hill from the house to the outskirts of the town, where Amichai kept his pottery
shop. Several potters worked near each other, and
the smoke from the kiln darkened the air as it rose upward.

I found Amichai sitting at the spinning wheel, moving it with
one foot as he molded wet clay with both hands. His apron was
splattered in clay, and I watched in fascination as he used a tool
to make patterns in the sides of the vessel.

He did not look at me but obviously sensed my presence.
"Nessa, you honor me with your visit. How can I help you?"

"I wanted to see you work. I've never watched a potter at
the wheel. The jars you have at the house are so beautiful." My
face flushed as I spoke, noting the smile he displayed despite
keeping his eyes on his work. "But I see that I've come when
you should not be interrupted."

"Nonsense. I can concentrate and listen at the same time.
I've done this task long enough that the pots fairly shape themselves." He chuckled, putting me at ease.

"I know it's messy work," I said, glancing at the row of
pots hardening on a shelf behind him. In another corner of

the shop, an apprentice worked new clay with his feet to soften it. "Do you think . . ." I paused, swallowed, and tried again. "Do you think that you would ever want to teach me how to mold the clay?"

He glanced up at that, but quickly resumed watching the spinning pot beneath his fingers. "I suppose a woman can learn to be a potter," he said lightly. "But it is not a task one can learn in a week or month or even a year. Wouldn't you prefer to do something that you're already skilled at doing?"

The thought of a loom of my own flitted through my mind. I hadn't expected him to deny me this request, but he was right. I missed the loom, and I hadn't had the courage to ask Hila for a chance to use it. Spinning was a mindless skill to me, whereas weaving took more expertise.

He slowed the wheel and removed the jar. He looked at me as he lifted it in his hands. "What is it, Nessa? Ask me for anything, and I will give it."

I swallowed the lump in my throat at such kindness. I did not deserve this man. I had despised our age differences for so long. Why should he give me what I wanted now?

I clasped my hands in front of me. "I do enjoy weaving. But I cannot ask Hila to give me that task. She enjoys it too."

He laughed, a pleasant sound, and his smile put me at ease. He carried the pot to a shelf, set it down, and faced me. "A household of our size can use two looms, my love. I will purchase another or have it built this very week. You do not have to muddy your beautiful face to work in a potter's shop."

Tears filled my eyes, and I wasn't sure I could speak, but at last I whispered, "Thank you." I might not love him, but I had come to appreciate him. "I'd best return home and help start the meal."

"Thank you for coming today," he said, and we shared a brief understanding look.

I bowed my head, then hurried toward the house. A new

purpose filled me as I climbed the hill, thrilled that I would once again be able to create the things I loved.

As I entered the house's cooking area, a child's scream pierced the air, followed quickly by wailing. A sigh escaped me. Rina's and Hila's children often fought and caused frustration for their mothers. No doubt one had hit another again.

The wailing quieted from the back of the house, and I released another sigh. Children were a blessing and a nuisance, and I wasn't sure I would make a good mother. Though after seven months of marriage, I wondered why I had not yet conceived.

No one had mentioned my lack of children . . . yet. But what if I did not bear a child after a year of marriage? Could I be barren like Rachel of old?

There was nothing to fear . . . yet. If I dwelled on it, the waiting would simply be worse. And after living with Amira and the other children, I was in no hurry for one of my own.

❖ ❖ ❖

Following the morning meal one day after we'd passed our first year of marriage, Amichai came behind me in the cooking area, placed his hands on my shoulders, and kissed my cheek. "Arieh, Ezra, and I are going into the hills today to chop wood to heat the kiln. We are running low, and animal dung only goes so far." He stepped away and I faced him.

"I will bring you something to eat later." I smiled. I would enjoy the outing to the hill country, and taking food to the men would be the perfect reason.

"We can just take nuts and raisin cakes along with our waterskins." He took a sack and began to fill it, but I touched his arm to stop him.

"Let me do this for you, please. I will fill the sacks if you like, but I may still bring you a treat. Felling a tree is hard work."

"Are you suggesting that I do not have the strength for it, dear wife?" Amichai's eyes twinkled as he spoke, and I laughed.

"Of course not! You just need me to look out for you." I had learned to tease him in return, because I knew he truly didn't take offense as Lavi might have and my sisters definitely would have.

He tweaked my nose. "You are too good for me, Nessa. I don't deserve you, but I'm very glad to have you." He handed me the sack. "If you will fill this and one for each of my sons, we will look forward to your visit. Especially if you bring your pistachio and honey treats."

I patted his arm. "I will do just that."

He left to gather what he needed while I hurried to fill the sacks from the jars of nuts and raisins and placed a small round of cheese atop each one. I tied the string to close the pouches and carried them to Amichai.

The men were putting their sandals on their feet as I handed the sacks to them. "Be careful," I said as they left the house.

"Always," Amichai said, smiling at me again.

When their footsteps receded, I called Dana. "Come and help me make pistachio cakes. We will take them to the men when the sun is hottest so they can be refreshed."

"Yes, mistress." Dana pulled the jar of flour we had ground that morning from the shelf while I grabbed the sack of pistachios and jar of honey.

We worked in companionable silence, and I was grateful that Rina and Hila had left us alone. They had taken the children to market, and I hurried to finish the pastry, hoping to be done before they returned.

"There. The cakes look perfect!" I smiled at Dana. "Thank you for your help. Let's put on our sandals and take them to the men."

Dana went to retrieve our sandals and cloaks, and I wrapped the pistachio cakes in a cloth, placed them in a basket, and then walked with Dana toward the hills behind the house. The sun beat down from its perch straight overhead, but the cool air made the warmth a blessing.

"It's a good day for working so hard," Dana said as we neared the edge of the woods. "Where do you think they went?"

"There is a clearing further in. Likely they found a tree to fell there."

We picked our way over dried underbrush and dead foliage. Voices drifted to us, and the ringing of axe hitting wood filled the air.

"We probably shouldn't get too close," I said softly. "We don't want to distract them."

Dana nodded, and we both stopped, waiting for the chopping to end.

A dull thud and a wild scream met my ears a moment later, jolting me. Raw fear ripped through me as the screams continued.

"Abba!" The voice was Ezra's.

I rushed into the clearing, Dana behind me, and stopped short at the sight before me.

"Abba!" Arieh cried. Both men bent over their father. "No! No! No!"

Terror coursed through me, but I slowly forced myself closer. "What happened?" Then I saw him, and my knees buckled. "Amichai?"

The head of an axe was embedded in his chest, and the light had gone from his eyes.

"Amichai!" The strangled cry came from my throat, and I rocked back and forth, barely feeling Dana's arms attempting to hold me.

"Why didn't you check the axe-head before using it? We always check it each time." Arieh's shouts pierced the air, and he rushed toward his brother, knocking him to the ground. "How could you!"

"It was an accident!" Ezra shouted in return, pushing to get Arieh off him. "I did check it."

"How long ago?" The accusation held such a bitter edge that it penetrated my shock.

"Not long. But I know . . . it's my fault." Ezra shoved Arieh to the dirt and stood. "Fighting about it now isn't going to bring Abba back."

At that, the news seemed to hit us all over again. Arieh returned to Amichai's side and wept. I could not think what to do next. Both men were inconsolable, and Amichai lay before me in a pool of his own blood. An accident. I would have seen it or perhaps been hit myself if we had entered the clearing a moment sooner.

"We need to get him home," Ezra said when he composed himself. "Prepare him for burial."

Burial? He'd just kissed me goodbye a few hours ago. I had made his favorite treat, still warm in the basket I'd dropped when I fell to my knees. How could this possibly be happening?

"We need a cart and a donkey. We can't possibly carry him," Arieh said.

"I can get it for you," Dana said, surprising me with her ability to suddenly take charge.

"We will go together," I said, though I didn't know where I would get the strength to stand. I looked at Amichai's sons. "We will hurry."

The men stared at me as if they didn't know what to say or what to do with me. I was their father's wife, but with Amichai's death, what would happen to me? Would they want me to stay in his house? I had no children to hold me there.

The thoughts intruded on my grief with every pounding step toward the place where Amichai kept the donkeys and carts. My father had taught me how to hook them up, and Dana also seemed to know what she was doing. I must tell Rina and Hila, but one glance at the house and I saw no movement or sounds coming from inside. No doubt they were still at market or had stopped along the way to visit with their families.

"I'll take the donkey to the hills," I said, numbly taking charge. "You run to the market and try to find Rina and Hila. They must know. I need them to help me prepare his body."

"Yes, mistress," Dana said. She touched my shoulder. "Are you all right?"

"Of course not! Nothing is right for either of us, and I don't know what will come." I met her gaze. "I'm afraid, Dana. For both of us."

The girl nodded, turned to the path, and ran toward the market, while I led the donkey as fast as it would go toward the hills to gather my husband's body. Married only a year and already a widow.

9

The rest of the day flew by in a flurry of activity. Rina and Hila burst into the house and took over the care of Amichai's body as if they had done the task hundreds of times. I watched, staring at this man whom I had come to care for though could not claim to love. I had appreciated him and how he treated me, and now he was gone.

My parents and sisters and brother and their families joined the procession to a cave outside of Sychar near the base of Mt. Gerizim. Amichai had buried his first wife there, and now he would rest beside her. If I died, would they place my body there as well?

The thoughts accompanied the many other tangled worries rushing through my mind.

Amichai's sons and sons-in-law managed to get the body into the cave before the sun set, and I walked with my family back to Amichai's house.

"I'm sorry, Nessa," Yaffa said, placing an arm about my shoulders. "This should not have happened to you."

"It is a great loss for everyone," Abba said, striding alongside us. "Amichai's pottery was among the best in the city, and none of his children can match his skill. I've seen their work." He lowered his voice so as not to be heard by Amichai's children, who walked ahead of us. I had preferred to stay back with my parents rather than deal with the grief of people I didn't really know all that well, even after a year in their presence.

"He bought me a loom," I said, not really thinking through what I was saying.

Abba gave me a puzzled look.

"They already had a loom, of course, but Hila used it, so when he knew I missed weaving, he bought another for my use."

Abba shrugged and continued walking as though my words were of no consequence. They probably were.

When we reached the base of the hill, I stopped. I looked at the house. My breath hitched and I felt faint.

"I can't go back there," I whispered. I pressed a hand to my middle. "What am I supposed to do?" I looked at Ima, who glanced from me to my father.

"Are you going to tell her?" Ima gave Abba a subtle glance.

"We have to go to the house first," Abba said, touching my shoulder. "Come, my daughter. We will let the neighbors pay their respects and gather your things. Then you will return home with us."

A rush of relief further drained my strength. Yaffa and Adva caught my arms. "Go home?" But wasn't this place my home now? I offered my father a look of bewilderment.

Abba released a deep sigh. "When Amichai signed the ketubah, he wanted you to be free to return home and remarry if he should die. You are young, Nessa, and he knew that he would not outlive you. He had no unmarried sons or brothers, and he wanted you to be free to wed another—someone not related to him."

I swallowed, my strength slowly returning. "He never told me."

"It's not something you needed to know. Until now." Abba ran a hand along the back of his neck as if the news troubled him. Would I be a burden to him by returning home? And would he hurry to find another husband for me so he didn't have to support me? But of course he would.

"I won't even stay here this night?" The image of Dana came to mind, and I caught sight of the girl waiting ahead of our party. Amichai's sons and daughters had already reached the house, and neighbors carried torches toward them. "Shouldn't I sit shiva with them first?"

My father held his chin, and by his look I knew he was considering that thought. At last he nodded. "You're right. Custom would have you sit shiva with them for seven days. Your mother can stay if you like."

"I would like that." Suddenly I did not want to be alone with Amichai's children. "But what of Dana? She is my servant. Amichai purchased her for me. Will she return home with me after shiva?"

Ima glanced at Abba while my sisters stood silent. None of them had servants as their husbands could not afford to keep one, even with Meital and Adva each expecting their second child.

"She is another mouth to feed." Abba frowned.

"She is a good worker. She doesn't eat much. I can't leave her here." I glanced again at the girl.

"Let me think on it," he said and began walking up the hill, obviously expecting us to follow.

I forced one foot in front of the other.

"We would stay with you," Yaffa whispered, "but we are needed at home. I'm sorry, Ness."

"It's all right," I said, looking from one sister to the next. "I will miss you." I said it to make it so. They *were* being kind to me, no doubt because of my sudden widowhood. But once I went home, Meital and Adva would probably resume their irritable attitudes. At least Yaffa treated me with respect. And I would have Gali to walk with to the well again.

We reached the house, and I found myself welcomed into the sitting room, where Amichai's family had gathered. Hila hung dark curtains on the windows and Rina lit lamps while neighbors brought food to share with everyone.

They spent the evening talking about Amichai, praising his kindness, his work, his generosity, and more. I listened, thankful that the numbness had settled over me once more. I had no energy to ponder all that had happened since dawn. When someone handed me a plate with the very pistachio cakes I had baked that morning to give Amichai and his sons, I pushed the offering away. Tears came then, nearly choking me.

I looked about the room and wanted to run from everyone and weep in silence. But I couldn't. If I let them see me cry, I would have nothing left to keep to myself. My feelings for Amichai were so mixed and confusing. I wasn't even sure if I cared enough to weep. The trauma of seeing the axe in his chest, the blood, the light gone from his eyes . . . I would never forget that lost light. I'd seen death among the animals and my grandparents had died when I was young, but I had not seen them like that.

"Are you all right, mistress?" Dana came and sat at my feet. "Can I get you anything?"

I shook my head and swallowed. I touched the girl's shoulder. "No. Thank you." Not even the wine a neighbor set beside me was touched. I had no desire to drink, even if it would help me forget.

Night deepened, and when Abba and Chen rose to leave, my mother and I walked with them to the door. Neighbors were leaving as well, for everyone had work to do in the morning. It was a sacrifice for Ima to stay with me, as my father and brother would have to feed themselves.

My father bent to kiss my cheek. "When I come for you in seven days, I will have a solution to your situation with your servant."

"Perhaps you could consider her like Lavi and have her work for food and a place to sleep," I said, hopeful.

A dark scowl crossed his brow. "Never mention that name again," he said, his voice a low growl.

My eyes widened. "Whyever not? He's our relative."

"He is a thief, and he's not welcome in our home." He paused and closed his eyes.

"I don't understand." Of course, I had heard that Abba accused him of stealing, but I secretly hoped that Lavi would return now and my father would have a change of heart and give me to him this time.

Abba sighed and touched my head. "Never mind, Nessa. I have my sources, and they tell me that Lavi ran off with my tools and your gold. He is not to be trusted. When you come home, we will find you a good man. As for your maid, I will tell you later." He walked off, Chen following.

I looked at Ima, but she only shrugged. "Better to talk about it later, my daughter. Why don't we get some rest?"

I nodded and led Ima to a guest room, while I entered the room I had shared with Amichai. But as I stared at the bed, I wasn't sure I could sleep there tonight or any night for the rest of shiva.

◆ ◆ ◆

On the eighth day, after seven days and nights of sitting shiva, I woke and saw that my mother was also up, dressing for the day. I had found a mat to sleep on in the guest room with her rather than stay alone in Amichai's room. The memories were too strange and raw.

"Are you ready to go home?" Ima asked as she tied her belt and straightened the bed.

I quickly dressed and did the same. "More than ready."

"You must say farewell to Amichai's children first and wait for your father. He will tell us what to do with your maid." Ima walked toward me and held me in a short embrace. "I'm sorry this happened, Nessa, but I will be glad to have you home for a little while."

Only a little while? "How soon will Abba seek a new husband for me?"

Ima shook her head. "I don't know, but I suspect he has already spoken to the men at the city gate. Everyone knew Amichai and you were a good wife to him. Your father should have no problem finding another to wed you."

We left the guest room and met Rina and Hila in the cooking area. The men sat about the table eating, and I felt the slightest twinge of guilt that I had not helped. But I was leaving, and I could not do so quickly enough. In anticipation, I had gathered my belongings the night before. Dana had done the same, but still I worried. What would my father do with the girl?

"I'll miss you," Hila said, pulling me into a warm embrace. "Amichai cared for you, and you were good to him."

Rina came behind and nodded. "I never understood why Amichai wanted someone younger than his children, but I am sorry for his loss. I know it was hard for you." She patted my arm, then turned her attention to one of her children, who tugged on her leg at that moment.

I accepted food from Hila and sat on a cushion next to my mother with Ezra and Arieh. They looked at me with expressions I could not quite define. I had been there, had seen the accident, or rather its aftermath. The truth was, I had seen nothing until I saw Amichai. I did not doubt it was an accident, but then, I would never know for sure.

"I wish you well," Ezra said around a bite of bread.

"Yes," Arieh said.

A knock sounded before I could respond, and Hila hurried to answer it. My father stood in the entry, and Hila welcomed him in.

Ezra and Arieh stood and greeted him. "I am sorry for your great loss," Abba said, embracing each one with the customary kiss on each cheek. "I have come for my family."

I jumped up and my mother stood. "And Dana?" I asked as we neared the door.

My father glanced at the girl and gave a slight nod. "She may come with us for now. We may have to sell her or let her return to her family."

"Thank you, Abba." I looked at Dana. "Come." We picked up the baskets filled with our clothing, spinning, and personal items and followed my father out of the house through Sychar's bustling streets.

We passed the markets, which had recently opened, and wove our way through the streets until we reached the poorer section I had known all my life. The humble home did not trouble me, and I would not miss Amichai's wealth.

"I need you to hurry to the well," Ima said after I had placed my things in my room. "Dana can help you. She can sleep where Lavi used to sleep."

I looked up and met Ima's gaze. "I thought we were not to speak his name." My father and brother were at the shop, so they were not there to overhear my words.

"That is your father's decision. Lavi was a troubled but good boy. He lost everything, and I do not hold his choices against him, though he did hurt us by taking your father's tools. He is young. He's my sister's son, so you may speak of him to me. Just not in front of your father." Ima shooed us toward the door. "Now hurry. We should have started hours ago."

I grabbed one of the water jars, and Dana the other. "I wonder if Gali would want to come with us."

"No doubt she has already been and her mother won't want her going again. You can go with her tonight," Ima said.

I did as I was told, but as I walked with Dana to the well, a strange restlessness settled over me. I didn't belong in Amichai's home any longer, but I didn't feel as though I belonged in my father's house either. After a year of marriage, I was too old to return to the days of my childhood. But until I married again, there was nothing I could do.

10

*L*ater that evening, I waited for Gali in her courtyard to gather her jar and walk with me to the well
as we had done most of our lives. How I'd missed
her! But one look at her face and I sensed something was wrong.

"I'm sorry I couldn't come to sit shiva with you, Ness," she
said before I could speak.

"I didn't expect you to. I know your ima needs you."

She said nothing in response, and I pondered her silence as
we kept a brisk pace through the city to the well. Gali filled her
jar before me, then set it in the dirt. I tied the rope to my jar
and lowered it to the depths of the well.

"We've been making things for my betrothal," Gali said as
she lifted her jar to her head.

"What?" I stopped mid-pull but decided the jar was too
heavy to wait. When it was securely out of the well, I lifted it
to my head and walked with Gali. "Tell me everything. Are you
marrying Harel as you'd hoped?"

Gali's brow furrowed at the mention of Harel's name. "My
father approached his, but he put him off. His father said Harel
has someone else in mind."

I gave Gali a comforting look. She kicked a stone in the path,
frustration seeping from her.

"I'm sorry, Gali. I know you want him."

"My abba is considering Rafael ben Elior. His family is new to Sychar."

"Have you met him?" My jaw clenched at the thought that Harel had not wanted Gali, considering she had wanted him for years.

"No." Gali moved slowly, and I wondered if she was avoiding returning home. Her ima made her girls work hard, and these walks were Gali's only chance to rest. "I've seen him at synagogue. He's pleasant to look upon."

"But not like Harel." I touched Gali's arm. "Do you know who Harel has in mind?"

Gali's gaze glanced off me to something behind me. "I've heard rumors."

"Then tell me!" How much I had missed in the year I had not gone to the well with my friend.

Silence followed my remark.

"What's wrong, Gali? Tell me what you know."

"Abba seemed to be close to making an agreement with Harel's father before Amichai died." Gali looked at me. "Tell me it isn't true."

A knot settled in my middle. I had just returned from sitting shiva for my husband. What could Gali possibly think she knew? Certainly nothing about Harel.

"Everyone knows you're a widow now, Ness. You are the most beautiful girl in Sychar, and don't you know that your father has been making inquiries for you from almost the moment Amichai died?" Gali's tone held accusation, as if I should know my father's business.

"My father has said nothing. I don't know what you're talking about. I just got home, Gali." I could not restrain the hurt in my tone. "I don't know what my father does or who he has spoken to."

"Well, my father does, and he said that Raanan has been to

the city gate and spoken with all the men of the town, seeking a new husband for you. And right then Harel's father suddenly stopped talking to my father because he is thinking of someone else? Who do you think that could be?" Gali's anger simmered in the air between us.

"You think Harel wants *me*?" My mouth hung open a moment until I snapped it shut. "That's ridiculous."

"It's not ridiculous at all. The worst part is that you were my best friend. I never thought you would steal the man I've wanted forever." She picked up her pace and walked ahead of me, leaving me stunned.

Were? Was Gali ending our friendship over a possibility that wasn't going to happen?

Would it?

Suddenly I was no longer certain. Would Harel have told his father he wanted me over Gali? Surely he knew that Gali cared for him. And I had been widowed barely over a week. I was not ready to start over again.

But Gali's straight back and stiff shoulders told me that she believed the rumors whether they were true or not. The only way I was going to keep my dearest friend was to prove her wrong. Even if Harel wanted me, I would refuse him. Insist he marry Gali. I owed her that.

But what if my father had already sold me to Harel's father without asking me? He'd done it before with Amichai. He could do so again.

The weight of the jar pressed down on me, and I felt overcome with grief. I could not lose Gali after losing Amichai and Lavi. There was only so much loss a person could carry and not be completely lost themselves.

❖ ❖ ❖

Morning came too soon, and with it the memories of my conversation with Gali the night before. I rose quietly and left to find my mother already at work preparing the morning meal.

"You're up sooner than I expected," Ima said as I took a date from a small dish and bit the end.

"I slept fitfully."

"Oh?" Ima began mixing the flour and starter in a bowl.

I met Ima's quick gaze. "I was troubled by something Gali told me yesterday."

"On your trip to the well?"

I finished the date. "Yes." I reached for the olive oil and handed it to my mother.

"Are you going to tell me?" Ima liked to know, but if I didn't want to tell her, she wouldn't push.

"Gali has always wanted to marry Harel. We've talked about it since before I became a woman." I looked about the cooking area for what to do next, still feeling out of place.

"Uh-huh." Ima did not look at me, and I wondered if she knew more than she was letting on.

"Gali's abba went to talk to Harel's father to make an arrangement, but Harel suddenly changed his mind and said he wants someone else. So Gali's father is considering other options." I rested a hand on the jar that held the cinnamon. "Do you know why Harel would do that, Ima? Gali says Harel wants to marry *me*! But that's not possible."

Ima stopped mixing the bread dough and faced me. "It is possible, Nessa. Your father has been talking to the men of the town, looking for a suitable husband for you since Amichai's death."

"Will my father give me no time to grieve? I'm not ready to marry again so soon, Ima."

"Betrothals and weddings don't happen the same day, Nessa. Your father could arrange a betrothal and you would have time until the wedding." She resumed her mixing, releasing a sigh. "Though I did tell your father to give you more time."

"He wouldn't listen to you?" The sinking feeling in my stomach made me look for a place to sit. I sank onto a nearby bench as Dana entered the room.

"Can I help with something, mistress?" Dana asked. She took one look at me and hurried to my side. "Are you all right?"

I nodded as my mother turned around. "Go gather more water from the cistern in the courtyard," she told Dana. The girl turned to do her bidding.

When she was gone, I gave Ima a look of misery. "I've lost Gali. She no longer considers me a friend because she thinks I took Harel from her. But I don't even want Harel. Why doesn't Abba ever ask who I want to marry? I wanted Lavi. If I'd been given to him, none of this would be happening."

Ima cupped my cheek with a flour-coated hand. "I'm sorry, my love. Your beauty was a blessing to us all of your life, but to you it must feel like a curse. Your father knows that he can ask for a higher bride-price for you than he did for your sisters because of it. So he does." She smoothed the hair behind my ears. "You have to understand, daughter, that your father has never made much money building tents. We don't live in the same area you lived in with Amichai. Losing you takes away the money you make with your weaving, so your father makes sure we are compensated. He just has an advantage because many men have asked after you."

My eyes widened. "Many?"

Ima nodded and wiped a stray tear from my cheek.

"Then why pick Harel and take him away from my best friend?"

Ima's brows scrunched in a frown. "That was not your father's doing. Harel thinks he can have you now that you are free. He broke it off with Gali's father before anything was even said to your father."

"Has Abba accepted him?" Hope rose. Perhaps I could yet

talk my father out of this ridiculous marriage that would make me lose Gali.

"I don't know." She turned back to the bread. "Help me now. Your father will be in from milking the goats and will want to eat before he heads to the shop."

I slowly stood and moved to the shelf where a knife sat with a pile of cucumbers and onions waiting to be chopped. I washed my hands in the water bowl Dana had just filled and dried them, then began to work. But my mind whirled. There must be a way to mend the rift with Gali and send Harel back to her. There must be.

❖ ❖ ❖

If I had hopes of stalling my father from seeking another husband for me because of a possible child I might bear Amichai, peace be upon him, they were dashed a week after Gali informed me that Harel wanted to wed me. The nagging ache from my cycle told me there would be no need to wait, despite the help I provided my family with weaving and cooking. Dana proved to be a big help in keeping things in order, but I could not determine my father's intentions regarding either Dana or my future. When different fathers came and went from the house, I held my breath and waited to be told another ketubah had been signed.

But after another seven days under my father's roof, I still had no answers. A sigh of relief filled me each evening when I went another day without anything changing. Each dawn, new dread filled me as I wondered what would be.

Three weeks after Amichai's passing, I rose and went to the courtyard to grind more grain, something I should have done the night before, but I could not make noise with my father entertaining one of the townsmen in our sitting room. I did not recognize him, and I knew Harel's father, Niv, so Gali must be wrong. *Please let her be wrong.*

I turned my attention to the grindstone. Surely today would be a good day. Gali would rush to our house and tell me Harel had wanted her after all. Or my father would find someone else for me, and Gali and I would mend our differences.

The sound of footsteps barely registered until I noticed the feet of a man standing over me. I jumped up at the unexpected intruder, then saw it was only my father. But a moment later, my heart pounded at the look in his eyes.

I sank onto the stone bench behind me. "Abba."

He sat beside me. "Nessa." He took my hand. "I have news."

I swallowed hard. *Don't tell me.* "Tell me," I said.

"I have been approached by several fathers of men who would like to marry you. I have listened to their comments about their sons. And I have come to a decision of which home would be best for you." He looked at me and smiled.

No doubt the person had offered him the most in return for me, whether money or goods. My hands shook. "Who is it?"

"Harel ben Niv."

I pressed my free hand to my stomach, fearing I would be sick. "Harel? But his father has not been here to visit. And, Abba, Harel is supposed to marry Gali." I searched his aging face, noting the new gray hairs along his temples.

He released my hand and leaned away. "I know nothing of an arrangement between Niv and Ilan for your friend's hand."

"But Gali said her father and Harel's were talking about it before Amichai was killed." The memory of that day still brought a pang to my heart and a vision I did not want.

My father ran a hand along his graying beard. He was not that old, but the new lines along his brow told me he worried. "Niv said nothing of this to me. Obviously he had not signed an agreement with Ilan or he would not be free to approach me for you." He touched my shoulder in an awkward attempt to comfort me. "This will be a good marriage, my daughter. Niv owns much land and farms it with his five sons. Admittedly, you will be in a larger household than you're used to, but there will be much to do, and Niv is an amiable person. I'm sure his son will be good to you."

A feeling of spiraling downward rushed through me. I gripped the smooth edge of the stone bench to steady myself, drew in a deep breath, and faced my father. "Abba, I don't want to marry Harel. Am I to never have a say in whom you choose for me? I'm the one who has to live with the man."

A scowl formed along his brow. He opened his mouth, closed it, then opened it again. "No. This is not a decision a woman should make. Did I not make a good decision when I gave you to Amichai? You were happy there, were you not?" His challenge brooked no argument. He expected me to agree with him.

"I accepted the arrangement because you gave me no choice," I said, knowing my words were risky.

He abruptly stood. "You should be grateful, Nessa, not question my judgment. I have chosen Niv's son Harel, and you will wed him within the month. The ketubah will be signed tonight, so I suggest you quickly change your thinking and accept this."

A month?

But he stalked off before I could say another word, leaving me shaken.

11

week after the ketubah was signed, sealing my betrothal to Harel, I walked with Dana to the well for the last time. My breath hitched on the panic growing in me after we passed the guards and drew closer to where Gali had gone ahead of me.

"I will miss you," Dana said, breaking into my whirling thoughts.

Even empty of water, the jar felt heavy on my head, weighted down by the sorrow filling me. I glanced at her, then stopped a moment, realizing that we might not have this chance again.

"I'm sorry that Niv's family did not find reason for me to bring you with me," I said. "But for your sake, I'm hopeful that you will be happy in the home of the rabbi." Sychar was not a wealthy town, but the religious leaders lived well compared to many of us. "You will have food to eat and a warm bed, at least."

Dana looked beyond me, but I did not miss the wistful look in her eyes. "I wish my parents could have allowed me to return home." She drew in a sharp breath. "But as they cannot, I hope I please my new mistress."

I knew nothing of the wife of the rabbi, so what could I say? "I'm sure she will love you as I do." At least I hoped it was true.

I had never actually met the man's wife, and she did not sit near our family at synagogue. She seemed to surround herself with her family and perhaps a few wealthy friends.

I touched Dana's arm. "I wish you well. I will miss you." Tears threatened, so I continued walking toward the well.

"I will miss you too," she said, her voice mingling with the crunch of stones beneath our sandals.

I glanced ahead at the group of women standing in a circular line about the well. When I spotted Gali, my heart skipped a beat. Would she speak to me? How could I explain to her that I did not want this marriage?

Dana pointed, and our gazes met. She knew what I wanted without speaking. "I will draw the water," she said. "For both of us."

I lowered my jar to the earth and nodded.

Voices grew louder at our approach. A few of the older women drew closer.

"We hear congratulations are in order," one said.

"Yet how unfortunate to have no time to prepare for the wedding."

"It's not like she's a virgin and needs time to make all that she did for her first marriage."

"I wish you well, dear."

The words all jumbled together as the women spoke on top of one another. I looked past them, longing to draw Gali into the circle, or better yet, pull her away and speak with her as I used to.

When she lifted her jar and began to walk toward town alone, I quickly excused myself from the women and ran to meet her. "Gali, wait!"

She did not stop, and I quickened my pace, knowing that I would have to return to the well to help Dana with the second jar. "Gali, please. Don't let our friendship end like this."

She stopped and slowly turned to face me. "You knew, Ness.

JILL EILEEN SMITH

You knew Harel was supposed to marry me. Why didn't you do anything to refuse this marriage?"

Technically, a bride could refuse a proposal of marriage—in a normal town with a normal father who didn't think he should control his family as mine did. Didn't Rebekah have the choice to go with Abraham's servant to marry Isaac?

"I tried, Gali. You know my father. You know how it was with Amichai too. He didn't let me refuse. He chooses for me, and even when I've pleaded with him, even when my ima has pleaded with him, he does not listen. Please understand. I don't want to lose you." I choked on a sob as the chatter of the women came near, all of them heading back to town, leaving Dana alone at the well waiting for me.

Gali watched the women look at us, shake their heads, and continue on, muttering things we could not hear. At last she looked at me and sighed. "I wish I could believe you, Ness. I'm not unaware of your father's greed to get the most money he can because you're so beautiful. Everyone in town talks about it. The women resent you, and the men fall over themselves wanting to reach your door to beg for your father to accept them." She drew a breath, clinging to the vessel that still rested on her head, and I could see her hand shaking and her cheeks flushed with emotion. "But of all the men in Sychar, you're telling me that your father *had* to pick Harel? After you told him that he was to marry me? Do you really expect me to believe that?" The hurt in her eyes turned to anger.

"It's the truth," I said, my voice dropping along with my gaze. I could not bear the look she was giving me now, a look I had never seen from her in all my life.

She scoffed. "Well, truth or not, you got the one man I wanted, and because men think you're so gorgeous you can have anyone you want."

"Not anyone." My voice was barely a whisper. I wanted Lavi, and if I'd had my way, we would not be standing here with Gali hating me.

85

"I have to go." She began walking again and did not look back.

I didn't attempt to stop her again, knowing there was nothing more I could say. At least not now. Maybe one day we could reconcile and get past this, but not today.

I returned to the well, scooped up my full jar, and walked in silence with Dana back to my father's house. Three more weeks and I would not see Dana or Gali again unless I saw them at the market or synagogue. But I had no idea what kind of home I was marrying into or how free I would be to have friends outside of Niv's family. And what I didn't know, I feared.

❖ ❖ ❖

Three weeks later, I found myself surrounded again by most of the city, pushing me closer to Niv's farm on the outskirts of Sychar. Harel, his four brothers, and his friends walked ahead, laughing and singing songs of praise to the groom and the bride.

Meital, Yaffa, and Adva walked with me—there was no litter to carry me this time—but Gali had not joined the procession. In the month of waiting, Gali had been betrothed to another, and Dana had left two weeks before my wedding to join the rabbi's family. The sting of both losses still hurt in a deep place in my heart.

"I hope you like farm life, Ness," Yaffa said, keeping in step with me. She carried a basket of my things while my sisters carried food to share with the neighbors in the crowd.

"I hope so too," I said, trying to see through the veil and to keep my hands from twisting my belt or readjusting the bridal crown placed so expertly on my head. "I don't have any idea what they do. We've had no time to discuss anything." I kept my voice low, not wanting to be overheard.

"At least you've met Harel a few times. Though I think you

saw Amichai far more often," Yaffa said, touching my arm. "It'll be all right."

I met her concerned gaze. "I've lost my closest friend over this marriage." I leaned closer. "This had better be a good choice." When had I grown so bitter?

Yaffa seemed to notice, by her raised brow and pinched expression. "Be careful, Ness. You know we have no say in who Abba picks. Learn to accept these things and life will be a lot easier."

"Are you happy with Yaron? He's so quiet. It's hard to tell." The songs around us nearly drowned out my question, but Yaffa nodded.

"Of course! He's given me Chana and Daniel and a stable home. What more could I want?" Chana and Daniel were two-year-old twins I barely knew, and I wondered if they were any easier to care for than Rina's and Hila's unruly children.

"I'm not sure I want children," I whispered.

"What?" Yaffa nearly forced me to stop walking, then seemed to think better of it, considering the people around us. We weren't far from the farm now, and through my veil I saw torches lining the path to the house, where light spilled from the open windows.

"I'm sure I will change my mind when it happens," I quickly answered before Yaffa could say more. "I didn't like Amichai's grandchildren overmuch is all. I can't imagine having children like that."

Yaffa laughed. "You will think differently when they're your own. A mother's love is unlike any other."

"I'm sure you're right."

Noise erupted as we stopped at Niv's home and the rest of the family met us in the large courtyard.

"Come. Come. Bring the bride and groom!" Niv shouted, motioning us toward the canopy where I would stand with Harel and listen to the words of his father blessing our union.

I moved through the familiar traditions, only this time I danced with Harel throughout the feasting before he took me to the bridal tent. Why the change in the order of the normal wedding ceremony, I did not know, but as I was in no hurry to be alone with my new husband, I didn't complain.

When the sun had fully set and the people were filled with food and wine, Harel took my hand and led me toward the bridal tent. I was not a virgin, so there would be no bridal sheet to give to my father, but Harel had not seemed to care that I had belonged to another.

The flap closed behind us and my pulse quickened, not in anticipation but in dread. I'd grown used to Amichai, but Harel was young and eager. And drunk, something Amichai had never been.

He came toward me on unsteady feet, then practically ripped the crown and veil from my head and the robe from my body. "At last you are mine!"

His kiss tasted like wine, and his hot breath on my face came fast. Before I could get used to his touch, he rose triumphant from the couch like he'd won some kind of race.

He donned his robe and left me alone in the tent, never saying another word to me. I pulled the blanket to my neck and stared at the tent's ceiling, listening to the laughter and music playing around me like I didn't matter. I was just a prize Harel had won in a game the men of the town had played to marry me.

I wasn't wanted for my abilities or my knowledge or even what I could bring to the family. I was wanted for my beauty by a young man too spoiled to know what marriage should be. Amichai had been too old, but at least he knew how to respect his wife and treat me like someone precious.

I bit my lip to keep from crying lest I ruin the kohl around my eyes and be found wanting in the eyes of my new family.

❖ ❖ ❖

The wedding lasted a week, and I breathed a relieved sigh when the last of the guests finally left. I stood in the cooking area, noting the herbs hanging from a beam above my head.

"Grab some rosemary and chop it for the bread," Harel's mother, Noya, said, giving me an assessing look. "I hope you know how to cook. You won't have servants to wait on you like you did when you lived in Amichai's big house. All of us work hard here."

My eyes widened at the semi-hostile tone in my mother-in-law's voice. "I cooked with Amichai's daughters-in-law. My maid helped, but she didn't do my work."

"Good." Noya turned to the table to begin mixing the bread, and Ela and Hodia, two of my four new sisters-in-law, entered the room from the garden behind the house, their children in tow. Each one held a basket of vegetables for the evening meal.

Moments later, Kelila and Ofra, two more sisters-in-law, came in carrying water from the well. It was a longer walk from Niv's home to the well than it had been from my father's, making me grateful that the women took turns drawing the water and bringing it home.

Home. How strange it was to look about this house with these people and think of any of it as my home. I blinked away the thought, grabbed a small stalk of rosemary from the larger bunch, and took it to the table to chop.

"With the dry weather, the lentils should be ripe today, and the gardens need weeding," Noya said after we prepared the food and set it before the men. "I will take Nessa to the lentil field and show her how to tell when the pods are ready to harvest. Hopefully we will have many that are mature and hardened." She glanced at me as I took a seat near the other women. "The rest of you can tend to your normal duties."

I nodded, then took a small bite of bread, hoping I would be able to eat. I looked from one sister-in-law to another. Would I find a friend among them like I did with Hila, however small the relationship? These women were near the ages of Amichai's children, but Harel was actually a year younger than I was.

"You'll get used to life on a farm soon enough," Ela said from across the table. "It's hard work, but when we bring in the harvest, it's also rewarding. We celebrate when the grain comes in."

I searched Ela's round, gentle features and smiled. "That sounds enjoyable. I haven't worked the land except for my mother's garden. I hope I learn well."

"I hope so too." Noya gave me another pointed look.

When the meal ended, Kelila pulled me aside while we put the leftovers in jars and baskets hanging from the ceilings. I looked behind me but found we were alone. "Noya will take some getting used to," Kelila whispered. She was married to Noya's second son, Shay, and already had three sons who were old enough to help their father in the fields. "She'll be hard on you for a while because you married her youngest. She's protective."

I put the leftover flatbread in a basket and hooked it over a beam to keep it from rodents that might sneak into the house, then faced Kelila. "I hope I please her. I have not had a mother-in-law before."

"That's right. Amichai was older and his mother and father were already gone, peace be upon them," Kelila said.

"Yes," I said, not realizing until that moment how very different it would be to have a mother-in-law.

"Is it strange for you?" Kelila led us to the courtyard. "Marrying again, I mean."

"It's different," I admitted. "But I'm sure I will adjust."

"Noya will be out soon." Kelila looked toward the house. "Let's grab a basket from beside the house to hold the lentils." She pointed to a stack of woven baskets meant for carrying produce from the fields.

I took the basket she handed to me.

"Marrying a man old enough to be your father had to be hard." Kelila seemed too curious about my previous husband, but I saw only kindness in her gaze.

I glimpsed Amichai in my mind's eye. "At first it was hard, but he was kind to me. I can't believe he's gone."

"Is Harel kind to you?" Kelila asked.

"Of course Harel is kind," Noya said, coming upon us unnoticed.

I jumped and looked at her. "Harel is kind," I said, feeling as though I was not being totally honest. "We are still getting to know each other."

"Well, you'll have plenty of time for that, but the crops won't wait. Let's go." Noya led the way toward the lentil field.

Kelila fell into step with me and gave me a knowing look. I smiled. Perhaps I *would* have a friend in this place. But Kelila was so much older than I was. Could I trust this woman? Or any of them?

I lifted my gaze heavenward. The cumulous clouds skittered across a bright blue sky, giving way to the sun. A cool breeze lifted my headscarf behind my back, but the day promised to be warm. I braced myself for the tasks Noya would give me, hoping I passed whatever test I might unknowingly be facing.

In any case, there was no turning back. I could not undo my marriage any more than I could bring Amichai back from the grave. Somehow I must learn to please Harel and his mother, and I wondered which one would be more difficult.

❖ ❖ ❖

SIX MONTHS LATER

I pushed myself up from the bed as light poured through the room I shared with Harel. I should have risen long ago to help with the morning meal, but when my feet hit the ground, I gripped the wall to steady myself. Nausea curdled in my middle, and a moment later, I bent over the water bowl and lost whatever was left in my stomach from the night before.

Shaking, I wiped my mouth on a linen towel and faced my reflection in the bronze mirror. The scent of vomit wafted to me, and I turned quickly away lest I be sick again. I was going to have to clean the bowl before Harel saw it, but I stumbled to the hook to gather my tunic and robe and told myself I would see to it later.

I made my way slowly through the house, one hand pressed to my middle as I entered the cooking area. The scent of fresh onion recently chopped assaulted me, and I ran from the room to the courtyard. What would Noya say? I was already late to help, and now I could not force myself to return to that awful smell.

I heaved, but nothing came up. Sitting on the bench, I tried to breathe. What was wrong with me?

Kelila appeared at the entrance to the courtyard and walked toward me. "Nessa. Are you all right?" She sat beside me and touched my knee. "You're pale and shaking. Are you ill?"

I nodded. "I threw up this morning in the water bowl. I haven't cleaned it yet. And now the onions . . . I can't go back in there."

Kelila looked me over, a smile curving her lips. "When did you have your last cycle?"

I forced myself to think. When had it been? Two months ago? I counted on my fingers. "Maybe two . . . three months ago? I can't remember. We've been so busy with the harvest that I stopped keeping track."

Kelila laughed, a pleasant sound. "Nessa. Don't you know what the problem is? I think in six months you certainly will!"

I stared at her, then turned at the sound of voices and the rest of the women entering the courtyard. My cheeks went hot at the look on Noya's face.

"Did I hear correctly? Are you carrying Harel's child?" She

clapped her hands and held them to her lips, joy lighting her eyes. "How wonderful!"

I looked at the faces staring down at me. "I don't know," I said, wishing I could recall the last time. "I think so?"

"If the smell of food makes you sick, you are definitely with child," Ela said.

"She can't keep food down," Kelila said. "I will clean out the bowl for you."

"You must rest, my daughter." Noya came close and took my hand. "We can do without you for a day or two, even a week if you must."

I wasn't sure I believed her. "No. No. I'm sure I will be fine, perhaps after some bread and water. I can still do my part." I could not let them think me weak. If I was carrying Harel's child, I must prove myself a worthy member of his family. Make his mother proud.

Was I truly with child? The thought brought a little thrill to my heart. In my year with Amichai I had not conceived, but perhaps he had been too old. Harel was young, as was I. This could be the first of many children with him.

Ima. A sudden longing to return to my father's house and tell Ima the news filled me. But I did not ask if I could return for a visit. I had never seen my sisters-in-law visit their families, and I wasn't sure my request would be met with favor. Perhaps I would find time at synagogue to tell her.

That wasn't how I imagined sharing such news. But I wasn't sure I had much choice.

12

As evening approached, I met Harel on his way in from planting the barley field. He smiled at the sight of me and quickened his step. Would he be pleased with my news? I hurried toward him, noting his sweat-streaked clothes and the empty seed basket tucked under his arm.

"Nessa, my love, what are you doing out here with Shabbat so close?" He placed an arm around my shoulders and continued walking. He'd come in early, as had his brothers and father, who were moments ahead of him.

"Your mother said I could come. They are preparing the meal so all is ready before sundown." Samaritans and Jews did not get along, but both honored Shabbat and kept the feasts, though Samaritans did not go to Jerusalem.

"Why would you need to see me before the meal?" His tone, however kind, held confusion. "It couldn't wait until we are alone in our room?"

"I wanted to tell you the news in case it's talked about at the meal," I said, trying not to breathe in the scent of his sweat.

"Tell me what?" He stopped to face me. "Why are you holding a hand to your face? Let me look at you when you speak."

"I'm sorry, my husband, but I'm finding that I am overly sensitive to smells of any kind, and your sweat . . . I will feel better in a few months, they tell me, but right now . . . please understand." Heat filled my cheeks at the look he gave me, but I felt a sense of relief when he took a step back.

"Tell me what makes my wife find me so unsatisfactory." He laughed. "A good day's work comes with honest sweat and smell."

I smiled. "Yes. Yes, it does. But your future son or daughter does not find it pleasant right now."

He stared at me, eyes wide. "Are you telling me . . . Are you with child?"

I nodded and laughed. "Yes! Your mother and sisters-in-law confirmed it today. I wanted to tell you as soon as you came home."

"I want to hold you and kiss you for this. Are you telling me to bathe myself so I can do just that?" He glanced at the sun. "I will have to hurry or be late for Shabbat."

I pinched my nose with my fingers. "You can if you're quick."

He swooped me into his arms and kissed my cheek, awkward though it was. He set me on my feet, handed me his basket, and motioned for me to walk ahead of him. "Go home and I will come quickly. Tell Ima that I went to the stream. I can't have the night go by and make my dear wife sick around me."

"Hopefully the sensitivity to smells will not last much longer." I glanced back at him. "Are you pleased with the news?"

"Pleased? I'm overjoyed, my love!" He shooed me away. "Now go!"

I hurried on ahead of him, my heart soaring. Harel was immature at times, but he was a good husband. A child would settle him and we would live a long and happy life together.

Memories of Gali suddenly hit me, and the pang of losing my best friend over this man still stung. But now, perhaps even Gali would find herself happily married and we could both bear children who would grow up together. I had to hope.

The house loomed ahead of me, and I slowed my step as I

approached. Hodia and Ofra carried freshly baked bread from the oven into the house. The sky beckoned the sun to take its rest beyond Mt. Gerizim.

I lifted my skirt, careful of the stones along the path, and noticed movement in the trees beyond the house. Would a wolf roam so soon? My thoughts turned to the oxen and donkeys housed in a cave behind the house, along with the few goats we kept for milk. Surely they were safe. Besides, it was too early for predatory animals to seek their prey, wasn't it?

One look about told me that I was alone. I quickened my pace, continually glancing toward the trees. A man stepped from the shadows, and I nearly cried out in surprise. Running now, I neared the courtyard and glanced back at him. Did I know him?

It wasn't Niv or any of Harel's brothers, so what was he doing here? Had he come to ask to share Shabbat with us? Perhaps a relative? But the familiarity I felt as he took a step closer caused my breath to hitch and my heart to pound.

Lavi? No. It couldn't be. Lavi had disappeared from Sychar when I'd married Amichai. He wouldn't have returned if he truly was the thief my father claimed him to be. Certainly not here at my home with Harel.

He did not move from where he stood, and I entered the courtyard, releasing a relieved breath. I glanced in his direction again, noted the shadowed expression on his bearded face, and hurried inside. Lavi's beard was not as dark. Whoever he was, he couldn't be the cousin I'd once loved. And if he was here, I would not speak to him.

I was a married woman and Harel deserved an honest wife, especially now that I was carrying his child. Never mind that Lavi's kiss was the only one that had made me swoon and long for more. Even Harel in his youth and vigor had never matched the way Lavi had made me feel in that moment.

But thinking of him would do me no good.

"What can I do?" I asked Kelila after removing my sandals, quickly washing and drying my feet, and entering the cooking room.

"You're back. Good. What did he say when you told him?" Kelila motioned me to a bench. "Sit. You don't need to do a thing. We are ready."

"He went to the spring to wash, but he is thrilled with the news." I twisted my belt, forcing my mind to the events of today and not to the man I'd seen near the trees.

"As well he should be!" Kelila laughed. "Did you send him to wash? I couldn't stand the smell of Shay's sweat when I was newly with child."

I smiled and felt myself relax. "Yes. He didn't want his future child to be disturbed by the smell of him."

Moments later the door opened, and everyone gathered about the table as the sun splayed its colors through the open window. Noya lit the lamps, and Niv called his grandsons Elias, Asher, and Zachary to his side.

"May you be like Ephraim and Manasseh," he said.

Noya called Eliana, Ofra's daughter, close. "And may you be like Sarah, Rebekah, Rachel, and Leah."

Together we all said, "May God bless you and protect you. May God show you favor and be gracious to you. May God show you kindness and grant you peace."

A hush fell over the room as the children returned to sit near their mothers.

Niv looked over the group, smiling at me. "There was an evening, there was a morning," he said softly. Glancing at Harel, he nodded.

Harel beamed at being chosen. He straightened before he spoke. "The sixth day: And the heavens and the earth and all they contained were completed, and on the seventh day God ceased from all the work that He had done. And God rested on the seventh day from all the work that He had done. And

God blessed the seventh day and sanctified it, for on that day He rested from all the work which He had done in creating the world."

"Blessed are You, Lord our God, Ruler of the Universe, who creates the fruit of the vine," Niv added after Harel finished. "Blessed are You, Lord our God, Ruler of the Universe, who has sanctified us with His commandments and favored us, and given us in love and favor His holy Shabbat as an inheritance, as a remembrance of the act of creation. For this day is the beginning of all holy days, a remembrance of the Exodus from Egypt. For You have chosen us and You have blessed us from among all the nations. And You have bequeathed us Your holy Shabbat in love and favor. Blessed are You, Lord, who sanctifies Shabbat." He ended his blessings with another glance at me, pride in his eyes.

Apparently having a child was the one thing I needed to provide this family in order to be accepted, and to make Harel proud. The harder part, though, was how I felt about all of them. After little more than six months of marriage, I still wasn't sure.

❖ ❖ ❖

Lavi stood frozen in the shade of the forest on the outskirts of Sychar. He had stayed away from the area since Nessa had married Amichai, since Amichai had paid him well to leave. But when word had reached him in Sebaste, almost a full day's walk from Sychar, that Amichai was dead, he had hoped. Would Raanan reconsider allowing him to marry Nessa now?

The thought had kept him awake at night, and as he'd worked for a local tentmaker doing what he'd done for Raanan, he turned a thousand thoughts over in his mind on how to convince his uncle to do just that. But he stopped short each time he remembered the night he'd left with Raanan's tools and Nessa's gold.

She didn't know the things he'd done. And just because she had allowed him to kiss her didn't mean she wanted to marry him. But the tormenting questions had caused him to return several months ago, only to find that Raanan had wasted no time in securing another husband for Nessa.

He watched the house lit with lamps as the sun grew heavier on its way to the west. Voices reciting the traditional Shabbat blessings drifted to him as darkness surrounded him, and he knew he could not continue to stare. But it was Nessa who had glimpsed him on her way into the house. Where had she come from? There was no jar of water on her head nor basket of food from the garden in her hands. Just an empty seed basket. Did they have her working in the fields planting? Clearly she had been on an errand of some kind.

Had she been visiting her mother? No. She wouldn't carry a seed basket all the way to Raanan's house. But if she did visit her family, might he intercept her and talk to her the next time? Hope lifted his chest but vanished a moment later. Nessa was wed to someone in this house, and by the looks of it, they were a large farming family. He would investigate to find out who owned this property, but there was no way he could talk to her without them knowing and telling Raanan.

And if they told Raanan he had returned to Sychar, Raanan could tell the Roman authorities or, if he was kind, the town elders. Either way, Lavi would not end up in a good place. He was not about to go to a debtor's prison or end up in the custody of the Romans. Nessa might be worth a lot, but she was not worth that.

He turned away from the house, ignoring the pang the traditional Shabbat prayers brought to his heart. He missed life with a family. It had been too long.

The forest sang its various mating songs as the crickets and other creatures began to rouse. He walked faster toward the road leading back to Sebaste. He would not make it until the moon stood high overhead, but its light would guide him, and he would return to work for the tentmaker there. It wasn't the life he wanted. But unless God had mercy on him or some kind of benevolence befell him, he wasn't likely to do any better.

❖ ❖ ❖

I walked the short distance to synagogue the next day, keeping in step with Kelila and Ela. "I can't wait to tell my ima the news about the baby." I placed a protective hand over my middle where the child grew in secret. "She will be thrilled." Though I still wished that Noya would allow me to visit my mother for part of a day to tell her privately.

"You'll have to tell her quickly. Remember, Niv doesn't like the family to stay long to associate with others after the reading." Ela pressed her hands to her robe to smooth a crease.

"Sit near your ima so you don't lose any time," Kelila added. "Niv won't wait for you."

I looked from one woman to the other. "Truly?"

They both nodded. My heart sank. I had never noticed Niv's hurry, but perhaps I had not thought a long talk with my mother or sisters necessary in the past. There was always something else occupying my mind. But now . . . I needed Ima. I didn't want my mother-in-law at a time like this. Or my sisters-in-law, nice as they might be.

Townspeople streamed from the city streets to enter the synagogue as we approached. I craned my neck to see if my mother and sisters had arrived, catching sight of them as they entered the area reserved for the women. Yaffa motioned me to join them, and she smiled as I took the seat between her and Ima.

I gripped my mother's hand and squeezed, smiling. Leaning close, I whispered, "I have news."

Ima looked ahead toward the rabbi, who now stood at the bimah to read from the scroll. "Tell me after the reading."

I released my grip and nodded as the people quieted and listened to the rabbi read from the first book of Moses.

"In the beginning God created the heavens and the earth . . ."

I half listened, my heart racing with the anxiety of not having time to tell Ima and my sisters before Noya hurried us away. Why the need to rush after service? And why had I not noticed Niv's behavior toward his family until now?

Irritation filled me as my mind wound backward over my six months of marriage. Memories of mealtimes where Niv or Noya commanded things of their sons or daughters-in-law. No requests. Just demands insisting the household, the plantings, the harvests all be done exactly as they wanted them done.

Had my father been as exacting with Lavi and Chen in the tentmaking shop? My mother had taught me to weave, and the craft was exacting in itself. My sisters had chided me about all manner of things when we were younger, but nothing had prepared me for Niv's insistent authority over his household.

A seed of rebellion toward Niv's and Noya's controlling ways settled in me as the rabbi continued to expound on the creation narrative. I had heard the same teachings from the same rabbi every year of my life, and many times a year at that. Was this how a person came to understand God?

If God had created the world and the life within me, did He care about us after we were born? Could I call on Him and be heard? Or had He left us to survive on our own?

At last the rabbi finished speaking and dismissed the crowd. I glanced at Kelila, but she was already following Noya out of the building.

"How are you?" Yaffa asked, taking my hand as we headed toward the door.

I faced Ima and my sisters and leaned close to Ima. "I am with child," I whispered. "I can't stay or visit to tell you more. Perhaps Abba can convince Niv to allow me to come home for a day or part of a day? I need you, Ima." A little sob rose in my throat.

"Oh my, Nessa! I'm so pleased." Ima kissed my cheek, then held me close for a brief moment. "I will talk to your father. When did you know?"

"I found out only yesterday, but I think I'm two or three months along. We work so hard on the farm that I had not kept track until I began to feel sick." I glanced behind me to see that Harel's family was already walking along the road. "I have to go. They will not want me to lag behind." I looked from Ima to my sisters. "I will see you next week."

I hugged each one quickly, then half ran to catch up to Kelila, my breath keeping pace with the growing anger in my heart.

13

The pains came early and suddenly when I was in the garden pulling weeds. I doubled over and pressed both hands into the dirt to keep breathing. "Ohh . . ." All I could do was groan, though every fiber of my being longed to cry out. I could barely breathe, and no one was within hearing distance to help me.

I pushed myself up from my knees, tears searing my cheeks, sweat trickling down my back. I braced my hands on my thighs against waves of pain. Something was terribly wrong.

I drew in short, labored breaths as another sharp pain attacked, and this time I forced the air from my lungs. "Help me! Please! Help!" I struggled to regain my balance as I cradled my protruding belly. "Help me." Weaker this time.

I awoke sometime later in the room I shared with Harel. Noya and Ima hovered over me. I blinked. Before I could speak, another wave of pain washed over me. "Ohh . . ."

"Nessa, my love, you must stay with us." Ima's voice sounded distant.

No. I didn't want to stay here in this sea of pain.

"Your baby is coming. You must help push him out."

My baby? This was all because of the child? Had my sisters ever lived through such agony?

"Come now, Nessa. Wake up!" Was Noya commanding me? Where was I again? This wasn't the garden. It was my room. Harel's room.

"My daughter, stay with us." Ima's voice drifted to me, comforting, drawing me. I rallied.

"Ima?" I managed to see Ima's concern and felt her hand on my shoulder.

"The baby is early and you need to push him out."

"It hurts." I could barely speak. Could they hear me?

"I know it does, my love, but we are going to lift you to the birthing stones and hold you up. All you have to do is push."

Several pairs of hands lifted me, and together they carried me from the bed to the place where women had been giving birth for generations.

My head drooped to the side, and I fought to lift it. I leaned into the strength of my sisters-in-law and both mothers and sought strength from a place I did not know. *Oh, God, help me.* The prayer came unbidden, as though I could do nothing more and nothing better.

I strained hard to push, then fell back against the arms that held me. Another push and wait. Push and wait. Until at last the child burst from my body, caught by my mother.

I closed my eyes, relieved. But as I rested against Kelila and Ela, exhausted, I wondered at the silence in the room. Shouldn't the baby cry? Why was no one speaking?

I lifted my weary head. "Ima? What's wrong?" Why were they hovering over the baby in a corner of the room, not saying anything? "Ima?"

My mother left the child with Noya and knelt beside me. "Nessa."

"Can I hold him? Is it a boy?" I heard the waver in my voice but begged myself not to cry. "Tell me!"

"It's a boy and he is dead," Noya said bluntly, coming beside me. "These things happen sometimes." She looked at me, showing me a brief moment of compassion. "Rest now, Nessa. I will tell Harel." She left the room while Kelila and Ela helped carry me to the bed.

"Ima?" The tears would not stop now. "I want to see him."

"I'm not sure that's a good idea," Kelila said.

"I want to hold him," I insisted. "Bring him to me."

Ima walked to the table where the stillborn child lay, wrapped him gently in linen cloths, and carried him to me. "This is your son." She placed him in my arms.

His skin held a blue tinge, but other than that, he looked like he was sleeping peacefully. My vision blurred and tears dripped onto the linen covering his body. I peeled it slowly away to examine every part of him. Perfect. There was nothing wrong with him.

"Why, Ima?" I searched her tortured face. "He looks perfect."

"Only God knows, my daughter. Sometimes children die at birth. Sometimes before birth. He came early. Maybe something was wrong inside of him. I am so sorry." She touched my shoulder and gazed with me into the baby's face.

"Will you name him?" Ela asked as she carried soiled linens to a basket for washing in the river.

I looked on the child with his full head of dark hair and his perfect eyes and mouth and nose. He had all his tiny fingers and toes and legs that should have been swaddled. Instead, he would wear a burial shroud. Harel would place him in the family cave, and I would miss it because I was too weak and unclean.

And I would never see this child again. Not in this life. Perhaps, if the rabbis were right, there was a place after life where we would meet again. Would it help if I named him?

"He is Raanan, after my father," I said, knowing that Harel would not want a dead child bearing his name.

Ima patted my arm. "Your father would have loved him."

I held the baby to my heart, not wanting to let him go. But as the sun sank lower, I at last released him to my mother, who carried him away.

I hugged my empty arms to my chest and wept.

❖ ❖ ❖

The soothing sound of the flowing stream barely registered as I scrubbed a tunic against a stone. Kelila worked beside me, thankfully silent. Though months had passed since I held my beautiful stillborn boy to my heart, nothing, not even my purification and return to synagogue or the visits from my mother, helped draw me from the pain of losing him. Did grief ever end?

"The day is pleasant at least," Kelila said.

I felt her looking at me, but I could not return her gaze as I worked the dirt from Harel's tunic and the sweat stains from the short sleeves.

"Are you happy working in the booth selling the family's wares?" Kelila seemed insistent on drawing me into conversation.

I glanced at her, catching her concern in that brief moment. She had tried to help, and I should be grateful, but the bitter taste of loss would not allow it. "It is easier than working in the fields," I said after a lengthy pause.

"I agree. And your weaving is better than Noya expected. I know she is pleased." Kelila smiled, but I could not return it.

"That's good." Did I care what Noya thought anymore? I supposed having her like my work meant something. I squeezed the water from Harel's tunic and carried it to some nearby bushes to dry.

"I'm glad you enjoy working the booth, though I miss working beside you in the fields." Kelila stood and rubbed the small of her back. "Normally, we all take turns. But I think Noya fears for you, so she wants to give you the easier tasks."

"Washing the clothes is not one of the easier tasks." Nothing in life was easy, so what did it matter? I frowned at the basket beside me, still piled with tunics and robes and undergarments from the household. "And just because I am late again doesn't mean I'm with child. I wish she wouldn't watch me so closely."

"Noya likes to know what is going on in her home and with her family. I know it can be annoying, but you get used to it as her way of caring after a while." Kelila touched my shoulder. "You *could* be with child. You did say it has been two months."

A dam broke inside of me. I wasn't sure I wanted to be with child. I couldn't bear to go through what I had just barely survived. "What happens if I lose another one? I could have another child die before birth. Will Harel blame me or put me out?" I kept my voice low, but the fear of what could happen and how I might be treated filled me.

Kelila's eyes widened. She knelt at my side. "Oh, dear one, are you worried about this?"

I nodded.

She took my wet hand. "Many women lose children in childbirth, or they come too soon. You are young and healthy. There is no reason to believe that what happened to you before will happen again. We will pray that all is well. You will be fine." She squeezed my hand and released it.

I met her gaze. Kelila was ten years older than I was, with three children all born without incident. She did not know what it was like. No one could relate to what I had endured, not even my mother. Even Gali had birthed a son shortly after her marriage, though my loss had not brought her around to offer comfort. Apparently her grudge against Harel and against me—as if I could have controlled the outcome—was not something that she would easily let go. If she ever would.

"I guess we will see in seven more months, if in fact a child has begun growing within me." Though I honestly did not want to think about this again. Not yet.

"All will be well," Kelila repeated. "You'll see." She returned to her basket and took the next tunic from the pile to scrub on the rock next to her.

I pulled Harel's undergarments from the basket and began the rhythmic scrubbing. The mindless, repetitive task of washing clothes was something I could do by rote, much like dressing, cooking, and eating. If I could just keep Kelila from talking, I could let the rhythm of sameness fill my soul and perhaps, if God was merciful, heal me.

Tomorrow, when I returned to the family's market stall, I could only pray that the well-meaning women of the town would not ask me how I was feeling. I was in no mood to hear their advice or watch their faces scrunch in sympathy. Even after six months, the people of Sychar did not quickly forget. And I desperately needed them to.

❖ ❖ ❖

THREE MONTHS LATER

The marketplace in Sychar boasted an entire street of shops selling the produce and wares from people of the city, along with a specialty shop carrying items brought to them by traveling merchants. I rose at dawn, though the burden of the child made it harder for me to do so, and led the donkey with the cartful of wool and woven garments to the shop in time to settle things the way I liked them.

Now, as the sun slanted toward the opening of the booth, I sat on a stool half hidden in the shadows. Noya had tucked food in a basket for me to eat at midday and packed another basket of pomegranates for buyers to add to their purchases.

"Be sure to eat well," Noya had said, pointing to the food and skin of water in the cart. "Harel's baby needs all of the nourishment you can give him." Her smile did not reach her eyes, and I wondered if Noya ever felt genuine compassion

108

or concern for me. Did she care only for Harel and his future heir?

"I will," I said, placing an ever-protective hand over the place where the babe grew. "Thank you."

"Anything for Harel's child."

Noya had walked away then, leaving a hollow feeling in my heart. What about me? This baby was as much my child as it was Harel's. But after nearly two years of living in Niv's household, I knew too well that Niv and Noya viewed the children of their children as their own. Daughters-in-law were accepted if they bore children and were treated well if they did what was expected. No one ever questioned or went against them, though deep down I feared how my child would fare as Harel's son.

If only Harel had married another. If only my father had given me to Lavi or if Amichai had not died.

"May I see that garment?"

The male voice startled me, and I looked up from my musings. I saw where he pointed, avoiding a direct look at him. I stood, lifted the man's robe from the pile, and held it out for him to see.

He touched the edge, and I pulled back, not wanting our fingers to connect. "Exquisite," he said, his voice low.

My head jerked up at the familiar low tone. I met his gaze, heart pounding as he looked from the garment to search my face.

"Lavi?" What was he doing here? I pulled the garment away and held it to my chest.

"Shalom, Nessa. Is this your work?" He leaned casually against the pillar holding up the booth, his lips curved upward.

Heat swept up my cheeks as memories assaulted me. "Why are you here?" I whispered.

"Are you not happy to see me?" He pouted, and I could not decide whether to laugh at him or smack him or run the other way.

"What do you want, Lavi? I didn't know you were back in Sychar." I leaned closer, but not too close. "It's not safe for you here."

"Are you worried about me, Nessa?" His smile widened. "How touching."

"You didn't answer my question." I leveled him with a stern look. "Are you interested in purchasing this robe, or did you just come to make a nuisance of yourself?" Irritation replaced my initial shock. I could not be seen with him, and he risked his life walking through the streets so brazenly.

"I'm here with my employer from Sebaste. And yes, I would like to purchase that robe. If you made it, that is." His dark eyes shone, and in them I saw the boy I'd once loved. Still loved, if I were honest with myself.

"It costs two hundred denarii," I said, placing the robe on the counter between us and holding it with my hand.

"So much!" His tone held complaint, but his eyes still smiled down on me.

"It took months to make. Consider it a bargain." I pursed my lips and glared at him. I would not allow myself to feel anything for him. I would not be disloyal to Harel even in my thoughts.

"Very well. I will take it." He pulled the coins from a drawstring bag at his hip.

"You've done well for yourself to afford such a garment," I said, wondering how he could have earned so much. But perhaps he worked for someone who paid more than food and shelter and the occasional denarius.

"The money belongs to my employer," he said, though by his look I wasn't sure I believed him. He held out the coins and placed them in my hand.

Our fingers brushed, and his touch sent a tingle down my spine. I forced myself not to shiver. I tossed the robe at him. "You should go."

"Aren't you even going to package it for me? I can't just walk off with it unwrapped."

I could not hold his gaze, my heart pounding, fearing that someone from Harel's family would see us talking. Or one of my sisters. But I grabbed the robe from him, folded it neatly, and tied it with burlap string. "Now go." I handed it to him, careful not to let my fingers near his, and sat on the stool again.

He stood there a moment staring at me, his gaze looking me up and down. His Adam's apple moved as though he struggled to swallow.

"Are you with child?" His words, a mere whisper, reached my heart.

I placed a protective hand over my middle. The insolence of his question! Such things were none of his business.

Still . . . if only I could have borne his children. But I could not think that way.

"You should know better than to ask me such a thing." Again I glared at him. "Now please go." But my voice did not carry the strength it had initially.

"It's good to see you again, Nessa. I will think of you every time my master wears this coat. If only I could have kept it for myself." Sadness tinged his words.

I let my gaze skip over his, then searched the market beyond him. "I'm sorry as well," I whispered. *Now go.* I begged him to read my thoughts.

"Goodbye, Nessa," he said, taking the garment and walking away.

I watched him leave, wishing another customer would come to distract me. But no one came, and my gaze followed him all the way down the street until he was out of sight.

14

TWO MONTHS LATER

I led a donkey and cart to the field where the men were harvesting wheat. I had filled the cart with food and skins of water for the men to refresh themselves and rest. The babe within me kicked as I walked, and I cradled my middle, marveling at the strength he possessed. Perhaps I truly had nothing to fear this time. But until I held the child in my arms and heard his healthy cry, I would fear.

"The food is here!" Harel's voice drew my attention, and I smiled and returned his wave.

Lavi had woven his way in and out of my thoughts since that day at the booth, but I had made a concerted effort to think only of Harel and his family. They were my family now, and I didn't want to do anything to risk my place here. What if I somehow sinned in my thoughts and God took my baby from me? Would He do that?

Harel hurried toward me, followed by his brothers and father. He wiped the sweat from his brow with a linen cloth and tucked it in his belt. "What did you bring?" His eager gaze made me laugh.

"Your favorite date cakes, and your mother made sweet millet balls for you all." I lifted the cover from the basket.

He reached for one of each and grabbed a skin of water. He stuffed the first cake into his mouth and moved away from me to sit with his brothers. They rested in the dirt at the edge of the wheat field, leaving me standing there. I watched them eat and talk and laugh, and I waited, hoping Harel would look my way. None of them thanked me.

When they stood to return to the harvest, I took the donkey's reins and turned him toward the house. I glanced back at Harel. For a brief moment I wanted to offer to help the men, but I shook the thought aside as quickly as it came. The women sometimes helped with the harvest, but Noya had given me strict instructions not to do tasks that were considered too difficult. Even the laundry and weeding had gone to the others now. If the other women could work thus when carrying a child, I should not be treated with such care.

All the special treatment just made me fear more. Work took the fear and shoved it to the back of my mind. But all I could do now that the birth was only about two new moons away was work in the market or at the loom. At least I enjoyed weaving, and I'd begun a good-sized pile of small garments for the babe.

The babe. He kicked again. Was it a boy? That would make Noya happy. And Harel. They didn't seem capable of thinking it could be a girl. I struggled with thinking about the babe as being real at all.

I removed the donkey from its cart and attached a lead to him so he could move freely, then entered the house.

"You're back. Good," Noya said. "We have an order for a man's cloak. A merchant from Sebaste, of all places! Apparently, he bought one from our booth a few months ago and now wants one for his son." She pointed to the loom. "He wants it to be red and brown. Can you handle that?"

I sat at the loom and bent to look through the baskets of colored yarn. *Sebaste?* My stomach dipped. Lavi had purchased that robe. Did his master want another? Or was this something else? "How soon does he want it?"

"As soon as you are able. Don't rush, but don't waste time. It won't hurt the child for you to work the loom." Noya walked away without another word, leaving me staring after her. Why was everyone so curt all the time?

I leaned over the basket of brown yarn. There were several shades of the color. Would the man like a mixture of reds and browns? I turned patterns over in my mind. When I at last decided on which color to thread onto the loom first, I reached to pull it closer and gasped at the pain.

That was not a normal kick. Was it? I took several breaths. Surely it was. Perhaps I had pinched the child. I straightened, concentrating on breathing. The feeling passed, and I leaned forward, slowly this time, and picked the brown yarn from the basket. I released a breath and let my fingers do the work of threading it onto the loom as I had done since childhood.

Hodia entered the weaving room and sat across from me. With her spindle and distaff, she turned the wool into yarn to be dyed for the weaving. "What are you making?" she asked as I fed the weft through the warp.

"Noya said we have a request for a man's robe from a person in Sebaste. I don't know how soon he needs it, but I hope I can finish it before the babe comes," I said, glancing at Hodia and offering her a tentative smile. Hodia was closer to my age than Kelila, but they were opposite in almost everything they thought and did.

"I'm sure someone else can complete the work if you don't. Sebaste, you say? I'm surprised they would come all this way for a robe. With a town the size of Sebaste, surely they have plenty of weavers." She looked me up and down. "I mean, you do decent work, but it's not like your garments are better than anyone else's."

"Of course not." But the words stung. Lavi had praised my

work, and Ima had considered me talented in my designs and my working with fine threads. But praise in this house was not something easily given. Why should I expect better of Hodia?

I continued to work until the sun headed toward the west. My back ached from sitting, so I finished the row and set the shuttle aside. Standing, I rubbed the small of my back. My hands moved of their own accord to my middle, longing to feel that strong kick again. But the babe seemed strangely quiet.

Hodia let the spindle come to rest and set it aside. "We should help with the evening meal."

I continued to gently rub my middle, my fear spiking.

"Is something wrong? You look pale."

I shook myself. "Do I? I'm just tired." That had to be the reason I felt the need to lie down and coax the baby to move. I would feel like myself again once I knew the baby was fine.

"Go and rest a little then," Hodia said, pointing to the hall that led to the rooms where each family slept. "Noya would want you to."

I nodded, suddenly grateful that Noya cared so much for Harel's baby. I would not be reprimanded for resting. "Thank you," I said as I walked toward the room I shared with Harel, all the while rubbing my belly. "Wake up, little one," I whispered, telling myself not to panic.

The room was not as spacious as I would like, especially once the little one came. Already the bed, stack of linens, and small chest of clothes took up one corner opposite our bed. I walked to the place where I longed to lay my sleeping babe, then made my way to the bed.

Perhaps if I lay still, he would delight me with a kick, however small. I'd grown used to stronger kicks, especially if I gently poked him. "Wake up, little one," I said again, lying still and drawing gentle circles over the babe's secret place.

A faint flutter as I'd felt in the beginning came beneath my roaming fingers. I waited, praying for more, but no matter how many times I prodded, gently then not so gently, he did not kick again.

He's all right. He has to be all right. But my pounding heart betrayed me. I feared. Desperately. "Please! Wake up and move!" My words, a mere breath, accompanied my tears. Had that one pain been an indication that something was wrong? Did other women have moments when their child stopped moving then began again?

Ima. I needed the comfort of my mother, not Harel's mother or the other women in this household. Should I send for her? Or try to slip away and walk home? Ima would know what to do and tell me what was wrong.

I swiped the tears from my eyes and slowly stood. The sun angled ever westward, casting its shadows through the window toward the eastern edge of the room. They would all wonder where I had gone. No one ever left Niv's home without permission.

But I didn't care. I needed Ima, and I wasn't going to wait for Noya to tell me what I could or could not do. Not this time.

I snatched my robe and tied the belt, slipped into my sandals as best I could, and walked out the back door of the house. I passed through the outer courtyard unseen and hurried toward the other side of Sychar to my father's house.

The sound of the men's voices coming in from the field drifted to me, making me pick up my pace. They would only stop me, and I was not about to be stopped. Perhaps the walk would awaken the baby. I had to try.

I arrived moments before the sun set and entered without knocking. My mother nearly dropped the plate of food she was carrying to my father and brother.

"Nessa! Whatever are you doing here? And so late and in your condition? Is something wrong?" Ima set the plate down and pulled me into a warm embrace.

116

My tears came so fast I could not stop them nor stifle a sob. "I think something is wrong with the baby."

Ima held me at arm's length and looked me over. "Are you in pain? Have the waters broken?"

I shook my head. "No . . . yes. That is, no, the waters have not broken, but earlier I had a sharp pain. I haven't felt the baby move since. I even lay down and tried to coax him to move, but I felt only a slight flutter. I'm afraid, Ima. I needed you."

"What's this?" My father rose and came close. "Why are you here? Lihi?"

"She's worried about the baby," Ima said. "Go back and eat." She took my hand. "Come, my daughter."

"Does Niv know you're here?" my father asked to my retreating back.

"No." I swallowed hard, unable to say more.

My mother took me to my old bedchamber and motioned for me to sit on the mat. "Lie back and let me examine you." Ima had worked as a midwife for many village women.

I did as I was told and waited, breath held tight within me as my mother checked me over. "You told no one you were coming?" she asked as she examined me. "Was that wise, my daughter? I know how Niv and Noya can be."

"They won't be happy, but I had to come. I'm so afraid, Ima. If I lose this child too, they will disown me." I choked on the words.

"Have they said that?" Alarm filled Ima's voice, and I did not like the look in her eyes.

"All Noya cares about is the child. I'm only given special consideration because of the child. I will be accepted when I deliver a healthy son for Harel." I was crying harder now, giving way to the pent-up tears.

"There, there. It might not be as bad as all that. They might keep you if it's a girl." My mother lowered my tunic and took my hand, pulling me to a sitting position. She smiled at me, but it seemed forced.

"Something is wrong, isn't it? Tell me the truth." I already feared the worst. Why not tell it to me now?

"I see nothing wrong, my daughter." She patted my knee. "But it is unusual that you feel no movement when you were feeling it consistently, yes?"

I nodded and hiccuped on another sob. "Yes."

"Then you will need to pay attention to the child. Rest as much as you can and see if the child moves in a day or so. It is possible he or she is simply asleep and too content to kick right now." Ima touched my cheek. "Now dry your tears and I will walk you back to your home. You don't want to anger Noya or Niv."

"Do you truly think everything could be all right?" A sliver of hope pierced my heart. Perhaps I was imagining the worst for no good reason.

"Let's wait and see. Only God knows for sure, and you still have two months to wait, so let's get you home." She pulled me to my feet, and together we walked to the sitting area. "I'm taking her home. I don't want Noya giving her a hard time. I will be back."

"Do I need to go with you? It's dark," my father said. The streets were fairly safe, but there was always the potential for harm in the night.

"I'll take a stick. If I'm not back soon, come for me." Ima led me into Sychar's streets, holding my arm the whole way. "Wipe your eyes, and let me explain your fears to Noya. She will take it better from me."

"Thank you, Ima. I only hope all will be well."

"That's what we all hope for, child. Trust Adonai and pray that He gives you the child safely."

She didn't tell me what I should do if Adonai did not say yes.

15

"top rolling so close to me, Nessa. I can get no sleep with you on top of me." Harel's irritated voice sounded distant, like an intruder of my dreams. "Nessa!" he hissed, pushing my shoulder to move me away from him.

I jerked awake. "What? Is something wrong?" I sat up too quickly and my head spun.

Harel rose and glared at me. "The problem is that you're impossible to sleep with in your condition. I will be glad when the child sleeps in a bed of his own." He grabbed his robe and headed to the door.

"It's still dark. Where are you going?" I shook my head, trying to clear it, still dozy from the dream. Why was Harel acting so upset in the middle of the night?

"I'm going to sleep on the roof. Maybe there I can get some peace." He left and closed the door, not waiting for me to answer.

I sank onto the bed again, confusion and exhaustion mingling within me. Why was Harel acting this way? I knew he needed his sleep for the long days of working the fields, but I needed my rest for the child.

The child. Fully awake now, I felt my belly for some sign of movement. Nothing. *Please, little one. Don't do this to me.*

Overwhelming dread filled me as it had the day before, and my heart sped up until I had to tell myself to breathe. *Adonai, do You hear the prayers of women? Should I go to the rabbi to ask him to pray for the child? If I have sinned in some way, please show me, but please spare this child.*

I closed my eyes, but no matter what I did, I could not get comfortable again. Not after Harel's irritation. Not with the fear coursing through me.

I pushed up from the bed and stood to pace the room. Walking was good for the child, wasn't it? But as I walked, my back began to ache as though I had just spent hours bent over weeding the garden. I rubbed the ache, but when a sharp pain crossed my middle, I could not withhold the need to cry out.

Clamping my mouth shut, I sat on the bed, rocking back and forth. It was too soon for labor and too early to wake the household. Moonlight filtered through the window, casting dappled light over the small room. Why was this happening to me?

More importantly, was there anything I could do to stop whatever "this" was? I wanted Ima, but I could not leave the house again—and not in the middle of the night.

Kelila's room was not far, if I could manage to get there and wake her without disturbing Shay or her children. I stood again. What to do?

Walking did nothing to ease my pain, and every step reminded me of how exhausted I was. If Harel had not awakened me, I could still be blissfully dreaming and not walking about our room trying not to panic.

Anger against my often-immature husband hit me hard. A moment passed before I heard footsteps coming toward my room. Had my pacing awakened someone? I stopped, and a moment later, Noya opened the door and peered inside.

"Nessa? What are you doing out of bed?" She stepped inside and looked about the moonlit room. "Where is Harel?"

"He went to sleep on the roof. Apparently, I bumped him and

woke him." Shame heated my face as I admitted such a thing to my mother-in-law, but I could think of nothing else to say.

"Humph." She looked me up and down. "So why are you not sleeping? Is it the child?"

My mother had explained my fears to Noya the evening before, but Noya seemed more upset that I had gone to see my mother than to think something might be wrong with her grandchild.

Another pain crossed my middle at the moment, and I clutched my belly, nearly doubling over. My waters broke in the next breath, and Noya sprang into action, waking the women of the household in hushed, urgent whispers.

"I want my ima," I said, choking on my tears. I hugged my belly, breathing hard.

Kelila stumbled into the room, carrying a lamp, and blinked at the sight of Noya gathering linens and me holding my belly. "Oh, Nessa, what's happened?"

"Her waters have broken. She's in pain and we need to check her. It's too soon," Noya said through clenched teeth.

"Can you lie down, Nessa?" Kelila asked, gently taking my shoulders and helping me onto the bed. "Let me check you."

I groaned at the attempt to lie flat but complied with Kelila's request.

"She's dilating." Kelila lowered my tunic. "The baby is coming whether we are ready or not."

"Can we send for my ima?" My voice was thin and hoarse to my ears, clogged as it was with tears.

"I'll send Shay for her," Kelila promised. "He won't mind." She hurried from the room to wake her husband, and moments later, I heard the entire household moving about.

Kelila returned, and Noya and my sisters-in-law prepared the room for the birth. A birth that should not be happening yet. Would the child live after it was born? Could it survive two months too soon?

I longed to pray, to beg God to make the child bigger than it would normally be, but my mind was full of the voices around me, the men clattering about the house, the cries of the children, and Harel's sudden appearance at the door of our room.

"What is going on?" His demanding tone carried fear.

"Your wife is giving birth too soon. And you cannot be here, so leave." Noya pushed him away, but not before I saw the look of terror in his eyes.

If the baby didn't live, he would blame me. His fear would turn to anger. I knew it just as I had come to know him too well.

Dawn crept up the eastern ridge, bringing my mother with it. Soon after I gave birth to another stillborn son.

I fell back on the bed, exhausted and despairing.

This time I did not ask to see the child. I could not bring myself to face the baby whom I had surely killed by something I must have done wrong. I was cursed, and soon enough the family's comforting words and sorrowful looks would end. They would need to blame someone, and who else but me?

There was no possible way that Noya would want me to remain Harel's wife after losing two children in less than two years of marriage.

"Ima," I whispered once the ordeal ended and I lay on the bed, cleaned and broken.

"I'm here, my daughter." Ima knelt at my side and took my hand.

"I'm a failure," I said, choking on a sob. "Harel will hate me after today."

My mother shifted to stroke my cheek. "There, there. He won't hate you. These things are beyond our control. I've seen it before. Some women are barren, others can't seem to bring a child to term. But you are young. You can still try again."

I shook my head. "I don't ever want to go through that again."

"Shh . . . Don't say such things, dear one. Of course you

feel this way now, but you won't forever." She leaned closer and kissed my cheek. "Rest now. I will stay with you. Sleep."

"Don't go, Ima."

"I said I wouldn't. Don't worry, my daughter."

Ima rested a hand on my shoulder and sang songs to me in her attempt to soothe. Noya came and brought chamomile tea to help me sleep. But my sleep was not sweet and my dreams caused me to jerk awake.

The house grew quiet as the men went to bury the child and the women went about their daily chores. I grieved yet again, only this time I knew nothing would return to normal. And I feared what was to come.

❖ ❖ ❖

The scent of freshly turned earth met my nostrils. I drew in a deep breath, grateful to be out in the fresh air working in the garden again. Planting the vegetables we would eat meant a lot of bending and making sure the seeds were spaced correctly, but the activity helped me to forget the days when I could barely see my feet and the household treated me as though I couldn't do anything but weave. Sometimes working in the dirt brought greater comfort.

"How are you feeling today?" Kelila called from a few rows to my right. Both of us held leather bags slung crossways over our shoulders to easily reach the seeds. "It's a beautiful day for sowing, don't you agree?"

I glanced at Kelila and offered a half smile. "Yes. It's good to be out here with the rest of you."

In the distance, I heard the children who were too young to help playing in the meadow as they picked wildflowers. Hodia sat watching nearby, spindle and distaff in hand.

Had my son lived, he would be tied to my back or resting in a basket nearby. "He would be three months old today," I said, not speaking to anyone in particular.

"You will bear one that lives soon," Ela said from my left. Both Kelila and Ela were within hearing distance, helping to plant different vegetables. "You're not the first woman to lose more than one child."

I ignored the attempt at comfort. Ela—and for that matter, all the women in the house other than Kelila—rarely knew how to speak in a truly comforting way. Apparently, speaking plainly or matter-of-factly *was* their way of comforting. I did not agree.

"Noya showed me that robe you wove for the merchant from Sebaste. It's beautiful, Nessa. It should bring a good price." Kelila knelt in the dirt, placed the cucumber seeds in her row, and gently covered them. "Are you pleased with your work?"

I focused on my own row, not wanting to see the pity in Kelila's dark eyes. "I think it came out better than I expected . . . considering." I had completed the work after the baby died as I awaited my weeks of ritual purification. Even after I was clean, I had continued working solely on that task until I finished, which was only a few days ago. I did everything in my power to please Noya, whose impatience filled every space I inhabited.

"Well, Noya was pleased, so you should be too." Kelila's voice sounded almost too cheerful, and when I glanced her way, her smile was too bright.

I gave her a curious look. The truth was that nothing had been the same in the three months since my second son had died. Harel had asked his mother to move me to a separate room, though the house barely had another space to spare. Noya eventually told Harel to make the best of what they had, but he no longer slept beside me. Another mat had been found and brought into our already small room and replaced the spot where any future children would sleep. Harel continued to sleep in the bed while I felt like a servant, sharing the space with him but no longer sharing his love.

Had he ever loved me? I tossed more seeds onto the next row, wishing I could move away from Kelila and Ela, who talked above me as though I was not there. I was glad of it.

In a way, I had pulled an invisible cloak over my heart, wrapping myself in a silent cocoon. The women still spoke to me, but Harel had said little since the day we fought.

"What did you do that caused the death of both my sons?" he'd demanded the day after my purification. He had not come near me until that moment, and when he did, his scowl penetrated like a dagger into the deep, hurting place within my heart, tearing the wound open again.

"I didn't do anything," I protested, raising my hands to protect myself from attack, verbal or physical.

"Ha!" His scoffing tone shoved the dagger deeper. "My mother doesn't think so. Surely you sinned in some way or did something to harm the child. Why else would you lose *two* children? I should have married Gali."

"Then why didn't you? You could have." How often had I wished he had given Gali what she'd longed for—to marry him—and spared me from living in this household. Perhaps they would have accepted her with open arms.

"Because you are the one every man in town thinks is so beautiful." He stared at me. "But they don't know that your beauty is outward, not inward, and you're not as good as they think. I never should have married you." He'd stalked off then, leaving my heart bleeding and me emotionally alone.

The memory, which had initially brought tears, carried no weight now. A sense of welcome numbness had filled me, and I no longer held any feelings, good or bad, toward this family who did not want me. How long would it be until Harel found a reason to discard me? Men gave women writs of divorce often enough. He would cite my inability to bear children as his reason.

Or what if he married another but did not set me free? The thought broke through with a kick to my gut. I would have no escape. Even if I complained to my father, he wasn't likely to do anything. Technically, Harel should still fulfill my marital rights even if he took another wife, but who would know but me whether he did so or not? People would assume me barren, and no one would believe the testimony of a woman against her husband.

Oh, God, don't let that happen.

The prayer caused the pain of loss to rush in on me again. I began to shake, and my hand could barely place the seeds in the soil. My heart raced as though I had run all the way home. Somehow I must convince Harel to accept me again. Or let me return to my father.

But would he listen? Harel did what he wanted, and no one stood up to him except his mother on occasion. He was too spoiled, even after two years as my husband, to see my hurt or care to understand that I had done nothing to cause the loss of my children.

A touch on my arm made me jump.

"Nessa, are you all right?" Kelila stood beside me.

I looked at her and shook my head. "No. Yes. I will be fine." I sifted through the seeds for another handful, telling my hands to obey me but barely able to make them comply.

As I sat with the women later that night, listening to them talking about the day or the children's antics, I felt Noya's gaze on me. I was being watched, and no doubt judged.

16

A month later, I was pulling my robe from its peg on the wall of our room when Harel barged in. Startled, I slowly faced him. His normally pleasant-looking eyes glared at me, and his brows drew down into a deep scowl. I cinched the robe tightly about me, all thoughts of working in the garden gone.

"Here," Harel said, thrusting a rolled parchment and coin purse toward me. "Take it."

I looked at the scroll, heart pounding. I swallowed hard. "What is it?"

But I knew.

"A writ of divorce. You can pack your things and go back to your father." He shoved the document into my reluctant hand, forcing me to take it.

My fingers curled over the parchment as he turned on his heel and stormed out of the room. "And be gone before I return from the fields," he said over his shoulder. "I never want to see you again."

I stared after him. Trembling from a place deep within me, I stumbled to my knees and bent forward, crushing the parchment beneath my hand. I longed to curl onto my side and hide from the world, but his words—and worse, his angry tone—shouted at me. *"I never want to see you again."*

Why? Because I had not borne him a living son?

My lips trembled, and I desperately tried to still the shaking as I forced myself to sit on my knees. Was this divorce Harel's idea or his mother's?

I'd seen Noya corner Harel more than once and talk to him apart from me during the past month. Had she deemed me unfit to be Harel's wife because of the two lost sons? Everyone knew that some women struggled to bear and some were even unable to conceive. I'd lived with this family's demanding ways for years and had never felt as though I measured up. If one of the children had lived, perhaps they would have accepted me. But now I would never know.

The pink light of dawn, whose colors normally soothed and warmed me, did nothing to help me now. My shaking continued, and I hugged my arms to my chest, silently shouting at myself to calm down. Secretly I had wanted this divorce over being a rejected first wife playing servant to a second. So why was I reacting so strongly when it was something I'd expected?

I could return to Ima and Abba and they would care for me, at least for a little while. Surely they would. Abba wouldn't rush me off into another marriage too soon. He would let me live with them and let my heart heal.

The thought calmed me. If I could not convince him to do so, Ima would. Especially after the loss of two babies. Would anyone even want me again?

I'm a complete failure. The thought would not leave, my heart sinking in despair as I gathered my few belongings, packed them into a basket, and lifted it into my arms. The loom and threads belonged to Niv's household. I had only the clothes on my back and the gold my father had held for me since the betrothal. At least I had that to help pay for my keep for a time.

I left the room, glancing one last time at the small pile of linens I had so lovingly made for the children who lay silent in the grave, and walked toward the door. No one roamed about the house, as everyone had already left for the fields. Even Kelila?

Noya and Niv had probably told the family that they could not even say goodbye to me. I was being sent away. Shunned. Unwanted. Like I had felt since the first day I entered this place.

I clung to the basket and walked slowly at first, then quickened my pace, longing for my mother, the only person who had ever really loved me. I needed her now more than ever.

❖ ❖ ❖

Darkness ignited the stars to light up the clearest night I had seen in a long time. Sitting by the crackling fire in my father's courtyard, wrapped in a shawl to ward off the cool night air, I shifted my gaze from studying the fire to watching the lights sparkle in the expanse above.

"I thought I'd find you here." Ima pulled her cloak about her and came to sit beside me. "It's beautiful tonight."

"Yes." I spotted the Bear and Orion high above, then searched Ima's dear, lined face. "We seldom sat outside after working in the fields. Niv wanted quiet, and after the evening meal we often went to bed."

"Every night?"

I looked away at Ima's incredulous tone.

"So much work can still be done by the light of the lamp. Or at the very least it is a time to rest and reflect on the day. I couldn't possibly sleep so soon after a meal," Ima said.

"Neither could I at first, but the men always rose before dawn, so we did as well. There was no changing Niv's schedule." I released a long-held breath.

"Niv and Noya were never my favorite people," Ima admitted. "Your father only gave in to Niv's request because he offered more for you than anyone else. If you ask me, they spoiled that son."

"More than you know," I said, feeling the sting of Harel's

rejection all over again. I swiped a stray tear from my eyes and stared again at the fire. I reached for a small log and tossed it into the flames.

"I'm sorry they treated you so poorly, my daughter," Ima said, patting my knee. "In time we will find a better husband for you."

"Not soon, I hope. Has Abba said anything?" I'd been home for two weeks and was not even close to ready to marry another.

Ima shook her head. "Not yet. He sees how hurt you are." She looked beyond me toward Gali's former house next to them. "Gali came by to visit her family a few weeks before you returned. She looks well." Her voice trailed off.

"She has three children now, or so I've heard." The thought hurt my still-broken heart, but I fought the urge to let myself give in to the pain.

"Yes. She has a son and recently birthed twin boys. They look like Gali. She seems happy."

"I'm sure she is happier than Harel would have made her. For her sake, I'm glad she never got her wish. I pity the woman Noya finds to replace me." I swallowed the lump of emotion and pulled the shawl closer about my shoulders.

Silence settled between us but for the night sounds of crickets calling for a mate and the occasional owl hooting in the distant trees. My father had gone to bed shortly after the meal, and Chen had returned to the workshop to finish a project for a buyer who was coming tomorrow.

"I saw Lavi in town when I worked at Niv's booth in the market, before I lost the second baby." I paused.

"Lavi?" Ima's voice held a hint of alarm. "In Sychar?"

I nodded. "Yes. He purchased a robe I had woven, claiming it was for his master in Sebaste. We received another order for a second robe later on, which I suspect came from Lavi's master, but Noya never revealed the buyer to me. I haven't seen him again."

130

"He would do well to stay away from Sychar lest your father hear of it. He still holds that boy accountable for the loss of his tools and your gold from Amichai." Ima shook her head and moved closer to the fire. "I assume you've said nothing of this until now?"

"I told no one. They don't know him in any case, and why would I cause trouble for him? He is still my cousin, and Abba would have done well to let us wed rather than put me through these last two marriages."

Ima sighed, shifting in her seat to face me. "Your father is only trying to do what is best for you, dear one. The failures of these two marriages have weighed heavily on him, and . . ." She stopped, putting a hand to her neck as if the words were too heavy to release.

"And what, Ima? Surely Abba does not blame me for either one, does he?" The very thought was incredulous. I could not have stopped Amichai's death nor kept my sons from dying.

Ima cleared her throat. "I don't know if you have noticed, Nessa, but your father is not well. Have you not seen that Chen works late hours while your father takes to his bed? It's not your fault that he's ill, but seeking a husband for you does take a toll. And this next one will be your third in not quite three and a half years. Pray that the next man keeps you until death parts you."

"Death already parted me from Amichai, Ima. God would have to strike me to make death's parting useful to my father." I stood and paced about the fire, agitated.

"That's not what I meant and you know it," Ima said, suddenly looking wearier than I had ever seen her.

I returned to the stone bench and sat beside her, taking her hand. "I know. What's wrong with Abba? Have the doctors been to visit? Has he seen the rabbi?"

"He has trouble breathing. It worsens during the rainy season, but he does not have the strength he once had because he finds taking deep breaths difficult."

131

"And my being here is a burden to him." I hated to admit what I feared, but by the look in my mother's eyes, I knew it was true.

"You are a help to me, so do not think such thoughts. But yes, your father will rest easier when you are safely in the home of a husband again. He just does not have the strength to look for one right now." Her shoulders hunched as though she was chilled.

My heartbeat quickened. I could not lose Abba too. I must help him find someone who would have me. But how? It wasn't proper for a woman to seek a man. Lavi's image came into my mind's eye, but I shook the thought aside as quickly as it came. Lavi would only add to my father's struggles.

"I will do whatever you ask to help, Ima. If I can do more of the chores so Abba can rest, tell me what to do." I had to help more, somehow.

Ima's smile held sadness. "You are a dear child, Nessa. I'm sorry that you have faced such trials." She tilted her head as though listening to the night sounds. "You can go to market for me later in the week. We need more wool for weaving. The more we can weave, the more we can help your father's earnings."

"I can do that." Relief filled me. A task I enjoyed and one that would make me less of a burden and a failure. "I will work hard to weave whatever is needed."

Ima smiled and stood, then took my hand between both of hers. "And pray for your father, my daughter. Pray that he has many more years on the earth. I don't know what I would do without him." The last words sounded hoarse as though she could barely get them out.

"I will pray, Ima." I squeezed her hand and released it, allowing her to return to the house.

I stayed a moment longer at the fire, wondering if God ever heard my prayers. They had done me no good anytime I had asked for favor or for the lives of my sons. Why would God lend His ear to me now, let alone answer me?

17

The market in Sychar buzzed with excitement at the appearance of a new merchant caravan. Goods from Damascus, Phoenicia, and even Jerusalem were loaded on camels bedecked with all manner of bangles and finely woven tapestries. The caravan was smaller than the one I had been to when Lavi had lived with us, but its wares were enticing just the same.

I walked with Yaffa toward the town square, purposely avoiding Niv's booth. I had not seen Gali in the last two months I had been living in my father's home. The thought troubled me. What gossip had she heard of my broken marriage to Harel? Did she have no sympathy for the sons I had lost? Then again, why should she? Gali had set me aside years ago and never looked back. The sting of rejection still hurt, but I didn't need to dwell on things I had no control over and could not change.

I glanced about, anxious to avoid anyone from Harel's family. Perhaps with most of Sychar milling about, I could stay clear of them.

"What are you hoping to find today?" Yaffa asked as we neared the booths where our father sold his tents and my weaving. Chen sat behind the curtained enclosure, waiting for customers.

"I'm looking for the finest wool I can find. I want to weave higher-quality robes and tunics and perhaps even a tapestry like that one." I pointed to a Phoenician wall hanging similar to the type Amichai had hanging on the walls of his home. How long ago it seemed since I had lived there. Truth be told, despite his age or maybe because of it, he had been a kinder husband than Harel ever was. I missed Hila and even Rina now and then. I didn't know how good my life had been.

"I'm looking for some new pottery," Yaffa said, interrupting my thoughts. I looked into her large dark eyes, so aware and yet so compassionate, and silently thanked God for her. "It's too bad Amichai's sons are not as skilled as their father was with their wares. Still, a few of our pots have broken and I need new ones."

We wove our way in and out among the crowd, easing past the camels bearing goods. I glanced at a tapestry as we passed, then stopped to talk to the wife of the caravan master.

"Did you bring any wool with you?" I asked, searching for a bundle tied to the camel's side.

"Oh my, yes. And not just any ordinary wool. Our sheepherders breed Awassi sheep, and their wool is wonderful for making blankets, carpets, and even heavy cloaks. Best you can find." The woman hurried to retrieve a bundle tied to one of the other camels in the caravan and returned to my side. "Touch it. You won't want any other ever again."

I felt the coarse, glossy fibers and pulled the wool apart to see its strength. "It's . . . interesting," I said, not certain it was any better than the wool from the shepherds of Sychar, or what I was looking for.

"It's the best!" the woman proclaimed again. "You won't find better."

"May I see it?"

I turned at the sound of a man's voice, a shepherd by the looks of him. My heart did a little flip at the way he glanced at me. How had I not seen him approach?

Yaffa leaned close and whispered in my ear, "That's Tamir. His family have been shepherds in Sychar for generations."

I turned to her as the man carried on a conversation with the merchant. "How do you know this?"

Yaffa shrugged. "Yaron knows them. They pasture their sheep near our fields sometimes."

"Your wool is good quality," the man said, drawing my attention, "but our local sheep produce a softer, fuller fleece." He shifted his gaze to me. "I can provide you with whatever you need at a better price, I'm sure." He looked back at the woman. "How much for a bundle?"

"Humph," she said. "You don't know what you're saying. Two denarii for the bundle."

"Two denarii? Two days' wages for that?" he scoffed, then faced me. "Come to my father's booth and I will show you better." He backed away and I glanced at Yaffa, who simply shrugged again.

We followed him, though I wasn't sure I wanted to, considering the uncomfortable feeling suddenly filling me. Why did every man look at me with a hunger in his eyes?

We kept some distance from the man as we parted from the merchant, who yelled after us, "If you change your mind, we are only here for one more day."

When we were out of earshot of the crowded caravan, the man stopped. "I'm sorry. I did not introduce myself. I'm Tamir, a shepherd in Sychar. I did not want to see one of our people cheated by those who carry more wares than they can possibly know the value of. Our wool is finer and less costly, if you are interested."

My cheeks heated, and I could not meet his gaze.

"I'm Yaffa, wife of Yaron," my sister said, "and this is my sister Nessa, daughter of Raanan."

I lowered my head in greeting, feeling strange about speaking to a man in public.

"Of course, Yaron. He is a friend." Tamir nodded at Yaffa, who returned the gesture. "And Nessa," he said, facing me again, "Raanan is well-known in the city for having beautiful daughters. I can see the rumors were not wrong."

"Rumors?" I crossed my arms over my chest like a shield.

"Never mind." He pointed beyond him. "Here is my father's booth. If you want wool, come."

I looked at Yaffa, uncertain, but she was already following Tamir. Why did my heart quicken in his presence?

"Here we are," he said, stopping again. "Ima, we have customers." He moved into the booth, and a short, stout woman emerged to meet us.

"Welcome," she said, her smile revealing a few missing teeth. "If you need wool for weaving, you have come to the right booth." She busied herself pulling a bundle from behind the curtain and set it on the shelf between us. "Here is our newest batch, already cleaned and ready for dyeing."

I stepped forward, aware of Tamir's watchful gaze, and fingered the wool. The fact that it was already washed would save me time, and the quality was softer than that of the traveling merchants.

"How much?" I looked at the woman who also watched me, giving me an uneasy feeling. She was probably about Ima's age, with similar graying hair though it was wispy and thin, and her round face held a weathered look.

"One denarius for the bundle."

Half as much? "It seems like it's worth more," I said, wondering if I would find something wrong with it once I began dyeing and weaving.

"I charge a fair price so the buyers will return. We live in this town, young woman, and we don't take advantage of our neighbors." Her voice carried a sternness despite the smile that accompanied her words.

"Of course you don't. Your price is acceptable," Yaffa said.

"We'll take it." She nudged me to produce the coin, shaking me from my thoughts. I fished in the pouch at my side and placed the denarius in the woman's open palm.

"Tamir," the woman said, nearly barking the order. "Tie up this bundle for our young women so they can carry it home."

"Yes, Ima." Tamir's smile, aimed at me, held humor, and I heard his soft chuckle as he bound the wool and handed the package to me. "Do you need help carrying it home?"

"No. Thank you. We are able to manage it." I hurried from the booth with Yaffa at my side.

"Don't forget I still need pottery. And I can tell you, I won't mind if a servant offers to carry it home for me." She laughed. "You should have taken Tamir up on his offer. He likes you, you know."

"Don't be ridiculous. He doesn't even know me." But my cheeks burned just the same.

"Mark my words. If Abba hears of Tamir's interest, he will not delay in arranging your next marriage."

We reached the booth Amichai used to run. I set the wool on the ground while Yaffa looked about at the various urns and jars. Hila sat at the booth and smiled at my approach.

"Nessa! It's been too long." She stood and joined us. "Do you need a new jar? How have you been?"

"My sister needs pottery. I came for wool. But I am well. I'm living with my father again for a time. My mother needs me." I could not bring myself to say that Harel had sent me away with a writ of divorce, though surely everyone in Sychar knew of it.

"We miss you," Hila said, touching my arm. "Rina and Devora have both had sons since you left."

The news felt like a kick in the gut as memories assaulted me. "I'm happy for them," I managed. I suddenly wished Yaffa would hurry and we could go home. I wanted to hide from everyone in Sychar so no one could see my shame and agony.

"We heard you lost a child," Hila said as though the topic was open for discussion. "I'm sorry. I know it's painful."

"Two children. Sons. And you cannot imagine." I bit my lip, appalled by my audacity to speak harshly.

"No. I suppose I can't. I'm sorry," she said again. Turning to Yaffa, she asked if she needed help, thankfully leaving me alone.

I left the shop and carried my bundle some distance away while Yaffa chose her purchases.

"Are you sure I can't carry that for you?" Tamir's voice startled me from behind.

I jumped and slowly turned to face him. "Are you following me?" How bold I was today! But he made me nervous, and I didn't want to think about Yaffa's comment that this man could be my next husband. Hadn't I considered looking for a man to help my father in his search, especially in his weakened condition? But I wasn't expecting this.

"You might say so. I didn't mean to frighten you, Nessa. I would not dream of making the sister-in-law of Yaron uncomfortable." He gave me a lopsided grin, reminding me slightly of Lavi. "I don't often come in from the fields, but I had heard that the daughters of Raanan were beautiful and the youngest the most beautiful of all. I never thought I would meet her."

"That's because she was married and living on a farm. And before that, living in a house of luxury. There would be no reason for you to know me." I should not be having this conversation, but suddenly I did not care.

"You were married twice already? You're so young." His brow scrunched as if he was thinking over my words. "Tell me."

I studied him. "Why? I don't even know you."

He raised both hands as if to ward off a blow. "You're right. You have no reason to explain. I can ask your father if you like."

I lifted a brow, eyes wide. "Why would you ask my father?" I already knew, but I wanted him to say it.

"To ask for your hand, of course. But I would send my father first. We would need to know the reasons you have had two husbands."

I curled a hand around my bundle, willing my nerves to still. "My first husband died in an accident. The second divorced me after I lost two babies. Does that satisfy your question?"

He smiled, then laughed outright. "You are spunky, I'll give you that. I can imagine that you would give my mother a hard time."

The image of his mother did not bring warm thoughts. Tamir himself was entirely too handsome for his own good, and I suspected he knew it.

"And you?" I asked. "Are you married?"

He shook his head. "Not yet. I have been waiting for the right woman to come along."

"You have waited a long time then, for you certainly look older than I."

Yaffa appeared at my shoulder just then. "Nessa, what are you saying? Be polite."

"It's all right, Yaffa," Tamir said, still chuckling. "Your sister is giving me back the same bold questions I've asked of her." His dark eyes twinkled as they assessed me. "I'm four and twenty, and yes, I should have married long ago, if my mother had approved of the woman. She is hard to please. But I've been known to prevail on her when I know what I want."

"I'm certain our father would be pleased to speak with your father," Yaffa said as she glanced back at a young boy pulling a cart with her purchases. "But come, Nessa. We must get home."

I glared at her, not sure whether I felt relief or anger at her audacity. I lifted the wool in my arms and moved away from Tamir, ever aware of him watching me.

"I will speak with my father," he called after me.

I did not want to acknowledge him, but Yaffa faced him and offered a bright smile. "I'm sure my father and Nessa will be pleased."

I continued walking, and it was Yaffa's turn to catch up with me. When the boy leading the cart moved past us toward Yaffa's home and our father's house came into sight, I stopped.

"Why did you encourage him? I don't even know if I want to marry again. And his mother—did you not notice how difficult she seemed? She did not speak as kindly as she should have to me, a customer." I set the bundle on the ground and glanced up the street. There was no sign that Tamir had followed or that anyone else lingered nearby.

Yaffa touched my tense shoulder. "You have to marry again, Ness. You know that Abba cannot support you forever."

"Ima says that he's ill and she needs me. My weaving brings in enough to help us both."

"Maybe so, but it's unseemly for a woman to remain unmarried. Abba would feel like a failure in the town if he could not secure you a bright future. And whether Tamir's mother is kind or not matters little. It is Tamir you would be marrying." Yaffa waved a hand as if to send her comment to the wind.

"A mother indeed has much influence, as Noya proved to me over and over for two years, Yaffa. I know of what I speak. And didn't Tamir say that his mother has not approved of women in the past? She is obviously in control of that household." I felt my stomach clench with the sudden fear of another marriage. "I'm not ready."

Yaffa's expression softened. "I know you're not, sister. I just want you to be prepared and understand that Abba will not wait forever to seek the elders to find men who might need a wife. Be grateful that Tamir is not wed yet and you would not be second wife in his home. His mother may end up being nicer than you know." She smiled, but I could not return it.

"You better go. That servant boy is already out of sight. He might take your wares to the wrong house." I picked up the wool and took a step toward the courtyard.

"He knows which house, but you're right. I must go." She

stepped forward and, in a rare display of affection, pulled me, bundle and all, into her arms. "Do not worry, dear sister. If Tamir is wrong for you, Abba will listen, and if not him, talk to Ima. But think long and hard before you put up any argument. There are only so many men left in Sychar who want to marry one who is no longer a virgin."

She released me and walked away while I slowly moved toward my father's house. I looked at the familiar stones and the court where I had spent so many years grinding grain or watching the fire at dusk. A pang of longing made me never want to leave this place, but Yaffa was right. I could not live under our father's roof forever.

But if Tamir's father came calling, I was not sure what I would say.

18

*L*avi wiped his brow as he picked a variety of aromatic flowers for the perfumes his master Eliav made. The summer's heat bore down on him at a time when he should be resting in the house with the man who had hired him a few years ago. But the orders for the man's perfumes would bring a tidy sum, and though Lavi would only receive a fraction of the amount, he needed every shekel, even every mite, if he was ever to leave this place and begin work on his own. He was skilled in tentmaking from his years with Raanan and then his time with a tentmaker in Sebaste, but he had switched to learning the art of perfuming when Eliav, a Sebaste perfumer, had taken him on. The work was far more interesting, and in time, he knew he could become as wealthy as Eliav if he could create the right scents from the flowers, resins, and oils and garner a good reputation for the business.

He released a sigh. Everything took too much time, and he felt as though his life was slipping from him. He still had little to support a wife, and the one he wanted was never free to have him.

He lifted his flask and took a long drink of the cool water the master's wife, Achinoam, had given him that morning. Sebaste was not a bad place to live—better, in fact, than Sychar. But Sychar bore his roots and held the only person he had ever loved. He needed to prove himself to her and earn enough to support her if he was ever going to convince Raanan that he was good enough to marry his daughter.

Was she still free? On his last visit to Sychar, he had learned that Nessa had been sent away from the farmer's family in disgrace. Divorced. But why? He'd been unable to find a reason, and no one he had discreetly spoken to had said anything against her, only that she had lost two sons at birth.

The tragedy of it all still pricked his heart. Was Nessa unable to bear children who lived? Or was it something else? He'd bristled during his conversation with the farmer's wife at the booth where he'd last seen Nessa. The woman did not strike him as kind, her expression pinched when he asked after Nessa. She'd sent him away with the robe Eliav had ordered and barely a word to gain his interest in purchases from them in the future. Good riddance, then!

Still, he needed to return to Sychar to see how Nessa was doing. But the plants in front of him would not pick themselves. He bent over and carefully removed the flowers, stem and all, and placed them in a wicker basket at his side. This work should really go to a newer apprentice, but he could not complain. It was good of Eliav to even consider taking him on when he had spent so many years at another craft.

He glanced heavenward, wiping his sweaty brow. Clouds scudded across the blazing sun as he worked, offering little shade or comfort. He had picked a few more stalks when the sound of his name caught his attention.

"Lavi, son of Erez, are you there?" Footsteps accompanied the voice, and he recognized his friend Aaron from Sychar, who had also moved to Sebaste.

Lavi lifted one hand and waved. "Over here." He carried the basket with him and met Aaron at the edge of the field, farthest from the house. "What's happened?" By the look in Aaron's eyes, Lavi knew something was amiss.

"I just returned from Sychar. I have news."

"I'm listening."

"Walk with me." Aaron headed toward a copse of trees.

Lavi glanced toward the area where he worked but saw no sign of Eliav, so he quickly followed his friend. "What is it? Has something happened to Nessa?" Aaron knew of his affection for his cousin. He was the only person Lavi had ever trusted besides her.

"Not Nessa, but they say her father is ill. He may not have long to live on the earth." Aaron drew a hand across his reddish beard.

"Raanan? He is yet young and strong." Lavi had always looked up to his uncle, until the day he had denied his wishes to marry Nessa. Then he had run off, leaving Raanan with only Chen to help him. Had the work been too much for him?

"He isn't gone yet," Aaron said quickly. "But he's been ill ever since Nessa was sent home from that farmer."

"Is Nessa still there with her parents? They will need her if Raanan is ill."

Aaron shrugged. "It is always difficult to discern whether the rumors are true. But I heard that there is a shepherd who has asked Raanan for her hand. I don't know if he has accepted."

"A shepherd?" Lavi's heart sank. He had not been swift enough. Not learned the trade quickly enough to go after her with means. "You must find out for certain."

"I'm going back at the end of the week. I can ask around again. Unless you want to go with me?" Aaron glanced beyond Lavi, causing Lavi to turn. But no one was coming toward them.

"I don't know if I can get away. I would need a reason to travel there again so soon."

"Tell Eliav that you are buying oil that grows near the sacred Mt. Gerizim for the perfumes. Even if the olives taste the same, convince him that they are better because of the mountain."

Aaron touched Lavi's shoulder. "Think on it. Let me know in a day or so. Right now I have to get back to work myself."

Lavi watched him go, his mind turning in a thousand different directions. Nessa. Would Raanan have already sent her off to marry another? If he was ill, he would want to secure her future. But who was this shepherd?

Suddenly Lavi knew that he had to get to Sychar. He would find a reason. Eliav wasn't likely to accept the olive oil excuse, but Lavi would do whatever it took. He had to convince him, even tonight. He must see if he stood any chance of capturing Nessa's hand in marriage before Raanan passed on or gave her to another.

❖ ❖ ❖

I sat at the loom in my father's house, working the various colors into a pattern I had never tried before. If only I would have time to finish the project. If only I could stay here forever. My father needed the income from my work, didn't he? I'd worked so hard not to be a burden, but my request to remain unmarried had fallen on unhearing ears.

The sound of the shuttle moved in rhythm with my despairing thoughts, until voices coming up the walk to our courtyard interrupted my work. "Who is it, Ima?" I called as Ima approached the door.

She glanced at me, then opened the door to Chen's newly betrothed, Malka, and her mother. "Shalom, Malka. Hadar. Come in."

I rose as Ima welcomed them into the sitting room, where my loom sat in the corner. "Shalom," I said. I smiled but received cool half smiles in return.

"Shalom," Malka said, taking the seat where my father normally sat. Could she not wait for my mother to instruct her where to sit? I had sensed that this new sister-in-law would not be easy to live with once the wedding took place. Why they were here when the wedding was nearly a year away made no sense.

I left the group to retrieve cups of cool water from the cooking area and returned to find them all sitting and talking about the upcoming wedding arrangement. I placed the cups on the table in front of them, then took my place at the loom once more. The noise would drown out some of their conversation, but I had no interest in listening.

"Nessa," Ima said as I took up the shuttle. "Can that wait until our guests leave?"

I held back the urge to sigh. "Of course, Ima." I took a seat closest to my mother.

"With Raanan's health in such a bad way," Hadar said, gripping her cup with both hands, "we have prevailed upon my husband, and hopefully Chen and Raanan will agree to an earlier wedding." She glanced at me. "You will need the help once Nessa weds again, if my guess is correct?" She sipped the water, looking at my mother over the top of the cup.

I stiffened, catching a glimpse of pride in Malka's gaze. She had captured Chen's affection months before, when he'd finally asked our father to request Malka's hand. The girl was newly nubile, at least five years younger than me, and haughtier by far. Perhaps marriage to the shepherd would be better than living with Chen's new wife.

"I can see where that might be prudent," Ima said. My heart sank. How quickly she agreed with this woman. "But Nessa is not leaving us just yet. There is time, and surely you need the year to make all the garments you will require for your new home here." She directed a look at Malka.

"We've been weaving and spinning and preparing for over a year already in anticipation," Hadar said. "She can be ready whenever the groom wants to call for her."

"Well, that is the groom's decision, is it not?" I said, irritated. The audacity!

146

"Yes, yes. Of course it is. But if your mother can influence your brother, knowing that his bride awaits him ready and willing, perhaps we can move things along," Hadar said, setting the cup back on the table.

"You seem in a hurry to be rid of your daughter," I said, studying Hadar.

"Nessa! Such a thing to say." Ima's reprimand stung. But I did not regret my words.

"It is just not normal to hurry along a marriage," I defended myself, crossing my arms over my chest.

"Unlike your marriage to the farmer? Did that not come sooner than the normal year?" Malka's tone dripped sarcasm.

"Those were different circumstances," Ima said, standing. "I think this conversation is one that should take place between Chen and his father, not us."

I joined her as Hadar and Malka stood. "Humph," Hadar said, turning to walk out. "Come, Malka. I hope your husband's family learns to be kinder once you live with them. I should have known . . ." She left the sentence unfinished as she reached the door.

Known what? But this time I did not say the words that dangled on the tip of my tongue.

They stalked away in a huff, and Ima closed the door behind them, then leaned against it. "Well, I never!"

"They seemed quite presumptuous," I said softly, searching Ima's face, praying she agreed.

"Yes. They think your father is near the grave, and I suspect they want to come in here and quickly gain some kind of control over Chen." She heaved a sigh and entered the sitting room to take up the spindle and distaff.

I moved to the loom again, my mind spinning. "Ima?"

"Yes, my daughter?"

"Is Abba truly going to accept the shepherd's offer?" Tamir's father had been here once, and Abba sent him away because he had not had the strength to speak with him. But I knew Tamir would send him again. He seemed the persistent type, and he would not stop until he had what he wanted.

"He is considering it, but you know they did not really discuss it much." She looked at me. "Do you want to marry the shepherd?"

I shrugged. Did I? After today I didn't want to live in the same house as Malka, but I was not quite ready to be thrust into another home with another man. Unless that man was Lavi.

Where had that thought come from? But hadn't he been on my mind since I'd seen him watching me from the shadows near the farm? And when I saw him in the market . . . foolishly I'd hoped.

But Lavi didn't even know I was free to wed again, and I had no way to get word to him. Unless Chen would go to Sebaste for me, if he could break free of the load he had to bear with Abba so ill.

"Nessa?" Ima's voice pulled me out of my musings.

"I don't know, Ima. He seems nice, but I'm not so sure about his mother." I held the shuttle still. "I wish I had more time."

Ima looked at the spinning spindle, then met my gaze. "Time, I am afraid, is what we do not have. Make up your mind about him, Nessa. Your father would be pleased to make a secure marriage for you before he goes the way of all the earth."

That thought brought a lump to my throat, and I did not miss the tear that slipped from Ima's eye. Abba truly was ill. Perhaps marrying again would be the last gift I could give him so that he could one day rest in peace.

19

Within the week, Tamir's father again paid a visit to my father, and this time they sealed my betrothal to Tamir. Tamir placed a ring on my index finger and brought me gifts, though it was not a normal betrothal with a gathering of family and friends. They would join us when we wed within the month. Given that I was not a virgin bride and had all that I needed to bring to his home, there was no need to wait—even if I'd wanted to.

I pondered my situation a few evenings later as I walked alone to the well, making sure to join the normal group of women who took the same path. Though it was not yet dusk, I never quite felt safe alone, and I missed Gali more than I cared to admit.

I kept to the back of the small group but didn't miss the raised brow here or the lifted chin there when the women looked my way. Why did they dislike me so much?

"You got the one man I wanted, and because men think you're so gorgeous you can have anyone you want," Gali had said the last day she had spoken to me after losing Harel.

I swallowed hard as I gripped the jar tightly against my shoulder. I glanced ahead, longing for a glimpse of Gali, hoping against hope to see her join us, but she never did. The gossips

149

said she had a servant who drew water for her, that her husband earned a good living. Like I'd had with Dana.

We reached the well, and I took my place in line and watched the sun edging closer to the horizon. Would I be the one to come here when I lived with Tamir? I had no idea how his family handled such things. Did the women take turns doing certain tasks, or were chores assigned to the same person every day?

"Nessa?"

I nearly jumped at the sound of my name. I turned to see Dana hurrying to my side.

"It's so good to see you!"

"Dana!" I set my jar in the dirt and embraced her. How I missed her company. "Are you still working for the rabbi's wife?"

She nodded. "Yes, and I got away late for the water tonight. I fairly ran the whole way here." She laughed, such a pleasant sound. "I heard the news that you are to marry again. I'm so happy for you!"

I smiled. How little she knew, but I couldn't tell her that marrying again did not thrill me. "Yes. Tamir. The wedding is in a month."

"So soon?" she asked as I approached the well. My turn came and I drew the water into my jar.

"Yes. There was no reason to wait the normal year." I stepped away from the well to let her fill her jar.

We walked together until we reached the place where our paths parted. "Are you happy where you are, Dana?" I asked before she turned to go.

"Very happy. Thank you for finding the place for me. I only wish you had not lost Gali when you married Harel." She looked at me, compassion in her dark eyes. "I'm sorry about the loss of your boys."

I looked away. I hadn't expected her to speak of them and was unable to keep the tears from rising up to clog my throat. I swallowed hard. "Thank you," I managed, then glanced at her. "I'm glad I saw you tonight. I must go. Be safe." I hurried away as quickly as I could with the heavy jar. I was pleased to know that Dana was doing well, but the reminder of my losses did not help my mood.

Later that evening as the moon rose high in the sky, I slipped from the house and walked about my father's land, glancing toward the shop where Chen worked by the light of a lamp. Would he hire someone to help him when Abba grew too weak to do the work? Abba's breath had seemed labored during the meal and his steps slow as he made his way to his bed. My heart hurt to think of losing him.

I bent to pick lavender from a patch growing near the trees that bordered the area we shared with Gali's family. Breathing deeply of the sweet scent, I felt my shoulders relax and released a sigh. I would place one of the flowers near my pillow tonight. Perhaps sleeping would be easier then. Should I take some to my father?

I tucked a few plants into the pocket of my robe as my thoughts drifted to my upcoming wedding. What would living with Tamir be like? We had not spoken since the betrothal, and though Yaffa had given her hearty approval, I longed to talk about it all with a friend. With Gali.

But Gali was caught up in her own life now and had no time for former friends. If only she had been at the well this night, perhaps I could have sought reconciliation.

Restless, I roamed aimlessly, picking more lavender and deciding to make a sachet for my father. *Oh, Adonai, let him live.* Even though I was moving away, I couldn't bear the thought of what was surely to come. I wanted to place grandchildren on his knee.

The sound of crunching leaves from the nearby trees startled me. I straightened and stepped back. Darkness brought out the wild animals and, worse, thieves. I moved slowly toward the house, not wanting to startle a predator.

And then I saw him. A man I would know anywhere stepped out of hiding among the trees.

"Lavi," I said as he came closer, gaze darting about.

"Nessa," he said, stopping within arm's length. His voice was deeper, husky, as if filled with emotion.

"What are you doing here? You shouldn't be here." My heart raced at his nearness, and in that moment, I wished I was free to run off with him. But the ring on my index finger suddenly weighted my hand, reminding me of my promise. I twisted the ring with my thumb, causing him to glance down at my hands.

"Is that . . . ?" He looked at me. "Tell me that's an old ring from a past marriage."

I slowly shook my head. "A few days ago, my father signed a ketubah, betrothing me to Tamir, son of Keshet. He is a shepherd in Sychar." I looked at my feet, unable to hold the hurt in his gaze.

"I heard you were free to marry again. I tried to come." He stopped. I watched the Adam's apple move beneath his beard. "I've worked hard for you, Nessa. I want to provide for you . . . Why do I keep hoping?" His expression moved from defeated to angry.

"There is nothing you can do, Lavi. The ketubah cannot be undone. The wedding is in a month." I searched his dear face, but he did not meet my gaze. "Lavi, if I had known . . . I would have asked my father . . ." I stopped, unable to continue.

Lavi lifted his gaze to meet mine, then took a step back. "Apparently God does not care about the concerns of the heart. Or if He does, He does not hear my prayers."

"Or mine," I whispered, my heart breaking as he stepped farther away from me.

"Goodbye, Nessa. I wish you a happy marriage with the shepherd." He turned and ran back to the path he had taken through the trees.

I watched him go, the lavender crushed in my hands, staining my fingers. Tears came then, and I did not bother to wipe them away. If only I had known sooner. If only he had come to Sychar before Tamir's father had pressed mine into an agreement.

If only my life, my choices, were mine to control.

❖ ❖ ❖

I entered Keshet's home surrounded by my family and the family and friends of my new husband. Neighbors had trickled into the street to join the procession, but the numbers were far fewer than when I had married Amichai and Harel. By the look on Tamir's face, he did not seem to care how many were in attendance, and I knew a sense of relief at the smile he sent my way.

After his father blessed our union, Tamir took my hand and ushered me into the bridal chamber while the guests ate and drank and danced the night away.

Tamir walked me to the center of the room. He stood before me. "My bride." He cupped my shoulders and simply looked at me, head to foot. When he met my gaze, seeming to take in the details of my face, I felt my heart skip a beat. "How lovely you are." He touched my temple and kissed my forehead, then slowly removed my veil.

One by one he removed the combs holding my hair, letting it tumble to my waist. He sifted both hands through my long locks and bent low until his lips brushed mine.

His kiss caused my pulse to race. As he deepened the kiss and pulled me closer, all thoughts of Lavi's stolen kiss that I could never seem to completely forget disappeared. Tamir's gentle touch as he led me to the wedding couch was nothing like Harel's or even Amichai's. And I had to remind myself to act like the virgin I was not and let him do as he wished with me. Yaffa had warned me not to show how familiar I was with the act of marriage. It would wound his pride, and I had no desire to offend this new husband but longed only to return his love.

I stiffened, reminding myself how I felt the first time, but moments later, his whispers of love and his tender kisses melted my resolve. I wrapped my arms about his neck and returned his kiss until he pulled away.

He looked down at me, and a shiver of fear passed through me. Had I angered him? Done exactly what Yaffa told me not to do?

"You are more than I expected," he said, breaking into a smile.

"You are pleased?" I said softly.

He captured my lips with his and enfolded me in his arms, completing what the men and women expected of him. He lay beside me afterward, holding me close. Was he not going to leave the tent and rejoin the party?

But he was soon sleeping beside me, and I pulled the covers over us both and rested against him. Tamir was not like any of the men I had known, and not even Lavi held such emotive power over me.

Oh, Adonai, let me please him. A sliver of anxiety entered my mind as I thought on the two husbands I had lost. I must make this marriage work. Must do everything in my power to satisfy Tamir and his mother and the rest of his family. I could not let myself or my father be put to shame again.

❖ ❖ ❖

When the seventh day came to an end and the guests left us, Tamir's young sister, Menuha, approached me and slipped her hand in mine.

"I'm so glad you said yes," she whispered, leaning close to my ear. "Odelia, Elkan's wife, is so much older than me, and she treats me like she's my second mother. But you are closer to Tamir's age, and I think we'll be friends." She offered me a tentative smile, enhancing her childish features. The girl was too young to wed and would become like the younger sister I never had.

I squeezed Menuha's hand. "I think we'll be great friends." I gave her an affectionate smile. "I hope you'll help me figure out how things are done around here."

Menuha glanced about, then leaned closer still. "Ima can be demanding sometimes, but there are ways to please her. She just needs to think that she is getting her way, even if she is not." She laughed softly and covered her mouth with her hand.

"What is my sister telling you?" Tamir asked, coming beside me and capturing my hand in his stronger one.

"We were just talking of girl things," I said, glancing at Menuha, wondering if the girl could truly be trusted. At the relief in her gaze, I relaxed. "Nothing that would concern you." I smiled at him and felt my pulse jump at the look he gave me.

"Well, little sister, if you will let me have my wife, you can continue your girl talk another time." He patted Menuha's head, then faced me. "Your parents are leaving."

We walked toward the outer courtyard hand in hand. Tamir released me when we approached my parents.

Ima hugged me close. "I hope you are happy, dear one. I will miss your help with your father . . ." Her voice trailed off. I glanced at Abba.

He approached me and held me close as well. "Be brave, Nessa. Work hard and all will be well."

"I will, Abba. Do not fear." I could not have him worrying over me, lest his health take a turn for the worse.

My parents bid Keshet and Derorit farewell, and I watched them leave.

Tamir came up and put his hands on my shoulders. "I will check on him, and you may come with me from time to time. I know he's not well."

I nodded but could not look at him for the tears filling my

eyes. Would I ever see my father again? "I wonder if Chen will hire someone to help ease Abba's load."

"That would be wise," Tamir said. He turned me to face him and rubbed the tears from my cheeks with his thumbs. "Do not fret, my love. Come with me to the sheepfold. I will show you what I do each day. When we shear the wool, you can weave it into garments and whatever else you want to make for the household or to sell. Ima will tell you what she wants you to make."

"Will your mother mind if I go with you?" I asked, grateful that we were alone.

"You are my bride. You obey me, not her. Though she will think you're meant to do both." He took my hand and led me toward the fields where the sheepfold stood. "A neighbor took care of the sheep during the wedding, but I doubt he did a good job, so the first thing I will do is inspect each one. If even one thorn or an insect is caught or embedded in their wool, it can cause damage."

"How do you treat them if they're hurt?" I hurried to keep up with his long strides.

He touched the flask tied to his belt. "Olive oil heals their scrapes and wounds. I pour it on their heads as well to keep insects away."

"It sounds like you take great care of them."

He smiled. "A good shepherd always will. It's not easy work, and sometimes I will be gone overnight or even longer. Do not let my mother intimidate you while I'm gone. I'll return and all will be well."

"Will I ever be able to go with you to the fields?" I realized that being alone with him in the open spaces would be more pleasant than being in the house without him, even with Menuha's presence.

"Perhaps." He chuckled. "Let's see how you like meeting the sheep in the pens, then spend the day with me. We will know after that."

We entered the pen, and one by one Tamir checked each ewe and lamb and led them out, calling them by name.

"I didn't know you named them," I said, touching the head of one of the lambs.

"Yes. The sheep know the sound of their shepherd's voice, and he calls them by name. There is much to shepherding, but I will teach you." He took my hand again, and together we led the animals past the pens toward the field until they reached a grassy knoll surrounded by trees. I sat in the shade, and once the sheep were all eating, Tamir joined me.

"I should have packed food," I said, but he lifted a sack to show me he already had.

"I always come prepared." He offered me a drink of water, and we sat in companionable silence. If only every day could be as peaceful. I could get used to the life of a shepherd's wife.

For the first time in years, my heart soared. Perhaps I had finally found my heart's home.

20

I woke aching from more than my work in the fields with Tamir and helping prepare the meals and clean the house. After six months of marriage, my time had once again come upon me, dashing my hopes that I would ever bear a child for Tamir. Had my two lost sons been the only ones I would carry?

I pushed up from the bed, grateful that Tamir had spent the night in the fields. He would sleep in another bed until my time was past and I completed my ritual purification.

Derorit did not impose restrictions on me or Odelia during our niddah, our time of the month. We couldn't sleep with our husbands or sit on any cushion they sat on, but we were too busy a household to care overmuch about not touching earthenware or wooden objects—a rule some Jewish women were expected to follow. As long as the men were not unclean, all was well. Our synagogue didn't even keep us from attending as long as we stayed away from the men, which we did anyway.

I donned my robe and walked to the preparation room, unable to keep back a heavy sigh. Derorit would ask when she saw me dragging my feet, and I would feel afresh the look of disappointment and even censure from my mother-in-law. Not unlike Noya, the woman was always watching, always counting. There would be no hiding a babe from her if I ever had the privilege of bearing one.

I grabbed the sack of grain and took it to the courtyard to grind the flour. Menuha saw me coming, hurried with the jug she carried from the well, and set it in its place near the house.

"At last you're up!" she said, coming to sit beside me. "Ima said to not disturb you in case you were ill with child. Are you ill with child?" She looked so hopeful that I hated to dash her hopes, but I shook my head regardless.

"Not this time." I poured the grain into the millstone and turned the wheel, crushing the grains beneath the heavy stones. I gave Menuha a compassionate look, noting the disappointment in her eyes.

"Oh, I wish this time you had said yes," Menuha said when I stopped grinding. "I know how much Tamir longs for a son and Ima worries." She clapped her mouth shut at that and looked about as if she had revealed a secret she was not supposed to tell.

"Why would she worry?" I kept my voice low, though I wasn't sure of the need for secrecy. Of course Derorit worried. She knew that I had lost two sons, and if it happened again, I would surely be to blame. I couldn't bear to go through that again.

"You know," Menuha said, touching my forearm. "She fears you might not be able to bear a son. But don't tell her that I told you."

The memory of my lost sons brought swift shards of pain. Would I ever be free of the grief? I swallowed, forcing back the emotion deep in my gut. "I won't tell her," I said, turning to the grindstone again.

Apparently satisfied, Menuha stood and ran into the house, probably to help her mother, leaving me blissfully alone. I worked the stone hard, as though the pressure against the grain would release the pressure of loss squeezing my heart. When the grain piled high enough, I stopped, winded. After sifting the grain, I poured it into the jar.

I lifted it to my shoulder as I stood, but stopped at the sound of running feet headed toward the house. I turned to see Chen rushing toward me.

My heart nearly stopped at his stricken look. Could this day get any worse?

"Nessa. You must come. All of you must come." He drew in a breath, and I stood there unable to move, my head spinning.

"What?"

"You must come," he said again, gulping a drink of water from the jar near the house. "Now! Go and get your family."

I ran to the cooking area and set the jar on the table. "My brother is here. Something is wrong. He is asking us to come."

Derorit tossed aside her apron and headed with me to the door. "Menuha, get Tamir and your father. Odelia, watch over the house and tell Elkan what happened." She looked at me. "What happened?"

I stared at her, realizing Chen had not said. "I don't know." I ran back to Chen. "Is it Abba?"

Chen nodded. "He's gone, Ness."

In that moment, I needed Tamir. I wanted desperately to cling to Chen's arm, but if I touched him, I would make him unclean. I kept a space between us, my heart stricken. "When? How?"

"Ima found him when she woke this morning. He died in his sleep." Chen noted the distance I kept and I knew he understood.

Derorit stood beside me while Tamir and Keshet emerged from beside the house, Menuha in tow.

"My father is dead, and we must bury him before nightfall," Chen said. "I have come to get Nessa to comfort my mother, but I was hoping that Keshet and Tamir would come to help me build the bier and move the stone from the family burial cave."

"Of course we will help," Derorit said, turning to Menuha. "Go inside. We have food to prepare. We will all sit shiva today." She looked at Chen. "Take Nessa with you. Odelia and I will bring food."

I gave Derorit a grateful smile. "Thank you." I had feared Derorit would be entirely too much like Noya, but the woman possessed more kindness than Harel's mother.

"Let me get my cloak," I said to Chen. I ran into the house to grab my cloak and a bag with some things I might need, then hurried to the courtyard to join the men.

We were headed toward the street when Derorit called after us. "Wait! Do you have enough spices?"

I looked at Odelia, who stepped into the house and returned with a jar of myrrh that the family saved for such a time.

"Can you spare it?" I hated to be beholden to them, but I doubted that Ima had purchased such a costly spice or had the money to do so.

"We can get more, and when you can," she said, directing her gaze to Chen, "you can replace this. But go now. Time is slipping away, and you will need every moment."

I did not argue. I ran with Chen toward our father's house, Tamir and Keshet behind. We slowed when we were some distance from Keshet's home, and I felt the dragging ache intensify with my running. I needed to rest, but rest was the last thing I was going to get this day.

◆ ◆ ◆

"Ima!" I placed the jar of myrrh on a table the moment I crossed the threshold and then ran into her arms.

Ima glanced at the jar.

"From Derorit," I said as she clung to me. Together we wept, until Ima straightened and pushed away. "We have much to do. Your sisters are already at the market purchasing spices, and Hadar and Malka and their family are on their way. But come.

161

I wanted you to see him before they arrive." She took my hand and led me toward the room my parents had shared all my life.

The windows were shuttered, and a lone lamp burned on a table near the bed. It took a moment for my eyes to adjust to the light, but at last I could see my father's prone form lying on the bed. I moved closer. Slowly. When I stood beside him, I sank to my knees, longing to bury my head in his chest. I did not care if it made me unclean. I was already unclean. But the father I knew was not there any longer, and I could not bring myself to touch his cold skin.

Tears spilled, dripping onto my robe. "He looks so peaceful," I said, glancing at Ima, who remained at the foot of the bed.

"Yes. I'm glad that he did not suffer. God simply took him in the night." She swallowed and paused for a lengthy breath. "We must remove his tunic and cleanse his body for the spices. I've had the linen wrappings waiting for this day for some time."

I faced her. "You knew it would be soon."

She nodded. "I've known for a long time. I'm surprised he lived so long after your wedding. I had hoped he would until Chen's wedding, but it was not meant to be."

"Will Chen marry sooner now that it will be only you and him?" I couldn't bear the thought of him marrying Malka, but there was nothing to be done about it. Somehow I would have to get along with the girl when our families interacted.

"I don't know." Ima looked again at Abba and moved into action. "Come. Help me get this tunic off him. The linens are in that corner. The water is in a jug on the floor, and towels are on the chair."

"Should we open the window for light to see what we're doing?"

"I think darkness is what he knows now, and darkness is how we will preserve his privacy and dignity. The lamp is enough."

I did not agree, but I followed Ima's instructions. We were

joined by Yaffa and Adva and Meital moments later. Together we took turns washing and lovingly anointing our father's body for burial. When the last strand of linen was wrapped about his face, Chen called from the front of the house.

The men had finished building the bier, and Malka's family and the townspeople had arrived. The trek to the tomb would take time, and the sun was already past its midpoint. I rubbed my back, ignoring the ache I had awakened with. Any physical pain I felt could not come close to matching the emotional anguish in my heart.

21

I stood in the courtyard of Keshet's home, stirring the freshly shorn and washed wool in a pot of red dye. Various pots of color formed a circle about me, and with Menuha's help, I mixed the wool with the dye to check the color consistency.

"I think this yellow is bright enough," I said, bending over the pot where Menuha stood. "What do you think?" She had grown into a beautiful young woman during my two and a half years of marriage to Tamir. Soon I would lose her close friendship, for Menuha was recently betrothed, and these wool yarns would be spun into a colorful bridal robe for her.

"I think it needs to be brighter," Derorit said, coming up beside us.

I jumped at the sound of her voice, but I shouldn't have, as I had become used to Derorit appearing when I least expected her. A trait I did not appreciate, along with the growing watchfulness and now criticism of my work. Had I done something to offend the woman?

"I like it how it is, Ima. If it's too bright, it will outshine the reds and greens and strands of blue. Or it will turn to orange, and you know that I don't like orange." Menuha gave her mother her typical persuasive smile, and Derorit nodded.

"Very well. Have it your way." She left us, and Menuha gave me a knowing smile.

"You do know that we would have to add red to the yellow to make orange," I said softly, chuckling.

"Of course I do. I'm surprised Ima did not say so." She lifted the wool from the dye and spread it on branches to dry.

"So am I," I said under my breath. I glanced behind me, grateful to find no sign of Derorit.

Later that evening as I put the fig pastries together, Derorit was continually underfoot. "You're mixing the filling all wrong," she said, with no attempt to curb her irritation. "There is not enough honey. Tamir likes plenty of honey."

I know. I bit my tongue to keep from saying the words. I knew Tamir better than Derorit did, whether she wanted to admit such a thing or not.

Derorit tsked and moved a short distance away to knead the dough for a different treat. Though sheepshearing had passed, the family enjoyed their sweets for weeks afterward. I didn't complain as the normal dinner fare was often rather bland compared to the way my mother had prepared it.

I finished the filling, mixed it into the pastry dough, and carried it to the oven in the center of the courtyard, where I stopped to stir the stew.

Derorit joined me, arms crossed. "What are you doing?"

Wasn't it obvious? Why was the woman so accusing? "I didn't want it to burn," I said, pointing to the pot hanging over the fire. "Is there something else you would have me do?" When had Derorit decided to command my every move?

"Odelia will handle the stew. Go to the well and get more water." Derorit returned to the house before I could respond.

I glanced at the sky. It was nearly midday, the hottest part. No one went to the well at this time of day, and we still had water in the cistern from the last rain.

But I picked up the jar, left the house, and began the long

walk to Jacob's well outside of town. Weariness dogged my
every step, and my thoughts spun in a thousand directions. Derorit had changed the way she looked at me in the past month,
after my last cycle showed that I had again not conceived a child.
Never mind that Tamir was often in the fields during the time
when conception might be possible. And could it be that my
mother-in-law's anxious fretting over it all might be keeping
me from bearing? Derorit's anxiety fed my own.

I passed the house where Gali now lived and glanced toward
the courtyard. At that moment, the door opened and Gali appeared at the threshold, a child on her hip. I stopped. Would
she speak? Should I?

But Gali turned and closed the door without a word, and my
heart sank yet again at the loss. *I have no friends.* The thought
deeply saddened me. Since Gali, Menuha had been the closest
I had come to having a friend I could talk with and enjoy, but
the girl was not one to confide in. No one in that household
could be fully trusted, not even Tamir, if I were honest. How
did I know what he said to his mother? Surely he had told her
of his desire for a child.

I shifted the jar to the other shoulder and continued through
the city gate, grateful that the Roman guards did not trouble
me. A woman alone in the middle of the day . . . was it safe?
But Derorit had not given my safety any consideration. What
would happen if I didn't return?

Suddenly thoughts of Lavi surfaced. How far was Sebaste
from Jacob's well? I had never been to visit the city with my
father or any of my husbands and had no idea how long such
a trip would take or how to find the way.

As quickly as thoughts of Lavi entered my mind, that old
nagging guilt followed. Tamir was a good, kind husband. I was
doing my best to please him. The only thing I could not yet
give him was a son, and I had no desire to be set aside or do
something to make him want another instead of me. He had

wooed me and captured my heart, and to think of any other felt like betrayal.

I set the jar on the ground and shook myself. *Stop thinking this way. All is well. Derorit is just in a strange mood right now. It's not your fault.* I lectured myself as I lowered the rope and filled the jar, then hefted it back to my shoulder. I carried it, slower now, back to Sychar, and set it beside the door to Keshet's house.

Sweat poured down my back, and I took a drink before composing myself and returning to the cool of the house.

"Nessa! Where have you been?" Menuha's shrill voice alerted me that something bad had happened.

"Your mother sent me to the well. What's wrong?"

Odelia joined Menuha in the sitting room, down the hall from the bedchambers. "Derorit has taken to her bed with a headache. I fear she is ill," Odelia said. "I've sent word to the men."

I glanced around. "Who did you send?" Menuha was standing there, and she normally took the messages to them.

"I asked the neighbor's son. I didn't want to be alone with her. I don't know what to do." Despite being older than me, Odelia did not seem to know how to take charge of a situation. Derorit had always been the one to order everyone around.

"Let us check on her." I led the way to the bedchamber.

Derorit lay on the bed with a cloth over her eyes. How frail she looked. Hadn't she just stood in the cooking room preparing sweets?

"Derorit? What can I do to help you?" I bent at her side.

Derorit did not stir, and I felt her head. "She's hot to the touch. Hurry. Get cool water and more cloths." My mind whirled. "And some willow bark. If she has a fever, it might help."

Menuha ran to get the water and Odelia the herb, leaving me alone with Derorit. How helpless she seemed.

Why do you dislike me so much? But now was not the time, despite the urge to ask.

"What's happened?" Keshet burst into the room just as Menuha returned with water and Odelia with willow bark.

"I don't know. Odelia said she took to her bed with a headache. She appears to have a fever." I looked at his stricken face.

"Should I send for a doctor?" He looked as helpless as I felt.

"That might be wise." Though Derorit might rue the cost of one if she turned out to be fine.

Keshet left as quickly as he'd come, and I replaced the cloth with a cooler one. "Let's take turns replacing these until her fever comes down. Odelia, help me lift her head and try to get her to drink the willow bark."

Odelia did as she was told, but Derorit choked on the water and fell back against the pillow.

Menuha came and knelt at her side. "Ima? Please get better. We have my wedding to plan."

I touched the girl's shoulder and felt her weeping beneath my touch.

"Will she be okay?" Menuha looked at me through her tears.

I lifted my hands. "Only God knows, dear one." What would I do if Derorit did not recover?

Tamir appeared at the threshold. "What can I do? Abba has gone for a doctor. Elkan stayed with the sheep."

A baby's cry drew Odelia from the room. Her young son was up from his nap, and the baby must have awakened at the same time. Why had Derorit not been satisfied with two grandchildren? But one look at Tamir and I knew. My husband wanted what his brother had, what all men wanted. A son to carry on his name. And Derorit had made it her mission to keep after me until it happened.

As if anyone could control such things.

The doctor arrived a short time later, and Derorit stirred at last, asking for water. After a thorough examination, the doctor said, "She will be fine. She has been working too hard and needs to rest. You young women can surely handle her work for a week or more."

"Of course they can," Derorit said, her normal controlling tone returning. "Now go and feed the men. You all made too much fuss over nothing." She slowly rose from the bed, a bit wobbly. "But don't think for a moment that I will just sit by and do nothing. Someone has to make sure you're all doing things the way you should."

She aimed her words mostly at me, the one who always took the brunt of her hostility when it was aroused. Odelia had her children and Menuha was her baby. Until I produced a baby of my own, I would always be expected to do the most, whether it pleased Derorit or not.

❖ ❖ ❖

Weeks passed and I assumed more of Derorit's duties, sometimes working myself to exhaustion. At dusk the day before Shabbat, I sat in the courtyard near the fire and stretched my legs in front of me, crossing them at the ankles. As it set, the sun wrapped itself from east to west in brilliant colors of golden orange and deep pink, something I'd never seen before, as though the Creator had sent it just for me. Had He?

Do You see me?

The rabbis told the story of Hagar, who gave God the name "the God Who Sees Me." But did He see everyone? Did He care for something as simple as a woman's longing for rest?

Voices drifted to me from the house, and I picked out Derorit's shrill tone beside Odelia's protesting one. What was the problem now? My shoulders drooped, feeling weighted from dealing with both of them. Odelia rarely said anything to go against Derorit, so why the anger coming from them now?

Tamir strode from the sheepfold and joined me in the courtyard. He did not sit but tilted his head to listen. "Why are they arguing?" He looked at me with a hint of accusation, as if I should know.

"I have no idea." I released a deep sigh. "I just came here to sit for a moment." Emotion rose and a tear slipped down my cheek. I swiped it away before he could notice.

"Ima shouldn't get so worked up. It's not good for her. Go and see what you can do to fix the situation as I'm sure it has something to do with whatever it is you women do all day." He pointed to the house, and I stared at him, disbelieving. Was he really asking me to come between Odelia and his mother when I had nothing to do with whatever this was about?

But his gaze never wavered, so I pushed myself up from the bench and walked into the house without a word. He did not follow me, and soon I heard him talking to his brother as they sat around the fire.

Another sigh rose within me. I was so weary. I followed the sound of Derorit's whining and entered the room where the women stood facing each other.

"Is there something I can do to help?" I faced Derorit, then glanced at Odelia.

"It's her fault that the robe isn't the way you wanted it to be. Ask Menuha. She did most of the weaving. Menuha will tell you." Odelia would not hold my gaze but looked at Derorit instead.

"I knew it," Derorit said, triumphant. "Why did you not just tell me in the first place? You know you don't have to keep these things from me to spare Nessa."

My eyes went wide. "What are you talking about? The garment isn't finished, and anything that is wrong, I'm sure I can fix."

Derorit scoffed. "Fix?" She held up the unfinished bridal robe. "Are you going to take out twenty rows of green in order to add *five* rows of blue, not three? How could you make such an error?"

I stared at the garment, then at Derorit. Where was Menuha? No doubt her mother had sent her from the room. She knew Menuha would side with me. She always did.

"I will make it right," I promised, feeling as though I had been punched in the middle. "First thing tomorrow, I will work on it."

"No! You will stay up tonight and fix it!" Derorit's face reddened with her cry. A moment later, I looked on in horror as the woman fell to her knees and then face down on the ground.

Odelia screamed, and I stood frozen, unable to move.

Footsteps sounded on the packed earthen floor. Tamir and Elkan rushed into the room. "What happened?" Tamir demanded.

Keshet soon followed and ran to his wife's side. "Derorit!" He turned her over, but her face was as still as stone. He shook her and tried to rouse her, but she did not move.

"Is she dead?" Tamir's voice sounded distant, and I still could not move forward or backward.

Keshet leaned against Derorit's chest, listening for breath, but when he found none, he rose and shook his head, his expression stormy. "What happened?"

"We were talking about Menuha's bridal robe," Odelia said. "She just collapsed."

"I heard a lot of shouting," Elkan said, looking at me.

"I thought I told you to fix this, not make it worse," Tamir said, his expression void of compassion.

"She found a problem with the colors, and I told her I would make it right," I said softly, barely able to find my voice.

"Ima!" Menuha burst into the room from wherever Derorit had sent her. "Ima!" She fell at her mother's side and wept bitterly.

The room fell silent at Menuha's outburst, and the men were suddenly subdued. They left the women alone, no doubt to build a bier. It was too late to take Derorit to the cave, but we could wash her and wrap her to take her there before dawn.

I told myself to do just that, but my legs would not cooperate with me. I stood still, watching, wondering. Derorit was dead? Was it my fault, as Odelia had suggested about the robe?

Suddenly I wasn't sure about anything anymore. I was needed for now, but how long would it be before someone in this household blamed me for Derorit's loss? What would happen to me then?

22

rose early each morning in the months after Derorit's death and Menuha's wedding to prepare food for the men. Odelia said little to me, and most nights when Tamir finally joined me, I was already asleep. Exhaustion followed me like an unwanted guest. I tried to be everything to everyone, especially Tamir, so why had he grown so distant of late?

"Is the food ready?" Tamir stood in the entrance to the preparation room, jolting me out of my thoughts.

I lifted the sack with the food I had gathered and handed it to him. "I hope it's enough."

"I won't be as late tonight. Elkan is taking the sheep while I am going to Sebaste."

My heart skipped a beat. "Sebaste?" What was in Sebaste that he needed?

"I have business there." He bent to kiss my cheek, then left without saying more.

I stared after him. "What business?"

Odelia came from the sitting room. "What are you asking?"

I did not trust Odelia, not after the way she'd lied about me to Derorit. "It's nothing."

She crossed her arms over her chest, assessing me. "Elkan

said Tamir has found a woman in Sebaste he likes. Is that where he's going?"

"Why would Elkan tell you that? Tamir has said no such thing." Anger flared that the family would know something about my husband that I did not.

"If he's looking for a second wife, you can't think he would tell you, do you?" Odelia lifted her chin. She'd grown haughtier since Derorit's death.

I turned away and mixed the flatbread to bake on the griddle in the courtyard. Three years I had been Tamir's wife, and not once had I conceived a child, even during the early days when he was consumed with me. Had my losses made me barren? Was Tamir looking for another wife to bear him sons?

I carried the batter to the stones and poured the mixture onto the hot three-pronged griddle. Normally, Tamir would have waited for the bread, but apparently Sebaste was a long walk and he wanted to start early.

Was he really going to find a second wife? Thoughts of Lavi surfaced, but I doubted Tamir would have business with him. I wasn't even sure if he was still making tents, and Tamir would have no need of such a thing.

Memories of Amichai and Harel followed my thoughts of Lavi. Had my father made an agreement that I would be Tamir's only wife? I searched my thoughts but could not remember those blurred early days. Women had so few recourses to deal with the choices of their husbands. I needed to talk to Chen to see what had been written in the ketubah. And I needed to find out if Tamir was really thinking of taking another.

Why hadn't he explained himself? I needed to know. Menuha would have told me if she knew. Would Elkan reveal the truth? Could even he be trusted?

Worry niggled my thoughts as I absentmindedly flipped the flatbread. When Tamir arrived home, I would ask him. I had a right to know his business. But I would ask humbly lest he think me too bold. He had grown more like his mother since her passing, and I wasn't about to risk offending him.

Then again, what did it matter? If he wanted someone else, let him divorce me. I didn't care what I said to him.

◆ ◆ ◆

The following morning, I rose before Tamir, waited for him to finish the morning meal, then followed him to the sheep pens. Forsaking his word, he had not returned early the night before and, in fact, came home so late I could no longer hold my eyes open.

I lifted my skirts and hurried after him now, reaching the sheep pen moments after he did. "Tamir."

He stopped, turning to face me. "Nessa. What are you doing?"

I wrapped my arms about me, though I didn't think I needed to protect myself from him. Did I? My fear made me suddenly unsure.

I swallowed and straightened, gathering my courage. "Why did you go to Sebaste yesterday?"

He looked at me for a lengthy breath. "I told you I had business."

"Odelia suggested your business was to obtain another wife." A shiver worked through me as my imagination ran in all different directions.

Tamir rested one hand on the gate, looked at his feet, then met my gaze. "You have not conceived even once in three years, Nessa. A man needs sons."

"I won't live with another woman who shares your bed." I stiffened, fearing that if I did not hold myself erect, I would crumble to the dust.

"Three years is a long time," he said as if that should explain everything.

"Abraham waited longer, as did Isaac and Rachel. Our God

can still give you sons through me." I clenched my jaw to keep from shaking. He was not denying Odelia's words.

"I've already made arrangements," he said softly.

"What? Without telling me or asking me?" My voice rose in pitch, and I hated the emotion he evoked in me. "I suppose you've found some young girl who hasn't been used up and isn't barren because she lost two sons." Tears came then, and I hated every one of them.

He touched my shoulder, but I shook it off.

"Tell me it isn't true." I glared at him.

"I can't, because it is. And I know this will break the terms of our arrangement, which means you can stay or you can return to your father's house and wait to marry another."

So, my father had made arrangements for me, peace be upon him. But what good did they do me if Tamir did not care that he was breaking the agreement?

He stepped closer, his expression that of the man who had wooed me. How charming he could be. How deceptive.

"I won't put you out, Nessa. You would still be first wife and have all the things you need. I would still provide for you. But Edna would bear me children."

"You don't know that. What happens if you find out that she is barren? Will you take a third? A fourth? I won't live in such a household. It is against Torah. God made them male and female, one man and one woman. This is wrong." I was shouting now, but I could not stop the rage rising in me. I whirled about and ran away from the house, toward the fields.

"Nessa!" he called after me, but when I glanced back, he did not follow.

He was letting me go. He was tired of waiting, and he would let me return to live with my mother and Chen and Malka, something I was loath to do.

But could I stay here without Menuha to give me comfort? Could I live with smug Odelia, with her perfect children, and

Edna, a likely spoiled child who would bear Tamir a son and then mock me as Hagar did Sarai?

Tears fell fast as I ran toward the foothills near the outer walls of Sychar. If only I had wings like a bird and could fly far away from this place, these people. Then I could be at peace. Because living with Tamir or living with Malka were not options I even wanted to consider, though I must.

◆ ◆ ◆

As the day waned and the sun passed its zenith, I made my way to my father's house, determined to speak to Chen, despite the fact that my heart was breaking with every step. Was this truly happening again? Another man rejecting me after such a short time? Whatever happened to patience? If my inability to bear a child was truly the cause, why not be like Isaac, as the rabbis taught, and pray for me to conceive? After Isaac's prayer, Rebekah bore twins. Wouldn't that be the better path? Better than to cast me out?

I glimpsed the edge of the shop where Chen would be working and slowed my step, framing my words. Was something wrong with me that I could not keep a man's interest? Everyone had always told me how beautiful I was, so it must be my personality that turned them away.

That thought felt like someone had stabbed me and turned the knife, accentuating the pain. And with the pain, I recalled the look on Tamir's face and his callous words.

I stopped as the shop drew close and lifted my gaze heavenward. *What's wrong with me, Adonai? Won't anyone ever love me for me?*

I expected no answer and wondered why I bothered to pray at all. One glance at the shop and the sound of voices coming from inside made me pause. Men's voices. Had Chen hired another?

Determined to speak to him regardless, I straightened and walked with purpose to the opening of the large tent workshop.

"Nessa, what are you doing here?" Chen rose from a small wooden chair where he sat stitching goats' hair and walked toward me. He held my arms but did not pull me close.

I searched his face. "May I speak with you alone, please?" I glimpsed a man slightly older than Chen carving tent pegs that would be needed to complete a project.

Chen led me outside some distance from the shop. "What's going on? Why are you here and not at home?" His dark brows furrowed, and he crossed his arms over his chest.

"I . . ." I looked away, swiping a tear, then faced him again. "Tamir is planning to take a second wife to bear him children. He is not happy waiting for me to conceive." I swallowed. "I think he fears I never will."

Chen's expression softened. He placed a hand on my shoulder.

"He can't do that, can he? He said that Abba made provisions in the ketubah to protect me, but he doesn't care."

Chen placed an arm about my shoulders and walked me farther from the tent. "Tamir would have had to pay a large sum if you had been a virgin. I doubt he is worried about paying much if he wishes to divorce you." He paused and turned me to face him. "Did he say he wants a divorce?"

I could not meet his gaze. But he tipped my chin up to look into my eyes. "Nessa?"

I shook my head. "He said that I can stay as first wife and he would provide for me. But, Chen, I cannot bear Odelia's smugness now that Menuha is wed. And this new woman he will marry will end up like Hagar and treat me with disdain the moment she conceives."

He looked at me in silence, then said, "You don't know that, Ness. She could be a kind young woman. Someone you could mentor."

"I will not share my husband with another!" Emotion rose, nearly choking the words.

Silence again settled between us, until at last he spoke. "What would you have me do? If you prefer he divorce you, you would have to live here again with Ima and Malka and me. And I don't know if I can find *another* man to marry you. You are beautiful, my sister, but you're going to be seen as damaged. Used. Is that what you want?"

Tears spilled over my cheeks faster than I could stop them, and he pulled me close, letting me weep against his shoulder as he patted my back like a parent would a child.

When my tears were spent, he held me at arm's length. "I don't know what to do for you, Ness. I know you don't care for Malka. Would you rather live here for a time with my wife or with Odelia and Tamir's new wife?"

I studied the dirt beneath my sandals. "I don't know."

The sun hid behind a spray of clouds, cooling the air about us. "Why don't you stay here tonight. Talk to Ima and see what she says. I will talk with Tamir to see his intentions, and then we can decide what is best for you."

I met his gaze, grateful for his compassion. "Thank you. I don't think I can return to that house alone regardless. I need your help to sort this out."

"You have it, dear sister." He kissed my forehead and walked with me toward the house.

For the first time since Derorit died, I felt a small sense of relief. At least for tonight I would feel loved and safe. If only it could last.

23

"Nessa, my love, why the long face?" Ima's arms came around me the moment I stepped into the house, but not before I caught the questioning look she aimed Chen's way.

"She is going to stay with us tonight. Apparently Tamir is taking another wife, and I must look over the ketubah and have a talk with him. For now, I said she could stay."

"Of course she can stay." Ima led me to the sitting room, where Malka sat at the loom I once occupied.

Malka's eyes widened at the sight of me. "To what do we owe this visit?" She did not rise to greet me but continued to work the shuttle.

"She is staying with us tonight," Chen said, giving his wife a warning look. Did he expect Malka to treat me poorly? No doubt he did, but I brushed that fear aside.

"I'm going back to tell Nadav that I have something to attend to." He left, and I followed Ima into the preparation area.

"Who is Nadav?" I accepted a cup of water from her and drank greedily. I had run far without food or drink and did not realize how parched I was.

"Chen found the work too much to continue doing alone, so he recently hired Nadav. Come, let's go to the courtyard where we can have some privacy." Ima lowered her voice and glanced behind her. The loom drowned out our voices, and I breathed a sigh of relief.

When we were far from the door, Ima faced it in case Malka appeared. "Tell me," she said.

"Tamir is tired of waiting for me to conceive, so he's gone to Sebaste and secured a young virgin to be his second wife. 'A man needs sons,' he said. I asked him to be patient, like Abraham and Isaac, but he does not wish to wait." I took another drink and swallowed, letting my heartbeat slow from the rapid pounding my fear had wrought. "I do not want another woman sharing his bed, Ima. And Odelia has become impossible to live with since Derorit died. She lied about me to Derorit before that moment and since then has grown proud and distant. I do not trust any of them now that Menuha is gone." I set the cup down and folded my hands in my lap. "Tell me what to do."

Ima looked at me for several moments. "I wish I had answers for you, dear Nessa. You have suffered much at the hands of others, and I wish we could go back in time and change the decisions that were made from the beginning."

"I've often wished that."

"But, of course, we cannot change what is past. Amichai would have passed on eventually, long before you, and Harel was an unfortunate choice."

"I wish my father would have chosen Lavi. Even now, I think Lavi would have me if Tamir divorces me. Would not Chen consider him now that Abba is gone?" The thought brought the first bit of hope I'd had in years. Could now be the time?

Ima's gaze grew distant as if she were seeing into a different time. "Lavi stole from us, Nessa. Your father asked Chen to never give you to that man should such a time as this ever arise again."

"He said that?" Anger flared that my father would be so uncaring.

"He died protecting you, child. He never trusted Lavi, and neither should you."

I met her grim expression with a frustrated one of my own. "People can change. He didn't know Lavi. Hadn't seen him in years. He had no right to ask such a thing of Chen." I bit back the words I wanted to say about having met Lavi several times over the years. My mother wouldn't understand, and if others heard, they could take my words and twist them.

"You have no way of knowing whether Lavi has changed, my love. He hasn't lived in Sychar in years." She took my hand and pressed it between both of hers. "Let Chen talk to Tamir. Stay here tonight and rest. Think about staying with him as his first wife. A first wife has privileges, and if he denies you any of your marital rights, then you can tell Chen and he will intercede."

Defeat settled in my heart. I couldn't pursue the idea of being given to Lavi unless he came to Chen and convinced him he was now able to provide for a wife and would treat me well. He wouldn't do that if he didn't know of my situation. And I had no way to tell him unless I went to Sebaste and found him. And I—a woman alone? Such travel held too much danger.

"Will you do as I suggest?" Ima coaxed me to meet her gaze. "Rest tonight with us. Things will look better tomorrow."

You can't know that. "I will stay," I said.

I could not run off to do any of the things I wanted without risking the wrath of Tamir or Chen or both. The last thing I needed was to have my family turn against me as Gali had done years ago. I had already been used and rejected by too many. If I did something rash, I would turn the entire town against me, and I absolutely did not want that.

❖ ❖ ❖

Chen returned to our father's home the next afternoon and met me in the garden behind the house, where I picked dill to mix with the sauce Ima was making for dipping the bread. I straightened, too aware of the kink in my back, and faced him.

"What did he say?" I searched his face, this brother who had played with me and Lavi when we were young. How long ago that seemed. "You do not seem pleased."

"I'm not." Chen motioned me to follow him to a bench at the back of the house. I sat, my stomach doing little flips. "Tamir is convinced that God is against you, and considering you have lost two children and have not conceived throughout your marriage to him, he doubts you ever will. He justifiably wants sons as every man does, and he is unwilling to wait."

"I already know that." I suppressed my impatience. "Tell me what he said to you."

"Besides that, he said that since you ran off, he does not want you to return to his house. His father doesn't want you to return either, and they paid the amount stipulated in the ketubah should he wish to divorce you." Chen pulled a small pouch of coins and a writ of divorce from the pocket of his robe and handed them to me.

I took the bag and tucked the writ of divorce into my robe. The weight seemed too light, but as Chen had said before, I was not worth the price of a virgin.

Silence grew heavy between us as I stared at the bag, the sum total of my worth. At last I lifted my head and looked into Chen's dark eyes. "I have things that belong to me there. Is he going to just keep them?"

Chen shook his head. "They will have them sent to you. Keshet has a neighbor boy who does errands for them sometimes."

I nodded. "I know." What more could I say? Tamir was done with me. He wanted someone else. Was Edna beautiful? Undoubtedly I would find out when I saw her at synagogue one day.

"What happens now?" I looked into Chen's concerned face.

He rubbed a hand down his bearded chin and sighed. "I will see if another man is willing to take you." His gaze went beyond me toward the shop where he worked. "Perhaps Nadav would take you as a second wife . . ." His voice trailed off.

I sank deeper into the bench, suddenly wishing I had never been born. Second wife? When I could have been first?

"I don't want to share a husband, Chen. That was the problem with Tamir in the first place." I clasped my hands about the coin purse. If only I could live on my own. If only I didn't need a man to survive in life.

"Ness." Chen touched my knee. "How many men in Sychar do you think are going to want a woman who has had three husbands and produced no living children? Nadav is a good man. He works for me, so I would be able to better protect you. He would treat you well, if he's willing to take you on."

Tears threatened at his earnest expression. I didn't want to disappoint him, but what of Lavi? Should I mention him? Ima's comments surfaced with that thought, and I could not bring myself to say the words I longed to say, so I simply nodded.

"Good. Let me speak with him. Then we will know." He patted my knee and stood. "I'm sorry, Ness. You've had too many terrible tragedies befall you, and I wish I knew why." He walked away toward the workshop.

So do I. Had I somehow offended the Creator that He would cause my life to be so utterly miserable, while my sisters all lived happily in the homes of their husbands and had been able to bear and keep children?

I lifted my gaze to the heavens. I was thirsty for love. Acceptance. Someone to keep me without censure or rebuke for the rest of my life. I wanted answers, but the heavens offered none.

❖ ❖ ❖

The following Shabbat I walked with Ima, Chen, and Malka to the local synagogue to hear a reading from the Pentateuch. I took a seat with the other women, pulling my headscarf closer to my neck, wishing I could hide from the stares of the women, who no doubt had gossiped about my divorce from Tamir.

I did not want their pity, but I could not escape the occasional haughty look sent my way. Were they happy to see me suffer? But why? Because men acted so foolishly, gawking at me in the market? I looked toward the men's section, catching at least one lustful glance my way. I wanted to sink into the seat and cover my face, but I forced my chin up and set my mind on the rabbi's reading.

"Now we know that our worship of the Almighty is best done on Mt. Gerizim, where our temple once stood," the rabbi said. "But since we no longer have a temple, we trust that God will accept our worship here. And now, a reading from the book of Leviticus, God's book of holy living and worship.

"The Lord said to Moses, 'Say to the Israelites: A woman who becomes pregnant and gives birth to a son will be ceremonially unclean for seven days, just as she is unclean during her monthly cycle. On the eighth day the boy is to be circumcised. Then the woman must wait thirty-three days to be purified from her bleeding. She must not touch anything sacred or go to the sanctuary until the days of her purification are over . . .'"

My mind wandered to the births of my two sons. I had followed the law and done all the things for purification. Noya would have had it no other way. So why had God not given me children again? Why not give me a living child?

Was our whole town in violation of God's laws because they couldn't worship on Mt. Gerizim? Or was I personally to blame?

The memory of Lavi surfaced again as the rabbi finished his reading. I should never have encouraged him. If I hadn't let him kiss me that long-ago day or spoken to him when I was married, perhaps my life would be different. Surely that was the reason. I had betrayed my husbands and father by caring for my cousin.

The thought sank like a stone in my middle, and I pressed a hand there to quell the bitter feeling. No wonder my husbands had stopped caring for me. I had been unfaithful to them in my thoughts. I deserved this life.

Heat flooded my cheeks with the realization, and I knew without a doubt that everyone who looked my way saw my shame. Why would Nadav want me as a second wife? Why would anyone want me at all?

"Nessa," Ima prompted, touching my elbow.

I looked up, aware that the service had ended and the people were filing out of the synagogue.

"Come," she said.

I walked with her as my heart beat with a new sense of self-loathing. I was not worthy of a loving husband or children. I was not pure in heart. Oh, I followed the laws and had been pure after each month and each child, but I was not a good person. If I was, good things would happen to me. Since nothing but hardship and hurt befell me, I must be the worst of sinners.

Was there a sin offering I could give to take away those sins . . . and the shame? Could I afford to give one? The coins I had would be nearly gone if I purchased a lamb for such a sacrifice. Would it be worth it?

"You're terribly quiet, my daughter. Is something troubling you?" Ima slipped her arm through mine.

I walked in step with her behind Chen and Malka. "Do you think I could purchase a lamb for sacrifice?" I leaned close lest Malka hear.

Ima stopped walking to face me. "Whatever for? It's a big expense and you don't have means to pay for it."

"I have the coins Tamir paid me." Would God bless me from now on if I did this?

"But why, my child? Can't you wait until the Day of Atonement and offer your sacrifice with the rest of us? Surely you have done nothing to be in need of a sin or guilt offering."

186

I looked away from the concern in her eyes. "I guess so." I shrugged.

Perhaps I was wrong to think such thoughts. Even if I paid every shekel to my name and offered a sin or guilt offering to God every day for years to come, I wasn't sure He would change my circumstances. Sacrifices might ease the guilt I felt over Lavi, but I knew I could never forget him or truly regret his kiss.

"Never mind," I said, walking again to catch up to Chen.

He intended to introduce me to Nadav after Shabbat, and I didn't want to cause another prospective husband to turn away before he even had the chance to meet me and decide for himself. Because one thing I knew was true. I needed the support of a man, and Chen could not keep me forever. So I would do what I must.

24

know you briefly met my sister Nessa," Chen said to Nadav the next morning in the courtyard of our father's house, "but I think it best to make a proper introduction." He looked at his apprentice, and I noted the lifted brows and spark of interest in Nadav's eyes. He seemed to like what he saw.

"Shalom, Nessa," Nadav said, slightly bowing in my direction.

"Shalom," I said, returning the gesture.

"Chen has told me of your situation." Nadav glanced at Chen, who nodded for him to continue. "I do not consider what has happened to you as right or just or fair, and I'm willing to accept you as a second wife if you approve. You'll be treated as any wife should be, though I do not expect you to bear me sons as your last husband did. I have several sons by my wife Ariel—four, in fact—so you need not worry about . . . that."

The blood rushed to my face, and I stiffened, praying I would not die of embarrassment at his comments about something so personal. We were not yet wed, after all. And what would his wife be like? His sons? I didn't even know his mother's name, only that his father had died shortly before Nadav came to work for Chen.

"Nadav is willing to sign the ketubah today and accept you into his home at the end of the week. Do you agree to this, Nessa?" Chen's words pushed past my swirling thoughts.

I shook myself and stared at my brother. I didn't miss the new lines that had appeared along his brow and mouth. I was a burden to him, and it showed.

I glanced at Nadav, forcing my smile to reach my eyes. "Yes." What else could I say? I could not continue to stay with Chen's family.

His family. I was part of his family, but a woman was supposed to join her husband's family, not remain with the family of her birth. Only the sons had such a privilege.

"Good," Chen said, moving with Nadav into the house, where no doubt he had already laid out the ketubah with its revised terms. I could not go into the marriage claiming to be a virgin, and the price Nadav would pay to me would be even less than Tamir had paid.

With every marriage my worth diminished, and I felt it deep in my soul. Would there be a wedding this time, or would I simply move into Nadav's home?

I followed the men at a distance, lifting my gaze to the familiar walls of the home I had known all my life. Multicolored rugs that I had woven in browns and yellows and reds were spread over the floor in the sitting room and the sleeping areas. The familiar cups and bowls, many of which Amichai had made, filled the cooking area. A deep sigh lifted my chest. I didn't want to leave. Not again.

"Nessa, help me, please," Ima called from the cooking area. "Take these to the men. They will celebrate once they sign the agreement."

I moved woodenly, carrying a tray with sweets my mother had prepared and cups of wine for the men to share. I placed the tray on a nearby table and retreated to a corner, where I picked up a spindle and distaff. Nadav, like Chen, was a tentmaker, but he also lived in tents, if I remembered correctly. I would probably be asked to spin the goats' hair for the tents rather than weave things for market. Then again, I had no idea what Nadav would ask of me.

I watched the men press their seals onto the parchment, then take up the cups of wine and drink. Laughter followed and Chen smiled, obviously happy to have found a solution for what to do with me. The thought stung.

After they finished the wine, Nadav took a pressed date cake and carried it to me. I looked up at him, let the spindle slowly wind down, and set it aside.

He sat beside me, and I took the cake from his hands. "Thank you." I lifted my shy gaze to his.

"I want you to know more about your new home," he said, smiling. "I am head of the household, as my father died several years ago and I have no brothers. My mother is Raziela, my wife is Ariel, and my four sons are Aviv, Eran, Haim, and Moti. They are young, but old enough to keep a small flock of sheep and goats, and soon I will bring Aviv here to apprentice under Chen and me."

I nodded, trying to remember each name and fearing I might forget. "What will you have me do?"

"You are a fine weaver, I'm told, so you may continue to do so and sell your wares at market. If needed, you can help Ariel spin the goats' hair or my mother with the food preparation." He searched my face, his gaze curious. "Do not be fearful, Nessa. I will treat you well."

"Thank you," I said again, though I could not bring myself to care about this union. Nadav was a pleasant-looking man, but to give myself to yet another did not evoke emotions in me. Not in the way Tamir had captivated me or Lavi had looked at me, quickening my pulse. Even Amichai had been so pleased to wed me that I had come to feel at peace with him. How could I give myself to another in any way other than out of duty?

Nadav stood, seemingly done with what he wanted to tell me. "Chen will bring you to my home in a week."

"A week. I will be ready."

He and Chen left the house for work in the shop. I set the

spindle aside as Malka entered the room and took her seat at the loom I should be using. She barely glanced at me except to offer a smirk.

I left the room for the courtyard.

"Nessa, wait," Ima called after me. She followed and took my hand as we walked toward the garden. "My dearest Nessa." She turned me to face her, pulling me into her arms. "You are still so young. Only twenty and already wed four times." She cupped my cheek. "You won't be far away this time, as Nadav's family has set up their tents near the border of Sychar's walls. It's a short walk just beyond the trees."

"That's nice," I said, feeling dead inside.

"This will work out. You will see." Ima tilted my head to look deeply into my eyes. "Try to see it as a good thing."

"I feel nothing, Ima," I said, meeting her concerned gaze. "I don't know Nadav or his family. He doesn't need me. He already has a wife and four sons. I'm just like a servant to him. He feels sorry for me." I looked away, suddenly ashamed.

"No doubt he is also attracted to you, as so many men are. In time you will learn to accept this," she said. "Nadav is a good man."

Ima entered the garden and began to pick vegetables for the evening meal. I watched her, my heart like a stone. I would do what everyone expected of me, what they wanted me to do. But I wasn't sure I would ever find enjoyment in life again.

❖ ❖ ❖

A week later, Chen escorted me along with my few belongings to Nadav's home without celebration or the usual gathering of family and friends. I did not even stand under the canopy or hear a rabbi bless our union. This was a fourth marriage as a second wife, after all. What was there to celebrate?

Chen left me at the door to Nadav's tent and greeted Nadav.

191

He set my bag on the ground, kissed my cheek, and told me to visit when I could. And then he was gone.

"Shalom, Nessa," Nadav said.

"Shalom," I said, looking from Nadav to the spacious tent behind him.

"So, this is the new wife." An older woman came from behind a curtained partition and looked me up and down. "Humph. Can you cook?"

"Nessa, this is my mother, Raziela." He touched my shoulder. "Be kind, Ima."

"I'm always kind." She scowled at her son.

"Yes, I can cook," I said, embarrassed at this exchange and trying to not squirm under Nadav's touch and the woman's scrutiny.

"Good. You can help me with the barley stew." She looked at Nadav. "Are you going back to work?"

Nadav offered me a sheepish look. "If you'll be all right here until I return."

Be all right? Did he expect something to happen to me? But what of coming together as man and wife? Was he to spend no time getting to know me better? Was I to have no type of wedding week? Even Rachel and Leah had their separate weeks.

"Let me put your bag in your room and introduce you to Ariel and my sons, then when I return, you will share my bed," Nadav said.

I hesitated a moment, then followed him to a small curtained room that held a mat on the floor and a small chest apparently for my use, as he set my things beside it. He led me outside to an area like a house courtyard but not as complex, yet it seemed to serve the same purpose. "Ariel. This is Nessa." He spoke to a woman a few years older than me and pointed to two young boys playing with carved animals in the dirt. "These are my two youngest sons, Haim and Moti. Aviv and Eran are with the sheep and goats."

"Shalom," I said, offering Ariel a smile.

The woman did not return it but simply nodded and continued her work.

Nadav's face flushed at the obvious rebuff, but he said nothing. Did his women control this home? I glanced at him, and he guided me back toward the tent, where his mother busied herself inside.

"Give her time. She is not used to sharing me."

"No doubt," I said, looking toward the tent. "I suppose it will take everyone time to adjust."

Nadav released a sigh. "So you understand. Good." He smiled and kissed my cheek, but the simple sign of affection felt awkward. "I will be back. Make yourself at home. Do whatever my mother directs you to do, and if you have questions for me, we can discuss them when we are alone." He took my hand and squeezed it, then hurried away toward my former home.

I stared at the open tent door, wishing I knew what to do, shoring up the courage to face his mother. Entering the tent, I met Raziela waiting for me.

"There you are. Come."

I followed in silence.

"This is where Nadav sleeps. And Ariel's rooms are here." She pointed to a curtained partition. "The boys sleep with Ariel. I sleep near the cooking area over there. And this large area is where we sit and eat and celebrate." She glanced at me, and for a brief moment, I saw compassion in her eyes. "You will adjust once you get to know us. But come. Help me to prepare a feast for your wedding. You may not have a week with my son as Ariel did, but we can celebrate as a family tonight. I trust you will bring him joy."

"I hope so," I said, so low I wasn't sure the woman heard me.

I took some small comfort in this kindness. Perhaps living here wouldn't be as bad as I'd feared, despite the awkward beginnings. I would thank Adonai for small favors.

25

I left the tent and glanced at the sky, but the clouds blocked any sight of the sun. My stomach rumbled with the scents of lamb and barley stew and freshly baked bread wafting toward me. My fingers ached from shelling pistachios and almonds for a honey-sweetened cookie Raziela had instructed me how to make. She insisted that this meal would be my wedding celebration. But when Ariel joined us to help with the preparations, the temperature in that part of the tent seemed to chill.

Hours later, I watched the road for Nadav's return, silently praying I could avoid contact with Ariel for the rest of the night. But the chatter of her children and their curious looks my way told me that this woman would be impossible to avoid.

The thought brought sadness, despite Raziela's slight attempts to make me feel welcome. I didn't belong here. Didn't want to be here. But I had no other options. Not any that Chen would abide.

I noticed Nadav approach but held back from running to meet him. What message would that send him? I didn't know him yet. We were husband and wife by contract only. A contract that had yet to be fulfilled.

My heart skipped a beat as he came fuller into view, his

smile capturing my gaze. He hurried forward and took my hands in his.

Leaning close to my ear, he spoke. "Tonight, my dear Nessa." He squeezed my fingers and then led me into the tent.

"At last you're home." Raziela tsked. "It's your wedding feast and you waited so long?"

Nadav shrugged. "We had to finish an order for a merchant who is leaving Sychar soon."

"Abba!" Moti rushed toward Nadav, who released his hold on me to scoop the boy into his arms. His other sons clamored around him, pulling him away from me.

I glanced at Ariel, whose smug smile made me wonder if she had told her sons to distract their father. How much of a rival would this woman be? Would we fight like Rachel and Leah? The thought made my appetite dim.

"Come now, boys. Let your father sit down. We are welcoming his new wife to our home, and you must be kind to her," Raziela said, glancing at Ariel. I could not decipher the look that passed between them.

Nadav sat on a cushion on the floor and bid me to sit beside him. Ariel's sons sat near their father, but Ariel stayed near the back of the room, apparently unwilling to join the meal or "celebrate" her competition.

What will I have to endure here, Adonai? I had taken to praying now and then, but I wasn't sure why. I saw little good come of my prayers. Perhaps it just made me feel better to think someone was listening, even if they weren't. Did God care?

Nadav and Raziela attempted to make the meal festive, Raziela telling stories of Nadav when he was young, and the boys filled their father in on how their day had gone.

When the last sweet and cup of wine were consumed, Nadav took my hand and led me to his room, leaving the others to pick up the leftovers and clean the area. His room was the largest, with a higher mat on the floor and tapestries hanging along the tent walls. The bright colors were cheerful, though they did not lift my spirits.

"Tell me how you like it here so far," Nadav said as he turned me to face him. He searched my face, one hand lifting the scarf from my hair.

My pulse jumped at his touch, but I told myself this was normal. He was my husband now. I no longer belonged to Tamir, the one who had become most familiar to me.

"I don't think Ariel likes me," I said softly. "But I cannot blame her."

He removed the combs from my hair, letting my long locks drape along my back, then cupped my cheek. "She will accept you. In time." He didn't sound so sure, but I simply nodded and let him slowly kiss me.

His kiss evoked little feeling, but as he led me to consummate the marriage, I did my best to pretend that he was everything I'd ever wanted in a husband. For years I had learned to play this part well, and none of the men ever knew that I didn't love them.

Or did they? Could they tell that my heart was not in the act of marriage or in the home I was forced to live in? How well had I hidden my heart from the men in my past? Was that why they had sent me away? Did they know?

Suddenly I wanted to make Nadav believe what I did not. I would give myself to him body, mind, and soul. Then he might come to love me, even if he loved Ariel more. Even if I never bore him sons.

I could not sleep as I lay beside him. Despite my best intentions, even longings, I could not shake the feeling that everything about this man was awkward and unfamiliar. As though I had given myself like a prostitute to a stranger. The thought only added to a despair that had begun that morning, and I wondered if I would ever be able to shake it.

❖ ❖ ❖

I took turns spinning and weaving with Ariel, though the atmosphere in the tent was anything but pleasant. Months had passed, yet the woman could not seem to smile my way or say a kind word to me. Noya had been better company, when I thought on it.

When market day came, I quickly volunteered to take our wares to sell there, grateful when Raziela agreed. "It will do you good to mingle among the people," she said as I loaded the donkey with blankets and linens Ariel and I had woven. "Don't purchase any goods with the earnings. We make what we need."

I busied myself in the booth the family used, setting the woven garments and rugs and blankets out to display. The scent of spices wafted to me, the cinnamon making me long for the delicate cinnamon pastries my mother often made when my father was living. Raziela knew we could not possibly make everything the family needed, spices being one of the many. We weren't potters. And we could only do so much with the goats' hair, the milk from the sheep and goats, the vegetables we could grow, and the fruit and nuts we found on nearby trees. But trying to convince Nadav's mother of anything had proven a waste of my breath, which I'd learned as I managed the role of second wife.

"Nessa!" A familiar female voice broke into my musings. I turned.

"Gali?" I looked her over, finding genuine interest in her smile. How was it possible?

"It's been too long," Gali said, coming close, basket draped over her arm. "How have you been?"

I gave her a curious look. "I am well," I said, feeling the need to hold back from trusting too much. "And you?"

Gali lifted her slight shoulders in a sigh. "I'm sorry I've lost touch with you, Ness. I was so jealous when you married Harel that I allowed it to cloud my judgment. I hope you can forgive me."

How earnest she seemed. But I had been hurt for so long. Dare I trust this former friend, apologetic or not?

"I never understood what I did to deserve your disfavor," I admitted after a breath. "I never asked to marry Harel, nor even wanted to. He should have been yours, though I do not wish his family on anyone." I looked about, suddenly fearful that someone from Harel's family might be nearby. When I saw no one, my shoulders relaxed. "But perhaps your experience would have been different than mine."

"He shouldn't have divorced you simply because you lost two sons. These things cannot be controlled. Surely his mother knew that."

Gali's sympathy soothed a desperately lonely place in my heart. How I longed to walk with her to the well and catch up on our lives and return to the days of old when we could trust each other. But so much had come between us. Gali had not been there to comfort me even when I lost my father. The thought still stung.

"How is your family?" I asked, diverting the subject from myself.

"They are well." Gali leaned against the shelf that held my wares. "My oldest son is five and often helps his father in our pottery shop or in the booth selling our wares. The twins are four. My mother-in-law is watching them today."

"I'm happy for you." Though I could not coax myself to feel anything for Gali's pleasant life.

"It's been a busy time, but they don't need me as they did before they were weaned. Rafael is teaching them to knead the clay. They love getting their feet dirty." She offered me a tentative smile. "Perhaps you could visit sometime."

"I remember the mess Amichai made making his pottery," I said, hesitant to respond too eagerly. If only I trusted Gali enough to say yes to her request. "I would need permission from Nadav's mother. I don't often get away to see even my mother."

"I'm sorry, Nessa. I wish life had been easier for you." She placed a hand on mine, her smile genuine and sad.

"So do I," I said, pulling away. "Perhaps we can meet sometime. It would be nice to hear about your family. Do you still visit your mother?"

"My mother passed a few weeks ago," Gali said, her gaze drifting to the things I had on display as if to distract herself.

"She did? I hadn't heard. I'm sorry, Gali." My heart softened, and I took her hand in mine and squeezed. "It's hard to lose a parent."

"It is." Gali blinked tears away. "It happened suddenly, and I had hoped you would come, but apparently no one told you."

"I'm surprised they didn't. Surely my mother would have known." Why had no one told me? And yet, I knew I would not have gone.

"Your mother was there with Chen and his wife." Gali lifted her gaze to mine. "They really didn't tell you?"

I shook my head. "Chen may not have told Nadav. Or Nadav chose to keep it from me. My life is not my own anymore. But perhaps it never was."

"None of us get to control what happens to us." Gali straightened as a group of women neared my booth. "Perhaps you can visit. We can talk more then."

"Perhaps we can." I gave Gali a parting smile. "I'm sorry about your mother."

Gali nodded and turned away while I spoke with some of the townswomen I knew only from synagogue. They haggled over the prices Raziela had set, but in the end, I sold most of the garments.

The sun rose to its midpoint, and I was ready to rest during the heat when two strange men approached the booth. "I'm closed," I said as I lowered the flap.

"Perhaps just give us a moment of your time?" a familiar voice said.

Lavi?

"Please, Nessa. Just a moment." Definitely Lavi's voice, which was impossible to forget.

I lifted the flap partway and looked from the stranger to Lavi. "What can I do for you?" My heart raced, though my whole body longed to rest in the heat.

"We are here looking for the person who made those beautiful robes we purchased several years ago. The merchant where we got them no longer makes such quality, but I suspect that is because you made them and are no longer part of that house." Lavi's dark eyes probed mine, his attraction to me still evident after all these years.

"I belong to Nadav's house now. These were woven by myself and my sister-wife." Saying the words made my cheeks heat. Why did being second wife still embarrass me? Everyone in town knew my status. But apparently Lavi didn't, by his raised brow.

"You're a second wife to a man? Who is this Nadav?" He looked as though he wanted to hurt someone, but perhaps I could just sense his buried fury. Something my father had not trusted in him.

"Nadav works with Chen. When—" I stopped. It was not his business. I glanced at the man standing beside Lavi. "Perhaps you should introduce your friend."

Lavi's stormy look did not abate, but he turned toward the stranger and pointed to him. "This is Amos, my brother-in-law. We are here to purchase new robes for my upcoming wedding to his sister Ilana."

My eyes widened at this unexpected news. Why was he so upset with me for marrying Nadav if he was betrothed himself? "When is the wedding?"

"In six months. We were betrothed last spring." He took

a sudden interest in the garments that remained on the shelf, fingering the fabric. "Do you have any robes left?"

I shook my head. "Only rugs and some tunics." I swallowed. "I'm happy for you." Was I? The knot in my middle said otherwise.

"Yes, thank you." He glanced at Amos. "Can you weave a robe for me and have it ready on time?"

"Just one?" I gave Amos a questioning look.

"He needs the groom's robe. I have what I need," Amos said.

"If you give me the details, the colors you would like, I can have something ready for you." I withheld the urge to release a sigh. Any hope I'd had of one day marrying Lavi drifted away on what little breeze remained during this part of the day.

"Something colorful with golden threads," Lavi said. "I trust you can design a groom's robe?"

"I think so." I smiled. "Come back in three months, and I should have it completed."

"Thank you, Nessa," Lavi said, suddenly formal in tone and demeanor. "Let's go, Amos." He backed away from me, then seemed to think better of it and pulled a coin pouch from his side. He handed me one hundred denarii. "This is for the down payment. I will give you the rest when I come to get it."

Lavi searched my face for one last moment, and I read regret in his gaze. How well I could share it. But I looked away so he could not read my heart.

As he walked away, I lowered the flap again and lay down on a pallet in the corner of the booth. Memories of growing up with Lavi, of loving him despite all the marriages I'd lived through and the losses I'd endured, spun through my mind, always ending with that long-ago stolen kiss. Somehow his kiss had given me hope that one day I would belong to him. One day I would be free to marry him and perhaps give him children, if God allowed. The truth was, Lavi had been the only man who loved me for who I was. He rarely mentioned my beauty and didn't act like it even mattered, unlike every other man in Sychar.

But obviously he loved me no longer. He would marry Ilana and I would remain Nadav's second choice, the lesser wife, for all my days. Unless God did something to again change my circumstances, I knew I had no choice but to give up on any hope of finding marital love.

26

ell me again why you lied to her?" Amos said, glancing Lavi's way as they took the road from the markets of Sychar to return to Sebaste. "It's not like she needed to think you were marrying Ilana instead of me."

Lavi shrugged, questioning his own purpose in lying. "I wanted to give her reason to forget me." Though he was certain he would never forget her.

"Why should she need help with that? She's a married woman, and from what you told me, this is her fourth husband. If she had wanted to marry you, don't you think she would have asked her father to allow it before now?" Amos pulled the skin of water from his side and drank as they walked.

"Her father is dead, and I'm fairly certain her brother would not allow us to be together." Lavi kicked a stone from the path to the side of the road, then ran a hand over his forehead, disrupting his turban. Frustration with the entire situation rose again.

"We could have chosen any number of weavers in Sebaste to make my groom's robe," Amos said, offering Lavi a drink.

Lavi waved it away. He was thirsty for far more than water, but the wine sat in the small house he used while he worked for Eliav. He would drown his sorrows later.

"You're mighty pensive, my friend," Amos said, as though oblivious to Lavi's pain in seeing Nessa again.

He hadn't realized that just the sight of her would cause his anger to flare. Why couldn't he simply let her go? She belonged to another and would likely never be free to marry him. Even if she was widowed or divorced again, God forbid, Chen would never allow him near her. How long did he really want to wait to find a decent wife?

"Lavi?" Amos touched his arm. "We did what we set out to do. Why are you so upset? And you still haven't satisfied me as to why you thought you had to lie to her."

Lavi walked faster, and Amos hurried to catch up. "Come on, Lavi. Talk to me."

Lavi stopped abruptly and faced his friend. "I love her, all right? I have loved her since we were young and lived in the same household. I thought when the time came, her father would agree to a match, but I was never good enough for him. I had no money, my parents were dead, and my uncle, her father, didn't want to support both me and his daughter for the rest of our lives. I would have proved him wrong. But he didn't believe me." Never mind that he had stolen his uncle's tools just to spite him. And taken some of Nessa's coins. But that was long ago. He had changed since then, but nobody believed him.

"Remind me again why my best friend insisted that his cousin make my robe? This is a journey I could ill afford to make. I'm missing a whole day's work." Amos's words held confusion more than anger.

"I wanted to see her again. I wanted to see her to put her out of my mind once and for all. Now she will assume that I'll no longer wait for her and I'll eventually find someone else. Perhaps Ilana has a cousin?" He laughed, but it held no mirth.

"None that are not already married. You've waited a long time, my friend. Too much longer and you will be too old to have sons." Amos slapped Lavi on the back, and Lavi knew he was attempting to draw him out, to lighten his mood.

"I'm not so old!" He smiled. "I have been pensive, though, haven't I?"

"That's what I've been telling you. Come now, when we return to Sebaste, we'll gather our friends and meet at one of the drinking establishments and forget about women for a while. You need to focus on something else." Amos led them down the road again. "Or perhaps I will ask Ilana to invite her virgin friends to her home so that you can meet them."

"That's not the way we do things and you know it." Lavi frowned.

"Without a father or your uncle, you don't have a normal way to do things," Amos reminded him.

"Well, I would still have to ask her father. And right now, no one compares to Nessa." He kicked another stone, sending it farther than the last.

"She is beautiful, I'll give you that." Amos placed an arm about Lavi's shoulders. "But beauty is fleeting. You will find someone else who is worthy. In fact, why don't I ask Ilana who among her friends might still be available. She knows nearly everyone in town. She would enjoy matching you with someone."

Lavi shook his head. "Maybe someday, but not now."

"Why not?"

"I'm not ready." A breeze lifted the hairs on his forehead as they followed the road through the hill country, where trees rose up on all sides. They had hours to go until they reached Sebaste, and Lavi had no desire to continue this conversation. "Can we talk about something else?"

Amos lifted his hands in surrender. "Fair enough. But you owe me a drink for dragging me so far from home."

"I can manage that," Lavi said, nodding. He was fortunate that Amos did not ask for more than that with the loss of a day's work. What had possessed him to think that Nessa had to make this robe?

The thoughts plagued him the rest of the way, while Amos talked about Ilana and the rooms he was building for her in his father's house. Lavi managed the appropriate nod or exclamation now and then, though he was barely listening. At least Amos was happy.

Why had he thought lying to Nessa was a good thing? The look in her eyes . . . Was it sorrow he had witnessed? Or relief? She'd been guarded, no doubt because of what he'd said and because Amos was with him.

Did her new husband treat her well? But how could he if she was a second wife? He could not be a man who followed the Torah if he would take more than one woman, though some of the patriarchs had done so.

And who was he to judge? He was a thief, though a repentant one.

Maybe God continually kept Nessa from him because of his past. If only he could sneak into Sychar and steal her away. Her husband would divorce her for unfaithfulness and they could finally live in peace. Unless, of course, the rabbis pursued carrying out the law and stoned them to death.

Lavi shook the wayward thoughts aside. It did no good to think such things. Nessa was lost to him, and he needed to accept that fact.

❖ ❖ ❖

"Who did you say ordered you to make a robe for a groom? Do we know these people?" Raziela stood, hands on her hips, watching me sort through the colored wool threads to develop a pattern for the robe for Lavi.

I looked up to briefly meet her gaze. "They were from Sebaste. Apparently the one man had purchased my wares in the past, and he wanted me to make him this special robe as well."

I dared not tell her that I knew Lavi or there would be questions I did not wish to answer. Chen need never know that Lavi visited Sychar now and then. He might hold him accountable for the loss of our father's tools all those years ago. If he could prove such a thing now.

Why hadn't Lavi ever paid my father back? If he had come to him contrite and with full reimbursement for what he'd taken, perhaps Abba would have relented and allowed us to marry. Was he so poor that he did not have the funds? But then how could he afford such a robe?

"He gave you six months?" Raziela asked, though she already knew the answer.

"He will be back in three to get it. Apparently he wants to be sure it's ready on time. The wedding is six months away." I pulled the blue threads apart from the others, then found the gold. I would weave the two colors next to each other to complement the greens and reds and the strand of black in between.

"Humph." Raziela started to walk away. "He better pay the full price for needing such a work so quickly."

"He will. He's already given a down payment."

Raziela whirled around and held out her hand. "Where is it? Why did you withhold it from me?"

"I gave it to Nadav." I forced myself to smile rather than groan. What I wouldn't give for a mother-in-law who was easy to get along with. In the more than six months of my marriage, Raziela had grown more controlling or took Ariel's side if we ever had a disagreement.

"You should have given it to me. He doesn't handle the sales of goods." She frowned. "Next time, be sure to give me the earnings."

I nodded. "I will," I said, silently praying she would leave me in peace to weave.

At that moment, Ariel's youngest sons raced through the tent, toppling one of the low tables before hurrying outside.

Raziela yelled after them, and again I silently thanked Adonai for small favors.

I returned to my work, my mind swirling with images of Lavi looking at me. If he was so happy to be marrying Ilana—Was that her name?—then why give me the feeling that he still cared for me?

Guilt filled me at the memories. I must not think of Lavi's marriage every time I worked on his robe. I threaded the loom, telling myself that this was for the best, and at the same time declaring myself a liar of the worst kind, for I was lying to myself.

◆ ◆ ◆

I worked the loom in the following months, hurrying to complete Lavi's robe amid squabbles and interruptions. Was Nadav's family trying to keep me from completing the project and earning the rest of the money for the household?

I was bent over the loom, working quickly, double- and triple-checking to make sure I had followed the pattern of colors I'd originally envisioned, when voices came from the inner rooms in the direction of Nadav's sleeping quarters. My heartbeat quickened.

The sun had nearly set, and most of the house had settled into their rooms, but my sense of urgency kept me working by lamplight. Was I being too noisy?

I stopped the work and tilted my head to better hear, but a moment later, no sound could have drowned out the words.

"How can you keep her around when you know she is nothing but trouble to our peaceful household!" Ariel's anger permeated the thin tent partitions.

"I keep her because I choose to," Nadav said, raising his voice to match hers. "Stop questioning me every time you spend time with me."

"I wouldn't have to question you if you avoided her bed. You spend more time with that *woman* than you do the mother of your sons!"

"You best know your place, wife. I do not take orders from you."

Had I ever heard Nadav's voice grow so stern?

"Well, perhaps you should! You have become worthless to me since she entered this home."

The sound of a loud slap met my ear, and I leaned back on the seat, my heart beating double time. Had Nadav hit Ariel? Or had she slapped him?

A louder, resounding smack came through the walls, followed by a shriek from Ariel. "How dare you! My father will hear about this!"

"Your father will hear that his daughter disrespected her husband. He will say nothing against me." Nadav's words held an undertone of venom. Had I come between them to cause such anger?

Stomping feet on the rugs covering the dirt floor told me Nadav was coming in my direction. Sudden fear of him nearly choked me.

In the distance, Ariel's weeping was impossible to ignore. This was not good. When Nadav left on the morrow to work with Chen, Ariel would surely take her frustrations out on me. Couldn't he see that he should do more to appease her?

Nadav stopped in the large gathering room and turned to see me sitting at the loom, the glow of one lamp illuminating my work. He stepped closer. "You're almost finished?" He sounded kind and genuinely interested. How could he change so quickly?

I nodded, swallowing a lump in my throat. "Yes. I have to complete it by the day after next Shabbat, so I'm hurrying to finish."

He regarded me, then looked at the cloth on the loom. "You do fine work," he said, running a hand through his hair. "But why not get some rest and finish in the morning?"

Was he commanding me? I couldn't tell by his hooded expression. "If that is what you wish, I will stop for tonight."

He offered a slight smile, his eyes brightening. I could not bring myself to mention the fight I'd just overheard, nor did I want to bring his wrath upon me. Was I truly safe here? Should I tell Chen what I'd witnessed? But what could he possibly do?

I stood, took the lamp, and moved toward the path to the sleeping rooms, where he still waited. "Come to my room," he said, louder than I wished. Did he want Ariel to overhear to spite her?

I nodded. "Yes, my lord." I moved toward his large quarters, my stomach twisting in knots.

He guided me inside with a hand to the small of my back, then closed the curtain, took the lamp from my hand, and placed it on a low table. "Come, my love," he whispered against my ear. "You are always so obedient and good. Share in my love for you."

He kissed me and pulled me roughly onto his bed, his actions urgent and far less enjoyable than they had ever been in our nine months of marriage. Was he taking his anger out on me instead of the wife he had just fought with? Was I to be an outlet for his near rage? I felt the heat of passion and anger pulsing through every part of his being, despite the tender words he whispered to me.

When he was done with me, he did not roll to his side and sleep. "Go to your room now," he commanded, as though I were nothing more than a servant or a concubine.

I quickly dressed and hurried from his room, forgetting the lamp in my haste. Stumbling in the dark to my smaller quarters, I heard Ariel still weeping. My face heated in shame that I was not only the cause but the weapon Nadav used against his first wife.

Humiliated, I fell onto my mat, buried my head in the pillows, and silently shared Ariel's tears.

27

I finished the robe within the week, moving around the women in the household and speaking only when spoken to. I could not escape the hurt and anger evident in Ariel's gaze, and I could not look at Raziela without feeling guilt for causing this turmoil. Ariel's sons refused to speak to me, whereas before they had begun to warm to my kind words and smiles. But Ariel had turned them against me.

I could not move fast enough the day I took the robe to market to meet Lavi. What I wouldn't give to run off with him to Sebaste and never return. But he had Ilana now, and I refused to be the cause of any more marital strife.

I slid behind the family's booth shortly after dawn. Searching the market, I hoped I did not run into Gali again or one of my sisters. Relieved to see only the other merchants, I sighed. Some glanced my way, but few waved or spoke to me. Had word spread that I had caused division in Nadav's household? Had Ariel gone to her father as she'd threatened to do and told him what Nadav had done?

I arranged and rearranged the garments Ariel and I had made in the previous months until I thought I would go mad waiting for Lavi.

"You look distracted."

211

I lifted my head, dread filling me at the sound of Yaffa's voice. This was not a good day to see her. She could not know about Lavi.

Yaffa picked up one of the rugs and studied it. "How are you?" She met my gaze.

A shiver worked down my spine. "I'm as well as can be expected, I suppose." I couldn't lie to this sister.

Yaffa leaned on the shelf between us. "What do you mean? Are you not happy in your new home?"

"It's hardly new. I've been with Nadav for nine months now. Though it feels like more." I looked beyond Yaffa toward the street. No sign of Lavi. Good. I let out a breath.

"Are you happy there, Ness?" Yaffa reached for my arm and touched me as though to comfort. "Tell me what's going on."

I looked about again. "I can't talk here. There are too many who might overhear." I really needed Yaffa to come back another time. "I'm waiting for a customer."

Yaffa raised a brow. "Indeed."

"Yes."

"Who?" Yaffa looked toward the other market booths, then turned back to face me.

"Two men from Sebaste. One ordered a groom's robe and asked me to make it. He is supposed to come pick it up." My cheeks burned, and I was unable to hide the embarrassment of my wayward feelings.

"Sebaste? Why would they travel here? Are there no weavers in Sebaste—such a large city?" Yaffa gave me a skeptical look. "What are you not telling me, Ness?"

"I'm telling you the truth." I smiled, willing my emotions to obey me, though I had never been good at hiding the truth from her.

"Hmm . . . not all of it, though."

Male voices drifted to us, and I cringed, fearing Lavi would appear at that moment. But when I craned my neck to see beyond the people milling about the market, there was no sign of him. Perhaps he would recognize Yaffa and stay away until she left. I could only hope that he would use such judgment.

"Things are not great at home," I confided, wanting to tell Yaffa something, just not everything.

Yaffa moved to join me in the booth. "I'm not leaving until you tell me."

I sighed. If Lavi showed up now, Yaffa would see him, but I could not control what would be. I glanced at her, then focused again on the goods that I moved and rearranged.

"Nadav . . ." I turned and leaned close to Yaffa's ear. "He hit Ariel about a week ago. But in his defense, she hit him first."

"What?" Yaffa's eyes went wide. "Has he hurt you too? Does Chen know of this?"

"No! And you will not tell him. Nadav . . . he has never hit me, but . . ." I looked at my feet, unable to finish.

"But what?" Yaffa's tone softened, and she placed a hand on my shoulder. "Tell me, Ness. Please."

"He seemed to take out his anger against Ariel on me right after he hurt her. He . . . he was not gentle as before." Shame filled me with the telling. With so many failed marriages, I could not help but wonder if I deserved such treatment.

"He should not treat you with such disrespect," Yaffa hissed. "Chen should know."

"What can he do? Tell Nadav to stop? It would ruin their working relationship." I had considered running to Chen the next day but thought better of it. "Things are better left as they are."

"And if he gets worse? What if he hurts you and Ariel again, and the children? Angry men can do awful things, Nessa." Yaffa cupped my chin and looked into my eyes. "You can seek a divorce from him."

"Only men can seek a divorce. The rabbis would never grant it." That was the truth, wasn't it?

"There might be an exception. Especially if you can prove he is hurting his family. Surely something can be done." Yaffa pulled me close for a moment, then held me at arm's length. "Let me ask Yaron. He will know if it's possible."

"No! I can't. What would such a thing accomplish, Yaffa? I would end up under Chen's roof again with Malka, and he would not be happy about it. Who would want me after four husbands? No." My voice weakened with the second protest. "No."

Yaffa held my shoulders. "If I find out he continues to hurt you—and I will ask again—I will not keep silent, Ness. We love you. We will not let men, no matter who they are, hurt you."

At that moment, a shadow blocked the light coming into the booth. "Am I interrupting?" Lavi's voice nearly made my heart stop.

I whirled around. "Lavi." I looked for his friend. "Where is Amos?"

"He couldn't come this time." Lavi glanced at Yaffa, his eyes lighting in recognition. "Yaffa. Shalom."

"Shalom, Lavi." Yaffa looked from Lavi to me. "What's going on here?"

"I came for the robe I asked Nessa to weave for me. I'm getting married in three months." He smiled at Yaffa. "Say hello to Chen and Yaron for me, will you?" He faced me. "Do you have the robe?"

My heartbeat would not slow as I pulled the robe from behind the curtain and spread it before him.

"Ahh, yes. It's perfect."

"Do you wish to try it on?"

Lavi shook his head. "I'm sure it will fit." He took the robe, glanced at Yaffa, and handed me a purse with the rest of the coins for its purchase. "Thank you."

"You're welcome. Shalom, shalom, Lavi," I said as he turned to leave.

"Shalom, shalom to you too, Nessa. Yaffa. It was good to see you both again." He walked away at a brisk pace.

"How long have you been in love with him?" Yaffa asked, watching him leave, then searching my flaming face.

"I'm not in love with him. He's getting married."

"Uh-huh. That doesn't change your feelings, though, does it?" Yaffa stood, arms crossed over her chest. "I should reprimand you, dear sister, but nothing I say will change anything. You've always wanted to marry him."

I nodded, fingering the tunics Ariel had made. "Abba would never allow it, and neither will Chen. Life could have been so very different."

Yaffa touched my arm once more. "I'm sorry it wasn't, dear sister. You should not have had to suffer so much. But put Lavi out of your mind if you ever want to be happy in the life you've been given. We often have to make the best of things, even if we cannot have what we want the most."

"Life is not fair or good," I said, tasting bitterness.

"No one ever said it would be." Yaffa moved to leave the booth. "I will come again and we can talk more. In the meantime, try to find a way to be at peace with what you have, Ness."

I did not nod or reply. I simply watched Yaffa walk away, knowing that I could never agree with what she'd said. But I also knew I could not change anything, so perhaps she was right. There must be a way to find peace.

❖ ❖ ❖

THREE YEARS LATER

I slipped from the tent, grabbed the water jug, and headed to Jacob's well before the sun spread its light over the city. I'd taken to rising before dawn as I had done in years past, and now I scurried through the city streets before the other women could meet me at the well. Except for Gali, who had made it her habit to join me for the past two years.

I tucked my headscarf tighter about me, concealing my face from the guards, who thankfully ignored the women. Rome would not be pleased if the guards attacked women on their way to and from the well, but their restraint likely had something to do with the men of the town keeping them satisfied with extra food and drink. Especially drink.

I lifted my head once I was a good distance from the gate, catching the gray light of predawn. Jacob's well soon came into view, with Gali waiting, sitting on the grassy knoll nearby.

I quickened my pace, set my jar in the dirt, and embraced my friend. How glad I was that we had renewed our friendship in recent years.

"How is it that I miss you when only a day has passed since we last met?" I laughed as I released my hold.

"I feel the same. Shalom to you, dear Nessa." Gali lifted her jar and lowered it into the well. "I would ask if things have improved since yesterday, but I can tell by the look in your eyes that they have not."

"I don't expect they ever will. Ariel grows more bitter by the day. Raziela snaps at me, and I have heard Nadav and Ariel or Nadav and Raziela arguing nearly every night during the past six months. I know I'm the reason they fight, but I don't know what to do." I took my turn filling my jug after Gali lifted hers and set it in the dirt.

"Do you think they'll prevail upon Nadav? Will he put you out?" Gali's brows knit in concern. "It seems to me that things have been miserable ever since you married him. I know it would be impossible to share a man, but shouldn't they be used to you by now?"

"I doubt Rachel and Leah ever really got along. Maybe later in life after Rachel had Joseph? But we can only guess." I often thought of the patriarch's wives and wondered how they put up with sharing Jacob not only with each other but their maids as well. "I mean, God created one man and one woman to marry. He didn't intend for us to share a mate. It only causes strife."

Gali placed a hand on my shoulder. "I still think you should talk to your brother about this. Living like you do sounds unbearable."

"It is. Why else do you think I get up before the household does to meet you? This is the only good part of my day." I released a sigh. "Gali, why is God allowing this? I try to pray, but I feel as though my whole life He has been punishing me, and I don't know why." Surely my secret love for Lavi could not be the reason. By now he probably had several children with Ilana. I hadn't seen him again since that day in the market, and my hopes of him had faded long ago.

Gali sighed, glancing heavenward. "I don't understand the Creator any more than you do, Ness. Why would He punish you and not everyone else? Your father is the one who chose your husbands."

I nodded, seeing Abba in my mind's eye. How I missed him! "He thought he was doing what was best for me," I said. I would always feel the need to defend him, despite everything.

We passed the checkpoint at the gate and came to the fork in the street where we parted ways. "Tomorrow at the same time?" Gali asked, as she always did.

"Yes. If one day I don't show up, you'll know something has happened to stop me. Otherwise, I will be there."

I turned in the direction of the fields outside the city proper where Nadav's tent stood. Perhaps a visit to my mother would be a good thing if I could manage it. I needed the counsel of one far wiser than me, and I was not going to get it in the home of my husband.

28

essa, my love, what are you doing here at this time of day?" Ima greeted me with a kiss to each cheek and welcomed me into the cool of the house.

"I needed to talk with you, Ima." I glanced beyond her into the sitting room, relieved to find that Malka and her sons were not in sight. I looked at Ima. "Where are the others?"

"As Providence would have it, Malka took the children to see her mother today. So come. We are free to speak openly." She poured me a cup of water and handed it to me, then led me to sit among the cushions of her home. "Now tell me. Something troubles you. What is it?"

I looked at the cup I held in both hands, took a long drink, and set it aside. Lifting my head, I sighed. "I don't know what to do or if anything can be done."

"Done about . . . ?"

"Nadav. He fights with Ariel and his mother nearly every day. While they are hidden behind one of the curtains, their voices still carry with ease. They fight about me. Ariel has turned her sons against me, and no one, not even Nadav, has a kind word to say to me. I try so hard, Ima. I don't say much. I do the work I'm supposed to do, and I give Ariel more time with Nadav than she should have, giving up my chances of ever conceiving a child." Heat filled my face at the last admission.

"He does not treat you as his wife, my daughter?" Ima folded her arms over her chest and narrowed her gaze. "You must speak to Chen of this."

"I can't! I would die of embarrassment. Besides, what could he do? I'm a second wife with little to offer Nadav. I should never have married him." I knew that now, but how could a wife possibly divorce a husband? It wasn't done.

"Then I will speak to Chen. Let him speak to Nadav. This must stop, Nessa. How long has it gone on?"

"Three years."

"Three years?"

"Well, it's gotten worse in the last six months, but life has been hard ever since Ariel . . . Never mind." I dared not speak of the day Nadav had hurt her. I couldn't.

"What did Ariel do?" Ima leaned closer, hands on her knees as if she were ready to jump up and rush to Chen that very moment.

I looked away. "I don't like to speak of it."

"Well, you will tell me. Now."

I hesitated, studying my feet. The whole thing made me continually sad, but I hadn't wanted to burden my brother or mother. Until now. Maybe it was time.

I drew in a deep breath and faced my ima. "Ariel fought with Nadav and slapped him. He hit her back. Things have not been the same since."

A gasp escaped Ima's lips. "Has he hurt you too, my daughter?" Her voice softened, and she came to kneel at my side and placed a hand on my knee. "Tell me."

Tears threatened. "Not in that way. But he is not . . . always kind."

Ima stood and pulled me to my feet. "We are going to tell Chen."

"But Nadav is with him."

Ima stopped. "That doesn't matter. He needs to be confronted. But first we will pull your brother aside and tell him in private."

My heart pounded at the very thought, but I allowed Ima to lead me outside to the shop at the back of the property.

Ima bid me stay some distance away, near the trees, while she approached. The breeze lifted my veil and pulled stray strands of hair from beneath it. I tucked them back in, willing my nerves to cease their trembling.

Moments passed until at last Chen and Ima emerged from the building and walked toward me. Chen's brows lifted at the sight of me. He glanced at Ima.

"What's going on, Nessa? Ima said there was something of import to tell me." Chen's look held a mixture of concern and . . . was that anger? No doubt he did not wish to hear that I was having trouble in another marriage.

"I . . ." I looked toward the shop, praying Nadav would not follow Chen.

"I don't have all day for you to tell me, Nessa. What's wrong?" He was definitely angry, and I suddenly did not want to tell him.

"Be kind, Chen. I brought her here," Ima said. "Nadav is not treating her as he should as his wife. His home is one of turmoil, and Nessa has not felt welcome there in three years. I think it's about time you knew and spoke to Nadav."

Chen reared back as if struck. "And you're just now telling me this? Three years, Ness? What has he done that's so bad? He acts as though all is well."

"It's not. He fights with his mother and Ariel daily, and I'm not welcome. I can hear their words. The women want me to go."

"The women don't decide such things," Chen said, teeth clenched.

"The women have far more influence than you know, brother. It's happened to me before, but this is worse." I hugged my arms to my chest, willing the shaking to stop.

Chen's expression softened slightly. "Has he hurt you? Fought with you?"

I nodded. "Some."

He blew out a tightly held breath. "What am I supposed to do?" he hissed. "You've had four husbands, Nessa. If this one divorces you, who will have you then?"

I shrugged shoulders that had grown too thin. I had lost weight in the past few years, my appetite little in such a household. Tears filled my eyes, and I could not speak.

He sighed again and pulled me into his arms. "There, there. Don't cry." He held me a moment, then released me. "I don't know what I can do or say. He is your husband. If he's not fulfilling his role as husband to you, perhaps we can go to the rabbi to show he has broken faith with you. Is that what is happening?"

Face flaming, I slowly nodded. "Ariel has him most of the time. I don't argue the point, for it would do no good."

"He is keeping you from conceiving children?"

Again I nodded, unable to say the words.

Chen spit on the ground. "I've heard enough. Go home and do whatever you're supposed to do. I will speak to Nadav."

Ima's arm came around me, and we hurried back toward the house. She quickly sent me on my way back to Nadav's tents. What would I do if he returned angry that Chen had spoken to him? Fear slithered up my spine, and I realized I should have remained silent. I should have simply lived with what was. And now I had ruined everything.

❖ ❖ ❖

I stayed in the garden behind the house, weeding and fussing over the plants. There was peace here, for Ariel and Raziela came only to pick food for the meals. I did so as well, but I lingered and cared for the plants—anything to stay out of the tents.

Weaving used to give me such respite, but I found Ariel claiming my favorite task more often than she used to, leaving little for me except cooking and washing the clothes. Tending the garden was my joy now, for it felt as though God was with me here.

I watched the sun slip behind an array of clouds, then skirt its way behind Mt. Gerizim. Nadav would be home any moment, and I would have to face him, like it or not. I straightened, brushed the dirt from my hands, made my way to the cistern, and dipped a bucket into the water to wash the remaining rich, dark soil from my fingers.

I heard voices within the tent, along with squeals of delight from Moti and Haim, who always greeted Nadav with joy. The prick of longing for a son of my own rushed in on me all of a sudden. The two I had lost would be old enough to help their father had they lived. Why had God denied me such pleasure?

The perpetual sadness I battled daily threatened to crush me again, an unwanted weight on my chest. I moved with sluggish steps into the tent and attempted to walk past Nadav toward the cooking area. His words halted me midstep.

"Nessa. Come here."

There would be no thwarting such a command. I slowly faced him but did not close the gap between us.

"Your brother spoke to me today." He stepped toward me, his scowl piercing, sending prickles of fear down my spine. "But you already know that, don't you?"

"What's this?" Ariel hurried closer, and Raziela entered from the cooking area.

"What's going on?" Raziela asked, holding a wooden spoon.

"Nessa has caused me much embarrassment with her brother today." He glared at me. "I assured him that you were mistaken, but somehow he did not seem to believe me. Explain to me, wife, why he thought such things?"

I found it hard to swallow, the words caught in my throat. I cleared it, then narrowed my eyes at him, facing down his scowl. "I went to see my mother today."

"And told her tales about our family?" He stepped nearer, and I wrapped my arms about me and moved back a pace.

"I only answered her questions." I could not tell him all that I'd said. Let him hurt me. I absolutely would not tell him everything.

"Well, those questions have caused a rift between your brother and me, and I no longer work with him. He seems to think that I do not treat you as a wife deserves. Is that what you told him?"

I lifted my chin, refusing to cry. Had his dark eyes ever seemed so dead? A shiver passed through me, but I stood my ground. I would not argue with him.

"Answer me!"

"I told him the truth," I said. I stiffened, waiting for a blow that did not come.

"You lie." I expected him to shout at me as he'd so often done with Ariel and his mother, but his voice barely broke a whisper. "And you have cost me more than it's worth to give you the divorce you seem to want so much." He whirled about and marched to his room, causing the three of us to stand where we were, unsure what to do next. Should we prepare the meal? Wait for him? What was he doing?

At last, after the boys grew fidgety, Nadav emerged with a small bag and a parchment. He handed both to me. "Here are the coins, the cost of this." He placed a familiar writ of divorce in my palm. "Go at once. Gather your things and return to your brother's house. You seem happiest there anyway."

I stared at the items in my hand, the very things Tamir had sent home to me four years ago. The price of my bondage and my freedom. For to be divorced put me in a kind of bondage to my brother but set me free from this man and his family, who had caused me to feel so unworthy for so long.

I curled my fingers around both items and walked past him and his wife and mother and sons without a word, entered the room assigned to me, gathered the few things I called my own, and left the tent. The sun seemed as anxious to make its descent as I was to return to Ima and Chen.

Tears blurred my vision as I picked my way along the familiar path, wondering how angry Chen would be now that he had also lost his business partner. But my thirst for something better, something lasting, caused me to half run, half stumble away from the last four years of my life.

Please, Adonai, let me stay with Chen and not have to marry again. I can't bear another husband or another rejection. Never mind that Malka would not make life easy. Malka was someone I could deal with as long as Ima was living. Pray God that she lived a very long time yet.

29

everal months later I sat in my usual place at the loom, trying to earn my keep under Chen's roof. I didn't want to become a burden to him, and with every passing day, I knew he grew anxious, wanting to find me a new home. Having an unmarried sister living under his roof did not make his life easy or acceptable among the people of Sychar.

"Nessa, you have a visitor," Ima said.

I stopped the loom at her call and walked to the door. "Hila?" What was Amichai's daughter-in-law doing here? Since my fourth failed marriage, most of the women of Sychar other than Gali wanted little to do with me. "Come in. Shalom," I said, finding my voice.

"Shalom," Hila said, stepping out of the breeze of the winter day. She undid her wrap and handed it to Ima. "Thank you for seeing me."

"Come, sit down," I offered, motioning toward the sitting room, which seemed so small in comparison to Amichai's home.

"I will bring refreshments," Ima said, disappearing into the preparation area.

"What brings you to see me?" I sat opposite Hila, giving her a curious look. "I hope all is well with you."

Hila nodded. "Everything is fine. The children are mostly grown now, all off helping their fathers, though the girls help

Rina and me. Ezra and Arieh are working at Amichai's pottery business and things are going well."

"That's good to hear." Of all my husbands, old or not, Amichai had been the best. I wished he had lived. Would life have been different? Would I have had children and lived a comfortable life? I would never know.

"I came to see how you're doing and to request a bridal robe for Amira. She's already old enough to wed, if you can imagine that!" Hila folded her hands in her lap, twisting the belt as though nervous about something.

I touched my cheeks in surprise. "So soon! Time has passed quickly." Amira had to be the age I was when I first wed. But at twenty-five, I was long past those days of my virginity. "When do you need it?"

"The wedding will not be for nearly a year as they were just betrothed, but we would like it completed a month before they marry, if you can manage that."

"I can. I would be happy to make it. Of course, you must tell me the colors and design you would like." Perhaps I could become the town weaver. Maybe more people would come to me for their bridal attire. Surely such income would help keep Chen happy.

"Yes, I will bring Rina and Amira next time and we can discuss it. They weren't sure you would want the work, so I offered to come to ask." Hila smiled, and I was carried back to a time when life was good and this sister-in-law was kind to me.

"I will be happy to help you." I returned her smile. "I enjoy the work and it helps us all."

"I thought it might." Hila paused and searched my face. "We have heard of your hardships since Amichai's death. If there is ever anything you need, please don't be afraid to ask. We all appreciated the way you treated Amichai despite his age."

A sense of peace filled me. "Thank you. I wish he had lived. Life in his home was good."

Hila smiled again, accepted the sweet treats and warm tea from Ima, and continued to fill me in on the life I had missed since I had lost contact with Amichai's family.

"You know," Hila said as she rose to leave, "Amichai has a younger cousin who lived in Sebaste but recently moved to Sychar. His family lives on the outskirts of the city near the pasturelands as they are shepherds, but I've heard that the cousin's son is looking for a wife. He is young, only eighteen, but perhaps you would consider him?" She offered me a compassionate look.

"Eighteen? I'm seven years his senior. Why would he want an older, used woman? Surely there are plenty of young girls to choose from." I couldn't tell Hila that I never wanted to marry again, for I knew that Chen would jump at the chance to send me to another. For Malka's sake.

"Osher is bright and mature for his age, and let's face it, Nessa. You are still as beautiful as you were when you married Amichai. The men in town, according to Arieh and Ezra, often remark on your beauty. You are blessed in that." Hila touched my shoulder. "Think about it."

"Thank you. I will." I led Hila to the door, handed her outer cloak to her, and bid her farewell.

My beauty was talked about in the city? Blessed? No. My beauty was not a blessing, as it had brought me nothing but trouble.

❖ ❖ ❖

One afternoon about a month after Hila's visit, I was working with Ima behind the house, weeding the gardens. "We will need to tend to the fig trees as well," Ima said, tossing a prickly weed into a basket to be burned in the fire. "They'll soon be ripe for picking."

"I will enjoy that task," I said, rubbing the small of my back. "My knees will appreciate not having to sit on them for so long."

Ima laughed. "My daughter, you are far too young to feel aches in your joints. Imagine how I feel!" She tossed me a bright smile, and I returned it.

I bent over another difficult weed with deep roots, chuckling at Ima's comment, when she suddenly cried out. "Oh!" The alarm and pain in her voice jerked me upright.

"Ima? What's wrong?" I hurried to kneel beside her.

"Something bit me." Ima rubbed a spot on her leg just above the ankle.

I looked just in time to see a small snake slither away into the underbrush nearby. I knew from the things my father had taught me that it was a viper.

My heart pounded. "Come, Ima. Let's get you inside."

I slipped my arms beneath hers and helped her to stand, but when she swayed and could put no pressure on her leg, my fear spiked.

"Chen!" I yelled as loud as I could. "Chen!" I faced the shop as I attempted to help Ima move toward the house. "Chen!"

He appeared in the door. "What is it?"

"Come quickly! Ima has been bitten by a viper." I glanced at Ima, whose face had paled, and she seemed to struggle to take a deep breath.

Chen ran toward us, and together we got Ima into her room and laid her on her pallet. Malka appeared at the door to the room.

"Hurry. Boil some water over the fire," I told her. "I'll get some cloths." I looked at Chen. "Stay with her."

"Where was she bit?" Chen asked.

"On her left ankle."

Chen knelt at Ima's side and examined the wound. I left the room and returned with cool cloths, though I knew boiling the water would help to remove any impurities.

"It's swelling and bruising," Chen said, meeting my gaze.

"We need a poultice. Go pick some figs and pomegranate leaves so I can make one."

Chen jumped up as if glad to be free of the room.

I smoothed Ima's hair from her eyes and placed a cool cloth on her head. I watched the rise and fall of her chest and looked into her frightened eyes. "Ima? Can you hear me?"

Ima wet her lips and nodded. "My mouth tastes strange."

I stroked her arm. *Hurry, Chen.* How long did it take to pick figs? I watched her closely, refusing to allow myself to fear. We would draw the venom from her body and all would be well. Then Chen would hunt down and kill the snake.

Please, Adonai. Save my mother.

Chen appeared at the door, his arms full of figs, and I traded places with him. I took the figs from him and hurried to the cooking room. Malka stepped into the room, holding the boiled water pot.

"Help me crush these," I said.

Malka set the water on the table and pulled the bowl and pestle from their place on a shelf. Together we peeled and crushed the figs and mixed them with the pomegranate leaves until a poultice formed. I wrapped the poultice in thin linen and carried it to Ima's room. Malka followed with the water and some wine. We washed the wound and placed the poultice over it, wrapping it around her leg.

"Replace the cool cloths on her head. How is her breathing?" I studied Ima's wan look, noting that she had paled further and her breath seemed labored. I took the wine and lifted her head, trying to coax her to drink some. But she swallowed little before the rest slipped down the side of her mouth to the pillow.

"What kind of viper was it?" Chen asked. "Are you sure that's what bit her?"

"I saw it slither away the moment Ima cried out. Yes, it was a viper. Abba taught me what to look for with them. It was a young one." I sank to the floor as we watched Ima.

A child's cry drew Malka from the room, leaving Chen and me alone.

"She can't die," I whispered.

Chen said nothing for a long moment. "I've never known snakes to enter the garden, have you?"

I shook my head. "I've never come upon one or feared one. Ima had just laughed at me for complaining about kneeling so much when she cried out."

Chen drew a hand down his beard, his expression weary. Tears threatened, and I knew if he broke down, I would too and never stop. I could not lose one more person.

The sun had begun its trek to the west when Ima's body began to shake. I felt her skin. "She's feverish." I rushed to check the poultice, but it had done no good. The bite area had swollen more and the figs had not pulled the venom out.

"Perhaps I need to replace it with another." I looked at Chen, who shrugged.

"I'll stay. Go and make another," he said. I did not wait to be told twice.

All night we stayed at her side, replacing cool cloths and poultices until weariness blanketed me and I had to force my eyes to stay open. *Please, Ima. Get better.*

Dawn broke through the dark house, waking Malka, who had lain down with her children to sleep, and jerking me from a fitful rest at Ima's side. I looked at her prone form.

"Chen?"

He was bent over her, weeping.

I joined him. There was no longer a rise and fall of her chest, and her skin was deathly cold to the touch.

"She's gone, Ness." The words were choked.

A bitter cry burst from my throat. I threw myself on Ima's body and wept, waking the children.

Malka stepped into the room, bidding the children to remain in their room. "She's gone?" she asked, coming closer to Chen. I barely heard her above my sobs.

"Yes. Just now." Chen's voice was husky, emotion close to the surface.

"We must prepare her for burial then," Malka said, stoic and void of the emotion Chen and I felt. "You must make a bier, and Nessa and I will prepare her body."

"Give us a moment," Chen said, sounding annoyed. "Go and feed the children and let us mourn."

Malka said nothing, and I felt relief as her footsteps receded. Chen placed a hand on my back, and I slowly rose from clinging to Ima. I turned instead to Chen, and he held me close as I wet his garment with tears.

When at last they were spent, I sat back on my heels. "Why, Chen? Why did God take her?"

He shook his head, wiping moisture from his face and beard. "Death is the end of all men and women, Ness. You know that. Only God knows when that day will come for any of us."

"She still had so much life to live and so much help to give us. We needed her." I heard my plaintive tone and wondered that at twenty-five I still needed my mother. Perhaps because none of my marriages had succeeded. If I'd had a husband to hold me close and love me through my grief, maybe this loss wouldn't seem so harsh.

"We will learn to manage without her," Chen said, slowly rising and pulling me to my feet. "Though she did help keep this household peaceful." He gave me a concerned look. "I don't know how well Malka will get along with you without Ima to help."

"Malka has never liked me much," I confided, keeping my voice low. "But I will do all I can to be at peace with her, Chen. I won't be a burden to you."

A fear I'd carried since I'd returned to this house surfaced.

What if Chen decided to send me away now that Ima was not here to intercede for me? Would he marry me off to the highest bidder as Abba had done, or just pick anyone willing to take me? Or would he let me stay?

Would Malka let me stay was the more realistic question.

30

*T*he week after sitting shiva with my brother and sisters to mourn Ima's sudden passing, I carried the water jug through Sychar's deserted streets to meet Gali at the usual early hour. My feet felt as heavy as the beams that held up a roof, every step accompanied by grief.

How could Ima be gone so quickly? One moment we were laughing and pulling weeds, and the next she was dying on her mat. It made no sense. Nothing in my life made sense, not since I was a young child and Lavi came to live with us. At the time I hadn't understood his grief of losing both parents, and he rarely showed it when he played with me.

How well I understood it now. I scuffed the stones of the street, noting the pinks of dawn peeking over the houses and buildings of the city. I quickened my pace, not wanting to miss Gali, who would surely be waiting by now. I didn't see the dung in the path until my foot landed on it, nearly making me lose my balance.

I cursed under my breath and rubbed my sandal on the stones as I walked. The stench wafted to me and I hurried along, angry now. How appropriate. Could anything else go wrong today? And yet the day had only begun. My first day after shiva. Why would I think life would return to normal?

I bit my quivering lip as I passed the guard standing half asleep at the gate and ran to the well across the plain.

"There you are," Gali said, rising from her usual place on the grassy knoll. "Is everything all right?"

I set my jar in the dirt, removed my sandal, and rubbed it in the grass. "I stepped in donkey's dung that someone left in the street."

"Here, wash it off." Gali lifted her filled jar and poured some water into my open palms. I cleaned the offensive sandal and then washed my hands.

"Thank you." A deep sigh escaped me. I lowered my jar and leaned against the well as it filled.

"How are you?" Gali asked after we had both finished our task. We stood for a moment before lifting the jars to return to the city. "I'm sorry about your mother. But you already know that."

I sat on the side of the well, my jar nestled between my legs. "I am numb, Gali. I'm twenty-five years old, and I feel as though I've lived a hundred lifetimes. I don't know what life will be like now with Ima gone. Malka has never really wanted me around, and even during shiva, within my sisters' hearing, she argued with Chen about me. It is impossible not to hear some of the words when they're spoken loudly in a small house. I wanted to run to the hills and never return, but I couldn't leave." I looked into Gali's dark eyes. "What am I going to do if Chen puts me out?"

"He wouldn't do that," Gali assured me. "Not without a husband to send you to. But no doubt Malka will convince him to find such a husband."

"I am weary of men."

"I don't blame you, Ness. Except for Amichai—and he was too old—you haven't been blessed with a good one yet." Gali touched my shoulder and squeezed. "What about that young man Hila mentioned to you before your mother died? The shepherd."

"Osher?"

Gali shrugged. "I guess so. I don't remember his name."

"Hila never mentioned him again, though she hasn't come to discuss the bridal robe more than once. And she had Amira and Rina with her, so the subject didn't come up." I glanced at the lightening sky, knowing that Malka would soon be up and I would be expected to have the water there to help prepare the morning meal. "I don't know, Gali. I've never met him and he's barely a man."

We picked up our jugs and began walking. "Eighteen is considered a man," Gali said.

"When the rabbis read the law in synagogue, men weren't numbered until they were twenty. So isn't he still a boy by those standards?" Why I thought of a synagogue reading in that moment, I wasn't sure, but any excuse to not marry again seemed like a good one.

"Men marry younger than that," Gali said. "I don't think the law meant marriageable age."

"Maybe not." What did it matter? If Chen found out about Osher and Osher wanted me, the matter would be settled without my consent. It had always been that way and always would be.

"Will you consider him if he asks? Not that you have much choice."

We passed the guards and were nearing the street where we parted. I shifted the jar and held Gali's gaze. "I hope he never asks. But I honestly don't know which would be worse—living with Malka or joining a new family again."

"God will give you wisdom." Gali turned to leave. "Tomorrow then?"

I nodded. "Tomorrow."

I headed home, pondering Gali's comment. Adonai had never answered my prayers. Why would I pray for wisdom when I would not be the one to decide? It was Chen who needed wisdom, and I very much doubted whether wisdom would even enter his mind when it came to making a decision about my future. He would simply appease his wife. There was no wisdom in that.

❖ ❖ ❖

I sat at the loom several months later, setting the next color in Amira's bridal robe. The work kept my mind occupied, though the house was far too quiet without Ima's presence. Hila's visits had lessened, but on her last one, she'd mentioned Osher's family again. And the following Shabbat, she had pointed them out after synagogue.

Unfortunately, Malka had heard Hila's comments, and she'd talked endlessly about him ever since. "You really should consider him, Nessa. You could do worse," she said.

"Really?" I retorted. "I think I've experienced my fair share of 'worse,' Malka."

Of course, my words had come back to haunt me the next day when Chen accused me of upsetting his wife.

I took to my room in the evenings far earlier than I normally would have. Anything to avoid spending time with Chen and his family. Never mind that I was his family too. But what good was an unmarried sister? My weaving helped support his family, and I was far better at it than Malka had ever been, but he would never admit that.

"How is it going?" Malka's question caught me off guard. When had she walked into the room? "The robe, I mean." She pointed to the loom and gave me a conciliatory look. "You'll finish soon, won't you?"

"It will take a few more months to weave the fabric. Then we have to fit the robe to Amira and sew it together. Why?" I narrowed my gaze, unable to keep the suspicion from my voice.

"No reason." Malka lifted her chin. "Can't I ask a question in my own home?"

I bit back the retort that lay on the tip of my tongue. This house had been mine long before Malka entered it. And my father's and Chen's. But I dare not say so.

"Of course you can." I focused on the shuttle and threading the weft through the warp.

"Good. Besides, I just wanted to be sure you finish before you move on."

Malka's words should not have surprised me. I was used to her sharp tongue and desire to needle me any chance she could. I had no desire to respond, so I pretended I hadn't heard her.

"Aren't you going to answer me?" Malka stepped closer. "I said—"

"I heard you the first time." I gave her a cool stare.

"You do know that you can't live here forever. Even now Chen is speaking to someone interested in an arrangement. I just thought you should know so you can begin to prepare." She tossed her head and whirled about, walking away before I could answer.

My heart pounded, and I wanted to scream at Malka and tell her that she didn't know what she was talking about. But what if she did? It would not surprise me if Chen spoke to someone without consulting me. At least with Nadav, I'd been given notice.

But Ima had been there when we talked about Nadav, and she was no longer around to protect me. Chen was my protector now, until he found another husband for me. I was at his mercy.

And he was at Malka's mercy, for Malka could drive him to do irrational things. I must talk with him to know whether what his wife said was true or not. This game Malka played could not continue. I had a right to know, and I would find out. I stopped the shuttle, set the weaving aside, and rose, determined to ask him.

I walked resolutely through the back door of the house to the shop. Grass curled around my sandals, tickling my feet, and I kept a watchful eye on anything that might hide in the grasses along the sides of the path. Though Chen had killed the viper, where there was one, there could be another. Funny, when we were children and Lavi lived with us, we never feared such things despite Abba's warnings. We simply played in the fields or picked wildflowers or chased each other.

What was Lavi doing now? Did he have children with Ilana? Would I ever meet them? I placed a hand over my heart to quell the pang such longings always brought. My hopes of marrying him had long been deferred. If he were free now, I would ask Chen to let me marry him. And perhaps now that Ima was gone, he might have agreed. Still, I wouldn't be second wife again to anyone, not even Lavi. Never again.

I brushed the thought aside and straightened as I reached the shop's door. Voices carried to me from inside, and I stopped to listen.

"My cousin's daughter-in-law pointed out your sister to my wife when we were at synagogue a few weeks ago. While I have heard that your sister has fallen on hard times in her past marriages, my younger son, Osher, was captivated by her beauty. I'm surprised that one so lovely has been unable to sustain a marriage. But we are willing to give you thirty pieces of silver for her. I would offer more, but obviously she is not a virgin."

The voice was one I did not recognize, but it set my teeth on edge. Malka was right, and I was too late.

"It is our custom to ask my sister if she agrees," Chen said, surprising me. Hope flared. Why would he say such a thing? Our father had never asked whether I agreed, though he should have. Even the matriarch Rebekah had been asked if she would go with Abraham's servant.

"Of course. I would expect no less," the man said. "I will return for your answer in a week, if that sounds reasonable."

"Yes. Very reasonable," Chen said.

The sound of shuffling feet made me scurry behind the building where I could remain unseen.

"Thank you, Dan. It was good of you to come. Shalom, shalom." Chen's voice drifted a little away, and I poked my head around the building to watch him walk with Dan toward the road leading back toward the city.

When Chen returned to the shop, I watched him coming. Was he happy about the proposal? Should I wait to ask him? But asking him now would be best, before Malka heard the details from him.

I stepped around the corner of the building and met him at the door.

"Nessa! What are you doing here?" He looked at me, and I noted the weariness and lines about his eyes. He stroked his beard as he often did, and I suddenly wanted to lift the burdens he carried.

"Malka told me you were considering another husband for me. I arrived as you were speaking to that man, so I heard what he said to you." I took his hand. "Tell me, brother, what you're thinking, please."

He walked with me into the cool of the shop, and we sat on benches that Chen had obviously set away from his work area to speak with Dan.

I settled my skirts and lifted my gaze to his.

"Dan is cousin to Amichai and has just moved here from Sebaste. He and his sons are shepherds and live on the outskirts of Sychar. His older son is married but his younger son is looking for a wife. When Hila pointed you out to Dan's wife, this young man, Osher, was interested. Of course, he didn't know at the time that you were not a young virgin." He looked away as if embarrassed. "You hold your age well, Ness, and every man in town talks of your beauty."

"I wish they wouldn't," I said, not agreeing with him at all. But I held back from saying more.

"Nevertheless, they do, and it has made it possible for you to continue to remarry. If you had crooked teeth and wrinkled skin, I doubt you would have found anyone to take you into their home after Amichai's death." He offered me a half smile. "Come on, Ness. I'm trying to lighten your mood. This is a good thing."

"Having five husbands is not a good thing, Chen. You can't believe that it is." I twisted my belt and looked at my hands. He was right. My skin still held the glow of youth despite eleven years since my first marriage and life with four husbands.

"Of course I don't. Not in that way. I wish you had married Lavi all those years ago, but Abba wouldn't hear of it. I know he loved you and you him. But he is not asking and Osher is." Chen folded his hands in his lap.

"Lavi is married regardless," I said, feeling the pang in my middle that came with every new marriage and every thought of my lost love.

"Dan will return in a week for our decision."

"I was surprised you offered to ask my opinion. Thank you." I met his gaze, a tear escaping. "I know Malka would like me gone. I hear your fights. It's wearing on you." I leaned close and touched his arm. "If it will make your life easier, my brother, I will marry Osher. I'm only sorry that I'm of so little value that he did not offer a higher bride-price."

Chen released a deep sigh, and I knew I had made him glad. "I would have bargained for more and gotten it if this wasn't—"

"My fifth husband," I finished for him.

He nodded. "Yes."

"I will finish the robe I'm making for Rina's daughter, then they can call for me. Will that work out for you?" I wanted to ask for the full year, but no one thought it was worth waiting so long for one who was not a virgin.

Oh, to be pure again and anticipate a groom who would love only me for all my life! Someone I could equally love. Like

Jacob loved Rachel and she him. But it was not to be, and the sooner I accepted my life, the better for all. Surely *this* time I could please Osher and his family and make Chen's life better in the process. Maybe the longings of my heart would finally be eased and I would find a little happiness living with shepherds, though I had not found it living with Tamir, the first shepherd I had wed.

Chen stood, pulled me to my feet, and kissed my cheek. "Thank you, sister. You have blessed me today."

I leaned close and kissed his cheek in return. "I must get back to work on the robe. And let you get a little work done before the sun sets. We can talk more at evening meal."

I left him, thoughts of what I had just done whirling in my mind. *Please, Adonai, let me like Osher and his family. And let them like me in return. Let this be the last man I have to live with . . . for Chen's sake. And perhaps mine too.*

31

*Y*affa, Adva, and Meital descended on Chen's home when word spread that Osher was expected to come that evening. Amira's wedding had taken place two months earlier, giving me time to weave a new robe of my own. I hadn't expected a true wedding with all that went with it—not after Nadav had simply taken me to his home. Osher's youth and excitement made him convince his father to have a wedding fit for a virgin, with the canopy and blessing and a host of guests. I felt a pang of guilt every time I thought on it. Would the people give me looks of censure? I didn't deserve to be treated so well.

"There," Meital said, placing the flowers in my crown atop the veil, which hid my hair and part of my face from view. "You make a beautiful bride, sister."

I looked in the bronze mirror Yaffa held before me. "I can barely see anything through this veil."

Yaffa laughed. "You're not supposed to. Be thankful you are not so hidden as Leah and Rachel were so as to deceive your husband."

I smiled. I loved the story of Rachel. How well I could relate to her longing for children and the pain of sharing a man. *Not this time.* This time I was determined to please Osher so well that he would never want to let me go, and he was certainly young enough that he should live a long life. And being Amichai's relative helped a little. *Please, God, let him be as kind.*

"I hope he doesn't keep me waiting until midnight," I said, looking about the sitting room I had lived in on and off all my life.

"I've heard he is anxious to get on with this whole thing, so if he is late, it will not be because he wants to be." Adva chuckled. "You do have a gift, Nessa, I'll give you that. Men never look at me the way they do you. I used to be jealous of you, you know."

I looked at her, the sister closest to my age. "I suspected as much, but thank you for admitting it. I would trade beauty for happiness and peace anytime."

All three sisters surrounded me and placed their hands on my shoulders. "May the God of our forefathers bless your union today, Nessa. May Osher love you and be the one to give you children. May you be like Rachel and Leah and fill their household with the laughter of little ones."

"And may your husband always love you," Yaffa added softly.

I swiped a tear from my eye as I turned to look at each sister. I stood and embraced them one by one. "I hope this is the last time," I whispered. "Thank you for blessing me. I only wish that Ima could have been here to see this."

Yaffa held on to me the longest. Moments later, the sounds of other women drifted to us. Gali and the women of Amichai's family—Hila, Rina, Amira, Devora, and Elke—descended on us. I laughed, greeting each one.

"We've come to be your 'virgin' girls," Hila said, smiling. "May Osher make you as happy as you made Amichai."

My heart lifted with the kind words coming from each of these women. And now, except for Gali, they would be family again in an extended sort of way. Perhaps God was finally smiling down on me and life could actually be happy and good.

And if the Creator chose to give me children through this union, I might actually begin to see myself as blessed.

❖ ❖ ❖

Seven days later, the wedding feast came to an end with Osher's parents, Dan and Elisheva, bidding the last lingering guests goodbye. Osher's sister Jaffe returned with her husband Binyamin to their home near his parents in Sebaste, as Binyamin's father had a lucrative pottery business there.

I stood with Osher at the back of the house, looking toward the sheepfolds. How like Tamir's family this one seemed, as both were shepherds. The thought of Tamir stung, so I brushed it aside, refusing to let the memories of past husbands ruin what was just beginning with Osher.

"Are you happy, my love?" Osher placed an arm about my shoulders and drew me close. He had shown me his affectionate side from the moment I entered the bridal tent, unlike the other men I'd known.

I fought the urge to stiffen in his embrace and instead leaned my head on his shoulder. "I am happy, my husband," I said, though I wondered if I could even define what it meant to be truly happy. Had I ever been so?

"Good." He kissed the top of my head. "Would you like to accompany me to the pastures today? My mother and Batel can do without you for one more day." He smiled. "Jaron will laugh at me for bringing you along, but if you can withstand his teasing, we can have an enjoyable afternoon."

"I would like that very much," I said, kissing his cheek. "Thank you. Shall I gather some food for us?"

"Yes," he said. "Meet me at the pens when you have packed us a basket of food and skins of water. If my mother or Batel says anything to you, tell them I requested your presence."

I nodded and hurried toward the cooking room while he left to gather the sheep. Batel, his sister-in-law, seemed nice enough, though we had rarely spoken. And Elisheva seemed pleased that Osher was so happy. How wonderful it would be if I could live in harmony with these two women.

"Where are you going?" Batel asked, entering the room with her youngest son on her hip. "Are you packing a midday meal for Osher? He doesn't need two skins of water."

I smiled at the child, who buried his sleepy head against Batel's shoulder. "Osher invited me to join him today. The food and water are for both of us."

"I see." She turned away from me and found some raisins for her son.

I glanced at her back, but when it appeared she would say nothing more, I hurried with the basket and waterskins to the sheepfold. At Osher's wide smile, my heart lightened. I would try to understand Batel another day. Today felt like one more day of celebration, and I intended to enjoy it.

"There you are." Osher called the sheep to follow him, and I hurried to walk beside him.

"I hope I packed enough." I glanced at him. "I'm still learning your favorite things."

He laughed, a delightful sound, and I felt relief pour through me. "I like everything, and anything you touch will be wonderful."

I blushed at the compliment. Had anyone other than Amichai told me such things? "Thank you."

He took one of the skins and tied it to his belt, then took the basket from me so I could do the same. "We'll be near Jaron with the goats, but never fear. He packs his own food. Batel is always too busy with their sons." He looked at me then with an ardent gaze. "Perhaps one day soon you will be doing the same and I will be left to fend for myself."

Again, heat rushed to my cheeks, and I looked slightly away. "I hope so," I whispered. "But I will always care for your needs, Osher."

He took my hand and squeezed it, glancing back to see that the sheep still followed. "And I yours, my love."

Contentment settled through me. Soon we came to a lush field with trees to shade us as the sheep grazed nearby. I settled in a mostly flat spot, spread a linen cloth on the ground, and set the basket atop it. Osher chased after a wayward lamb, gently using his staff to guide it back to its mother.

He returned to me and sank onto the grass. I spread the food before him, and he grabbed a wedge of cheese and took a bite. He leaned against a tree trunk, his gaze shifting from the sheep to me and back again.

"Tell me what you love to do when you're not with the sheep," I said after swallowing a nibble of bread.

He pulled a piece of wood and a flint knife from a pocket of his robe. "This." He showed me the carving of a small animal. "I make toys for Jaron's sons. Sometimes I make flutes or other small objects. I don't quite know how to make a lyre, but I hope to try one day."

"So you are musical. That's wonderful." I reached for the carving and he placed it in my palm. "I used to sing when I was a young girl. I haven't done so in a while, and I would love to learn to use the flute, if you'll teach me."

He beamed. "Another thing we have in common. I knew you were the right woman for me the moment I saw you." He touched my knee. "Thank you for marrying me. I know I'm young and not your first . . ."

"It is I who should be thanking you, Osher. For wanting me after . . ."

"It seems we both don't quite know what to say. But never fear. All is well." He broke off a piece of flatbread and stuffed it into his mouth.

We sat in companionable silence for a while, until we spotted Jaron leading the family's goats some distance from us.

"We don't usually mix them," Osher said, "as the goats can

246

be temperamental and trouble the sheep. Though sometimes, when only one of us can shepherd them, we watch a little more carefully. Goats can eat faster and wander off."

"Will he bring the goats and join us?" I pointed, noting the space between us.

Osher nodded. "He will, but he won't stay long." He stood. "I'm going to walk among the sheep to make sure none have strayed."

"Should I come with you?" I wanted to do what pleased him, but he waved me off.

"I'll be back shortly. You can stay here."

"All right." I wished I had brought my spinning or some stitching to give my hands something to do. I gathered the food and straightened the linen, then folded it and placed it back into the basket.

"Do you have anything left over?" Jaron's voice startled me. I hadn't noticed him coming.

"There are some almonds if you want them." I opened the basket and handed him a portion.

He tossed them into his mouth and sat beside me. "How do you like your first week with our family? Of course, most of that was your wedding. Osher has been anxious to bring you home. I think he spoke of it at evening meal every night." He laughed and I joined him.

"I'm glad he is happy." I glanced at Osher among the sheep.

"He married the most beautiful woman in Sychar. Why wouldn't he be happy?" He smiled, and I sensed appreciation in his gaze.

The comment embarrassed me as such things always did. "Batel is also beautiful," I said. In my mind it was the truth. Batel was older than me, but her smooth skin did not show her age, and on the rare occasion that she smiled, her dark eyes sparkled. Of my many sisters-in-law, Batel was the prettiest.

"That she is. Don't worry, she lets me know it too!" He

laughed again and so did I, though I wondered if I should. Would he tell Batel that I laughed at his teasing, causing a problem between us? But why would he?

"What's so funny, brother?" Osher joined us and took my hand in a possessive hold.

I sidled closer and smiled at him, praying he would feel at ease. The last thing I needed was for the brothers to vie for my attention. Jaron wouldn't do that, would he?

"I was pointing out to your bride how anxious you were to get on with the wedding, even when Father kept telling you the house wasn't quite ready. Trust me, brother, we are all glad that the wait is over for you both." He chuckled, and Osher did as well.

"I was a bit impatient, wasn't I?" He pulled me against him and kissed my cheek. "But now all is well."

"Yes, indeed." Jaron stood, thanked me for the almonds, and walked back to tend the goats.

Osher released his hold slightly but tipped my chin up. "I love you, Nessa." He kissed me like he had the first night of our marriage.

I returned the kiss to please him, but when he left me to tend the sheep, the memory of my first kiss with Lavi surfaced out of nowhere. Osher's kiss could not compare to that memory. But Osher was the one in my life now. I simply had to stop remembering the only boy who had ever stolen my heart so completely and instead let my husband win my love.

32

One morning six months after my marriage to Osher, I hurried from the well, having stayed too long talking to Gali. My breath came fast, and I wished not for the first time that I'd awakened earlier. Elisheva didn't seem to mind so much when I was delayed, but Batel always raised a brow as though questioning my reasons.

Never mind the fact that I had conceived after only a few months and was now in my third month. I'd worried that carrying the water might cause me to lose this child too, but Elisheva assured me not to fear, and Batel insisted that she could not leave her sons to make the trip. I thought that excuse a poor one, but Elisheva allowed it, so there was nothing I could do.

I entered the courtyard out of breath and set the jar in its place.

"There you are at last," Batel said in her slightly accusatory tone. "I suppose the jug was too much for you again."

"I never said that." I felt my defenses rising. I had voiced concern over this child to Osher, and I knew he had gone to his mother, anxious for me. But never to Batel.

"I think you're forgetting what you say, Nessa. I clearly heard you tell us at evening meal over a month ago. Don't you remember?" Batel tilted her head, looking at me as if she was concerned for my memory.

"I remember telling my husband alone," I said, pouring some of the water into a smaller jar to carry into the house for baking. Why did the woman always question me?

"This isn't the first time, you know." Batel followed me and began chopping dill for a dipping sauce. "You do remember that you're part of a shepherding family, don't you? Not a tentmaker or potter as you were before."

"Of course I remember." I took some of the ground flour and mixed the water with it.

Elisheva entered the room holding Batel's youngest son, Gideon. "What are we talking about?" she asked, bouncing the child on her hip.

"Oh, nothing important. Nessa just forgets things sometimes." Batel glanced at Elisheva, avoiding my gaze. "It's probably because she's with child, or perhaps she's had so many husbands that she can't keep them straight."

"What are you talking about?" Angry now, I swiveled to face her. "I have not forgotten anything. Perhaps it's you who does not remember correctly."

Batel laughed, but the sound held no mirth. "Oh, I remember everything quite well. But don't fear. Your memory will surely return when the baby is born." She pushed the chopped dill aside, took Gideon from Elisheva's arms, and walked out of the room to nurse him.

I bit my lip, refusing to allow emotion to rise, and pushed my palms into the dough, kneading it over and over again. I felt Elisheva's touch on my shoulder. "Don't worry about her, Nessa. Batel has her moments. We just let her be."

She moved to finish the sauce Batel had started and worked beside me. Was I truly becoming forgetful with this child? I had never told the entire family about my fear of losing this one—only Osher. Hadn't I?

I had compared his family to my past marriages a time or two, though I had told no one—or had I? I had determined to keep my past in the past and do all in my power to make a life with this husband. I wouldn't have said something to jeopardize my place here.

I told myself that Batel was the one who was confused, but as the day wore on, I couldn't shake the niggling doubt. Was I slowly losing my ability to keep things straight? I hadn't dealt with such feelings during my last two pregnancies, but I'd been younger then. Could this one have changed my thinking?

As I lay beside Osher that night, unable to sleep, I smoothed my hand over the place where the babe grew in secret and wondered who was right—Batel or I?

I pondered the thought for too long. Though dawn awakened me early, I forced myself to concentrate harder today to be sure I remembered everything correctly. I could not bear another night of fear that I might be losing my mind.

❖ ❖ ❖

Six months later I stood in the courtyard, rubbing my protruding belly and groaning with each new pain that crossed my middle. The child kicked between the pains as the sun sank in a colorful rainbow-like array across a cloudless night. A fire burned in the pit, and I paced, knowing that I needed to call Elisheva soon. I knew the signs, and I didn't want to be too soon or too late. And I hoped to avoid needing Batel's help, but surely it was too dark to send for Yaffa or Adva or Meital. How I longed to have my sisters with me now.

"Are you all right?" Osher said, standing in the doorway of the house, watching me. "Is it time?" Excitement and fear filled his wide-eyed gaze. "Shall I get my mother?"

I nodded, and he hurried to my side. "Yes?" he said. "She won't be sleeping yet."

"I wish you could send for my sisters as well," I said, knowing he would want to please me.

"Anything for you, my love. But let me get my mother first."

251

He ran to call her, and soon Elisheva and Batel stood with me in the courtyard.

"Let us get you inside," Elisheva said. "Osher, go for her sisters, or at least one of them."

Osher looked uncertain.

"Go now," his mother said.

He kissed my cheek and ran out of the courtyard into the night.

I released a sigh, then stiffened at another pain, this one longer than the last. "Oh," I groaned.

"Have the waters broken?" Batel asked, suddenly showing concern.

"Not yet," I said through clenched teeth.

"Come, my dear." Elisheva took my arm and helped me into the house. "You will want privacy when the time comes."

I stopped, waiting for another contraction to pass, then walked slowly with Elisheva to the room I shared with Osher. Batel did not follow but stopped in the preparation area, no doubt to heat water. I was grateful for her absence, however short a time that could last.

In the room, Elisheva arranged the birthing stones and told me to lie down to be examined. "You still have a way to go. But with the pains coming this close together, it will be soon."

"I hope Yaffa can come," I said, desperately longing for one loving face to welcome my child into the world. While I had grown fond of Elisheva, who was mostly kind to me, I was still unable to understand Batel. It was like she purposely tried to confuse me at almost every turn.

Several times I had talked to Gali about it at the well, but she could not understand the woman's behavior either. Was Batel jealous of me? But why? She had Jaron and Baruch and Gideon. She should be happy.

"Ohh!" Another rush of pain ripped through me, and with it the gush of breaking waters spilled onto the rug.

"There! At last," Elisheva said as voices came from the hall. "It won't be long now."

The sound of Yaffa and Adva speaking with Batel caused my worry to lessen. When Yaffa rushed to my side and Adva started asking questions of Elisheva, I knew I would be all right. *Please, God, let this baby live.* If only this time both of us would survive.

Hours passed, and the birthing process came to the point where I sat on the stones and pushed the child into the world. The crying child!

"It's a girl!" Yaffa said, laughing. "A healthy girl!"

A flurry of activity followed as I finished the birthing and the women cleaned me and the baby. I lay on clean linen sheets and held the tiny child in my arms. "She's beautiful," I whispered, staring into the dark liquid eyes of the infant whose mouth moved hungrily for sustenance.

I laughed, guiding her mouth to my breast. The pull of longing and the feeding of new life filled me with joy such as I'd never known before.

Yaffa knelt at my side. "What will you name her?" She touched the child's dark, downy head.

"Aliyah," I said, glancing at Yaffa before quickly gazing on my daughter once more.

"To climb? An interesting choice, sister." Adva came and peeked over my shoulder at the child.

"It's been a long climb to get to this point in life. To have a child and a husband who loves me," I said softly, looking from sister to sister.

I caught Batel looking on, her expression unreadable, while Elisheva beamed. She had been the one to clean the child and the first to hold her.

"Our first granddaughter. Osher will want to see her soon," Elisheva said, smiling at me. "You did well, my daughter."

My heart swelled. To hold my living daughter and hear my

mother-in-law call me "daughter" and have my sisters here beside me—was anything better? I didn't need to worry about Batel's strange expression or her odd behavior of the past year. Now that I had borne a living child, Batel could not claim I was losing my memory because of my pregnancy. She would no doubt make up some other claims against me. Or perhaps she would soften now that we were both mothers.

As my eyes grew heavy and the baby nursed contentedly, I said a silent prayer of thanks. And that God would look down on me with continued kindness in this house.

33

I settled comfortably into the role of mother, and Osher took great delight in his first and thus far only child. He carried Aliyah on his shoulders and pranced around the house, making her laugh, and often carved wooden blocks and other things for her to play with. I found myself chasing my running toddler through the fields when I worked in the garden or accompanied Osher with the sheep. I had never known such happy times.

But when Batel drew near or her sons played with Aliyah, I worried. And watched. Always watched. I wasn't exactly sure what caused my feelings of unease, as Baruch and Gideon were kind to Aliyah, even seemed protective of her. Still, when Osher and Jaron joined the fun, I breathed easier. Batel did not give me such pointed looks or say hurtful things when the men were near.

To mark the third year since Aliyah's birth, Elisheva and I planned a special sweet treat and celebration at the evening meal. "Aliyah will love this," I said to Elisheva when the raisin cakes finished baking.

"She is such a dear child," Elisheva said, smiling at me. "I hope one day she will have a brother or sister as well." It wasn't exactly a question, but the reminder that I had not yet conceived another troubled me, and I feared that my lack somehow displeased Elisheva.

"We hope so as well," I said, not wanting to talk about the personal nature of such things or my own hidden fears. Was this child to be my only living one?

"It is strange that you have not conceived again, though, isn't it?" Batel's haughty tone made me turn. She stood at the entrance to the room, hands over her middle. "Jaron and I just discovered we are going to have a third." She looked at Elisheva. "Perhaps this time you will have another granddaughter."

I stiffened as Elisheva raised her hands in the air. "Praise be to Adonai! Another grandchild!" She embraced Batel, who returned the hug while I looked on.

Leave it to Batel to announce such news on Aliyah's special day, which also happened to be the day Aliyah was officially weaned. But of course she would do such a thing. For reasons I could not understand, Batel had never liked me. And nothing I did seemed to change her thinking. Had she lied to Jaron about me and Jaron told Osher? Was that why Osher was not as attentive to me as he'd been at first?

Angry, mind whirling, I walked past Elisheva and Batel toward the room where Aliyah napped. I couldn't bring myself to congratulate Batel. Perhaps later.

I reached the room to find Aliyah just waking from sleep. She rubbed her eyes and lifted her arms for me to pick her up. She rested her head against my shoulder, filling me with such love I could barely stand it. How grateful I was for this child! I held her close and kissed the top of her head.

"Are you ready to play, sleepy one?" I led her to where she had learned to relieve herself, then carried her to the sitting room and set her down with a basket of toys while I retrieved a cup of water for her.

"Where did you go?" Elisheva asked as I walked back toward the room where we worked and ate. "Batel thinks you're angry and jealous of her." She touched my shoulder. "Tell me she's not speaking the truth, my child."

I sighed. "I am not jealous of Batel. I simply went to fetch Aliyah." I smiled and patted her arm in reassurance, despite the conflicting emotions rushing through me. I lowered my voice, hoping I was not making a huge error in judgment. "I find Batel difficult to understand," I said.

Elisheva looked me up and down as if searching somewhere for the truth. "Batel is always loving and kind." Her curious, uncertain look pierced my heart. The woman actually believed her own words.

"She is loving and kind to you," I said, choosing my words carefully. "But I have not found her looking on me with the same kindness. I don't want to cause a problem. I'm sure we will eventually learn to care for each other." I didn't truly feel that way, but I said so to appease Elisheva.

"I do hope so." She looked so stricken that I embraced her.

"Don't fret. I will try harder." I turned and carried the water to my daughter.

Elisheva followed and hurried past me to greet Aliyah. "There is my sweet girl," she said, getting down on her knees to sit with her.

"Savta!" Aliyah scrambled over to Elisheva and hugged her before I could give her a drink.

Elisheva laughed. "Savta will play with you. Would you like that?"

Aliyah nodded, then hurried to her basket and carried it to her grandmother.

I stood holding the cup, irritated and not knowing what to do. "Are you thirsty, sweet girl?" I touched Aliyah's shoulder.

Aliyah took a quick gulp of water, then returned her attention to Elisheva, all but ignoring me.

"Looks like it's time for you to think about having another." Batel's voice carried a note of sarcasm. "Unless, of course, you are trying *not* to conceive another, though why anyone would do that to her husband . . ." She shrugged and walked away.

I watched Batel for a moment, then caught Elisheva's puzzled look. "I would never do such a thing," I told her, taking a seat and picking up my spindle and distaff. "For reasons I don't understand, I have simply not been able to conceive again." To admit such a thing to my mother-in-law stung, but Elisheva simply nodded.

"Sometimes these things take time. And you are getting older." She turned her attention to Aliyah's chattering.

I absently worked the spindle, my mind doing its own spinning. *Older?* I was thirty. I was not nearly as old as some women were when they conceived. Even Batel was older than me.

Was something else keeping me from bearing? Or was I not meant to have more children? Would Osher be pleased with only one daughter the rest of his life?

The thought brought sudden fear to my heart. My other husbands had divorced me for less. Memories of a conversation over the evening meal the week before surfaced.

"Well, my man," Jaron had said, smacking Osher's back as we sat around the low table to eat, "when are you going to give the family another daughter or a son? Aliyah is almost weaned, after all."

Osher stiffened at the comment, and I coughed in embarrassment.

"Keep your comments civil," Dan said, frowning. "Jaron, you know better than to discuss such delicate topics in front of the children."

Jaron laughed. "I'm just giving him a hard time, Father. He's used to me by now." He glanced at me again, making me uncomfortable, though I tried to laugh it off.

Batel glared at both of us, and later that evening Osher asked me what Jaron had said that was so funny.

"He made me nervous is all," I'd said, and it was still true.

Jaron often looked at me in a way that made me wonder what he was thinking, but by Batel's reaction I knew. And his interest, friendly or not, made his wife jealous and Osher angry.

A sigh escaped as I watched my only child thrilled to be playing with her grandmother. I was the one who wanted to play with her. How was it that Elisheva so often came along and took my place?

Would having another child help matters? But I was not God to bring about such things. And Osher had been less ardent of late. Had Batel turned him against me somehow?

I shook myself. Impossible. Osher loved me. Batel was just jealous because Jaron was not the man Osher was. I must make Osher see that. Perhaps he could talk to Jaron and convince him to pay less attention to me and more to his own wife.

Bringing up such a conversation, however, was not something I quite knew how to do.

❖ ❖ ❖

That night after I finally put Aliyah to bed, following an exciting celebration that kept her awake too long, I waited for Osher to join me. When he didn't come as expected, I glanced at Aliyah's peaceful sleeping form, then walked through the quiet house to find him.

Voices drifted to me from the courtyard, where the adults often gathered after the children were in bed. When I heard my name, I stood to the side of the door and listened.

"Nessa seems to think that you don't like her," Elisheva said. "Tell me, my daughter, that it isn't true. We can't have our family at odds with each other. It isn't right, and Adonai, may His name be praised, would not want that of us."

I felt as though I had been kicked in the gut. I had told Elisheva that I found Batel difficult to understand in confidence, not as something for her to twist and share with the entire family. And since when did she care what Adonai thought?

The family went to synagogue, to be sure, but I rarely heard His name other than during the morning and evening prayers.

"Ima Elisheva," Batel said, her tone sweet like honey, "Nessa confuses things far too often. I have never said that I don't like her. I think she is a lovely woman, though I do wish she would stop eyeing Jaron the way she does." She paused, and I imagined her looking into Jaron's eyes.

"What are you talking about?" Osher asked, and I longed to rush to his side and tell him to listen to his heart. Surely he knew Batel's manipulative ways by now.

"Oh, come now, Osher. Have you not eyes to see?" Batel's tone dripped with scorn. "She laughs at the most inappropriate times whenever Jaron says anything, even if it *isn't* funny."

"She's just being kind," Jaron said. Was he hurt by his wife's words?

"Kind? She is tempting you, husband. And your brother is too blind to see it." Did Batel hate me so much that she would lie about me in this way?

Osher cleared his throat and I silently begged him to defend me too, but a moment later, he simply said, "I will speak to her."

Speak to me? And here I was the one who wanted to talk to Osher to ask why he'd seemed so distant of late. Had the family had these conversations without me in the past?

I drew in a slow, painful breath and tiptoed back to the room where Aliyah slept in peace. What I wouldn't give in that moment to scoop her into my arms and run back to the only home where I'd ever felt secure. Instead, I lay on the bed I shared with Osher and stared at the ceiling, hearing again the conversation in the courtyard and Batel's bitter words.

Had I tempted Jaron in some way to make Batel jealous? Was I the one at fault, truly? I knew men were attracted to me by the way they nearly fell over themselves when I passed them at the market, though thankfully they rarely spoke to me. Just gawked, making me uncomfortable. And I did nothing to enhance my features as Batel often did by adding color to her cheeks. She was attractive. She had no reason to feel jealous of me. Why did women so often turn away from me when all I wanted to do was live in harmony with them and my husband? Would I ever know such peace?

A sudden longing for life to be different, to end if it had to, startled me. No one knew joy in the grave. I had many more years left on the earth. I must. For Aliyah's sake. But as I lay there wondering if Osher would ever join me, I pondered my life and wished I had never been born.

34

The conversation with Osher that I had expected that night or the next day never happened, and the fragile peace I sensed with him kept me from asking. The months of Batel's pregnancy passed quickly, and Jaron appeared more attentive to his wife, to my great relief.

Their baby, another boy, came early, though not dangerously so, and the household rejoiced. I secretly thanked Adonai that Aliyah remained Elisheva's only granddaughter. Perhaps having the only daughter would keep me in everyone's good graces.

How mistaken I was. The suddenness of Osher's change in attitude toward me, six months after Batel's son was born, caught me completely off guard. He found me in the garden teaching four-year-old Aliyah how to pull weeds and how to tell them apart from the food. The child was smart for her age and learned quickly, giving me a continual sense of pride and joy.

The afternoon was warm after Aliyah's nap, but I knelt in the dirt beside her regardless, to give me a reason to stay out of the house. I looked up at the sound of approaching footsteps and turned to see Osher coming our way.

"Abba's home!" I said to Aliyah, who turned and squealed and raced into his arms. What was he doing home so early? Had something happened?

He scooped Aliyah into his arms and lifted her onto his

shoulders, holding her hands as he approached me. I stood, brushed the dirt from my knees, and smiled. He did not return the gesture. My stomach did a little flip, a feeling of foreboding rising within me.

Osher stopped and placed Aliyah on the ground. "Go and find Savta, Aliyah. Abba will come for you again in a few moments."

I looked at him, confused, and my heart beat double time at his expression. When Aliyah ran off and I turned to watch her enter the house, Osher took my hand. "We must talk," he said, pulling me toward the trees near the sheep pens. He turned to face me and released my hand.

"Is something wrong?" I searched his face, noting the new lines along his brow.

"Apparently everything, though I am the last to know it." He stood with arms crossed, looking down at me.

"I don't understand." At the look on his face, I feared I would be sick.

"I think you do. I've seen the way you look at my brother and the way you treat Batel. She warned me not to marry someone who'd already had four husbands, but I thought I could be the one to make you happy. I didn't blame you for the past. In my naivety, I thought it didn't matter that you were not a virgin." He ran a hand through his hair and stared at the sky. "I trusted you, Nessa."

I swallowed hard. "Trusted? Don't you trust me now?" The words nearly choked me. What had I done?

"I think my brother is far too friendly with you and you lead him on. But I can't very well send my brother away from my father's house." He let the words linger.

"What can I do to convince you that I have never encouraged Jaron? I laugh with him as the rest of us do." My words sounded wrong even to me, and I somehow knew that defending myself would do no good.

"Batel doesn't. And I don't either. You are oblivious to us." He stopped, his anger seeming to abate a little.

"Please, Osher, I have never cared for anyone here but you and our daughter. I mean, I love your family, but I don't want any man but you." I clasped my hands in front of me.

Sadness filled his eyes, and he slowly shook his head. "I loved you, Nessa. I love Aliyah. But you must go. You are causing too much discord in my father's house, and I can't let it continue. In time, I pray God will give me a compliant wife who doesn't cause dissension, but that woman is not you."

My heart nearly stopped beating. I stared at him, dumbstruck. "You're sending us away?" What would Aliyah do without her father?

"Not us," he said, his jaw clenched. "Just you."

"What?" My eyes widened and fear clawed at my throat. "You cannot keep my daughter without me."

"Cannot?" He almost smirked, but stopped himself and grew stern again. "I have every right to keep my daughter. My mother cannot be parted from her only granddaughter."

"But you would part her from her mother?" This could not be happening.

"You will see her at synagogue, though I do not permit you to speak to her unless we approach you."

I stared at him, this stranger in my husband's body. This was Batel's doing. Osher would never have treated me this way if we had lived without his family. "She is *my* daughter, Osher. I gave her life."

"You have no rights, Nessa. I will give you the money from the dowry, but you are to pack your things and leave. I will allow you to say goodbye to Aliyah, but she stays here." He crossed his arms over his chest again, brooking no argument.

"I suppose Batel will be her 'mother'? She has wanted me gone from the beginning, but I thought better of you. I thought you could see the way she controls all of you!" Anger made my whole body shake, but I told myself I could not give in to despair with him standing there watching.

"Gather your things," he said again. "I want you gone before the sun sets."

"I will fight for my daughter, Osher. I will go to the rabbis and Chen will help me. You will not get away with this."

I whirled about and ran toward the house, calling Aliyah's name. I did not care what anyone said. I would hold my daughter and, if possible, snatch her and take her with me.

I could not live without her.

My tears would not stop as I rushed into the house, found Aliyah, and pulled her into my arms. I carried her to the room where I'd slept beside Osher for the past five years and sank to the floor, rocking her.

Aliyah stroked my face, brushing a tear away. "Something wrong, Ima?" She placed her small hands on my cheeks and looked into my eyes.

I gulped on a sob and kissed Aliyah's forehead. "Ima has to go away for a while," I said softly, fearing that Elisheva or Batel or even Osher might follow me and listen to this private exchange.

"When?" Aliyah asked, giving me a puzzled look. "Take me with you?"

My tears fell faster as I smoothed my daughter's hair and kissed her cheeks, drinking in the scent of her small body. "I have to go now, but you will stay with Savta and Abba."

"But when will you come back?" Aliyah must have sensed my despair, for her lip quivered, and I feared she would cry out and alert the household.

"I don't know," I said, taking Aliyah's hands and squeezing. "I need for you to be brave, my sweet girl. Even if I can't return right away, be good for Savta and Abba, and perhaps one day God will make a way for things to change."

"But why? I don't understand." Her voice dropped in pitch

as she leaned close to my ear. "Ima, why can't I come too? Are you going to see Uncle Chen?"

I nodded. "Yes, my love. I'm going to see Uncle Chen and Aunt Malka, and perhaps you can come soon, but not now."

How I longed to promise her that I would return and take her with me. But I would not make a promise I didn't know I could keep. I would do all in my power to keep her, but what if the rabbis or even Chen sided with Osher? What if they considered me unfit to be a mother because I'd had so many husbands?

Oh, God, why is this happening again? I can't lose Aliyah!

"Ima?"

"Yes, my love?"

Aliyah leaned closer still and cupped her hands to my ear. "Auntie Batel does not say nice things about you. Gideon told me so."

The shock of my daughter's admission caused me to rock back on my heels. I clutched Aliyah's hands. "My love, I want you to promise me something."

Aliyah nodded, wide-eyed.

"I don't want you to tell anyone what Gideon told you, not even Abba. It must be our secret, okay?" I had no doubt that Batel and the others would twist Aliyah's words, making my attempts to take her away harder than they already were.

"I won't, Ima." She pressed two fingers to her closed lips.

"Good girl." I pulled her to my chest one more time. I wanted to say so much more, but footsteps coming toward the room made me pause. I looked up to see Elisheva standing in the doorway.

The look she gave me was a mixture of sorrow and relief. I'd never thought ill of Elisheva and had no doubt that she would care well for Aliyah, but the woman was blind to Batel's manipulative ways. As was Osher. Did Jaron not see it either? Or Dan? But I could not ask, for Elisheva would side with her son above all.

"I need you to go with Savta now," I said loudly enough for my mother-in-law to hear. "Be a good girl and always know how very much I love you." I hugged Aliyah one more time, kissed her cheek, and turned her toward her grandmother.

Aliyah stood torn, seeming unwilling to move.

"Come, child," Elisheva said, opening her arms.

Still Aliyah did not move.

"It's okay, Aliyah," I said, choking on her name. "Go with Savta."

Aliyah shook her head and clung to me.

Elisheva looked at me. "Have you packed your things?"

"Not yet." I glanced at the baskets holding my clothing and personal items.

"Let me help you." Elisheva moved into the room. "I assume these are all the items you brought with you?"

I watched her pull the baskets to the center of the room, where Aliyah clung to me, crying now. My heart wrenched as I saw the despair in my daughter's eyes, matching my own.

"That's everything." Never mind all the cloth I had woven for the family. They would claim it as their own.

"We will saddle a donkey for you. You cannot possibly carry these all alone. I will send a servant to help you." Elisheva hired a neighbor boy now and then, as the family had no permanent servants.

Thank you was on the tip of my tongue, but I could not utter the words.

Elisheva left the room to carry out what she'd promised, leaving me with Aliyah a little longer.

"I don't want you to leave," Aliyah cried.

"I don't want to leave either, sweet girl. I want to stay with you always." Could my heart break any more than it already had? A part of me told myself this was real while the other part warred within, knowing it could not possibly be happening again. I'd tried so hard.

Aliyah clung to me, and I did the same to her. We sat in silence until the neighbor boy came to gather my things to load on the donkey. Elisheva appeared in the door again, her expression filled with more pain than I thought I would ever see from her. Perhaps someone in this house truly had cared for me.

She came close and knelt beside Aliyah. "Aliyah, Savta will take good care of you, and we will play and make sweet treats. Won't that be fun?"

Aliyah shook her head. "No! I want my ima!"

Elisheva sighed. "It would help if Osher does not hear this," she said to me, "but I promise to do all I can to let you see her from time to time. I am not against you, my daughter. This was not my choice."

I looked at her, wondering if I could believe her. I searched her expression and saw no guile there. "I will hold you to that promise," I whispered. "What he's doing is wrong."

Elisheva nodded, though I was not sure she would ever go against her son if it came down to a fight for the child. That is, if I had any right to engage in such a fight.

"It's time, Nessa. Osher is waiting with the donkey to give you the dowry. I am truly sorry." Elisheva reached for Aliyah's hand.

But suddenly I could not release it. Her little arms wrapped around my legs, and I held her to me, unable to break free. This was so wrong. Osher was the weakest, cruelest man I'd ever known. Not at all like his cousin Amichai. Amichai would have never sent me away.

"Please, Nessa," Elisheva said. "Come, child."

Aliyah shook her head against my knees. I felt as though my body had broken into two pieces and my heart had been ripped from me.

Elisheva attempted to take her arm, but the child pulled away. "You don't want Osher to force this," Elisheva said softly.

I couldn't look at my mother-in-law, but I pulled Aliyah's

grip free and gazed at her with blurred vision. "It will be all right," I said, not believing a word of it. I placed her hand in Elisheva's. "Aliyah, Ima needs you to be brave, remember?" I choked on the tears clogging my throat. "Savta will watch over you and take care of you. And Ima will always love you." Those final words felt like a death sentence.

"You will see your ima at synagogue," Elisheva promised, then leaned close to my ear. "I will make sure of it."

The promise did nothing to alleviate the intense grief coursing through me in that moment, but it was the only good thing I had to cling to. *Please, Adonai, let her mean it.*

"Come along," Elisheva said to both of us.

I rose, and Aliyah held both our hands as we walked to the courtyard. Elisheva scooped Aliyah up and kissed my cheek in parting.

"No! I want to go with Ima!" Aliyah screamed, and my heart broke yet again with every step toward Osher and the waiting donkey.

Osher's stern gaze did not soften, and when I glanced back at my squirming daughter, I glimpsed Batel in the window, a smirk on her face. She had gotten exactly what she'd always wanted. For me to leave and her to be the only beloved daughter-in-law. What would she do when Osher married another?

"Here." Osher handed me a writ of divorce and a purse of coins, the thirty pieces of silver he'd paid as a bride-price for me. I had been worth so little, and now I felt more worthless than I ever had in my life.

I took the purse and followed behind the donkey. The neighbor's son led it down the path toward Sychar's streets as the sun descended toward the west. We would have to hurry if we were to make it to Chen's home by nightfall.

But I didn't care to hurry. I walked with deliberately slow steps, listening to Aliyah's cries until I could no longer hear them. I did not look back at Osher, nor give him the satisfaction of goodbye. Bitter hatred filled my entire being until I wanted to call down all manner of curses on everyone in that family.

As we neared Chen's home, the bitterness turned to absolute grief, deeper than any I had ever known. No man, aside from Lavi and Amichai, had ever treated me well. They saw me as a prize to show they'd married the "most beautiful woman in Sychar." I would leave this world an old woman, or pray God let death come sooner, never feeling truly cherished for who I was.

And I knew without a doubt that I absolutely could not bear it.

35

*L*avi led a donkey loaded with jars of spices and oil that he'd earned under the tutelage of the town's perfumer and continued his journey toward Sychar that he'd begun the night before. Sleeping in the fields allowed him to arrive in Sychar earlier in the day—a day that he needed to begin his new life and return to the place where his heart had remained despite the time that had passed. He should have returned home years ago with his uncle's tools and Nessa's gold, but he couldn't. Guilt about hurting Nessa coupled with his anger toward his uncle had held him back, especially when Raanan had continued to give her to husband after husband.

A sigh escaped him. He patted the pouch that held double the gold he'd taken and glanced at the tools hanging over the donkey's back. Consequences or not, he would return them now. He only hoped that he could convince Chen of his remorse and in making restitution be allowed to at last marry Nessa.

The warm breeze lifted the fabric of his robe, a robe Nessa had woven for him years ago without realizing his true reason for wanting it. He had never intended it for his employer but for himself. Of course, the robe that he'd told her was for him was for Amos's wedding, not his. Ilana and Amos were now happily married with three children.

271

But he had never found a woman in Sebaste to win his heart. The heart that Nessa had stolen years before. He quickened his pace at the thought of her. Word had come to him from Rafael, a friend in Sychar, that Nessa's fifth husband had sent her away and she'd lost a child in the process. How could anyone be so cruel? None of the men she had married could have possibly loved her as he always had. He loved Nessa because he knew her. She was fun and laughed at his teasing, always good-natured and yet so empathetic. She'd cared what he thought, how he felt, when no one else did. Her beauty was inner, not simply outward. Couldn't those men see that? They'd all thrown away a wonderful gift, and he hoped they paid for it!

So when he'd heard that the fifth man had sent her home to Chen, he knew he had to return no matter what anyone said against him. Even if Chen gave him a hard time, he would still seek out Nessa. It was time to fight for her because obviously no one else would.

The city came into view as the sun rose above the hills. In a few weeks the men of Sychar would likely climb Mt. Gerizim to worship. They still considered it the only true place to worship God, not Jerusalem as the Jews believed. Lavi, though raised in Samaria and of Samaritan blood, did not care about such things. God had done little for him over the years.

He clucked his tongue to urge the donkey along, anxious to find the booth he had secured where he could set up a shop to sell the perfumes and oils he made. Once he established himself as a merchant in Sychar and found a house to purchase or rent, he would approach Chen. In the meantime, he still intended to visit Nessa—today if possible. He had to know if the rumors he had heard were true. Was she finally free to marry him? Could he convince her to do so? Could he convince Chen to let her?

He fisted his hands, his knuckles whitening around the donkey's reins. When he reached the gate, he allowed the guard to inspect his wares and clenched his jaw as he paid the necessary tax. *Robbery!* he thought as he handed over coins he did not wish to part with. Taxation thievery was what it was.

His own feelings of guilt no longer accompanied the thought of other people's dishonest ways. Yes, he'd stolen once, but he had long since paid Nessa back by saving for this day. Her father would have understood. Or so he told himself, because to think anything else was useless.

He reached the street of merchants as the shops were beginning to fill with customers and led the donkey to the street where the perfumers and potters sold their wares. He found the booth he had purchased from the family of a man who had passed on and tied the donkey to a post next to it. The curtains were drawn, and it took some time for him to lift them and tie them into place.

Dust filled the air, and the dirt floor held animal droppings. He would need to clean the place properly first and make a spot at the back to sleep until he found better lodging. After retrieving a broom and pan from among his belongings, he set about sweeping, listening to the sounds of those around him. The scent of freshly baked bread made his stomach growl, and he took a moment to find the baker and purchase a loaf and then a round of cheese from the cheese maker nearby.

He watched the crowd a moment as he popped the cheese into his mouth, then returned to his booth to retrieve a skin of water. His friend Rafael, Gali's husband, approached him, smiling.

"Lavi, my friend, you finally came!" He embraced Lavi and kissed his cheeks, fairly crushing the food in Lavi's hands. He backed away. "I'm sorry to interrupt your meal."

Lavi waved away the remark. "Shalom, Rafael. It's good to see you here. I just arrived. Thank you for securing this spot for me, though I will say it may take me all day to clean the booth and set up my shop."

"I have to meet my sons who are watching the pottery shop."

Rafael pointed a few booths down. "But I can help you for a short time."

"Would you? Thank you, my friend." Lavi hurriedly finished his food and handed the broom to Rafael, then searched for a rag to scrub the wooden shelf that would display some of his wares.

"I have to admit, after all Gali has told me of what happened when you lived in Raanan's home, I never thought you would return to Sychar. Have you truly been pining after Nessa all these years? Gali said you had married another." Rafael swept as he talked, keeping his voice low.

"Nessa thought I married another. I wanted her to believe it so she would forget about me," Lavi admitted. He cleared his throat and looked up and down the street before glancing behind him at Rafael. "But I could not forget her."

"You have waited a long time, my friend. I can't imagine all that you've suffered, hearing Nessa being given to one man after another. Gali struggles to understand it, and sometimes we both wonder if Nessa is doing something to cause these men to turn away from her." He shrugged as he scooped rodent dung into a pan and carried it behind the shop to toss into the line of trees in the distance.

When he returned, Lavi met his gaze. "Nessa could never be anything but good. I blame the men her father and brother chose, not her. And how could this last one take her daughter away? That is what made me return. I will do everything I can to see her reunited with her child. To keep them apart is simply cruel." His pulse jumped as he spoke. Ever since he'd heard the news, he'd fought bitter anger toward the man who'd done such a thing.

"You will be hard-pressed to succeed, my friend." Rafael set the broom in a corner of the shop and the pan beside it. "The place is swept and I must return to my sons. But we will talk again."

Lavi touched his arm before he could leave. "Why will I be hard-pressed to help her? Please explain."

Rafael sighed and glanced about as if to be sure they were still alone. "Gali told me that Nessa went to Chen and Chen went to the rabbi at the synagogue, but no one could find anything that gave Nessa the right to her child. It was her husband's decision, and he has the power to keep her. Nessa sees the girl at synagogue, so they say. Gali said that her former mother-in-law tries to make sure that the child has at least a little time with Nessa each week. But Nessa cries nearly every time she meets Gali at the well." He shook his head. "We live in a harsh world."

Defeat rose, wanting to dig its claws into Lavi's emotions, but he stiffened, fighting the urge to give up. He could not do so. Not without trying. "Nevertheless, I will speak to Chen and Nessa and the rabbi if I must, and if I can I will find this man who called himself 'husband' and speak to him myself."

Rafael raised a brow. "Be careful, my friend. You have just returned, and no one here really knows you anymore. Only a few remember you. Gali because you lived next to her family, but not many more. You will not get far with anger."

Lavi nodded. "You're right. I will plan my course, and I will proceed with caution. I'm a patient man. I've waited for years for a chance with Nessa. I'm not going to let this time slip away. If she will have me, we will make a way."

"I wish you the best," Rafael said, turning to head toward his booth. "Shalom, shalom."

"Shalom, shalom," Lavi said almost absently. Perfect peace. If only he felt what the words were intended to mean.

❖ ❖ ❖

I sat at the millstone, grinding the barley into flour to be made into loaves for the evening meal. Shabbat was two days away, and I was counting the hours until I could see Aliyah again. If only our visits weren't so short. But Osher had found another wife in the three months since I had returned to Chen's house, and nothing Chen or I had done had been able to bring Aliyah home.

I pushed the stone in a continuous circle, though the task, which was once easy for me, drained the little energy I still had. Food tasted dull and my clothes hung loosely about me. Adva and Meital had commented on how wan I looked, and Yaffa had held me close, allowing me to weep in her arms.

I had so little to live for. Shabbat was the only day of the week that gave me any pleasure, and only when Osher's family brought Aliyah to synagogue. There had been a few times when they claimed Aliyah was sick and did not bring her, but I never believed them. Especially if the person telling me was Batel or Osher. Elisheva always stayed behind at such times.

I stopped the stone to sift the grain, brushing away the hair that had fallen over my eyes. Footsteps sounded from the street that ran in front of the house. I looked up to see who it was. When a man stopped at our courtyard, I covered my hair with the scarf that had slipped to my shoulders and wrapped it around my neck.

He stepped closer, and I squinted at him through the blazing sun as it angled westward. I blinked, certain that I was not seeing correctly. "Lavi?"

He came closer, set a wrapped sack on the nearby bench, and squatted beside me. "Yes, Nessa, it's me."

I looked from the sack to him, curious. "Are you alone or is your wife with you?"

He reached for my hand, but I did not allow him to take it. "Come sit with me?" He motioned to the bench.

"I have to finish the flour. It is time to bake the bread." What was he doing here? "You shouldn't be here." I lowered my voice and glanced at the house. "Though if your wife is with you, I suppose I might ask Chen to let you stay to eat."

"I would love to stay. I want to talk to Chen, but my wife is not with me." He stood and looked down at me, studying me.

I turned to the flour, sifted it, and poured it into the jar to carry into the house. "I have to go, Lavi."

"May I join you? Ask Chen, if you will." He sounded so earnest.

"Why are you here?" I met his gaze and saw longing in his dark eyes.

"I will explain at the evening meal if you'll allow it." He clasped his hands, then seemed to think better of it and offered to take the jar from me into the house.

I shook my head. "I've got this. Come."

He snatched the sack and followed as I led him into the house and carried the jar to Malka, who was busy preparing some of the dishes.

"I thought you would never finish," Malka said in her typical snide tone. But a moment later, she became aware of Lavi and startled. "Who is this?"

"Malka, this is our cousin Lavi. Chen will remember him. He lived here before you joined the family." I addressed Lavi. "Lavi, this is my brother's wife, Malka."

"Shalom, Malka." Lavi bowed, and Malka flushed and gave a brief nod.

"I've invited him to stay to eat the evening meal with us." To Lavi I said, "Take a seat in the sitting room while we finish preparing the food. Chen will be in shortly."

Lavi nodded and walked past me to the place he would barely recognize for all of Malka's furnishings, which had changed since my mother died. I had nothing of my own to adorn this place, not even my room, which Chen and Malka had given to their children. I slept in a small area where they dried herbs and hung wineskins to ferment. But I had not cared where they put me. I would have slept in the shop if I had to. Life had no meaning without Aliyah.

Malka said nothing to me as I made the flatbread and she finished the plates of cheeses and pickles to go with the barley stew. The silence was nothing new, but with Lavi in the next room, I could not stop wondering why he had come. And where was his wife?

When I'd heard he had married, I had forced myself to stop thinking of him. Even my memories, the ones I'd cherished, had been pushed from my thoughts.

The door creaked open and Chen entered with his sons, who now helped him in his business. "The food is almost ready," Malka called as they washed their feet.

The boys hurried into the house. They stopped short at the sight of Lavi, and Chen followed, also stopping to stare at their guest.

"Lavi?" Chen's voice did not betray his feelings.

I carried the tray of bread to the table. "I invited him to stay. He said he has things to tell us," I said as I passed Chen.

"Shalom, Lavi," Chen said at last, taking the seat next to him. "It has been a long time."

"Too long," Lavi said. "Thank you for letting me stay with you for this meal."

"We are always willing to have guests," Chen said.

Malka and I soon joined them, bringing the rest of the food, and the boys sat at the end of the low table.

After Chen introduced Lavi to his sons and said a prayer over the food, we ate in relative silence. When the boys ran off to play and the adults sat together drinking the last cup of wine, Chen turned to Lavi. "So, tell me now, what brings you to Sychar?"

"I have moved my business here. I no longer wanted to stay in Sebaste when this is my true home." Lavi glanced at me, then faced Chen.

"Go on," Chen said, taking a sip of wine.

"I have a perfumers booth at the market and plan to purchase or rent a home as soon as I can find one that is suitable for a family," Lavi said, again glancing at me. He pulled the sack from his side and set it next to Chen, then reached into his robe, pulled out a smaller pouch, and handed it to me. "But first, I wanted to return these. They are the tools that belonged to your father, and Nessa's gold is double what I took. I regret my actions. I should have returned them long ago."

Chen opened the sack and examined the contents, but I sat there numb, unable to untie the heavy pouch in my hand.

Chen cleared his throat and lifted his gaze to Lavi's. "Why now, Lavi? You would never have been caught if you'd stayed out of Sychar. We are grateful to have these returned, of course, but I thought you had sold them by now."

Lavi shook his head. "I couldn't. I didn't touch Nessa's gold either, though on days when I had no food, I was sorely tempted." He looked at me. "I knew that you would never accept me if I didn't return more than I had taken."

Accept him? "You are family, Lavi. There was no need to double my gold," I said, unnerved by the look he was giving me.

"Yes, there was," he said, turning to Chen. "I want to find favor with you."

My mind whirled with his words. What was he talking about? "Where is your wife? Did she stay in Sebaste?" I asked, voicing my confusion.

Lavi cleared his throat. "The truth is, Nessa, I have no wife. It was Amos who married Ilana, and they have three beautiful children now. But I have never married." He looked at Chen. "All my life I have wanted to marry your sister, but your father would not allow it. I heard that she is free to wed again, so I came to see if you are willing to let her marry me. I can support a wife now. Before, I could not."

"You lied to me?" I stared at him. "You stole from me and then lied to me? All these years I thought you were married."

"I didn't want you to think about me," Lavi said, color rising in his cheeks. "I should not have done so, but since I knew

I couldn't have you, I tried to find a way to forget you. I could not." He looked again at Chen's scowling expression.

"Because of these," Chen said, lifting the sack of tools, "my father asked that I not allow Nessa to marry you, Lavi. What you are asking . . . it's not possible." Chen crossed his arms over his chest. "Believe me, I would like nothing better than for Nessa to find a man who will keep her forever, but I cannot in good conscience do what I know my father would not have done."

Lavi stared long and hard at Chen while I watched, my mind churning. I knew Lavi well enough to know that if he had waited this long, he would not take no for an answer.

"Then let her live with me as a concubine. It's not as binding as a wife, but I would still treat Nessa as my only woman." Lavi tapped one foot on the floor, his bearing stiff.

Chen sighed deeply and uncrossed his arms. "You are not making this easy. How can I give my sister to you without the full legalities of marriage? What if you treat her as all the others have done?"

"What if I want to go with him?" I interrupted, suddenly realizing that I must say something. His lying to me and stealing from me was no worse than how anyone else had treated me, and I would be away from Malka and her sulking ways. With Lavi, it would be just the two of us. No mothers-in-law to convince him how awful I was, or jealous sisters-in-law who hated me. I might finally feel free. Except for the loss of my daughter.

The thought made me pause.

"If you go with him without the benefit of marriage," Chen said to me, "don't you think Osher will hold that even more against you? He will find any reason he can to keep you from seeing Aliyah, Nessa. Living with Lavi would make things worse."

Tears threatened, and it was suddenly all too much. "Would it? How can it be worse than it already is?"

"I can help her fight to get her daughter back. Aliyah could live with us," Lavi said, as if he had already planned it all out.

"Not if you aren't married," Chen said, sitting up straighter. "I can't allow it. Aliyah means too much to her."

"But, Chen, don't you want our home to be just ours again?" Malka interjected. She had not been pleased to see me enter their courtyard again with nowhere else to go.

Chen shook his head. "I cannot." He stood. "I think you should go, Lavi. Let us think on it. Give Nessa time."

"There has to be a way," Lavi said. "You know it's the best thing to do."

But as he left, I didn't know any such thing. If I ran off and lived with Lavi without the benefit of marriage, I could lose any chance of ever bringing Aliyah to live with me. Osher would use it against me.

Yet if I didn't live with Lavi, I would be stuck with Malka the rest of my days, or until Chen found someone else to wed me to. Something I would not allow. Not again. If I had to have another man, it would be Lavi or no one. I could not bear the thought of living with other women who hated me or turned my husband against me.

36

eeks passed, but despite my questioning him, Chen gave me no answer to the dilemma of marrying Lavi. Why did he have to be so stubborn?

"Did you really agree with Abba to keep me from Lavi?" I asked one afternoon when I found Chen alone in the shop. His sons had taken one of the tents to a nearby neighbor who had purchased it, leaving him alone in this rare moment.

"I didn't exactly disagree with him," he said, looking guilty, as though I had caught him in a lie. "But I let him believe that I would do as he would, Ness. I never said the words in promise, because I sensed that he wasn't thinking clearly." He paused and ran a hand along his beard. "Abba loved Lavi, Ness, and if Lavi had returned the tools and gold while Abba was alive, he might have changed his mind." Chen stood before me and searched my face. "As it stood, when he died, Abba had not forgiven him."

"Well, I have forgiven him, Chen," I said. "I have always loved him, and if you will not allow me to marry him, especially after what you just told me, I will find a way to be with him regardless."

"To live with him outside of marriage would be wrong."

"Then let me marry him."

His wavering look gave me hope, but a moment later, he shook his head. "I can't."

"Can't or won't?" I stomped out of the shop, knowing by the stubborn tilt of his jaw I would never convince him. It would be up to me to choose between living with Lavi, hoping that somehow I could still see Aliyah and one day have her live with us, or staying with Chen and Malka with no hope of change.

If only I could have kept Aliyah. Then I would have taken her to live with Lavi, marriage or not. We wouldn't need a legal document if I became his concubine.

My head spun as I walked toward the well to meet Gali the morning after my argument with Chen. The cool mist of early morn was a welcome change from the heat of the past months. As I approached the well, Gali smiled in greeting.

"Shalom, my friend," she said, giving me a quick embrace.

"Shalom to you as well," I said, "though I'm not feeling very peaceful of late."

"Has Chen made no decision then? Rafael said that Lavi found a house not far from the merchants' street. It's small but adequate, he said. I haven't seen it, of course." She looked me up and down. "Have you?"

I shook my head. "I haven't seen Lavi since the night he visited. I didn't know he had a house."

"We can stop by and look on the way back." Gali lowered her jar into the well, then tugged it back to the top. "Is Chen really so against Lavi that he would keep you from marrying him?"

I nodded. "He's being unreasonable, and I don't know why. He claims that living with Lavi could cause Osher to keep Aliyah from me for good, but he doesn't know that." A sob rose, but I covered my mouth, holding it back.

When we both lifted our jars to our shoulders, we took the street that led to Lavi's place, saying little. "I think that's it," Gali said, pointing to a small but quaint home some distance from the market. "It looks nice."

"Yes." I looked it over, admiring the small but useful courtyard and the fact that it was not as close to his neighbors as Chen's house was to Gali's former home. "It's slightly secluded."

"Perhaps he likes privacy." Gali continued walking. "I have to get home."

I did not follow at first.

Gali stopped. "Are you coming? Malka will be waiting."

Let her wait. "I'll come. Give me a few moments."

"You shouldn't stay here, Ness. What if he's inside and sees you?" Gali returned to my side.

I stood in indecision. I *wanted* Lavi to see me here, but I knew Gali was right. People would talk if they saw me get too close. I couldn't morally enter his house without Chen.

I turned and fell into step with Gali. "You're right, as always. Let's go home."

As I entered the courtyard of the home of my birth, I could not stop thinking about Lavi's house, and Lavi himself. Why had he not told Chen that he finally had a place to live? Would it make any difference to Chen?

If Chen would not even listen to Malka, who I knew was as anxious as I for him to make a decision, what would it take to convince him?

I was beginning to wonder if I even cared to convince him. What would it be like to have someone truly love me? If I couldn't have my daughter—and I would never stop trying to—would having Lavi be enough?

❖ ❖ ❖

Another Shabbat passed, and Elisheva brought Aliyah to see me after the service. We stood in front of the synagogue while the men talked some distance away, Lavi and Chen and Rafael in one group, with Osher and Jaron and Dan waiting impatiently nearby.

"I miss you, Ima," Aliyah said, wrapping her small arms about my neck when I knelt at her level. "When are you coming home?"

I swallowed hard. *Home.* Aliyah considered her father's house to be her home, which she would, of course. It was the only home the child knew. But it was not so for me. How to make her understand, though?

"Ima cannot come home, Aliyah. Your abba has a new wife, and though Ima wants you to come and live with her, she cannot make that happen right now." I whispered the words, hoping the child would not repeat them but at the same time not caring if she did.

"I don't like Abba's new wife. She wants me to call her Ima, but I already have my ima. I want you." She clung to me and kissed my cheek, then leaned toward my ear. "I know it's our secret."

"Good girl," I said, kissing her forehead. "Remember that I will always love you."

"I do," she said as Elisheva came toward us.

"It's time to go, Aliyah. Tell Ima goodbye."

"Shalom, Ima," Aliyah said instead, surprising me.

"Shalom, my sweet," I said, rising to my feet. I watched Elisheva take Aliyah's hand and walk away, and though Aliyah glanced back at me, when she reached her father and he scooped her into his arms, she giggled. I heard her laughter as the family walked home.

"She's a beautiful girl," Lavi said, coming up behind me. "I'm sorry for all you've suffered, Ness."

I turned to face him. "Why does God hate me so much?" I searched his expressive face, longing for someone to give me an answer to that nagging question.

Lavi shrugged. "I have asked the same thing, Ness. Why has He allowed us to be kept apart for so long?"

"And still allows it," I said softly.

Lavi looked at me, then glanced at Chen in the distance. "He won't reconsider, but there is a way," he said, leaning close.

I gave him a quizzical look. "How?"

"Come and live with me. Once you step into my home, no one will question that you belong to me. We will be one, and no one can say anything about it." He touched my shoulder.

I should have pulled away, but I couldn't. His touch was gentle and sent little shivers up my spine. "I would be considered immoral and a prostitute. I would lose everything."

"You would have me. We could make a home, Ness. I would take care of you the rest of our lives." He discreetly stroked my cheek, then lowered his hand. "Think about it. I will claim you as my concubine if anyone asks. Come to my home and bring your things. Why wait for Chen, who only wants to keep us apart?"

"I can't," I said, but I knew deep down that I absolutely could.

"You can," he corrected, his ardent gaze making my heart beat double time. "Let me show you what real love is."

Real love. Did anyone know what that looked like? But Lavi had waited for me for a very long time. And he'd saved himself for me.

"I'm damaged, Lavi. I've known five husbands. Can you live with that?" I had to push the truth on him no matter how he made me feel.

"Chen asked me the same question."

"You spoke to him again?"

"I've spoken to him many times in the past few weeks. He is a stubborn man." He looked deeply into my eyes. "Nessa, I don't care about your past. Neither one of us is perfect. But we can start over and make a good life."

I swallowed hard. "We could," I admitted barely above a whisper.

"Then you'll come?" Hope lifted his countenance.

"I will think about it." I turned quickly and walked away, unwilling to admit the pull his words had on me. He would wear me down, and eventually I would give in to him. I knew it as well as I knew the day would dawn tomorrow.

But what consequences would I face if I did what he was asking? I needed time to think long and hard before I threw myself away for love.

❖ ❖ ❖

For the next month, I worked beside Malka in growing tension, saw Aliyah at synagogue for a few moments each Shabbat, and met Gali at the well six days a week at dawn. The routine of my life might have felt normal if not for the friction in the house whenever Chen entered a room where I worked or served a meal. This brother who was once my closest ally when our parents were living had become hardened, almost cold, toward me, and I didn't understand why.

The reality of my situation weighed heavily on me, for I could make no sense of it. Sukkot would soon be upon us, which made more work for all of us, but one afternoon when Malka rested, I wrapped my scarf about my head and walked to Yaffa's house. She had always cared about me. And she was wiser than I was. Perhaps, unlike Gali, she could tell me what to do.

I walked along the deserted streets until Yaffa's courtyard came into view several streets over from Chen's home. Yaron had done well for himself, and since his parents were no longer living, Yaffa enjoyed a home where she was the older woman, as Yaron was the oldest son. His brothers' wives listened to Yaffa. My sister had known peace and safety for years, things I could only dream of having.

I knocked on the door and waited. Footsteps came from inside, and soon the door opened. One of Yaffa's sisters-in-law answered.

"Is Yaffa home?" I asked before the woman could speak.

She smiled. "Please come in." She allowed me entrance, and moments later a servant motioned me to sit on a bench and washed my feet.

Yaffa hurried toward me and pulled me into her arms. "Nessa, my dear sister, what brings you here?"

I glanced at the servant, who removed the dirty water. "I didn't know you had a servant. Yaron's business is doing well then."

Yaffa brushed the thought away with a wave of her hand. "He has worked for us only a short time. His family needed the money, and we find small things he can do to earn it and help them." Yaffa motioned me into the sitting room. "But tell me, what brings you to see me in the heat of the day when most of us are resting?" She called the servant to bring us cups of cool water and settled in a chair opposite me.

After the servant brought the water, I wrapped my hands about the clay vessel and drank. I wiped my mouth and set the cup down, then straightened. "I need your advice."

Yaffa raised a brow. "I don't have many answers, but I will help if I can."

"I want to marry Lavi," I said after a lengthy pause. "Chen refuses to entertain the idea because Father didn't want Lavi to marry me. So Lavi offered to make me his concubine. I wouldn't be labeled a prostitute if he did that."

"But a concubine is normally a second wife, though not a true wife. Lavi has no wife, so could he really call you that?" Yaffa sipped her water.

"I suppose he can call me what he wants. But if Chen will not allow me the benefit of marrying him, then what choice do we have?" I crossed my arms, suddenly feeling chilled.

Yaffa studied the water in her cup as though the answer was buried in the bottom. I waited, the silence growing, until at last she sighed and looked into my eyes.

"I can't tell you what to do, Ness. I don't agree with Chen.

I think Abba was wrong to keep you from Lavi when he knew how you both felt. He wanted the money he knew he could get from the very fact that you are truly the most beautiful woman in Sychar, maybe in all of Samaria, and he used that to his advantage." She glanced beyond me a moment. "You still are, Ness. And that makes men attracted and women jealous."

"But after five lost husbands, why not let me have Lavi, who has loved me all these years? He waited for me, Yaffa!" Just the thought caused my heart to beat faster.

"It's incredible, I know. But Ness, he's been gone for years. You haven't seen him until recently, so how can you trust that he means what he says? If he stole from Abba, what makes you believe he's being honest with you now?" Yaffa set her cup down and leaned closer, elbows on her knees.

"I have seen him a few times over the years. You know he came to order that robe from the booth when I was married to Nadav. But he stopped by the house, at the back near the trees, before that. He has visited Sychar a number of times, just privately. I think he's been biding his time."

Was that truly what he'd been doing? He'd claimed to wait for me, but did I believe that he'd kept himself pure for me when he knew he might never have me?

"What if he's lying to you?" Yaffa asked as if she'd read my thoughts.

"I could have said the same of any one of the men I married," I said, my defenses rising. "I didn't know any of them at the time, and they all turned against me except Amichai, peace be upon him. I would take my chances."

"It sounds as if you've already made up your mind then." Yaffa clasped her hands in her lap. "You aren't really asking for my advice, Nessa."

I stared at my hands, then at my sister. "I wanted to talk to someone I trusted about this. Someone who also knows Lavi."

"I haven't seen Lavi in so long. Yes, he's our relative, but I don't *know* him."

I smoothed my robe, my mind turning with a hundred different thoughts. "Will the town scorn me if I live with him as his concubine? Without Chen's approval?"

Yaffa shrugged. "I wish I could answer that too, but I'm not really sure. I think it will be hard for the women to accept. Then again, many of the women have never accepted your beauty or the way it turns the heads of their men. The men won't care, unless they decide they don't want their wives associating with you. And what of Aliyah? Will Osher find you unfit to even see her anymore? Are you willing to take that risk?"

I leaned back in the chair and sighed, defeat settling over me. "That is my dilemma. I don't know how Osher will react. Perhaps Elisheva will see that I live in a stable home and she will convince Osher to let Aliyah visit us. As it is now, Malka doesn't make life easy for me, and I don't think Osher likes Chen, so I doubt he wants Aliyah around either of them."

"He told you this?"

I shook my head. "Chen gave me the impression, but Osher is a foolish, immature man with a streak of stubbornness. Two stubborn men trying to come to an agreement is getting me nowhere."

Yaffa looked uncertain. "I don't know what to tell you, Ness. I want to see you happy, though . . ." She looked toward an open window and sighed. "I can't tell you not to do what your heart longs to do. I don't know how God feels about it all."

"God has never helped me before," I said, tasting bitterness. "I am on my own."

"God hasn't left you, Nessa." But Yaffa's words lacked conviction.

"God has never been with me," I said. "Not since Lavi left and Amichai died. I've been betrayed too many times to believe

He cares, Yaffa." I stood. "I should go. Malka will awaken soon and wonder where I am."

Yaffa walked with me to the door. I strapped my sandals on, hugged my sister goodbye, and walked away hearing Yaffa's "Shalom, shalom, Nessa. May God go with you."

I repeated the words, minus the part about God. If He was with me, I couldn't find Him. I knew no one could see Him, but surely if He cared, He would answer even one of my prayers. Instead, my words felt like dry reeds turning to dust. Lifeless words that God did not hear. If He did, His answer was always no.

And I was tired of living with no for an answer.

37

wo weeks later I rose before dawn with purpose in every movement. I had wrestled with a decision on what to do with the rest of my life since my talk with Yaffa and subsequent conversations with Gali. Neither woman had been able to guide me with conviction, and Chen's attitude toward Lavi had not changed.

But Malka's attitude toward me had only grown more strained until we barely spoke to one another. If not for Chen and Malka's sons to speak with now and then, I would have lived in a house of silence. Malka had plenty to say to Chen when he was home, and most of the time I heard them fighting in their room.

I couldn't continue to allow strife because I was no longer wanted here.

I stuffed my nightclothes into the basket I had packed the night before, added my cosmetics, ointments, and spindle and distaff along with the wool attached to them, and looked about the small room. Nothing was left except my pallet, but I would not need it in Lavi's home.

Walking to the sitting room, grateful that the household still slept, I looked longingly at the loom I had used since childhood. Perhaps Lavi would build one for me or purchase one if he could afford to do so. Strange that I had never asked him for details of what our living arrangement would be or how I would help him support us. All I could think about of late was my need to escape this house and finally make my own choice of a mate. Such as it was.

I walked to the door, grabbed my cloak from a peg on the wall, slipped into my sandals, and left the house, baskets in hand. Osher had sent me off with his donkey, but Chen had later returned it. I couldn't take one of Chen's animals with me. No, I would carry all that I needed. One glance at the water jar told me I would miss seeing Gali today, but I had warned her that this day might come. Would we continue meeting at the well once everyone knew what I had done?

A pang of regret hit me, but I pushed it aside as I had with every other negative feeling. Aliyah was my only uncertainty, but I had to think about my own happiness too. One day when she was grown, if not before, she would see me again. Hopefully sooner if Lavi had anything to say about it.

Dawn barely crested the horizon as I walked the quiet streets of Sychar to the opposite end of where Chen lived. Lavi's home was near the merchant district, far from my family and from the families of the men I had married. Good. I would miss my sisters, but not the others.

Of course, I couldn't avoid the censured looks when we attended synagogue, but I would simply have to endure whatever came my way. I couldn't bear to miss my chance to see Aliyah.

I passed the shops and came to the street leading to Lavi's house. As I took the path and gazed on the small house, I paused. My heart beat harder, and I fought the indecision that had plagued me for months. I could do this. I *would* do this. But what if I was wrong and this was my worst idea yet?

The door opened at that moment as if Lavi had been watching for me, and he walked toward me, smiling. He stopped within arm's length. "You came."

I nodded, unable to speak past the lump in my throat.

"I'm glad." He touched my face, trailing a finger along the side of my cheek, sending chills through me. He deftly took my baskets in one hand and placed the other at the small of my back, ushering me toward the door.

At the threshold, he set the baskets just inside the house, then took my hands in his. He lifted them to his lips and kissed each finger, then slowly pulled me into his arms.

"I know it's not a huppah with your father or a rabbi, but I hereby claim you, Nessa bat Raanan, as mine." He kissed me lightly, temptingly, and wooed me to follow him into the house.

He touched the mezuzah on the doorpost and kissed his fingers, a practice I had seen now and then among the families I had lived with, but never before with Lavi. His simple act touched my heart, as if he wanted God's blessing on our union even if we weren't strictly obeying the law.

He shut the door behind us, bent to remove my sandals, then stood facing me. "Come," he said, taking my hand.

My feet landed on plush rugs, surprising me with the simple elegance, as he led me to the only bedroom in the house. "We must make this official before I leave for the shop," he said, his voice husky.

I nodded, looking deeply into his dark, expressive eyes.

"I've wanted you for so long, Nessa." He removed my headscarf, not a bridal veil as I might have worn if Chen had allowed us to marry. "I'm sorry you're missing out on a real wedding."

"Those 'real' weddings meant nothing to me, and the traditions hardly kept them from lasting," I said, hearing the hint of bitterness in my tone.

"Consider this truly real then," he whispered as he kissed my temples and undid the combs holding my hair.

When he found my lips and his kiss deepened, memories of our first kiss disappeared, replaced by one far more emotive. He cupped my shoulders, pulled me down beside him, and slowly, gently showed me his love until I felt as though I would melt from his achingly tender touch.

My tears spilled onto the pillow when he rose up on one elbow to look at me. He brushed them away. "What's wrong, my love?" He kissed my cheek. "Did I upset you?"

I shook my head. "No," I said too quickly. But I couldn't tell him the thoughts that filled my heart. I wanted to throw my arms about him and make him promise to never leave me. At the same moment, I had the awful fear that he would one day ruin the brief joy we'd just shared.

He stroked the hair from my forehead. "Nessa. I know you cannot trust me yet. How could you? Every man you've ever known has let you down. But I will prove to you that I am not like them."

I swiped the tears and offered him a wobbly smile as I held the bedsheet over me with one hand. "I know," I whispered. I desperately wanted to believe him, but I couldn't. Not yet. Maybe not ever.

But I would stay and see if he could keep his promises, unlike everyone else in Sychar.

"I will never leave you, Ness. I will leave to go to work, but I will always return. I promise." He kissed my forehead. "Never fear."

I nodded, hoping he believed me.

He pulled me up to sit with him on the bed. "You are mine, Nessa, and I am yours. No matter what anyone says." He stood and dressed, handing my clothes to me to do the same. "Let us eat something quickly so I'm not terribly late opening the booth."

"I brought some flatbread with me and a cheese that I purchased yesterday. I didn't know what you might have." I hurried from the room, and he chuckled, following me.

"While I'm gone, feel free to set your things wherever you want to. Here are some coins so you can go to the market and purchase whatever we need. I don't have much, I admit, but I trust you to make our house a home."

Our house. The words felt wonderful to hear. I had never had a home that belonged to just me and my husband. "I will make it beautiful for you."

He searched my face as I handed him some bread and cheese and poured him a cup of water. "I know you enjoy weaving, so I'll find a loom or have it built for you. I want you to have everything you have always wanted, my love."

His smile warmed me as I bid him farewell for the day. Surely I had made the right decision. Except for one thing. He could not give me Aliyah. Only Osher held that power, and he was not likely to ever do so now. But I refused to grieve over all that was lost because the past was something I could never get back.

❖ ❖ ❖

I moved through Lavi's home, *our home*, and searched for places within easy reach to set the things I had brought with me. Lavi had extra pegs on the walls of his room and a chest in which to place my cosmetics and other items. He had thought of everything I would need, more than a man alone would normally think to have.

I searched the food preparation area, making a mental note of the spices I would need and the grain and lentils he lacked. What had he eaten in the days before I came? No doubt he had purchased food from the merchants as he had only a sack of nuts and another of raisins.

I donned my sandals as the sun was halfway to its midpoint and wrapped the scarf closely about me, in part to hide from anyone who might notice me, and in part to keep the warm breeze from pulling my hair about. I had hastily replaced the combs Lavi had removed but had not taken the time to fix my hair as I normally would. So I covered it well, lest anyone think me a loose woman.

The street of merchants was the next one over from our home, and I noted Lavi's shop nearest the end of the row. I glanced his way but did not wave when I saw him interacting with a man I didn't recognize. I made my way to the spice merchant, purchased what I needed, and continued on until my basket was nearly too full to carry.

"Can you have a bushel of wheat and another of barley sent to my home?" I asked the woman behind the grain booth.

"Certainly," the woman answered, peering closely at me. "Where shall we have it sent?"

I paused, suddenly uncertain. What would she think when I asked for it to be sent to Lavi's house? Everyone who had met him knew he was unmarried and alone. I cleared my throat and straightened, telling myself it didn't matter what anyone thought.

"The home of Lavi ben Erez, the perfumer. It's the next street behind the street of merchants." I pointed in the general direction, then pulled my coin purse from the pocket of my robe and handed the woman the money.

"Lavi," the woman repeated. "The new merchant from Sebaste."

I nodded. "Yes."

"Are you his sister? I thought he lived alone. Surely he didn't suddenly take a wife." Skepticism filled her tone.

My heart beat faster. I had not expected to answer such questions so soon. "I belong to him," I said, my voice low. "That's all I need. Please have these things sent." I hurried away to the next booth, heat flooding my face.

I paused before entering the cheese maker's booth to draw in a steadying breath. *"I belong to him"?* Was that how I wanted to be known? Could I say "concubine"? I fanned my face despite the gentle breeze.

Indecision warred within me. I needed cheese, bread for tonight, almonds, and pistachios. And wine. Lavi had one skin but he would want more. I fingered the purse he had given me. He had not been skimpy with his wealth but had trusted me. I couldn't let him down.

Bracing myself, I entered the next booth without incident and moved on, feeling slightly better. I had added the sack of almonds to my basket when I heard my name.

"Nessa? Is that you?" Amichai's daughter-in-law Hila waved at me from across the street, hurrying toward me. "It's been too long."

I'd seen Hila now and then during my marriage to Osher and still saw her briefly after synagogue, but it had been some time.

I nodded at her. "Shalom, Hila." I pulled my basket closer like a shield between us.

"Shalom." Hila studied me and sighed. "I'm sorry things went so poorly for you with Osher, Nessa. I thought he was a good man. He was Amichai's relative, after all."

"Yes, well, he was a decent man at first," I said, glancing about and longing to escape this conversation. "I believe others had a hand in changing his opinion of me." My knuckles whitened on the handle of the basket. "I really must be going," I said when Hila said nothing in response. "It was nice to see you again. Give my love to your family."

Hila took a step closer, blocking my intention to walk away. "Before you go," she said, meeting my gaze, "are you well? I'm sorry about Aliyah. If I could do anything to help, you know I would."

I nodded, my expression softening. Hila *had* been kind to me in the past. "I know. Perhaps one day things will change."

"Are Chen and Malka treating you well?" she asked as if wanting to find something to keep me from leaving.

I hesitated. If I said yes, I would be lying. If I told her I no longer lived with them, the gossips would hear about it and word would spread throughout the town before I could return home.

"You know, if they're not happy with you being there, you could return to live in Amichai's home. We would welcome you. Of course, there is no husband for you to marry, but it would be a place to stay, and perhaps you could see Aliyah more often if we could arrange it." Hila's words were rushed, as if she feared I would flee before she could say them.

My heart skipped a beat, and I felt my body drain of warmth. If I had moved in with them instead of Lavi, would I have seen Aliyah more often? On feast days and other gatherings of the family? But I had made my choice.

"I don't live with them anymore," I said at last, keeping my voice low.

Hila raised a brow. "You don't? Where do you live then? I didn't hear of another marriage arrangement."

"There wasn't one," I said, the heat returning in a rush and making my palms sweat.

Hila waited, confusion in her expression.

"I moved in with Lavi today. He is my cousin and he took me in." Dare I mention the true arrangement we had? He was not simply being an older cousin watching out for me. The rabbis might consider what I was doing sinful.

"Oh," Hila said. By her look, I was certain she had guessed the situation. "I remember Lavi. Amichai convinced your father to let you marry him, but he knew Lavi wanted to be your father's choice. That's the cousin you speak of, isn't it?"

I nodded, this time lifting my chin in a hint of defiance. "Yes. We belong to each other now. Call me his concubine, for we are not married as I was with the others."

"Concubine," Hila said. I did not get the impression she believed it in the legal sense. "Would not Chen sign a ketubah to allow you to marry Lavi?"

I shook my head. "Chen is stubborn. He would not." I leaned forward, not sure if I should say more but determined to say it regardless. "I cannot bear another marriage to a man who does not love me, Hila. So I made my own decision."

Hila's eyes widened. Such a thing was unheard of in Sychar, though men were sometimes unfaithful to their wives and too often sought divorces. Still, no one in Sychar had been through as many marriages as I had.

Hila touched my shoulder. "I'm sorry for all you have suffered. Perhaps you can go to the rabbi for something to make your arrangement official."

It was too late for that as far as I was concerned, but I offered Hila a half smile. "Perhaps we will. But I really do have to go. I'm almost done with my purchases and have to finish setting things up before Lavi returns home."

"Of course," Hila said, stepping back. "I wish you well, Nessa." She hurried away.

My heart raced after the encounter, and I stood a moment in the street, not sure what to do next. I glanced at my basket. I had enough to make a nice meal for tonight. I would come again early tomorrow before most of the women were about, to avoid another encounter.

I needed water. The sun was already nearly overhead, bringing the heat with it. I would go home and hurry to the well, despite the heat of the day. Tomorrow I would go at the early hour to meet Gali. Things would return to normal, and soon the people of Sychar would forget. Still, I had no doubt they would talk about us in every home at evening meal tonight.

But there was nothing I could do to stop what I had now set in motion.

38

entered my new home, set the basket of food on a shelf in the cooking area, then hurried to the courtyard to grab the jar I needed for water. The sun's heat caused sweat to trickle down my back. This was the worst time of day to go to the well, but what choice did I have? Lavi had successfully interrupted any thought I had of going early the moment I'd entered his home.

The memory of his kiss heated me more than the blazing sun. Never had a man made me feel so much emotion. Even Tamir with all his wooing ways had not made me care for him as Lavi had done this morning. Would our future continue to be so full of love and caring? Or would Lavi eventually tire of me like all the others had?

The thought that even he might not keep his word dampened my mood, which had already been soured by my discussion with Hila and the skeptical look of the woman who sold the grain. Even now, I sensed the whispers in the houses I passed and saw the curious stares of the few women who worked in their courtyards rather than rest in the cool of their homes. They knew. They had to know.

Today should be a joyous occasion, and I should have come here with Gali before dawn. But how could I rejoice when guilt plagued me? Did I have to feel this way so soon after my decision?

I lifted my chin and walked toward the gate, passing a group of men I did not recognize. They appeared to be travelers, and as I gave them a closer, subtle inspection, my heart jolted. Jews? What were they doing in a Samaritan town?

I hurried past, not wanting them to speak to me, though they undoubtedly had seen me. I rushed through the gate and past the guards, thankfully without inquiry. Relief filled me even as the heat shimmered over the dusty ground, and I trudged toward the well on suddenly weighted limbs. Could this day become any stranger? Jews had nothing to do with Samaritans. This could not be good. Were they spies?

I glanced ahead as the well came into view and noticed a man sitting on the grassy knoll where Gali often waited for me. What was he doing there alone at this hour? Thoughts of Jacob meeting Rachel at a well surfaced, but this man could not possibly be searching for a relative to give him shelter.

I watched him as I approached, wary now. And then I saw his distinctive clothing. Another Jew? And why had he stayed behind? One glance told me that he looked strong and capable and yet . . . weary.

He lifted his gaze to mine as I reached the well. I kept to the side away from him and quickly lowered my jar.

"Will you give me a drink?" the man asked.

I looked him up and down and suddenly realized that though I was alone with a strange man, probably about my age of thirty-one years, I did not fear him. I should have, shouldn't I? But his manner did not evoke such fear.

I lifted my chin and boldly met his gaze. "You are a Jew and I am a Samaritan woman," I said. "How can you ask me for a drink? Jews have nothing to do with *Samaritans*."

I flinched at the depth of compassion in his gaze. As if he

knew me. But he didn't know me. I shook myself and focused on pulling the jar from the well.

"If you knew the gift of God and who it is that asks you for a drink," he said, his voice gentle, "you would have asked him and he would have given you living water."

I stared at him. *Living water?* What was he talking about? Who was he? I almost turned away to walk home and ignore his request, then thought better of it and faced him, holding the jar to my chest.

"Sir," I said, looking about at his lack of belongings or a vessel with which to draw water. "You have nothing to draw with and the well is deep. Where can you get this living water? Are you greater than our father Jacob, who gave us the well and drank from it himself, as did also his sons and his livestock?"

The man shifted but did not stand, for which I was grateful. He was showing me that he posed no threat to me. Wasn't he? Why then did my heart pick up its pace at this conversation? A conversation I did not understand.

"Everyone who drinks this water will be thirsty again," he said, "but whoever drinks the water I give them will never thirst. Indeed, the water I give them will become in them a spring of water welling up to eternal life."

I stared at him, utterly confused. Was I speaking to a madman, one of those possessed who wandered the hills? There were no springs close enough to Sychar to draw from. Did he know of one that no one else did? How could this man offer me living water if it did not exist here?

"Sir," I said, wary and carefully framing my words, testing him. "Give me this water so that I won't get thirsty and have to keep coming here to draw water." I would gladly go to a spring closer to home or, if he was telling me the truth, be even happier to never thirst again. But water was necessary for far more than thirst.

Thirst. If he only knew the thirst I'd had for more than water all my life. For love. Safety. Security. Home. But he didn't know, so I watched him, waiting for a logical answer to explain his illogical comment.

He searched my face, and for a breathless moment I wondered if indeed he could read my thoughts. Impossible.

"Go, call your husband and come back," he said quietly.

The request felt like a punch to my middle. But of course he would ask such a thing. Men didn't normally talk at length to women, nor explain the answers to any questions to them alone. Particularly a Jewish man, who should not even be sitting here talking to me at all.

I cleared my throat and lifted the jar to my shoulder as if to leave. "I have no husband."

"You are right when you say you have no husband." He paused and folded his hands in his lap. "The fact is, you have had five husbands, and the man you now have is not your husband. What you have just said is quite true."

My heart nearly stopped. I stiffened. How could he possibly know this? Surely God knew my sins and my miserable life's story. Could He have told the man? No one else in Sychar knew all the details yet. The gossips had not had time to tell everyone!

I swallowed and set the jar in the dirt. "Sir, I can see that you are a prophet." He had to be. My mind whirled, and I didn't know what else to say. I lifted my gaze to Mt. Gerizim in the distance and searched for something to ask him to prove that he knew more than my personal history. The mountain seemed to speak, reminding me of the difference in our histories and the constant debate the Jews and Samaritans had bickered about over the years. Hadn't the rabbis spoken of it often at synagogue?

I squared my shoulders. "Our ancestors worshiped on this mountain," I said, pointing to Mt. Gerizim, "but you Jews claim that the place where we must worship is in Jerusalem." I leveled him with a taunting look, certain he would never be able to settle that debate. I hoped it took his mind off my personal failings, which were none of his business. Why did I stand here continuing this conversation?

"Woman," the man said, "believe me, a time is coming when you will worship the Father neither on this mountain nor in Jerusalem. You Samaritans worship what you do not know; we worship what we do know, for salvation is from the Jews. Yet a time is coming and has now come when the true worshipers will worship the Father in the Spirit and in truth, for they are the kind of worshipers the Father seeks. God is spirit, and His worshipers must worship in the Spirit and in truth."

His words nearly knocked the breath from me. "Are you saying that Jews and Samaritans will all worship God in the same way? Our people would never agree with you." I dared him to argue with me with a nearly contemptuous look.

"Whether they agree or not, I speak the truth. God doesn't dwell in temples made with human hands. He is spirit, and those who worship Him must worship Him in the Spirit and in truth." He shifted in his seat, but he kept a respectful distance from me.

"I have never found that God cares anything about me," I said, unable to keep the bitterness from surfacing. "He has never answered my prayers or kept my husbands from sending me away or given me my children . . ." My voice broke, and I could not continue. I looked away, for I could not bear to see pity in his eyes.

"The Father does not always give us what we ask, Nessa. But that does not mean He hasn't heard our prayers."

I jerked my gaze back to his. "How do you know my name?" My heart beat double time in my chest.

"You rightly said that I am a prophet," he said, his dark eyes searching and filled with . . . kindness. Not scorn or rebuke or censure.

I swallowed back a sudden burst of emotion. I put a hand

to my throat to keep from weeping. "I know that Messiah is coming," I said at last, desperately trying to change the subject. What better way than to put off this heated discussion to some distant future? "When he comes, he will explain everything to us." If I lived to see that day, perhaps he would be able to make sense of my life as well. But not now. Not in my lifetime.

The man slowly stood and extended his hands to me in supplication as if what he was about to say next was of great import. As if he cared that I listened and believed him. His intense dark eyes captured mine, and I gasped at the light emanating from them. "Woman, I, the one speaking to you—I am he."

Messiah? I held his gaze for one amazing moment, and suddenly, as though someone had turned me completely around, I knew I would never be the same.

The sound of male voices interrupted us. I looked toward the town and saw the same Jewish men I had passed walking toward us. I looked back at him.

It couldn't be. But the longer I held his gaze, the more all the hurt and bitterness I'd carried within me for years slowly unraveled. The tenseness I'd felt since I entered Lavi's home that morning against my brother's wishes melted away. His gaze pierced my heart, cracking the walls I had built around it, and without a word I felt what could only be healing of all the hurt I had suffered. Could it be?

I cleared my throat, anxious to say something before the men drew up beside us. "You truly are the Messiah? Why would you tell me this? Me. A woman of Samaria."

"Because you need to know that God has not abandoned you in your struggles. He sees you, as do I. Only the Messiah can give you what you have always longed for, Nessa. Love. Security. Safety. A home."

I gasped. He had read my thoughts. "I have never felt that He heard my prayers because my circumstances have never improved."

"God has heard every one, my daughter."

That he would call me by that name made tears spring to my eyes. Even my father had not treated me as well as he could have. I saw the man smile, and in his smile the rest of my fears and shame and guilt and anger disappeared.

"You truly are the Messiah," I said, joy bubbling within me. "I'm going to tell everyone!"

At that moment the other men joined him, the Messiah, and I could only assume they were with him. Disciples perhaps? But I didn't wait to find out. I left my jar near the well and ran back toward the town, my feet no longer weighted but light as air.

I reached the town gate, passed the guards, and climbed the stairs to the city gate where the elders gathered. I stopped, out of breath, and looked about, seeing the fathers of a few of my former husbands suddenly silent at my approach.

"Come, see a man who told me everything I ever did," I said, looking from one man to another. All of them knew my life's story, as many of them had played a role in it. "Could this be the Messiah?" I added. I turned to hurry down the steps and into the streets, shouting the same message, certain the men would follow simply out of curiosity.

I made my way to the merchants' street and found Lavi sitting in his booth. "Come, my love," I said, again out of breath from running. "Come to the well and meet a man who told me everything I ever did. Could he be the Messiah?"

Lavi stared at me as though I'd struck him. "Nessa, what are you talking about?"

"I went to the well to gather water for tonight, and this Jewish man was sitting there. He asked me for a drink and then talked about living water, but I didn't understand, so I asked him about where we're supposed to worship—in Jerusalem or on Mt. Gerizim. I didn't want to talk about myself, but he told me I'd been married five times and the man I had now was not my husband. But, Lavi, how could he know that?

I only came to you today! The whole town does not yet know it, so he couldn't possibly know unless God told him." I drew in a breath, unable to slow down. "So I told him he must be a prophet and he told me he was the Messiah! Me!" I extended a hand to him. "Please, Lavi, you must come."

Lavi's expression had moved from humor to interest to concern. "Yes, I will come. I don't want someone telling you lies. Let me see for myself."

He closed the booth and took my hand, and together we joined the throng from the town and hurried to the well where the Jewish men still waited. The crowd surrounded the area near the well.

"This woman," Tamir's father Keshet said, pointing at me, "said that you told her everything she has ever done. Are you a prophet? And why have you come to Samaria?"

"I am Jesus of Nazareth," the man said, looking from one person to the next until he had captured everyone in his gaze. "Nessa is correct. I met her here and asked her for a drink. She asked me questions that normally are things taught by a rabbi to his disciples. So I asked her to call her husband, and she told me she had no husband. She spoke the truth, for she has had five husbands and the man she has now is not her husband." He looked at Lavi and me in that moment, again with a look full of compassion.

A collective gasp came from the crowd. Of course, very few of them knew I had moved in with Lavi that morning. I glanced at Lavi, whose stricken expression made my heart break. Did he feel the same guilt I had when this Jesus had looked at me? What we had done was wrong, and we both knew it deep down. We should have waited for Chen to agree to let us marry.

"I did not come here to reveal everyone's secrets," Jesus said, lifting his hands toward heaven. "I have come that you may have life. I am the way to that life. I am the truth you are seeking. I am the living water that has come from heaven to offer the world eternal life if they believe in me and accept my words."

"Nessa said that you claim to be the Messiah," Harel's father Niv said. "Is that what you are telling us?"

"Yes," Jesus said. "I am the one who is coming into the world. I have come to bring reconciliation between the world and the Father."

"Are you going to bring about the kingdom and set us free from the Roman oppression?" Chen asked.

I whirled about at the sound of his voice. How had he heard the news so quickly? When I glanced at the crowd, it seemed as though all the men in Sychar were crowding closer to see Jesus of Nazareth.

"Come, please, stay in our town and speak more to us about these things," Niv said. His words were followed by nods and yeses from the others.

"Very well," Jesus said, though the men with him did not look too comfortable with the idea.

"You can stay with us," Amichai's son Arieh said. Of all the homes in town, Amichai's would have the most room.

As the crowd moved to walk back into the city, I could hear the men asking questions of Jesus, but I was not close enough to catch them all. I glimpsed my water jar still near the well, so I hurried over to snatch it up and walked with Lavi behind the others.

"What do you think of him?" I asked, glancing into his eyes.

"I don't know what to think," he said, his look pensive. "If he is truly the Messiah, then I think we have a lot of things to learn from him."

"Yes, I think so too." I watched the road, longing to catch up with the crowd to hear every word he had to say.

If only I could stay with Amichai's family tonight. I would sit at Jesus' feet and listen. Perhaps he would answer even more of my nagging questions, the ones that had troubled me for years. Like why had God allowed me to suffer the loss of so many men? Why did He take my two sons from me and then not allow me to keep my daughter?

Please give me a chance to hear more from him. My silent prayer accompanied a quick glance at Lavi, who seemed to be thinking about and processing all that he had heard.

"Do you think you should return to Chen's house tonight?" Lavi said after a lengthy silence. "I mean, until we can properly wed."

I stopped walking to face him. "I don't know. We are already one in God's eyes."

"But we didn't have the blessing of the rabbi or your brother."

"I know." I swallowed. The fear of losing him was not as strong as the sudden desire to do what God might want. Had Jesus' words changed my heart so quickly? Deep inside I knew they had. "Perhaps that would be best. But let me take this jar to your house. I have food for us to eat. Then I will return to Chen's home until we can make things right."

His smile warmed me, and I knew he would not abandon me. This was not like my previous marriages. This was the start of something much better and new. And I realized that only the Messiah could have changed my heart for me to believe this was possible. Only God could make me trust a man again or love him without fear.

39

*J*esus spoke to the crowd in the town's square the next morning, where men and women and even children clamored to hear his words. I had managed to stand near him with Chen and Malka and their children. Lavi kept himself slightly apart from us, but I sensed his nearness and knew he was also drinking in every word that came from this man's mouth.

"Suppose one of you has a hundred sheep and loses one of them," Jesus said, drawing my thoughts only to him. "Doesn't he leave the ninety-nine in the open country and go after the lost sheep until he finds it? And when he finds it, he joyfully puts it on his shoulders and goes home. Then he calls his friends and neighbors together and says, 'Rejoice with me; I have found my lost sheep.' I tell you that in the same way there will be more rejoicing in heaven over one sinner who repents than over ninety-nine righteous persons who do not need to repent."

"What things must we repent of?" Lavi asked, drawing Jesus' attention. "I mean, I know the law and we all try to keep it. Is that not enough?"

"The law is good and perfect, but it was given to show men and women the impossibility of keeping the whole law, because if a man keeps the whole law and yet stumbles in just one point, he is guilty of all." Jesus searched the crowd.

"Then what is the purpose of the law?" I asked, causing the men to glance my way. "If we cannot keep it, why did God give it to us?"

"It was given to show you that God is holy and you cannot meet His standards. Abraham was justified in the sight of God by faith, not by obeying the law. The law was given to make sin evident to everyone—to show you that you need a savior. For instance, when the law says, 'Do not steal,' it convicts those who have stolen even the smallest thing. But faith trusts in God to forgive that sin. Abraham believed even before his redeemer came, and God counted his faith as righteousness to him. Faith gives you eternal life when you place your faith in me."

Murmurs moved through the crowd. Older men and women nodded in understanding, while the younger among them seemed curious and pondering.

"Let me explain this faith and the kingdom another way," Jesus said, moving to sit on a step that led to the town's governing offices. His disciples also sat, surrounding him. Then one by one the people sank to the paved streets.

"Suppose a woman has ten silver coins and loses one," Jesus said. "Doesn't she light a lamp, sweep the house, and search carefully until she finds it? And when she finds it, she calls her friends and neighbors together and says, 'Rejoice with me; I have found my lost coin.' In the same way, I tell you, there is rejoicing in the presence of the angels of God over one sinner who repents."

I glanced about. The people were enraptured by his words, but I caught discomfort in many expressions. Surprisingly, even Tamir, Harel, and Osher looked uncomfortable. Were they sorry for the way they had treated me? Or were they convicted of other sins?

As I pondered the hope that they felt the sting of guilt because of the hurt they had caused me, a swift sense of conviction filled my own heart. I was in no position to judge even them. I knew my own traitorous, bitter thoughts. I may not have purposely caused my broken marriages, but I could have been more loving, more giving. I could have believed God cared about me instead of always looking upon Him as though all my life's circumstances were His fault. A sigh escaped me as Jesus continued.

"I will tell you one more story. Listen carefully, as this will tell you of the Father's heart. He loves the world, all of the world, and He has sent His Son as an atoning sacrifice to show you that love. Anyone who runs from Him but then returns repentant and believing will be welcomed home." He lifted his hands toward the heavens, then toward the crowd. "There was a man who had two sons. The younger one said to his father, 'Father, give me my share of the estate.' So he divided his property between them."

Little gasps came from some of the men. For a son to ask such a thing was unheard of.

"Not long after that," he continued, "the younger son got together all he had, set off for a distant country, and there squandered his wealth in wild living. After he had spent everything, there was a severe famine in that whole country, and he began to be in need. So he went and hired himself out to a citizen of that country, who sent him to his fields to feed pigs. He longed to fill his stomach with the pods that the pigs were eating, but no one gave him anything.

"When he came to his senses, he said, 'How many of my father's hired servants have food to spare, and here I am starving to death! I will set out and go back to my father and say to him: Father, I have sinned against heaven and against you. I am no longer worthy to be called your son; make me like one of your hired servants.' So he got up and went to his father.

"But while he was still a long way off, his father saw him and was filled with compassion for him; he ran to his son, threw his arms around him, and kissed him."

Another collective gasp rose from those listening. What father among them would ever welcome back such a wayward son? My own father had never accepted Lavi after what he had done, and his crime seemed so much less than this man's. How could a father do such a thing? I leaned forward, my heart yearning to understand.

Jesus opened his arms as if to encompass us or draw us near. "The son said to him, 'Father, I have sinned against heaven and against you. I am no longer worthy to be called your son.'

"But the father said to his servants, 'Quick! Bring the best robe and put it on him. Put a ring on his finger and sandals on his feet. Bring the fattened calf and kill it. Let's have a feast and celebrate. For this son of mine was dead and is alive again; he was lost and is found.' So they began to celebrate.

"Meanwhile, the older son was in the field. When he came near the house, he heard music and dancing. So he called one of the servants and asked him what was going on. 'Your brother has come,' he replied, 'and your father has killed the fattened calf because he has him back safe and sound.' But the older brother became angry and refused to go in."

In that moment, Jesus looked at Chen. Color rose in Chen's cheeks. "A logical reaction," he said softly.

I expected Jesus to respond to Chen, but he simply gave him that same look of kindness he'd had for me and continued. "So his father went out and pleaded with him. But he answered his father, 'Look! All these years I've been slaving for you and never disobeyed your orders. Yet you never gave me even a young goat so I could celebrate with my friends. But when this son of yours who has squandered your property with prostitutes comes home, you kill the fattened calf for him!'

"'My son,' the father said, 'you are always with me, and everything I have is yours. But we had to celebrate and be glad, because this brother of yours was dead and is alive again; he was lost and is found.'"

Jesus paused, his eyes alight with compassion and something I could not define. Earnestness? Pleading?

"That, my friends," he added, "is true repentance. I have come to preach that the kingdom of heaven is near, so you must repent if you want to have any part in it. Repent and believe in these words I have told you."

Excited murmurs filtered through the crowd, and my heart soared.

"Will you stay longer and teach us more?" the synagogue ruler asked. "Your words have stirred our hearts."

Jesus nodded. "We will be in town for one more day." He stood then and dismissed the crowd.

I stayed with Chen, Malka, their children, and Lavi as the others dispersed to their places of work. I longed to speak with Jesus, to ask more, but would he talk to me again without the crowds?

At that moment, Jesus walked closer to me and smiled when he met my gaze.

"Rabbi, we are honored to have you among us," Chen said, placing an arm about Malka's shoulders, his sons standing close to them both. "We would be honored even more to have you come to our home for a meal."

"Oh yes," I said, silently praying he would accept.

"Thank you, my friends." He motioned to his followers. "Are you sure we will not be a burden?"

"Not at all," Chen assured him.

"Then let us go," Jesus said.

Chen led the way and I followed, but Lavi held back. Would he not join us?

"You come as well, Lavi. I think we have much to discuss." Jesus beckoned him, and Lavi did not hesitate.

With Jesus there, Chen could not easily send Lavi away. And perhaps Jesus would bring healing to our family now. If only he could bring healing to my relationships with all of my past

315

husbands' families. And perhaps help me see Aliyah more often. But I refused to hope when my heart was still so full of his words. There was too much to comprehend, but I rejoiced in knowing that Chen and Lavi were willing to hear him out.

❖ ❖ ❖

Lavi followed the teacher at a distance toward Chen's home, his heart and mind full of questions. As they entered the court-yard and the men took seats along the benches, encircling Jesus, Lavi glanced at the house. How he had loved it here when Uncle Raanan had taken him in after the death of his parents. He'd felt accepted, like a son, though not quite as favored as Chen. Even the laughing and bickering sisters made him feel as though he belonged, especially when he teased them. They all took his remarks in fun and gave back as well as he'd given.

But Nessa had always been his favorite, the one closest to his age, and as she matured, his affection for her slowly changed from brotherly love to a longing to make her his wife. Uncle Raanan's rejection of his request still stung if he thought on it too long. And when Uncle Raanan gave Nessa to that old man Amichai, Lavi had wanted to pay him back for the hurt he'd caused. His hurt only increased when Amichai paid him to move away. He hadn't wanted Lavi near to cause discord in his family.

The memory had always fueled Lavi's anger and made him want to do whatever it took to win Nessa back, even if he had to wait for the old man to die. He hadn't expected him to go the way of all the earth so quickly, or for Raanan to continue to pass Nessa from one wealthy man to the next before his death. He'd never chosen a man who truly cared for Nessa apart from her beauty. Everyone wanted to show the world that he had won the heart of the most beautiful woman in Sychar.

How many times had Lavi wished Nessa was not so pleas-ant to look upon? Perhaps he would have stood a chance much sooner if she looked more like her sisters. He had always loved her for who she was at heart, not because of her beauty.

His thoughts whirled as the men about the court talked among themselves. What was he even doing here? This man, Messiah or not, wasn't going to be able to make things better with Chen or allow Lavi to make up for his sins by marrying Nessa. His sins, if he were honest with himself, went deeper than the stealing. He'd hardened his heart against Nessa's father and brother and sought some way to make them pay for what they had done to him. Was that why he had coaxed Nessa to come to him without the benefit of marriage?

He shook himself and glanced about the group. His gaze rested on Jesus, who was watching him with an expression of compassion, as if he could read Lavi's thoughts. Could he?

At that moment, Jesus stood. "If you will excuse me for a moment," he said to his followers and Chen, "Lavi and I have some things to discuss." He motioned for Lavi to follow him.

Lavi's heart lurched at being singled out, but he slowly stood and followed the teacher behind the house toward Chen's shop, the place where Lavi also used to work and had stolen those tools. Did Jesus know what he had done?

They stopped near the tree line where Lavi had come to see Nessa years before. Jesus turned to face him and placed a hand on his shoulder. "I know what you fear, my son. But it is not too late to repent of your sins and give your heart to the Father."

Lavi couldn't hold that penetrating, loving gaze. The words said in such sincerity and the acceptance in Jesus' eyes accompanied the gentle conviction he felt at the man's touch.

"How do you know?" Lavi choked back the rest of what he wanted to say.

"I know," Jesus said. "I know you were hurt by your uncle, Nessa's father, the one you thought would give you what you were sure you wanted. But Nessa would not have completed you, Lavi. Only the Father's love can give a man what he truly needs. A wife is a gift from the Lord, but loving God with all of your heart, soul, mind, and strength is of greater importance than loving any woman."

Lavi lifted his eyes to meet Jesus' tender gaze. "I've never felt that God loves me, so I have never known how to keep that command to love Him."

"Lavi, God loves you more than you will ever know. He is the Father in the story, waiting to welcome you home. Will you run to Him and confess the sin and pain in your heart? All the Father wants, all that I want, is your love. Your undivided love."

Lavi lowered his head, unable to continue to hold Jesus' gaze. He glimpsed his past in the space of several breaths—the lies to Nessa, the anger and bitter hurt. He sensed Jesus watching him even as he removed his hand from Lavi's shoulder. He swallowed back sudden emotion. "How do I do that?" he whispered.

"To repent is to tell God you recognize your need of Him, Lavi. Admit that His law is just and that you have broken that law. Turn from the past and surrender your will to the Father's . . . whatever that may be."

Lavi looked up at Jesus' words. "Even if He asks me to let Nessa go to another?" The temptation to lift his chin in defiance surfaced, but he could not escape the love and understanding emanating from this man. Why had he singled Lavi out? Shouldn't Chen and the men Nessa had married be required to do what Jesus was asking of him?

Lavi shook his head. "You desire a hard thing." Dare he tell him the truth? But he sensed that this man already knew him completely, which made no sense, unless what Nessa said was true. "Are you truly the Messiah?"

"I am," he said softly.

"Nessa and I are already one," he said after a lengthy pause. "How can I let her go now?"

"Give your longings to God. Surrendering to His will means letting go of your wants for your life. He may grant your heart's desires, or He may give you something better. He is good. He wants to bless you, if you will let Him determine how to do so. Do you have faith to trust Him with your life and your future, Lavi?"

The question hung between them like a barrier separating Lavi from all that God had waiting for him, whatever that might be.

"I love Nessa."

"I know you do."

Lavi turned slightly and glanced at the shop. If only his life had been different. But he still needed a savior if he was to ever know God. That's what Jesus really meant, wasn't it?

He lifted his hands, palms up, to Jesus and sank to his knees. "I want what you say can be mine," he said. "I want to receive God's love . . . and forgiveness for all that I've done. Including taking Nessa before we were wed."

His tears came as Jesus knelt beside him and clasped his hands. Then he felt Jesus' arms around him, holding him close. He wept as he never had before, not even when he'd lost his parents as a child. Not even over Nessa's loss. The release of pent-up shame and regret was swiftly replaced by an intense yet gentle sense of peace.

Jesus held him at arm's length and helped him to stand, then embraced him once more. "All is forgiven." He patted Lavi's back, then stepped away.

Lavi wiped the tears from his eyes, wanting to laugh and cry again at the same time. After several moments of trying to collect his emotions, he searched the face of this Jesus Messiah. "Will I ever be able to marry Nessa?"

Jesus gave a slight shrug. "That is something you must work out with her brother. Follow the law's requirements for sacrifice and sign the appropriate documents. Watch and see what happens."

They walked back toward the courtyard together as Lavi

asked one more question. "Rabbi, how do I ask Chen when I know what he'll say? He has already rejected me so many times."

Jesus looked into his eyes, the clear light so unlike that of anyone he had ever known. As if no darkness resided within him. "Ask again and see."

Lavi simply nodded and walked beside Jesus in silence, anxiety warring with his newfound peace. But no. He would not fear Chen's answer. He would trust God this time to work it out. If he was meant to have Nessa as his wife, Chen would agree to his request. If not, he would accept God's choice.

40

I stood under the arch of the door to the courtyard, a tray of cups filled with water in my hands. At that moment, Jesus and Lavi emerged from the side of the house. Jesus sat on the bench, but Lavi approached Chen. My heart leapt in my throat.

"May I speak with you, Chen?" Lavi asked, his voice humble, unlike other times I had heard him speak.

Chen looked up, surprise filling his expression, but after glancing at Jesus, he nodded. "Come inside," he said as he stood.

I moved away from the door, hurriedly passed the drinks to the men sitting there, and then debated with myself. Should I sit with Jesus, as I longed to do, or return to the rooms where I might listen in on Chen and Lavi's conversation?

"Nessa," Jesus said, making the decision for me. "Come. Join us." He pointed to an empty seat not far from him, next to one of his men.

How strange it felt to be among so many men while Malka prepared food inside. I should join her, but I could not pull away from the look in Jesus' eyes.

"Let them work this out," Jesus said, and I knew in a heartbeat that he not only understood what they were discussing but must have said something to Lavi to bring it about.

I nodded, set the tray beside me, and tried not to wring my hands. "The rest of the townspeople will want to hear more of your teaching, but thank you for joining us today. We are honored to have you here," I said.

I glanced from his homespun garment to his leather sandals. Nothing about him seemed remarkable or would make anyone notice him. He did not have the kind of beauty I had felt cursed with all my life. But the light coming from within him drew people, and I knew he did not need to be the most handsome man in Samaria or Judah to be their redeemer. He already had what he needed—such compassionate love for everyone he came into contact with. Even a woman like me. The fact that he would even speak with me filled my heart with joy and longing. Two days with him was such a short time.

"I came to seek you," he said, causing me to look into those unusual eyes.

"Why me?"

The men around me, his followers, seemed to lean closer, as if they wanted an explanation too. Certainly they could not be comfortable in the home of a Samaritan.

"Because you needed me. After all you have lived through, you questioned God's goodness and whether He could possibly care for you. I came to show you that He can and does." Jesus smiled, and my heart lifted, feeling lighter than the air escaping my lungs.

"I'm glad you came," I said just above a whisper.

Silence followed my remark, and a moment passed before Chen and Lavi emerged from the house. My heart hammered as I looked from one to the other. *Tell me.*

But Lavi remained silent, turning to Chen, who approached Jesus. Malka entered the courtyard, watching them.

"Rabbi," Chen said, "you have caused a stir in our town and turned the hearts of many of us back to God in a way we had never thought possible. You have made me realize that I and my father before me, peace be upon him, have not acted in my sister's best interests and have caused her great pain." He stepped over to me and placed a hand on my shoulder. "I should have protected her from the men who set her aside without so much as an apology for things she could not control. My father should have made better choices, as should I. I know that my pride kept me from seeing the truth, thinking I was simply doing what my father would have done, but I should not have seen Nessa as a means to gain wealth as he did. She is worth far more than that. Is it too late to make things right?"

Jesus stood and placed his hands on Chen's arms. "My son, it is always best to do the right thing, to obey God rather than men." He released Chen.

Chen swallowed and blinked back emotion. Malka took a slight step closer to Jesus. I met her gaze. Even her expression had softened, and she offered me a half smile. What was happening to our family?

A commotion from the street interrupted us as my sisters and their families entered the crowded court to sit in a circle at Jesus' feet. I noted their smiles and the earnestness in their eyes—all of them—as they settled the children with them.

"It looks like we have gathered more of your family," Jesus said, still facing Chen. "Perhaps you need to express your desire to them as well."

Chen nodded, glancing from Jesus to Lavi.

"May I speak first?" Lavi asked Chen.

Chen motioned for him to speak, and we all waited while Lavi lifted his hands in supplication. "I want you all to know that I have sinned against your sister. I have loved Nessa for years, but yesterday I convinced her to live with me. She came and . . ." He looked away and swiped a tear from his eyes. "In the eyes of God we are one." He faced them again, glancing at me.

I stood beside him, took his hand, and squeezed. "I came

willingly," I admitted. "Lavi did not have to convince me. I wanted this too."

"But we should have wed first," Lavi countered. "We should have waited for Chen to allow it."

"And I should not have repeatedly denied you," Chen interjected. "I was wrong to keep Nessa from a life with someone who truly loves her."

"I want to make it right," Lavi said, glancing at Jesus. "I want to marry Nessa today, if she'll have me. I promise that I will never leave her or put her out. We will wed until death parts us. And we will offer a sacrifice for our sins," he added, "for they are many."

"I will have you," I said, meeting Lavi's tender gaze. "For always. Until death parts us."

Jesus looked between Lavi and me, smiling. His pleasure warmed me to my toes. Oh, how wonderful it felt to know we were doing what God wanted us to do!

Tears of joy filled my eyes, and Yaffa jumped to her feet and embraced me. "I knew this day would come!"

Adva and Meital surrounded me, and Gali burst from the crowd, which had gathered outside our courtyard, to embrace me. "We must get you ready for your wedding."

"And I must draw up the ketubah," Chen said, then stopped. He turned, meeting Jesus' gaze. "But I don't want to do this if it will stop your teaching."

Jesus laughed, and I saw his wide smile. "Weddings are one of my favorite things," he said. "We celebrated one in Cana at the beginning of my ministry."

"We won't take long," Lavi said, "so that you have plenty of time to still teach us."

"Why don't you get the rabbi, Lavi, while Chen gets the ketubah, and I will teach once the rabbi has blessed your union. Then"—Jesus glanced at each one sitting near—"we will celebrate!"

"But surely, Master, you did not come here simply for a wedding," one of his followers said as I entered the house. I turned back to hear what Jesus would say, for I felt as though I had stolen too much of his time already.

"Simon," Jesus said, "a wedding is one of most perfect examples of how the Father shows His love for His people. When the bride is finally clothed in her bridal attire and made ready, the groom comes and carries her away to his father's house. There is much rejoicing when the bride and groom are finally together with the father. One day you will understand."

I slipped away with my sisters and my best friend, wishing I could stay to hear what else he would say, but I also didn't want to miss this moment. Tonight I would truly belong to Lavi, but I sensed in a greater way, I would also belong to God and to His Messiah. And after we were wed, Lavi and I would do as the law required for a sin offering and finally be made right, something I had not felt in a long, long time.

I looked lovingly at my sisters and Gali and pondered this amazing man called Jesus. His presence here was even changing my closest relationships for the better. And to think that he, the Messiah, had just blessed the one union I had always wanted. He had come to Samaria just for me, and now he had given me the favor and love I had longed for all my life.

❖ ❖ ❖

"I think the entire town has gathered outside of Chen's house," Yaffa said, glancing through the window. "They are spilling into the streets and beyond."

"They want to hear Jesus. They don't care about me."

"Don't be so sure, Ness. Things are different already." Yaffa strained to see, then let out a little gasp. "Osher is here with Aliyah!"

My heart leapt. My daughter was here? "Why would he bring her to this?"

"I guess you'll find out," Adva said. "Come. They are waiting in the courtyard. Lavi is already standing under the huppah."

The men had thrown things together so quickly that my head spun. Was this really happening? Would Osher's feelings toward me change now as well? But I had no time to think as my sisters ushered me through the door to join Lavi beneath the canopy.

His wide smile made gooseflesh tingle along my arms. Jesus stood behind the rabbi, his eyes dancing with delight.

The rabbi's blessings were shorter than any given at my previous weddings, and before I knew it, Chen and Lavi had sealed the ketubah. I drank from the cup Lavi offered me, then finished the wine in one gulp.

People rushed forward, and I thought I might be squeezed to death from so many hugs. When Aliyah ran toward me, arms outstretched, I bent to lift her into my arms. My thoughts spun, and my heart longed to hold her always.

Osher approached, and Lavi placed his arm about my shoulders. Osher glanced at Jesus, then lifted apologetic eyes to me. "I should not have kept her from you," he said, all coldness and hard-heartedness gone. "In fact, I want you to have her. You're her mother and she should live with you—after your wedding week has passed." He looked once more at Jesus. "We've been talking," he admitted to me. "I know this is the right thing, but will you bring her to see my mother . . . and me . . . from time to time?"

I knew my heart could not hold one more ounce of joy. "Of course," I said, pulling Aliyah closer. "She can stay with you now and then too, if you'd like." To say so seemed like the worst thing ever after so long, but I knew it was also right. Aliyah needed both her mother and father and her grandparents.

"Thank you," he said. "I will bring her to the market after your wedding week."

For a brief moment, I had the horrible thought that he might change his mind once Jesus returned to Israel. For only the

Messiah could have brought so many changes to this city, these people, in such a short time. But would they last?

"I promise," Osher said. He looked at Chen. "You can hold me to it."

I caught Jesus' expression and saw his slight nod. "All right," I said, kissing Aliyah. "Ima will see you in a week, my love. Then you can live with Lavi and me. Would you like that?"

Aliyah bit her lip a moment, then nodded. "I miss you, Ima."

"We will be together again."

She smiled as I handed her back to Osher. Lavi's hand captured mine, and together we moved to one of the benches as the huppah was removed.

Jesus sat among the crowd and spoke of the kingdom of heaven. Enraptured faces looked to him, and my heart soared with every single word. One day the kingdom of heaven would be even better than this day, this wonderful day of marriage to the man I had loved all my life. And soon my daughter would sleep near me again and my life would finally be full of joy.

I blinked away a handful of tears as I listened to Jesus' amazing words. How had he known how much I needed him? I still couldn't take it all in.

When Jesus paused to take a drink, Niv, Keshet, and Dan, my three former fathers-in-law, approached me, awe and humility in their eyes.

"We no longer believe just because of what you said," Niv said.

"Now we have heard for ourselves," Keshet added.

"And we know that this man really is the Savior of the world," Dan said.

"He truly is," Lavi whispered in my ear.

I smiled, my heart full. "No one knows that better than I do."

Note to the Reader

Most of the teaching that I've heard of the story of the woman at the well has come with the belief that she was a moral outcast, no better than a prostitute, in her village. Why else would she be at the well in the middle of the day, avoiding the other women? And when Jesus told her that she'd had five husbands and was living with a man who was not her husband, His words seemed to cement this interpretation. Or do they?

When I began to research her story, I questioned these age-old beliefs, matching them against the culture of her day. Could a woman be married five times by choice? Did a woman have the right to seek a divorce, and if she did, why would she want to unless she was living with abuse? Marriage was meant to last a lifetime, but it appears that even the Samaritans practiced Moses's allowance for divorce, though Jesus declared that Moses only allowed such a thing because of their hard hearts.

So why would five men have hardened their hearts against this woman? Then again, perhaps she wasn't divorced but widowed five times. It is possible, I suppose, though it seems unlikely. I wouldn't paint this woman as a black widow. So if she was divorced more than once, why? If she'd been unfaithful, she would more likely have been stoned than divorced.

While I do not believe this woman was completely innocent, as no person living is without sin, I do see her more as a victim of her society and her circumstances than the cause of most of her problems in marriage. The hard part was creating six separate households, occupations, and reasons for her falling out of favor with someone in those homes. And why would anyone want to marry her after two or three divorces? Unless she was beautiful beyond words.

I could be wrong, but beauty seemed like a plausible reason for why men would want her and women would hate her. These attitudes prevail even today. We tend not to think of how the beautiful person who is both hated and adored may feel. So I explored those feelings in this story.

What struck me most was that Jesus did not condemn this woman. He simply stated the truth. What is even more amazing about our Lord is that He went out of His way to a hostile city to meet a woman who needed Him. And she was the first person to whom He revealed that He was the Messiah.

Doesn't it amaze you to think that God, holy God, cares *that* much about women? He spoke truth to them, appeared first to them after His resurrection, and here, inconvenienced Himself and His disciples to reach one lost, broken woman and give her the truth. The truth that changed her forever.

The Catholic church chose a name for her—Photina—many years after the Gospels were written. She is considered one of their saints and is said to have become a missionary and a martyr. Because these things are traditions not written of in Scripture, I chose to give her a different name. What became of her, only God truly knows. But she was the first missionary, because the moment she believed, she ran into the town that had probably shunned her and told them about the Messiah.

I hope you have enjoyed my interpretation of the story of this remarkable woman who met Jesus at Jacob's well two thousand years ago, and whose story still resonates with us today. May God meet you in your place of deepest need as He did with her, and may you believe as quickly as she did.

In His Grace,
Jill Eileen Smith

Acknowledgments

The year that I wrote this story was a challenging one. My husband faced a number of health issues, particularly a few bouts of Covid, one of which landed him in the hospital. How grateful I am for praying friends who covered us during those trying days. Even more, I am grateful to the Lord for allowing us to still have each other on this earth.

That one event caused us to cancel two trips, and it took a toll for months. In the middle of it all, I was editing *Dawn of Grace* and trying to complete the first draft of this book. What helped me get through it all was that for the first time in over twenty books, I had plotted this one in pretty good detail. I knew where it was going and where I wanted it to end. That was a huge blessing because if I hadn't had the plot to guide my scattered thoughts, I would have struggled to finish it on time. I did not want to ask for an extension. I wanted to finish it early, and by God's grace, I did!

We never know where life is going to take us year to year. People come and go from our lives. Health issues arise unexpectedly, and life is more fragile than we realize. Our times are in God's hands.

So the first people I want to acknowledge are all my friends, family, and readers who prayed for us during those dark spring days. We both appreciate you all very much.

Of course, every book would never become what it is without the great team at Revell—Rachel McRae, Jessica English, Karen Steele, and Raela Schoenherr. Thank you to each one of you!

Wendy Lawton, my agent and dear friend through every book, thank you for being there for me!

Jill Stengl and Hannah Alexander, thank you for pre-reading the second draft and for all the great suggestions. The book is better for you having read it first.

To our family, kids, in-law kids, and grandkids—there are no people on earth I love more than you! And, of course, Randy—love of my life! God has blessed us so much, and I'm so glad we get to do life together and have eternity to look forward to one day.

Jesus Messiah—I can't wait to see you face-to-face. What an amazing privilege it was for those who walked the earth with You back then, and for the woman at the well to hear You say that You are the Messiah. A woman, outcast and broken, whom You blessed with such knowledge before You revealed Yourself to the world. How amazing You are! Thank You for allowing me to be called Your own.

Jill Eileen Smith is the bestselling and award-winning author of many biblical novels, including her first series, The Wives of King David. After twenty years of closed doors, she has since published twenty-five fiction and nonfiction books. She loves Jesus and His Word and all things related to learning more about the women God has immortalized in Scripture. Jill has been married to the love of her life for forty-eight years and counting and lives in a quiet neighborhood in southeast Michigan. Learn more at JillEileenSmith.com.

Meet
JILL EILEEN SMITH

at **www.JillEileenSmith.com** to learn interesting facts and read her blog!

Connect with her on

- f Jill Eileen Smith
- X JillEileenSmith
- JillEileenSmith

Be the first to hear about new books from Revell!

Stay up to date with our authors and books by signing up for our newsletters at

RevellBooks.com/SignUp

FOLLOW US ON SOCIAL MEDIA

  @RevellFiction